BLOOD TYPE:
AN ANTHOLOGY OF VAMPIRE SF ON THE CUTTING EDGE
Edited by Robert S. Wilson

All net proceeds of *Blood Type: An Anthology of Vampire SF on the Cutting Edge* go to support: The Cystic Fibrosis Trust.

You can learn more about The Cystic Fibrosis Trust from their website at: http://www.cysticfibrosis.org.uk/

First Trade Paperback Edition

ISBN: 1-938644-17-4
ISBN-13: 978-1-938644-17-7

Nightscape Press, LLP
http://www.nightscapepress.com

Table of Contents:

TYPE O NEGATIVE
An Introduction to Blood Type

A while back, I promised a good friend (whose name I will keep private) that I would do a charity anthology to help fight Cystic Fibrosis. Her daughter has the disease and the more she talked about it, the more I realized just how many great things The Cystic Fibrosis Trust was doing to help. It didn't take a whole lot of connecting the dots from there. At first, the idea to do a vampire anthology was a completely separate one.

At the time, late in the process of co-editing HORROR FOR GOOD: A CHARITABLE ANTHOLOGY, I knew at some point, I wanted to do an anthology on my own. And with having broken into the horror scene initially with my first novel, SHINING IN CRIMSON: EMPIRE OF BLOOD BOOK ONE, a vampire novel, it seemed only a natural choice.

The problems I often see with most vampire fiction out there today is that it lacks either one of two things; originality or that truly dark element that had always—in the past—made up some of the best vampire stories of all time. So, I figured that was a hell of a start. A vampire anthology consisting of only the most original dark stories I could find. I liked the idea a lot... and then life went and sped up, and I was forced to move on to other things.

And then one day the idea came crawling back into my mind and the more I thought about it, I realized that the vampire stories that had made the most significant impact on me were both also technically stories of science fiction. One is more commonly known as a masterpiece of horror and the other is known simply as a work of hard science fiction. Both have made one hell of a mark on their respective genres.

Richard Matheson's 1956 short novel I AM LEGEND was the first of the two to truly grab me by the throat and well... do what any good dark, original vampire story should. But it did one more thing... It intrigued me with one hell of an interesting scientific concept that, although pretty run of the mill now-a-days, had to have been controversial as all hell still in the '50s. I won't spoil it for those of you so unlucky not to have read it before. And as much as I hope you'll keep reading this tome of varied dark vampire SF, I have to advise that you put this book down and read that one first!

The other major spark of inspiration for this book has a more personal tie to it. Peter Watts is and shall likely always be my favorite living writer. His novel BLINDSIGHT not only took vampires to a new scientific level but it also turned the concept of what it means to be conscious and how that affects our abilities and accomplishments as a progressive race of beings and turned it on its head. And now that I think about it, both books have a similar theme of humanity not quite being as superior as we petty humans would like to think. But I digress...

I've been waiting for years for Peter's second novel in the BLINDSIGHT universe, the novel he has been referring to as the coming *sidequal* as opposed to a sequel: ECHOPRAXIA. One of my biggest hopes when I started working on this anthology was that Peter would be willing to contribute something. Not only was he willing, in the spirit of the overall concept of the anthology, he wrote a story called "Orientation Day" based in the BLINDSIGHT universe that ties into his upcoming novel ECHOPRAXIA! I couldn't have been more pleased with how this worked out and the fact that Peter so graciously contributed this story.

So there you have the reasons behind why this anthology came into being; I wanted to do a charity anthology to help support The Cystic Fibrosis Trust and I wanted to do an anthology of dark science fiction. The glue that holds the two together was my good friend whose daughter has CF. She is one of the many friends I have today who started out as fans of my own vampire fiction. So, when I thought about the two things I wanted to do, it made perfect sense to put them together and make a science fiction vampire anthology for The Cystic Fibrosis Trust and for my friend. Hence the anthology you're just about to read.

When first considering stories for this book, I had a much more restrictive criteria for acceptable stories; I wanted stories with more of a hard science fiction core. But as I read through submissions and found some amazingly brilliant science fantasy tales, I started to stretch my original boundaries and in the end I'm glad that I allowed myself to not be too constrictive. And the result, whether you're just about to dig into this entire book or just sample a story or two at random, is a nice mix of various kinds of science fiction and fantasy pieces with the vampire theme or idea used in a multitude of interesting ways. I hope you enjoy it as much as I've enjoyed putting it together and that you'll maybe find a few new favorite authors to read further as I have.

Robert S. Wilson
Smyrna, Tennessee
October 27th, 2013

THE UNDYING
William F. Nolan

*B*lood. My own. Sweet Christ, my own! Seeping along my chest, soaking my white pullover, a spreading patch of dark red. So this is how it finally ends? With the stake being driven in another inch, each blow of the hammer like a thunderclap... closing my eyes in Paris with blood everywhere on the tumultuous streets, tasting it on my cool lips, with the guillotine hissing down, severed heads thumping wicker baskets... King Richard there (was it the Third Crusade?), his battle axe cleaving through the enemy's shoulder, sundering down through muscle, bone, and gristle, and watching the stricken rider topple from the tall back of the sweating gray horse... in Germany's Black Forest, barefoot, my flesh lacerated by thorn and stone, pursued by the shouting villagers, the flames of their torches wavering, flickering through the trees, a strange, surreal glow... gulls above the sunswept English Channel as I lower my head toward the child's white, delicately tender throat, with the warm sweet wine of her blood on my tongue. (So many myths about us. They call us creatures of the night, but many of us do not fear the bright sun. In truth, it cannot harm us, although we often hunt at night... so many myths)... on the high seat of the carriage, pitching and plunging through moonlit Edinburgh, wheels in thunderous clatter over the narrow, cobbled streets, hatless, my cape blown wild behind me as I lash at the straining team... the impossibly pink sands of the beach, with a stout sea wind rattling the palm fronds, the waves blood-colored, sunset staining the edge of horizon sky and the young woman's drugged, open, waiting flesh, and my lips drawn back, the needled penetration, and the lost cry of release... the limo driver's rasping voice above the surging current of Fifth Avenue traffic, recounting the intensity of the police hunt, and my quiet smile there with my back against the cool leather, invincible, the girl's corpse where no one can ever find it, with the puncture marks raw and stark on her skin... the stifling, musky darkness of the cave, the rough grained face of the club against my cupped fingers, the fetid tangle of beard cloaking my face, my lips thick and swollen, the hot roar of the saber-tooth still echo-sharp in my mind, and thinking not of the dead, drained female beside me but of the brute eyes of the beast... the stench of war, of cannon-split corpses, the blue-clad regiment sprawled along the slope, the crackling musket fire in the cool air of Virginia, the stone wall ahead of me in the rushing smoke... the plush gilt of the Vienna opera house, the music rising in a brassy tide and the tall woman beside me in blood-red velvet as I watch the faint heartbeat in the hollow of her arching throat, flushed ivory from the glow of stage lamps... the bitter-smoked train pulling into crowded Istanbul station, the towers of ancient Byzantium rising around me, the heavy leather suitcase bumping my leg, the thick wool suit pressing against my skin, the assignation ahead with the dark-haired little fool who trusts me... the bone-shuddering shock along my right arm as my sword sparks against the upthrust shield, the gaunt Christian falling back under the fury of my attack, the orgasmic scream of the Roman crowd awaiting another death... the long, baked sweep of sun-blazed prairie, suddenly quiet now after the vast drumming of herded buffalo, the young, pinto-mounted Indian girl riding easily beside me, with the flushed red darkness of her skin inviting me, challenging me... standing with Rameses II among the fallen Hittites, with the battle-thirst raging through me like a fever, the sharp odor of spilled blood everywhere, soaking deep into parched Egyptian sands... the reeking London alehouse along the Thames, the almond-eyed whore in my lap, giggling, her breath foul with drink, her blood-rich neck gleaming in the smoky light... the slave girl in Athens, kneeling in the dirt at my booted feet, begging me to spare her wretched life as the pointed tip of my sword elicits a single drop of crimson from her fear-taut throat... at the castle feast, soups spiced with sage and sweet basil, the steaming venison on platters of chased silver, the hearty wines of Auvergne aglow in jeweled flagons, with the Queen facing me across the great table, my eyes on the pale blue tracery of veins above the ruffled lace at her neck... and, at last, here—with all the long centuries behind me, their kaleidoscopic images flickering across my mind—hunted and found, trapped like an animal under a fog-shrouded sun along the soft Pacific shore, in this fateful year of one thousand nine-hundred ninety-two, as the ultimate anvil-ringing stroke of the hammer sends the stake deep into my rioting heart... to a sudden, unending darkness.

The final blood is mine. . .

. . .until the year of two thousand eight hundred and seventy-two—when I am, at last, reborn. . .

William F. Nolan writes mostly in the science fiction, fantasy, and horror genres. Though best known for coauthoring the acclaimed dystopian science fiction novel *Logan's Run* with George Clayton Johnson, Nolan is the author of more than 2000 pieces (fiction, nonfiction, articles, and books), and has edited twenty-six anthologies in his fifty-plus year career.

Of his numerous awards, there are a few of which he is most proud: being voted a *Living Legend in Dark Fantasy* by the International Horror Guild in 2002; twice winning the *Edgar Allan Poe Award* from the Mystery Writers of America; being awarded the honorary title of *Author Emeritus* by the Science Fiction and Fantasy Writers of America in 2006, and receiving the *Lifetime Achievement Award* from the Horror Writers Association in 2010. Nolan resides in Vancouver, WA.

TAXING YOUTH
Rebecca L. Brown

They marketed it as 'Anti-'tax' — *who wants to be a slave to taxing*, the adverts said. *Income taxing; council taxing; eotaxins...* Even at the time, Anya didn't find that funny.

At nineteen, she didn't need some injection or other to help her live forever. She was immortal, just like every other teenager. Seventy years — maybe more — was forever. Longer, even. Seventy years was all the time in the world.

"Is it like botox then?" her mum asked. "Chemical peels and all that?"

"Probably." Anya didn't bother to explain. The only kind of plasma her mum cared about was the widescreen kind. The Kings had one and Anya's parents didn't.

There are times, her mother had told her, *when three inches makes all the difference*. When she said it, Anya had almost choked on her coffee.

"Maybe I'll give it a go. Reckon it'll perk up an old cow like me?"

"It might." Or, at least, it couldn't hurt to try — except the money. Even thinking about the cost made Anya wince.

Designer skincare, her father called it. *A waste of money*.

They both knew her mum would buy it anyway. She always did.

~

"So what is it, some face pack or something?" Anya's mum peered over her shoulder at the blister pack. Five needle syringes. Each with 'CCL11-chemokine rec.' printed on the side. Each completely filled with the same off-white liquid.

They bought the injections online. A home kit, complete with latex gloves and instructions in twelve different languages.

Anya had already explained what it was twice.

"You do it for me," her mum said. "I'll only get it wrong."

So it was Anya who injected the eotaxin blockers into her mum. Afterwards, that would give her an excuse to blame herself.

~

They withdrew the Anti-'tax from the market just three months later.

Potential side effects, the product recalls claimed. What those side effects were, nobody seemed to know.

"Probably want to keep it to themselves," Anya's mother said. "Selfish. Greedy." She had three unopened packs left and one half empty.

"We could sell them for a fortune," Anya's father suggested.

"No chance!" Anya's mum wasn't about to sell eternal youth at any price — not now that there was so little of it left.

Eternal youth — a three month supply.

Something about that made Anya want to laugh — although there was nothing funny about it.

~

"Do I look younger?" Anya's mum asked. "Do I *sound* younger?" There were only two injections left from the last box. Anya had heard they were worth hundreds of pounds each—maybe even thousands by now.

"Hmm?" The adverts never claimed to make you younger, only to keep you from aging so quickly.

They're being modest, Anya's mum had told her. *I'm five years younger by now at least. Soon I'll be as young as you!*

Only two injections left. And after that…

"They'll start selling them again I reckon. Soon," Anya's mum kept telling her. "There's a market for them. They'll sell them again."

~

A single treatment would have cost them two thousand pounds—and Anya's mum would have paid it if Anya's father hadn't stopped her.

"What're we going to do?" she kept asking, over and over, until Anya would have done anything to shut her up. "What are we going to do?" As if this was Anya's problem too.

She looked up eotaxin online just to make her stop asking.

"It says here it comes from a gene on chromasome eleven," she told her mother.

"Where's that? Can we cut it out?"

"No, Mum." Anya sighed.

"How do we get rid of it?"

Anya laughed. "You'd need to get rid of your blood, Mum. That's where it is—in your blood."

"How do we do that then?" It had taken Anya a moment to realise she was serious.

~

As far as Anya could tell, there were two ways to stop the effects of eotaxin—and neither of them seemed like a good idea.

"It must be there for a reason, Mum."

"Yeah—to make me old. Older. Huh!"

"No, but listen—"

"Just—find a way to get rid of it," her mum snapped.

The Anti-tax had been an inhibitor. A blocker. It bound itself to the eotaxins and stopped them from working. When you stopped using them, the eotaxin would start back up where it left off.

The only way to get rid of it was a plasma transfusion.

"You'd need to get plasma from someone young. Some way of getting it out of them and into you. Um, it just isn't practical."

"If you loved me, you'd find a way." She sniffed dramatically. Over-dramatically.

"Mum..."

Anya's mum folded her arms. "If you loved me, you'd find a way."

~

There were plasma clinics now, for those who could afford it. If you took in a donor, it was cheaper.

"Come with me," Anya's mum said. "Just for moral support."

You had to go private to get it—the National Health Service considered it a 'cosmetic procedure'.

Immortality at a price! The headlines said. *How much will you pay?*

Too much, Anya thought. Far more than they could afford.

~

Nobody really knew—or cared—when the first girls went missing. Most of them were prostitutes or illegals. All of them were under twenty five.

If the papers reported it, it was as an afterthought.

"Anya, if you loved me..."

"No. I'm not -"

"See this? See this here? That's another wrinkle. I'm getting old, Anya. I'm dying. And—and you could stop it. But you won't, will you? You've got your youth, haven't you? You've got it and you don't want to share!"

She didn't ask when Anya's father was there anymore. He had lost his temper with her weeks ago.

"Stop it, Hayley! Stop it! Just... stop it. Why should she have to do it?"

"I don't want to die!" I don't—"

"You're a grown woman, Hayley. Behave like it." He picked up his newspaper and opened it at random.

"I'll pay you, if you like," Anya's mum told her. "I'll pay you... I don't know, how much do you want? It'll grow back, won't it? You'll get more—plenty enough to share with your mum."

The leaflets said that you could donate plasma twice a week. Anya's mum had brought them home with her one evening and scattered them around the house. The leaflets said it wouldn't hurt. That it wouldn't do any lasting damage to the donor and there was no risk involved.

Anya's father had collected up the leaflets and put them outside with the rubbish. No one mentioned them again.

~

There was an article in the paper about a man who killed his nephew.

"I needed the plasma," he was supposed to have said. He

9

had collected up as much blood as he could and taken it to one of the private donation stations.

"It was all over his arms," the witnesses said. "All over his face."

Anya dreamed that her mother did the same — that she would wake up one morning to find a knife pressed against her throat. She started looking for a flat of her own and locking her door at night.

"Anya, I want to talk to you." Her mum's voice was muffled through the thickness of the door. "Anya, unlock the door please."

When she knocked — hard and then softly when her fists started to hurt — Anya cried. The dreams stopped. The knocking meant she didn't sleep.

The abductions were making the headlines by then. A few young men but mostly women. Pretty girls — maybe people thought they could transfuse good looks. A few bodies turned up, but not many. The papers speculated — 'plasma farms' was the most popular theory — but there was little to no evidence.

"Anya, I'm your mother! Doesn't that mean anything to you? I brought you into this world…"

When Anya moved out, her father helped her pack.

"Take care of yourself, love," he told her.

"Tell Mum — "

Her father sighed. "I'll tell her."

~

It was four weeks — just under a month — before she visited them. Unpacking seemed to take her forever.

"In here, Anya!" her mother called. She was smiling — Anya couldn't remember the last time she'd seen her mother smile like that.

"What do you think?" Her mum twirled.

New hair? New dress? Anya couldn't tell. She wasn't sure.

"Very nice," she said. "Where's Dad?"

"No more wrinkles. Can you tell?"

"That's —" There were two glasses in the sink, both of them stained red. The kitchen smelled like copper and rot. Like rotten meat.

"Dad?"

"He sent his love, Anya. He had to —"

"Dad? Dad! Mum, what did —?"

"If you'd bloody cared I wouldn't have had to —" her mum snapped. "Only five years younger, but I took it all. I figure that'll make a difference. Don't you?"

Two glasses in the sink — the price of immortality, one pint at a time.

"Will it work? Do you think that it will?"

If it did, the price was too high.

One pint at a time, Anya's youth drained away.

Rebecca L. Brown is a writer, model and businesswoman. She takes her coffee very seriously.

THE SOULS OF STARS
Amelia Mangan

There was a girl with a bruised arm on Earth, and that was why I had to leave. I saw her through the limousine window. Standing at the lights. Waiting to cross. She was leaning on the post and adjusting the strap of her bag and there was a bruise on her arm, dark and blotchy and big. It was purple in the centre, a dark angry purple, paling to red, until there was nothing left but a thin sick aura of yellow. Her skin was so pale the bruise seemed obscene, an insult to her flesh.

The car moved on and my gown fell between my thighs. I pulled off my glove and started to rub my arm, right where her bruise had been. I kept rubbing and rubbing until the car stopped and I was told the party was here. By then my wrist ached and my skin had begun to burn. I smiled and thanked the driver, but the bruise was still there, lodged in my brain. I kept thinking about blood under the skin, about internal bleeding, about how that sort of thing could never be treated, that wound never dressed; all it could do was bleed and bleed and bleed inside her, and spread, and grow fat, until she was nothing but blood, nothing but a swollen mass of blood bound in thin, pale skin.

I entered the party and had my picture taken, but people weren't looking at me. They were crowded in the middle of the room, gasping and sighing and asking questions I didn't understand. *Does it bite? Can I touch it? It's so beautiful.*

I pushed ahead and looked down. Someone had brought a dragon to the party.

It crawled on thick fat legs and flicked its tongue and hissed. Its tongue was purple. Paling to red. Muscles coiled under thick, scaled hide. Diamonds encircled its neck. "What is that?" I said, to no one. "What is it?"

"A Komodo dragon," someone said, probably its owner. He looked very proud. "Largest lizard in the world."

My stomach knotted. "In the world."

"Uh huh. You can touch him if you like."

"No," I said, very fast. "No."

"It's safe. They only eat rats, rabbits. Small things."

The dragon looked at me. Its eyes were black and dull, heavy with hunger. *I should touch it,* I thought. People were looking at me, expecting it of me. My glove was off. I'd left it in the car. Why had I left it in the car? People were waiting for me to touch the dragon.

I put my hand out. The gloved one.

"You wouldn't want it to bite you, though," the owner went on. "Their mouths, you see. Almost a hundred different kinds of bacteria in there."

I snatched my hand back. Stared at the dragon. It stared back.

"It's not the bite that kills you," said the owner. "Not the bite itself. But the germs. Those germs would kill you stone dead. Right where you stand."

I smiled and excused myself and ran to the bathroom and puked until I was empty.

14

~

After that it was impossible to think without thinking of them. The girl and the dragon. The arm and the mouth. The bruise and the germs.

Everything was dark, and everything was dirty. Dark like the bruise; dirty like germs. I couldn't look at anyone without seeing one or the other. All the world was blood, and all the world was sick. There was nothing else.

I tried. I went out with friends. I went to more parties. I had more pictures taken. I smiled harder. But as soon as I got home I'd leap into the shower and scrub and scrub and scrub until the skin flaked, until it came away from the flesh. Snakes slough their skin. This, I told myself, was natural.

I took meds. A few at first, mild ones. Then more, and not so mild. I stopped taking calls and locked myself away. The apartment was air-conditioned, climate-controlled. All the flowers were under glass. Nothing could hurt me there. I made sure there was no dust, no dirt.

I am going to hurt myself, I kept thinking. Or: *I am going to hurt   other   people.* I started saying a lot of prayers. I am not religious, but it calmed me to say the words. Every time the panic rose, I chanted, like a witch: *God grant me the Serenity to accept the things I cannot change, the courage to change the things I can, the wisdom to know the difference.* After a while the words stopped meaning anything.

The calls stopped too. Things grew quiet. I began to wonder if this would be the way my life would end. If I would die soon. The thought was a comfort.

I watched a lot of news reports. Most of them confirmed what I knew, about the world, the people in it, all the blood and all the sickness. But one of them was different. One of them felt like something. Felt real.

It wasn't very long. Only a couple of minutes. One of those human-interest things, an oddity, something to make people laugh. I didn't laugh. I rewound it and watched it again, and again, and again.

They called it "the McCaul Ghost Ship". Created and fired up into space by eccentric billionaire RJ McCaul thirty years ago. Shots of the ship: huge, massive, leviathan. A giant twisted on his back, drowned in a black bath.

Shots of RJ McCaul. Young, handsome. Nervous blue eyes. Planed cheekbones. Swan neck. No one ever understood, the announcer said, exactly why he made the ship; he refused to explain. Some said it was guilt, over the people his family's munitions company had killed in the last war. Some said he'd gone mad. Whatever that means. Either way, he fired the ship deep into space, with himself inside, and was never heard from again. They'd tried to find him. But the ship wasn't designed for anyone in it to be found. McCaul had followed plans (shots of scattered blueprint, scrawled graying ink) that no one understood; plans that corresponded to no dimensions save those inside his head. Corridors led nowhere. Staircases looped back on themselves. Rooms tapered into forever, or ended at the doorway.

McCaul was dead. Had to be. He was never found, and no one could live like that. Suspended in nothingness. Lost in floating steel.

The ship could not be brought down. Not legally. It had drifted outside Earth's jurisdiction, into unregulated space. The area was a minefield of black holes. Far too dangerous to venture out there, to try and recover the Ghost Ship. It might, the announcer said, hang there forever. High above the world. High above everyone and everything. Empty and vast and silent.

I called my father. I asked him to buy the ship for me. He did it. He did it because he owes me.

Seventeen and a half minutes after I saw the news report, the McCaul Ghost Ship was the property of Yoshida Salvage Inc. Nineteen minutes after that, it was the property of Angela Yoshida. It was mine.

Leaving Earth was not a sacrifice. I took very little. Food would be sent to me each week. The ship's lights and water still worked. The only clothes I needed were the ones that I wore. I could be naked, for all it mattered. No one would — no one will — ever see me again.

~

I am lying on my back in the middle of the floor. My ear is pressed to the steel. The McCaul Ghost Ship hums with silence. Floor upon floor of no sound, no song, no words; nothing loud and nothing soft. Silence stacked on silence. Outside is space, cold and dark and forever. Nothing lives but me. Nothing breathes but me. No heart beats but mine. I take a breath and hold the generated air in my lungs until they start to ache. I breathe out softly and listen to my breath as it gusts through the ship, waltzes down tubes and conduits, slithers through metal cracks and echo-chamber vents.

This, I think, is how it was always meant to be. Just me. Alone. Only my heart for company. Only my heart, and my breath, and my mind.

I wander the ship. I follow its twists and its turns, expecting nothing. I follow one corridor to its end; it tightens around me as I walk, growing smaller and smaller, tapering to a vanishing point, until I am jammed eye-to-eye with a miniscule door. I open the door and peer inside. A tiny room, unfurnished, except for an even tinier rocking horse. The horse grins, mindless, wooden teeth brown and peeling.

I climb a staircase and find myself staring at a ladder. I climb the ladder and find myself staring down an empty elevator shaft, sheering into solid blackness. A twisted velvet rope hangs above the shaft. I climb down the rope and find myself standing once more at the foot of the stairs.

I open a hatch on the ground and inside there is a spiral, cast in pearlescent white, the inside of a conch shell. The spiral curls down and down and I try to follow it but it's impossible.

I pluck a coin from my pocket and toss it in. It dances on its rim, looping the spiral, tinkling like a bell. It grows smaller and smaller and vanishes and I listen for the sound of it landing somewhere, but the sound never comes.

I pass the days this way. Or I pass hours this way, or minutes, or weeks, or months. I didn't take a watch. I have no idea how long I've been here. Time gets caught in the cracks here, loses itself in the geometries that make no sense, in the rooms that vanish, in the halls that stutter and trail away like forgotten words. I am no longer tangled in my own mind; I am tangled in someone else's.

It doesn't feel too bad.

~

I don't dream these days, which is how I know I'm not dreaming the sound that wakes me up. I sit up and listen. There shouldn't be any sound. There shouldn't be anything at all.

I breathe and swallow and breathe. My heart thuds, dull and slow, but getting faster.

Godgrantmetheserenity, I begin, *toaccepttthethingsIcannot...*

There. There, again.

Difficult to describe. A hollow *thoom,* someplace unidentifiable. This ship is uncharted territory, *terra nullius.* Perhaps some faulty machinery? The ship is old. Never undergone maintenance, as far as I know.

My heart is speeding now. My meds are in the bathroom, and I wish to God I had them with me now. They'd slow things down, blunt the edges. Might be helpful.

I twist my hands against each other and think about blood under flesh. If I look down, I can see the cells through my skin, swirling and churning, waiting to break free.

I can't keep thinking about this. I won't. So I get up. *Godgrantme. Theserenity. Toaccept. Thethings.*

I open the door and walk out into the corridor. My feet

slap metal. I would like to stop twisting my hands but they seem to be twisting themselves.

I slept in my clothes. I am glad of this. I wouldn't like to be naked now.

Senseless configurations of iron and steel. Broken shadows all around.

Thoom.

It's closer. Or I am closer. I don't even remember moving.

I open a door, and behind the door there is a wall, and on the wall there is a hatch. So many hatches on this ship. This one is huge, the metal heavy with rust. The size of a person. A lever beside it.

I put my hand out. I should have worn gloves.

I pull the lever. A snake-hiss; decompression.

Behind the hatch, there is a tube, and inside the tube there is a body. The body falls out and hits the floor.

Breath leaves me and I gasp and claw for more and stagger back and hit the wall and slide down and stay there and stare. I will stay still. I will stay very very still and I will not touch anything.

He is wearing what was once a tailored suit. A fancy label, the kind my father wears. His hair is thin as dry grass. His nails are black with filth. At first I think they're long talons, but quickly realize it's just that the skin of his fingers has worn away to the bone.

He has a long neck. A long white neck with a long red wound.

He's dead. He's very, very dead and I start to think about all the bacteria he must be leaking into the air, all the germs, *Godgrantmetheserenity* and I think, Oh God, I have to get him off the ship and Oh God, that means I'm going to have to move him, I'm going to have to put my hands on him and hold him and touch him.

And then his head turns. And he raises himself. On his arms, his fleshless arms. And he looks at me.

The eyes are different than I remember. The eyes are like

nothing at all. It's the cheekbones I recognize. The cheeks are collapsed hollows but the bones are the same.

RJ McCaul. Missing, RJ McCaul. Thirty years dead, RJ McCaul.

He sits there like that, raised on his arms, looking at me. He casts a shadow. His shadow is wrong. Its shape is very wrong.

I pull myself up, slowly, and I stand there, looking at him looking at me.

He raises one hand, slaps it down on the floor in front of him. His body shifts. Closer to me. Still looking at me. His eyes. His eyes are eaten away.

His lips are parted. I can see into his mouth. Pale gums pulled back over gray teeth. Filmed with red. *Almost a hundred different kinds of bacteria*, I think.

The lips are peeling back. His hand. His fingers at my leg. The nails, brushing my ankle. He's so cold. So unbelievably cold.

I get out. I get away.

I slam the door and I lean on it. I lean on it as hard as I can.

I listen and I hear nothing. Pad down the hall to the kitchenette. Make myself a cup of coffee. I drink it slowly, unhurriedly, and once my cup is empty I sit holding it in both hands, palms absorbing the fading warmth. I stare out into the black. The black which I now know not to be empty. The black in which I am no longer alone.

I left Earth because there were dragons there. But there are dragons out here, too.

I shower. I shower again. I shower over and over again.

Eventually I go back to bed. I don't think I'll fall asleep but I do, instantaneously.

~

My eyes open and I am out of bed and walking down the hall

and standing outside the door.

I slide into a crouch. Press my ear to the door. Tapping. Rhythmic, patient. Almost soothing. Like a metronome. I think of those dirty nails again.

"Hello?" I say.

The tapping stops.

"Hello," I say.

Silence.

I think about going away. Leaving this door closed forever. In time, I'm sure I would forget.

I lift a hand, extend a finger, and tap on the door.

"Hello."

That wasn't me.

It takes me a moment to recognize it as a voice. As a word. I imagine his vocal cords, stringy rotten meat in a gouged-out throat.

"Can I open the door?" I ask. "Will you hurt me?"

Silence. Then:

"I'm hungry."

I sit back on my heels. "Is that a yes?"

Tap. "Open the door."

"Answer the question. Will you hurt me?"

Silence.

"Listen," I say. "I have an offer for you. Okay? Can you hear me?"

Tap.

"Yes."

"Good." I sit down. "Good. Okay. How about this? You can stay here." My hands twist. Twitch. The thought of having to touch him. The very thought. "You can stay. But we won't go near each other. All right? You stay in whatever part of the ship you've always stayed in, and I'll stay around here, and we won't...we won't be close to each other. It'll be like I don't even exist to you. How does that sound?"

Silence.

"That's what you want?"

"Yes," I say. "That's what I want."

Tap.

"All right."

I hear shuffling. Stumbling feet. Fading away.

Silence. Real silence. Empty air, unstirred by sound or motion.

I start to breathe again.

~

No life signs. That's why they never found him.

I think about this in bed. I can't seem to get to sleep.

They would've scanned the ship for signs of life. A heartbeat, a heat signature. Maybe they even went in and looked for him. Impossible. The whole point of this ship is that it's someplace to get lost.

I could ask him why he built it. I'd be the only person alive who knows.

I turn over and try to sleep.

He must have spread germs all over the ship. He must be spreading them now.

The walls whisper all around me.

~

I am sitting on the floor in the kitchen, counting out my meds. I have twenty-four left. That covers me for twelve days, but I don't feel good knowing that's all I have. I'll have to wire Earth to have some more sent up.

I thought I did have more. I wonder how many I've been taking. More than I should.

I gulp one down. You're supposed to take them with water but I don't like turning the faucets on and off. RJ McCaul might hear me.

What is he doing? What *has* he been doing? Thirty years gone. Thirty years dead. And not.

Twelve days does not seem a long time at all. I get up and send the wire.

~

All of my books are read. All of my movies watched and re-watched. I am bouncing a tennis ball off one of the bulkheads. Its fuzz has worn away; the hard bald surface cracks when I hit it too hard. The noise it makes is satisfyingly solid.

I hit the ball and catch it. Hit and catch. Hit and catch. Hit and miss, and it rolls down the corridor and into a pool of shadow.

I take a step forward.

The ball rolls back. Hits the side of my foot.

I stop. Look at it. Look around.

Everything is dark and still.

"Thanks," I call.

Nothing moves, but I feel something stir.

I reach down and pick up the ball, toss it from hand to hand.

"I'd feel better if I could see you," I say.

He melts out of the wall. His flesh is so white, I can't believe I didn't see it before. It glows in the dark.

"You said you didn't want to see me," he says. "Ever."

I drop my arms to my sides. "I might've changed my mind."

He nods. The motion is too broad, the muscles in the neck loose and floppy. I think of puppets on strings.

"I know you," I say. "You built this place. You're RJ McCaul."

The head inclines. "I am. And I'm not."

"What does that mean?"

"What's your name?"

"Angie," I say. "Angie Yoshida."

"Yoshida. The salvage company?"

"You know us?"

"RJ did."

My head is beginning to hurt. "But you're...Wait. Are you RJ McCaul or not?"

He smiles. It's horrible. "Yes."

I give up. "Are you still hungry?"

The smile dies. "Always."

I gesture at the kitchen. "You like pop tarts?"

~

We sit facing each other at the butcher's block. I place one foot on the floor and angle my hip outward, ready to run. I eat slowly and watch him, and he watches me eating, and doesn't touch the pop tart in front of him. His hands are folded on the tabletop. This close, I can see that the dirt beneath them isn't black, but a very dark, gritty red.

"Thought you were hungry," I say.

"I am."

"Then why don't you eat?"

"RJ's stomach doesn't digest food anymore."

I take a sip of milk. "You keep saying things like that. Like you're not really RJ McCaul. If you're not him, then who are you?"

"No. I am RJ McCaul."

"Oh, Jesus." I set down the milk and rest my head in my hands. "This is pointless."

"I'm also Sacha Kreznikov," he continues, "and Lisa Marks, and Henriette Leduc, and Andrew Talbot, and Vincent Tarbuck. Those are just the ones who have names. Names a human tongue can pronounce. But right now, RJ McCaul's body is the one I'm wearing." He shakes his head, looking down at his hands. "The body just won't seem to die. Not completely. It's very inconvenient."

I stare at him. His nails. His eyes.

"Your body," I say, "seems pretty dead to me."

"It is and it isn't," he says. "The lungs don't draw breath.

24

The heart doesn't beat. There isn't a pulse. But I can't leave it until it either wears out completely or I find another one to replace it. That's why I'm so hungry. There's no food for me here, and I can't go anywhere else."

"What do you eat?"

"It varies. But when I'm human? Oh, it's blood."

I should probably be running. I really, really should probably be running.

"Why do you have that gash on your throat?" I ask instead.

He reaches up and strokes it. The tips of his nails probe under the skin, into the meat. "That's how I do it. With humans. The carotid artery, that's the key. That's how I get inside them. They give me their blood and I give them me. I fill them up inside. We...it's hard to describe. We become each other. Eventually the body wears down and we transfer to the next one. And on and on."

"How long have you...existed that way?"

"Millennia. Aeons. As long as there's been time to measure."

"There haven't always been people. Hasn't always been blood."

"No." He leans forward. I move back. But he's only resting his head on his palm, staring out the window. "I've worn a lot of bodies. A lot of forms. Stones no hand has ever touched. Plants no tongue has ever named. A speck of dust in a comet's tail. A mote of ultraviolet from a sun gone nova. Acid rain on Titan, lava on Upsilon Andromeda B. Sometimes I had no form, and when I had no form I drained the light from stars. They're still inside me, too. We're all still here."

He looks back at me. "Why are *you* here?"

"I wanted to be alone," I say.

"No one's ever alone," he says. "Nothing exists all by itself, not ever. I've been almost everything in the universe, and almost everything's been me. RJ made the same mistake. He came here because he was lonely."

"Is he lonely now?"

"No." He moves, and I flinch, but he's only reaching out to the window. Dirty nails clink cold glass. He leaves no fingerprint. "I'm not."

I watch. I consider.

"You won't hurt me?"

"No."

"Then," I say, "I guess we can hang out."

~

We're approaching a black hole.

One morning I wake up and it's the first thing I see, right outside my window. It's far enough away not to be an immediate threat. The ship doesn't seem to be drifting toward it. But it's there. It's there and I feel its pull, the gravity of the thing, the weight of it. Solid darkness. Thick and irrefutable. Endless.

I stare into it for hours. For a whole day. By the end of it my mouth hurts, and I realize I haven't stopped praying once.

~

"It won't harm you," RJ says. Easier to call him RJ.

I roll the dice and move my tiny metal shoe up Boardwalk. "It's right out there," I say. "I can feel it. Everywhere I go. All over the ship. Can't you feel it?"

"Of course," he says. "But it won't harm you. Its gravitational pull might draw us in, eventually. Suck us down. That's just what black holes do. But it won't harm us."

"That's reassuring."

"I've won a beauty contest," RJ says, holding out a card.

"Good for you. I think I'm going to take my meds now."

"I'd like to go through a black hole," he says. "I once had a lover on the other side of a black hole."

I pause. "You had a lover?"

"Yes. We were each other, for a while. Part of the Lover is still in me. I suppose part of me is still in the Lover. We'll find each other again. It's impossible that we wouldn't."

"What if the Lover's dead?"

"Not possible. Nothing ever really dies."

I sit back down. "That some sort of religious thing?"

"No. It's physics. When it comes to energy, there's no such thing as creation or destruction. No death. No new life either. It's all right there, laid out in front of you. Like this board." He taps it with a nail. "Everything exists in a permanent state of living and dying. It's all the same thing, really. Open space is the same as a black hole. A rotting body is the same as a pristine one. You, me. We're not separate, you know."

"I'm not you," I say. My voice grates in my ears. I become aware that I am rubbing my arm.

"You are," he says. "Everything inside you. All those cells, those tissues. Webs of nerves; prisms of bone; seas of muscle and fat, oceans of germs and antibodies. A whole universe. So loud I'll bet it gets hard to hear yourself think. And all of it decaying. Decomposing. Your skin cells die and regenerate every single day; you're never the same person you were when you went to sleep as you are when you wake up. Every day you die. Every day you rot. Just like everything else."

My arm hurts.

"So you're saying it's all the same," I say. "You're saying nothing really matters."

"Everything matters," he says. "Everything is matter, so everything matters. You're bleeding."

I look down. My nails have broken the skin of my arm. Three little runnels of blood trail down to my elbow.

RJ looks away. "You probably shouldn't be near me now."

"No," I say. "Stay. I'll clean myself up. I'll fix it."

I get up and go to the bathroom. I wash myself off, bandage my wound. Open the medicine cabinet and take out my pills.

I look out the window.

The black hole seems closer now.

Thinking of nothing, I walk out into the corridor. I find the hatch, the one that opens onto the pearly conch-shell spiral. I kneel down and open the bottle and pour the meds out. They skitter on the white, rattle away into black.

~

I wake up clawing at the sheets, gasping for air. My throat feels wet. *RJ*, I think, and touch a hand to the side of my neck. It's sweat. My whole body is drenched. The bed is sopping wet.

I was dreaming. First time in years. I can't remember it: something about RJ's nails and a blotch on an arm and a dragon's open mouth and my father. Something about gravity and decay. Something about germs and blood. Metal angles that make no sense, empty doors and endless spirals.

I get up. Check the window. The black hole is still there. The black hole has always been, will always be, there.

Godgrantmethe, I begin, and stop. God will grant me nothing.

I left Earth to escape decay. To escape blood and sickness and constant, omnipresent death. It made no difference. It follows you. It follows you as far as you could ever possibly run.

I'm up, and I'm moving. The corridors whirl around me. I follow them wherever they want to go. I travel up staircases that lead to staircases traveling to staircases. I open a door and find a window and climb through the window and open another door and find myself staring down into another spiral, a greater spiral, so white it dazzles.

I climb into the spiral. I thought it would feel like the inside of a shell, but it doesn't. It's just hard, hard metal.

I hurtle down into the black. Wind screams in my ears. A song of rusting steel.

I slam hard onto the floor. Something cracks. White bone,

white tile. My nose drips red onto white bathroom tile. Everything is horribly, achingly, beautifully white. My eyes stream salt, and through the salt I see a long white curtain, shielding a long white tub. Nothing else in the bathroom. No toilet, no sink. Not even a mirror.

Something glints behind the curtain. I crawl to it. My bones move inside me, loose as unhinged doors.

I grab the curtain and pull it aside.

The bathtub is full of gleaming razor blades. A thin blanket of dust rests over them, but none seem rusted, none seem dirty. *Stainless*, I think, and am glad.

I reach up and pluck the very topmost blade from the pile, hold it to the light. It winks at me, as if we share a private joke.

This room has never been touched. Never been entered. RJ designed it, but never had the guts to use it. Some instinct. Some sense of self-preservation.

RJ isn't me. No matter what he says. I have no instincts left. There is nothing of me that I wish to preserve.

I lie on my back and stare up at the blade, held high, refracting light. The light slips beneath my eyelids and blinds me, and I don't see myself lowering the blade, don't see how it looks against my flesh. I barely even feel it as I draw it across my throat.

Gouts of red arc high into the air. Salt, more salt, and thick dark metal, curdling at the back of my throat. Everything is white now. Everything is red.

I swallow and taste myself. Bitter. Hot and bitter.

My head lolls to the side and I see myself, pouring out onto the white. A small, still pool. Spirals in the red. The curl of a conch shell, of a neverending loop. The swirl of a galaxy. Stars drowned in space. It's all going. All gone. It was all inside me, and it's gone.

Tap.

I sense, not see, the door swing inward. The outstretched hand, the outstretched nails, dirty red claws.

RJ slumps against the door and pushes forward. Falls to

hands and knees. His elbows stab the air. Muscles coil under flaking skin. He is so slow. So slow.

Black tongue unfurls, scrapes the floor clean. He takes my blood. Takes it all inside him.

He crawls to me. Lies down beside me. I see nothing in his eyes. I see everything in his eyes.

He waits. His lips are flushed with my blood. Red and purple and parted. Germs dance on the tip of his tongue. Almost a hundred different kinds of bacteria. The dragon waits.

My face is wet. I am crying. It takes me a moment to realize this, now that there will be no more moments, now that this is the only moment left.

I stare into RJ's eyes and I move my head. The hole in my throat closes, opens again.

RJ gazes back at me, and moves his head, too. If you weren't watching him the way I am, you would never know he'd moved at all.

He raises his hand and slips it into mine. He feels so cold. He feels so good. So good.

All I see is his mouth. The opening hatch. The widening gyre. His mouth, red and purple and black. He's drained the souls of stars, but there are no stars, not tonight. Not ever. There's only white. Everything is white. I am turning to white, and I am turning to red, and I am turning and turning.

And I am gone.

~

The ship sings me awake. Generators vibrate through Angie's flesh, through her bones, up and down the rivers of vein, the streams of blood. Nerves twang like plucked strings. Electric sparks in red darkness. The body, her body, my body. Our body. Everything hums.

I get to my feet and the air parts around me, washes over me, through me. I hold my hand up to the light, fingers splayed. Delicate webs of flesh, glowing pearl-pink.

RJ's husk lies on the floor. I see the cells shriveling, curling in on themselves like burning paper; feel the rot lacing the tissue. The scent of violets fills Angie's nose. I pull it inside us, taste it at the root of the tongue, every atom, every molecule.

All the pain is gone. All the world is new. And the same. The stones I have been, long crumbled, tell me so; the plants I have been, long withered, tell me so. The stars inside me have burned out, and burn forevermore.

I remember my life, Angie's life. Joys and triumphs, sorrow and fear, needs and wants and yearnings undefinable. It is all so small, and it is all so terrible, and so lovely.

I take a step. Another. RJ knows where we're going. I built the ship, after all. No one knows it better than I. Him. Us.

Hatches and ladders and stairs. We're in the ship's heart, now. The steel welcomes me. I punch in coordinates and feel the metal heave below my feet as the ship changes course. Lets go. Gives itself up to gravity, to that which cannot be escaped. Should not be escaped.

I stand at the window and watch as we slip into the mouth of the black hole. Stars speed past, stretched to thin white thread. The thread snaps. No more light. We are in the dark, and we are the dark. We are falling, falling into forever, and this is what it is to fly.

~

The ship touches down in thick orange dust, and the Lover is waiting. I would know the Lover anywhere. My own face in a mirror; my own hand, clasping the other.

Triplicate moons throw my shadow to earth. Angie's pores open in the autumnal light, tiny mouths sucking down alien air. Dust slips through the other mouth, too, the mouth she opened in her throat; sifts down her esophagus; settles gently in still gray lungs.

The Lover moves toward me. Stands before me. We touch.

We speak in tongues of flesh, of muscle and bone, nodes and cells and microbes. Behind walls of skin, blood whispers to blood.

Universes move around us, and inside us. We stand together, perfectly still.

Amelia Mangan is a writer originally from London, currently living in Sydney, Australia. Her writing is featured in Attic Toys (ed. Jeremy C. Shipp); X7 and No Monsters Allowed (both ed. Alex Davis); The Bestiarum Vocabulum and Phobophobias (both ed. Dean M. Drinkel); When Darkness Calls (ed. Emma Audsley); Charms Vol. 3 (ed. Sally Odgers); Carnival of the Damned (eds. Henry Snider & David C. Hayes); Mother Goose is Dead (eds. Michele Acker & Kirk Dougal), The Willows Magazine, Twisted Dreams Magazine, Cthulhupalooza Magazine, and Akujunkan: The Infinite Process 2003 Anthology (ed. Roseanna White). Her short story, "Blue Highway", won Yen Magazine's first annual short story competition and featured in its 65th issue. She can be found on Twitter (@AmeliaMangan) and Facebook (http://www.facebook.com/amelia.mangan).

EVERGREEN
Peter Giglio

1.

Years before the world started to change, Rachel had gone to the grocery store. A routine trip, nothing unusual...until she didn't return.

The case turned cold fast. And so, in many ways, did Chance's heart.

The one thing he clung to was a holdover from his beloved wife. Her affection for living things: vibrant greens and cherry-red roses, beings as trivial as dandelions and those as magnificent as pink peonies.

"Watch where you mow, dear," she'd always warned.

And he did, always. The yard, the garden, the flowers: these things were her legacy; one cut short by the cruel currents of time, by a cold case and a warming world.

An old man, he thought, was entitled to simple joys, more than memories and photographs. Something he could feel, touch, smell; something that pulled the past closer.

So for decades, Chance Freeman kept a plush, green yard. He tended her roses.

He carried on.

To countless compliments, he proudly beamed, "Just growing nature's carpet."

He loved the soft, sticky feel of fine cool blades on his bare feet: Kentucky Blue, Bermuda, Centipede... Any species was fine, as long as it was green and his to tend.

He spent many nights on the deck, sipping wine, enjoying the sweet scents of flowers and a fresh mow; aromas that, for many years, were the only constants in a progressively lonely life.

But being alone wasn't exactly loneliness, as long as he could pay tribute to Rachel.

Then the world took a sharp turn for the worst. Temperatures spiked higher with each passing year, until four seasons were reduced to three: hot, hotter, and terminal.

People in uninhabitable climates fled to other stars in vessels that moved faster than light. And those who stayed behind forlornly witnessed Mother Earth's untimely demise.

Great Lake states like Minnesota, where Chance called home, became deserts.

Some installed artificial grass and staked ersatz trees, clinging to the look and feel of a bygone era. But most people dropped the façade altogether, settling for barren vistas.

Chance did neither.

He fought the unfavorable tides of time tooth and nail. He used the latest, greatest chemicals, spent hours watering a desolate yard, and tried to drown out the stern rebukes that had replaced compliments.

"You're wasting water on nothing..."

"This must be costing you a fortune. You're a fool..."

Despite bruised pride, Chance smiled from inside his cooling suit as he toiled beneath the blazing sun. Long retired from a lucrative career, he had enough time and wealth to pursue whatever madness brought him comfort. And if not *true* comfort, at least a shred of solace.

Some years his rectangle of earth sprouted a few clumps

of Buffalo Grass. In good years, he cultivated entire patches. Regardless of yield, every blade that cheated fate was a giant victory.

A victory for Rachel.

Now, things had worsened. Record high temperatures and his failing back kept him indoors. He watched through the great windows of his sunroom, the last blades withering under the December sun...

And thought about the short and happy life he'd led once upon a time.

Even the years between had served a purpose; had been better than this.

Something had to be done.

So he scrolled through the yellow listings on his handheld vid-com and landed on lawn services. He started at the top of seven entries, remembering how the old phone books contained hundreds. The first six attempts produced the same result: a recorded message that said the business had gone under. Resigned to more of the same, he clicked the last entry.

A jaunty man with a bright smile appeared on the screen.

"Thank you for contacting Zellman Lawncare," the man said. "My name is Nigel Zellman, here to assist you with all your lawncare needs."

Chance's eyes widened. "Hello," he said. "Is this a...a recording?"

Zellman laughed. "No, sir. This is yours truly, Nigel Zellman, in the flesh. Well, at least I'm in the flesh here in my office." He laughed again. "How can I help today?"

"I...I—"

"Let me guess, you can't grow grass, right?"

Chance nodded.

"Not to worry, friend. I've recently procured a new product from Rigel, a treatment sure to remedy your barren-Earth blues. And I'm proud to report that Zellman Lawncare is the sole distributor in the state of Minnesota. You're in Minnesota, aren't you?"

"Duluth."

"Great! You'll be my first customer in Duluth. That is, if you decide to go with Evergreen."

"Evergreen?"

"That's what we're calling it. Great name, eh?"

"Yeah, well, uh...does it grow grass?"

"Thick, lustrous, weed free grass, just like grandpa used to grow and mow, and the best thing about Evergreen, it only needs to be applied once a year. Go with Evergreen...I'm sorry, I didn't catch your name."

"Chance."

"Go with Evergreen, Chance, and you'll be mowing in no time. When would you like me to come by for a free consultation?"

"Uh...anytime that's good for you."

"Nights work best for me."

"Nights?"

"When it's cooler, of course."

"I go to bed pretty early, Mr. Zell—"

"Please, call me Nigel."

"Tonight's fine, Nigel." Chance tentatively returned the man's smile. "Tonight is just fine."

2.

Chance was awakened by a beep from his vid-com.

It was dark, his head foggy. He glanced at his wristwatch, a fifty-year-old Timex he kept in perfect condition ("takes a licking, keeps on ticking," he liked to say, though no one seemed to remember the now-defunct watchmaker's once famous slogan), and squinted until he made out the time. "It's almost ten," he groaned, pulling himself upright on the couch.

"Sir," a pleasant female voice said, "you have a visitor."

"Who bothers an old man this time of night?" he asked.

"Remember," the voice said, "your appointment with

Zellman Lawncare."

Chance rubbed his head and considered his place on the couch rather than his bed. "Of course," he said with a dry chuckle. "Where's my mind? Please disengage the antechamber door, Rachel."

"Yes, dear," she said.

He'd programmed her voice into the house's communication circuit a decade ago, using an old DVD recording he'd stumbled upon in the attic. The system had analyzed the recording in less than five minutes and produced a remarkably lifelike facsimile that was sometimes calming and other times eerie. Still, it wasn't much. Not her legacy, of course, just a cheap electronic imitation. He was capable of programming it to say anything, even "I love you," but he never did. It already felt aberrant to keep her around in such a counterfeit manner, and just like he didn't carpet his lawn in turf, he didn't like pretending artificial intelligence could possess his wife's soul.

A light knock sounded.

"I'm coming," Chance said. Cracking the door open, he said, "I'm an old man, don't move as fast as I—" Peering into the antechamber, he gasped at the sight of his visitor.

"May I come in?" asked the Rigelian male at the door.

More than ten feet tall, the *alien* wore a poorly-fitted business suit of earthly origin. His florescent, green skin pulsated, giving off its own light in the dimly-lit corridor. And when the man—the *thing*—smiled, Chance felt panicked as he fixated on its—*his*—incredibly sharp fangs.

He'd never seen a Rigelian in the flesh. After all, he'd never been to Rigel, and as far as he knew only dignitaries from their planet's four nations ever traveled to Earth.

"My name is Tim," said the visitor. "I'm a representative of Zellman Lawncare."

Chance swallowed the dry lump in his throat, eyes never leaving his caller. "Tim?"

The fangs became more pronounced as "Tim" laughed,

and Chance's heartbeat, pounding in his head, grew dangerously arrhythmic. "Not my real name, of course, but I like it. I like human names very much. Take yours, for instance. Chance. Such a *daring* moniker."

As far as mankind at large was concerned, these creatures were heroes, having opened the door to their world, inviting millions upon millions of human refugees to live free on their soil. Who was he to deny one of them entry through his front door?

"May I come in?" Tim repeated.

"Of course, of course, you'll have to forgive me…" Chance stepped aside as Tim ducked his head beneath the relatively short door frame and entered, his flesh taking on a more normal appearance in the halogen glow of the living room.

"You're the first man from Rigel I've ever met," Chance said.

Tim nodded. "Yours is a forgivable and common reaction, Mr. Freeman."

"And your English is—"

"Perfect," Tim said with another hearty laugh. "I hope you won't take this the wrong way, Mr. Freeman, but human languages are not complex."

"No. Not at all. I studied French for years in college and still have no fluency to show for my efforts, so I wish I could say the same."

"Ah, French. One of my favorites. Your human tongues have the elegance of simplicity, and I'm happy you didn't consider my remark condescending. As you know, we admire you in many ways. The ability to walk in the light of your sun is a far greater gift than our intellect, wouldn't you say?"

Chance considered the question for a moment. Although his pulse had returned to normal, his muscles tensed at the irony of the question. "Perhaps," he said, "but that gift has been rendered somewhat pyrrhic now, wouldn't *you* say?"

"Ah, but not for those who come to Rigel, Mr. Freeman. Our world blooms with the most beautiful flora and fauna in the universe, and the mildness of our seasons makes it a paradise, particularly for humans who are able to enjoy the long Rigel days."

"I'm sorry, are you a travel agent or a lawn-man? I'm confused."

"It is your turn to forgive me, if you will be so kind. It was my understanding that humans often enjoy a thing called 'small talk.'"

Chance laughed his first real laugh in years, and it felt good. "Language is logical, Tim. Not culture."

Tim arched a bushy eyebrow, raised a long, sharp finger, and said, "Very true." Then he walked to the sunroom, Chance following closely behind. There, he stared through the large windows, into the desolate backyard.

"Can you help me?" Chance asked.

"Yes, Mr. Freeman. I can help you."

3.

The fee for the service was shockingly low, and Chance couldn't help but be suspicious. "And this really works?"

"Evergreen is guaranteed to work within twenty-four hours or you pay nothing."

His father's advice rang through his mind: *If something's too good to be true, run!* But these were different times. And he—here in his living room, talking to a man from another star—was desperate for a modicum of normalcy.

Chance nodded. "Okay, you sold me."

"Excellent," said Tim. "Our team will apply the treatment tonight as you sleep."

"Thank you. Should I pay you now or—"

"We'll send you a bill, Mr. Freeman. We never accept payment until the customer is completely satisfied."

As Tim ducked through the front door on his way out, he paused and glanced back at Chance. "Would you mind if I asked you one last question?"

"No. Go ahead."

"Why do you stay?"

"This is my home, Tim. At my age, memories are fleeting enough. This place...well, it keeps me in touch with the past. Happier times."

"How's that working out for you?" Tim said with a smile...

A somewhat wicked smile, Chance thought, not to mention a *second* "last question." His mouth turned down as he tried to shake off prejudice. Cultural differences, he reminded himself, then with a greater degree of happiness, he thought about the promise of a green lawn. He forced a weak smile and said, "If you do what you claim you can, everything will be...much better."

"Of course. Goodnight, Mr. Freeman."

"Goodnight, Tim."

4.

The next morning, Chance ambled into the sunroom, sipping coffee. He pressed a button on the wall and watched expectantly as shutters rose. A sliver of green widened until it was a sea of bright perfection. Tears streaming down his face, body weak, he spilled coffee down his nightshirt. But the painful burn on his chest couldn't weaken the fullness of his heart. He dropped his mug, ignored the crash-tinkle of shattering ceramic, and stepped out of his slippers. Then he unlatched the door and rushed into the yard in his pajamas. Even though the morning air was blistering, the earth beneath his feet—draped in lush, velvety greenery—was intoxicating on his toes and in his nose.

"I need to mow already," he said with a smile. He couldn't believe how fast Evergreen grew.

He pushed the electric mower over the yard three times a

day, breathing deep the scents of rediscovered hope.

"A man your age should be more careful," Miranda Sicuro, a neighbor, warned through a thin crack in her sliding glass door. "You're going to dehydrate out here."

He smiled. "Ah, Miranda, such neighborly concern. Let me ask, did you bring me something cool to drink?"

"Well, no, I—"

"Then kindly shove your concern up your ass, dear." His eyes widened, smile implacable.

Miranda slammed the door shut.

As the days ticked by, Chance's back began to feel better. He discovered muscles he'd forgotten he had. And he was happier than he'd been in decades.

He spent his evenings in the sunroom with an old family photo clutched to his chest and watched Rachel's roses miraculously—and rapidly—bloom in the narrow space her garden had once graced. His eyes filled with joyful tears.

This was more, so much more, than promised. Far more than he'd dreamed. Although the growth defied logic—not a single drop of water was used to yield this fruitful bounty—he didn't care.

Logic told him long ago to set course for Rigel, as so many others had, and he'd ignored it. Logic was useless; it was the way of math and language and science. What he was experiencing was so much more important.

This was *spiritual*.

One day, tired of electronic-Rachel replying to his out-loud ruminations, he deactivated the house's communication circuit. She was alive in his mind's eye, and he could almost see her tending the garden again. Could almost see the curvaceous outline of her form through her sundress. Could almost smell her Channel No. 5, and the secret, feminine fragrances—the more powerful aphrodisiacs—that hung under her store-bought allure.

At night, when the temperatures cooled below one-twenty, Chance rolled around in the grass. He breathed deeply the sweet fragrance of Rachel's roses, as well as the lilacs and peonies that had started to bloom around the house, and he imagined he was young again, holding his new wife close, wrestling playfully with her in the yard.

He felt more than alive.

He felt immortal.

Two weeks after Evergreen was applied, Chance noticed other unexpected changes that went far beyond *feeling* younger. Every morning in the mirror, he *was* younger. Just as grass had returned to the yard, hair returned to his once barren head. Wrinkles faded. Aches and pains all but retreated. Gray gave way to brown. Teeth whitened. Nose and ear hairs receded. Waste flowed without protest. And morning boners returned with a vengeance.

Within a month, he looked and felt like a twenty-five year old man.

Then, one morning, the most incredible thing happened. When the sunroom shutters opened, Rachel stood in the backyard clothed in her favorite sundress, which fluttered gracefully in the hot dawn breeze.

He stared at her, shocked beyond reason. When she stared back at him, deep and abiding love in her soft emerald eyes, shock vanished and joy danced with every molecule of Chance Freeman's existence.

He opened the door to her.

"May I come in?" she asked.

"Rachel?"

"Yes," she said, tears brimming in her eyes as they were in his. "I'm home."

"Rachel?" He held his arms out to her.

"May I come in?" she repeated.

He began weeping. "Is it really you?" He made a move toward her, but she held up a halting hand.

"It's very hot out here," she said, "you shouldn't come out; I should come in. May I...may I come in?"

"Of course," he sobbed. "Of course. Please, this is your

home. Come inside. Come inside."

As soon as she entered the house, he threw his arms around her. "Where did you go?" he cried. "What happened?"

"Are you satisfied?" she asked coldly.

"What?"

"Are you satisfied?"

"Of course, of course I am. I'm overjoyed. But, but...what happened to you?"

She didn't respond with words; rather, with her sharp long fangs sank deep into his neck. Pain burned trails through his head, and he knew in his dying moment, watching the opulent greens and reds of his backyard fade to brown, feeling his wife's soft body transform into something hard and alien, that this was no reunion.

It was a cruel game of predator and prey, and he wouldn't let them win. Wouldn't let them shatter *all* hope. Somehow, perhaps by virtue of the same psychic link that had fooled him, he knew his lifeforce would taste sweeter if he surrendered the lie completely.

He closed his eyes, pretended the thing in his arms really was Rachel, and waited for death.

5.

"So run this by me again, Mr. Zellman," Detective Saunders said. "How exactly did you know the victim?"

"Like I told you," Nigel said in a quivering voice, "I didn't. He called me some time back about treating his lawn, but my daughter fell ill and I wasn't able to make it up to Duluth for our appointment. When I was able to return to my professional responsibilities, I tried to follow up with Mr. Freeman, but I couldn't reach him. The recordings all said his communication links were temporarily out of service. I was in the area this morning, calling on another client, so I swung by. His backdoor was open and...I found him...found him just like he is…a husk…a, a shell."

The detective shook his head. "Doesn't make sense. None of this makes—"

"I swear," Zellman pleaded.

"Calm down, Mr. Z," the detective said. "I'm not saying you did anything wrong. This is the fourth case like this I've seen in the last month."

"Really? But I haven't—"

"It's been kept out of the papers for now, at the insistence of the governments of Rigel, and I must warn you keep your mouth shut. They don't want to start a planet-wide panic—that's their official position—but they think it has something to do with a virus. They want us instead to double our immigration efforts. Damn fine of them to do this considering the potential for contamination, but who are we to question our saviors. I'm only telling you these things because…well, you seem like a good man, and I would strongly recommend you to take your family and get off this dying rock as fast as you can."

"No," Zellman choked. "I won't leave."

"Do it for your daughter," the detective said. "Her sickness was due to the heat, wasn't it?"

The salesman nodded glumly.

"See it all the time, Mr. Z. Kids need to play outside without getting sick, without falling down dead."

"I understand. I agree. But…but we won't be leaving."

"Why. My family is scheduled to immigrate two weeks from tomorrow. It's perfectly—"

"No," Zellman insisted. "Don't go."

"What do you know that you're not telling me, Mr. Z?"

"Have you ever met a Rigelian?"

"Of course not. No."

"Well, I have, and I don't trust them. Take it from a natural born salesman. I know when someone, even some*thing*, is selling a false bill of goods. And I know when I look in a man's eye who I'm dealing with. It's a gift. Maybe a curse. These creatures, they're cagey. They like to play games."

Saunders threw Zellman a dismissive wave. "Listen to yourself. You sound like one of those revolutionary nuts in the days of first contact."

"I think they were right," Zellman said. "The revolutionaries, I mean. I've denied it for a long time, but I think they were right not to trust the Rigelians. Please, don't take your family to Rigel."

"I've had family and friends immigrate already, Mr. Z."

"As have I. We all have."

"I talk to my brother almost every day through interstellar-com. Everyone there is fine. Hell, they've never been happier."

"Look in their eyes, Detective. Listen closely to their words. Think of all their quirks, the things that made them human, then ask yourself if you see those odd, almost imperceptible features articulated now. Like me, observation is your specialty, understanding people, body language. Our goals are different, of course, but the psychology is the same."

Worry swept the detective's face. "What are you saying?"

"I'm saying that the immigrants are all dead. That the…the communications are all…they're all A.I. facades. And if I'm right, though I pray I'm not, the Rigelians are some kind of…of *vampires*."

"Vampires?" the detective bellowed, worry replaced by an incredulous look. "That's ridiculous."

"Maybe you're right," Zellman said in a defeated voice. "Maybe you're right."

"Go home, Mr. Z. Give your daughter a big hug. Then get some rest. You need it."

Nigel Zellman turned away from the detective and stared into the blood-red sky through the windows of Chance Freeman's sunroom.

He thought about his family.

And he wept.

A Pushcart Prize nominee and an active member of the Horror Writers Association and the International Thriller Writers, **Peter Giglio** is the author of five novels and four novellas. His works of short fiction can be found in a number of notable volumes, including two comprehensive genre anthologies edited by NEW YORK TIMES Bestselling author John Skipp. With Scott Bradley, Peter wrote the author-approved screen adaptation of Joe R. Lansdale's "The Night They Missed the Horror Show," and an established screenwriting team in Los Angeles holds the film option on Giglio's SUNFALL MANOR. Peter's next novel, LESSER CREATURES, will be released in December by DarkFuse.

WELCOME TO THE REPTILE HOUSE
Stephen Graham Jones

I t didn't start the way you might think.
This is where I kind of pause, look off, bite my lip into my mouth so I can come up with the next big lie. With what my dad, talking loud for my little sister, would call Jamie Boy's next big excuse.

Let me try it again: it started pretty much exactly the way you'd think a thing like this would get going.

I was twenty-two, still flashing my high-school diploma at job interviews. Still doing stuff like stealing an extra bag of ice from the cooler if the clerk's not eyeballing me. Hiding a litter of mismatched puppies for the weekend for my friend Dell, and not asking any questions. Bumming smokes outside the bars, but sometimes having my own pack.

I was just getting into tattoos, too. Not on me — my arms had been choked blue not four months after I moved into my own place — but *from* me. That was the idea, anyway. I wasn't officially apprenticing anywhere, and nobody'd offered their skin to me yet, but I'd always been drawing. My notebooks from junior high are like a running autobiography in doodles, and I'd worked one summer applying decals and pinstriping at my uncle's bodyshop, and finally graduated to window tint before he trusted me with the front-door keys.

He should have known better.

But, tats, they were kind of the same as those junior high notebooks. They were the one thing I could concentrate on. Just for hours. Planning, sketching, tracing. For now I was practicing on the back of my right calf, the side of my left I could reach. Snakes and geckos mostly, though I could feel a dragon curled up inside me, waiting for the right swatch of skin. I've talked to the grizzly old-timers, the real gunslingers of the wild west of body art, and they say you go through phases. You get stuck on something, and talk all your clients into it. What you're trying to do is get it right, what's in your head. You want to get it right and make it permanent, and then watch it walk away.

Like I say, though, tattooing was strictly a sideline, and, as I couldn't afford supplies, it probably wouldn't have been just superhygenic for me to draw on anybody, either. It was just me so far, so I guess that didn't matter too much. But I could already see myself ten years down the road. My own shop, a girlfriend with my ink reaching north out of her bra, circling her shoulder, everybody but me having to imagine what the full image was.

Anyway, where it started: one night, to pay me back for the thing with the puppies, Dell's on my phone, has a shiny new job.

"Seriously, *morgue* attendant?" I said, turning away from my living room of three people with names I hadn't all-the-way caught.

"Different," he said.

I told him maybe, sure, but was there two hours after midnight all the same, a cigarette pinched between my thumb and index finger.

"Leave it," Dell said, opening the door on me and looking past in his important way. Into the parking lot.

Saddleview Funeral Chapel and Crematorium.

I rubbed my cherry out on the tall ashtray, followed him in.

~

On the way through the maze of viewing rooms to get to the back, Dell told me how he got this gravy gig. His uncle had worked here forever and a day ago, sitting up with dead soldiers mailed back from war. Or, not sitting up, but sleeping in the same room with, like a guard. It was because there had been some political vandalism or something. Anyway, the boss man now had been the boss man then, and remembered Dell's uncle, so here Dell was. His job was to buzz the alley door open for deliveries, and not touch anything.

He was Dell, though, right?

We toured through the cold room. It was slab city, naked dead people everywhere, their usually-covered parts not nearly so interesting as I'd kind of been hoping. We put those paper mouth-masks on and felt like mad scientists drifting through the frost, deciding who to bring back, who to let rot.

"Hell yeah," I said through my mask, and, ahead of me, Dell nodded that he knew, he knew.

I told him about who-all'd been at my place earlier, maybe lying a little, and in return, like I owed him here, he asked me for the thousandth time for my little sister's number. Not permission, he'd always assumed he had permission to do what- and whoever he wanted. But he wanted me to middleman it.

"Off limits," I told him, about her, trying to make my voice sound all no-joke. Because it was.

"Fruit on the limb," Dell said, reaching up to pluck her. Except more graphically, somehow. With distinct pornographic intent.

"She's not like us," I said, but before we could get into our usual dance where my sister was involved, the lights dimmed. A second later, a painful buzz filled the place, coming in from all sides, like the walls were speakers.

"Delivery," Dell said. "Hide."

Alone in the room with the dead moments later, I looked around, breathing harder than I was meaning to. All fun and games until one of those bright white sheets slithers off, right? Until somebody sits up.

Finally I held my breath and crawled in under one of the tables, onto that clangy little shelf, some guy's naked ass not two feet over my face, his body bloated with all kinds of vileness.

After ten minutes in which I got terminally sober, the double doors slammed back. They were the same kind restaurants have, that are made for crashing open, that don't even have handles.

A gurney or whatever was rolling through, no legs pushing it. Just exactly what I needed, yeah. Finally it bumped into a cabinet, stopped. I breathed out but then its wheels started creaking again. It lurched its way over to right beside me, parked its haunted self inches from my face. Just far enough away for a hand to flop down in front of my face. It was pale, dead, the beds of the fingernails dark blue.

I flinched back, fell off my shelf, and Dell laughed, stepped off the belly of the new dead dude he'd been using like a knee board.

I flipped him off, pushed him away and lit a cigarette. Not like anybody in there was going to mind. Dell took one too and we leaned back against stainless steel edges, reflected on our lives.

Another lie.

What he did was haul a laser tag kit up from his locker.

It was the best war ever, at least until, trying to duck my killshot, he crashed a cart over, a dead lady spilling out, sliding to a stop at a cabinet.

I read her toe tag, looked up to her face.

On her inner thigh was a chameleon.

Everything starts somewhere, Dad.

~

Before you get worried, no, this isn't some necro-thing about to happen. I never asked Dell what those puppies were for, but I'm pretty sure he'd nabbed them from about twelve different backyards—people in the classifieds give their addresses over so willingly—and would guess he sold them from a box in the mall parking lot. Meaning they all have good lives now. He wasn't sacrificing them out on some lonely road or anything. He wasn't trying to conjure up a buddy to rape dead women with.

However, if what he was looking for was somebody to trade him rides and cigarettes and ex-girlfriends' numbers for some quality time alone in his cold room with a tat gun, well: there I was.

When you're looking to hire onto a parlor, to rent a booth—hell, even just to lure a mentor in—one thing you've always got to have, it's an art book. A portfolio. What you can do, your greatest hits, the story of your craft.

Problem is, every two-bit dropout can pull something like that together.

But. What if, say, you'd moved to the city only a couple of months ago. And had always just done ink for friends, but were looking to go legit, now. And, what? Did I snap pics of any of those mythically-good tats?

Yeah, yes, I did.

Here.

Play with the hue a bit on your buddy's computer, and a gecko crawling up a dead guy's shoulder, his skin will look so alive. And there won't even be any rash, any blood. Like you've got that light of a touch.

At first Dell would only let me practice on the bodies that were queued up for the oven, as that would erase evidence of our non-crime, but one night he left me alone to make a burger run—it's cliché that morgue attendants are always eating sloppy food, but I guess it's cliché for a reason—and I unplugged my gun, plugged it back in under the table of this woman I was pretty sure had been a yoga instructor. And recently.

Her skin was tight, springy. Most of the dead, I was having to really stretch their flesh out, then get Dell to hold it tight while I snapped the pic, so that night's lizard wouldn't look like it was melting off.

With her, though. I was just halfway through the iguana's tail by the time Dell got back.

He had to let me finish, because who conks with only ten percent of a tattoo done, right?

It was a beauty, too. Just like in my head, I made the tongue curl the opposite direction the tail was, for symmetry. And where it was reaching, only her boyfriend would ever know.

Pretty as it was, though, I didn't get any burgers—this was Dell's punishment (like I would want to eat something his hands had been touching on)—and, to make him laugh, I inked X's over the eyes of the guy at the front of the line for the oven. He was skinny, pale with death, still cold from the freezer, his two gunshot wounds puckered up like lips. He looked like a punk reject from 1977.

Dell shook his head, walked away smiling. I could see his reflection in all the stainless steel, and, as it turned out, Dell's uncle's reference didn't mean much when the boss man's just-dead, honor-student, choir-singing, yoga-bunny niece he'd been saving for the morning to embalm *personally* turned up with an evil bug-eyed lizard of some kind trying to crawl up her side, its tongue reaching up to circle her nipple in the most lecherous fashion.

Some people got no sense of art, I mean.

Dell in particular.

~

Like he had to, he came over, did what he needed to do to my face, to my television and my lamp. The television wasn't mine, but I wasn't saying anything. And then, so I would remember, he dug my tattoo gun up from my backseat, came back in and pulled me off the couch by the shirt I wasn't wearing, sat on my arms with his knees so he could drill some bathroom-wall version of a penis into my chest. Or maybe it was a novelty sprinkler, or a leaky cowboy hat, I don't know.

Chances are I could have bucked him off, but I kind of deserved it too, I guessed. Though if he'd been a real friend, he would have lit a cigarette for me. And maybe done a better job.

When he was done he threw my rig into the corner, slammed through my screen door, told me to forget his number if I knew what was good for me.

I spent the next two days turning his punishment tattoo into a Texas bluebonnet, because that's where I'd been born. At least that was the new story I was going to have ready.

How a flower was going to fit with the iguana theme I'd been studying on lately, I had no idea, but maybe it didn't matter so much either. Soon I wasn't going to have any skin left.

A week passed, then another, and, standing outside a bar one night with my shirt already gone, I saw the last girl Dell had been shacking up with. I'd taken her to prom once upon a time, when prom still existed. She was riding by on the back of another guy's motorcycle. Really pressing herself into him. Glaring us all down.

"She thinks we care?" I said to whoever was beside me.

"Probably thinks we did it," whoever it was said back, taking a deep drag and holding it, holding it.

I narrowed my eyes, looked over through her smoke: Sheila. From when I was a community-college student for three weeks.

"Story?" I said, offering her one from my pack.

She held it sideways, ran her fingers along the white paper and sneered about it like she always did, like she hated cigarettes, like she was just smoking them to kill them. But she threaded it behind her ear all the same. Your monkey's always whispering to you, I guess.

She shrugged, told me about Dell.

He'd been found not just normal-dead, like OD'd or stabbed or drowned in vomit in a bed across town. No, he'd been like *exploded* behind a club. A dental-records-only kind of thing. Smeared on the brick, important footsteps leading away, the whole trip.

I eeked my mouth out, stood on the stoop for more smokes than I'd meant.

The bluebonnet on my chest was waving with each inhale.

I went home, watched it in the mirror. Added red buds in the blue, in memoriam. I think that's the word.

When I searched Dell up on the newspaper site, two hits came up.

One was his obituary, the funeral I'd missed, and the other hit was about impropriety with the dead.

The blotter had nothing at all about the late-night, involuntary tattoo on the owner's car-wrecked niece — I guess I could have been famous, started a career right there — but it did mention how Saddleview was getting the funeral home version of an audit. Evidently, one month it had taken in more bodies than it had buried.

I shook my head, clicked away. Dell.

He'd probably got the orders wrong. Pushed one too many into the oven one night, then tried to fix the manifest, had to burn a to-be-buried stiff as well.

It didn't have anything to do with me, anyway.

That part of my life was over.

Lie number ten-thousand, there, I guess. But who's keeping count.

~

As for why Dell had turned inside-out behind the bar, I had no clue. He'd always been high-strung. In junior high, he'd always been the first one to put his lips to the freon tube, the first one to spray thinner into the rag, press it against his mouth, so I figured it was some accumulated chemical reaction. Something the military would probably pay big bucks to the get the formula for. They should have been monitoring us the whole time. Every night, we were out there, experimenting.

And, just because Dell was gone, that didn't mean the lab was closed.

One night maybe three weeks after the funeral where I probably should have been a pallbearer, there we all were, miles out of the city, in a field with a bonfire, like the bonfire had always been there, waiting. There were sparks and, when the wood started to run out, everybody had to donate one article of clothing. And then two.

It was interesting in a decline-of-the-world kind of way. I was kicked back in a lawn chair, zoned out, just mellow, my shirt burning, keeping us all warm. I was watching this one girl named Kelly, already down to her pink clamshell bra, and thinking I might have to wait this situation out when another car pulled up and we all kind of sighed.

Too many cars meant the cops wouldn't be far behind.

Then, too, depending on who was in that car, it could all be worth it.

I shrugged to myself, leaned back to see who the new victims were going to be: first was a guy who could have been a surf bum in a movie ten years ago, second was his clone, and third was a red-headed girl I thought I knew from somewhere.

When the fourth stepped out, I knew where I knew Red from: my sister's friend from down the street at the old house.

Gigi was here.

"Hey!" my non-buddy Seth called out, dancing behind her, pointing down to her with both hands.

I settled deeper into my chair, looked back to the fire like maybe I could blind myself by staring.

Soon enough she found me, stood there with a silver can in her hand and said, "Dad's been trying to reach you."

"Dell?" I said.

"You were his best friend."

"He was a punk. A wastoid."

"And what are you?"

"You should leave," I told her.

"I'm the one who should be doing things, yeah," she said, and that was it.

For a while some guys were running at the fire and jumping over it, but that was short-lived. It was mostly quiet and surly, at least for me. Just music and muttering, and too many snapshot flashes of my sister with surfer boy two, his arm draped over her in a way that was making me swallow hard.

Before the night was over, there were going to be words. And probably more. But first I'd need to make sure he was eighteen—too old to press charges, according to Dell, who would have learned the hard way.

I was nodding to myself about how it was all going to play out, how I was about to step across to the cable spool they were using like a love seat, and was even halfway counting down in my head when a chainsaw pulled up to our little gathering in the sticks.

It was Dell's ex. On her new guy's motorcycle. She stepped off—dismounted, more like—and he just sat there still holding the grips, inspecting us all, the fire dancing in the black glass of his helmet.

I swallowed, looked away like I'd never seen them, tried not to track Gigi even though I did register the t-shirt she'd had on at one point. It was in the fire. The first chance I got I went to pee in the tall grass, never came back, just stopped at a convenience store, called the party in.

You do what you can to save your little sister, I guess. Even cash your friends in.

In my living room the next morning, still awake—I hadn't planned on coming home this early—I ran my hand over the elaborate, dragon-scaled salamander on the right side of my left calf.

I tried to keep the hair there shaved down, to really show it off, but, running my hand over it, it was crackly. And smelled worse than bad.

I sleuthed through my head, made the necessary connection: this was the leg I'd had kicked up on the cooler, close to the fire. On purpose, to show off my work, show what I could do. I'd even been wetting down the scales with beer when nobody was looking, just waiting for anybody to say anything.

Nobody had.

Instead I'd just curled all the hair on my leg, and singed the heel of my favorite shoe.

Everybody had to have seen, though. It was beautiful, it was crawling, it was alive.

I smoothed it down, passed out on the couch with that lizard warm under my hand, its eyes open for me, wheeling in their orbits, the pupils just slits, like rips you could climb through, into another world.

I should have tried.

~

I woke at dusk and flinched back hard, deeper into the couch.

There was a black motorcycle helmet on my coffee table. Watching me.

"Recognized your work," a guy said from the kitchen, and punctuated it by closing my refrigerator hard enough to rattle the ketchup.

Dell's ex's new boyfriend.

"Be still my heart," I said, clutching it, sitting up.

"Don't be stupid," he told me, and stepped in, my tub of butter in his left hand, his right index finger smeared glossy yellow.

He ran it into his mouth, pulled his finger out like he was sneaking frosting off somebody's saved-back cupcake.

"Dairy," he said, running his finger along the edge of the tub again, then shaking his head to get his oily bangs out of his face.

I nearly screamed.

His eyes.

There were two crude X's tattooed over them. Two X's I'd done. When he was cold and dead on a rolling cart, two bullets punched through his chest.

"Been looking for someone with your particular . . . talents," he said, downing another fingerful.

I shook my head no, no, saw Dell smeared on a brick wall and stood to crash my way to the screen door, escape out into the night, into some other life.

The boyfriend's helmet caught me in the back like a bowling ball, threw me into the wall by the door, the whole house shaking when I hit.

He turned me over with the toe of his boot, stared down at my chest. Eating butter the whole while.

"Thought you were into reptiles," he said, about my bluebonnet, his accent tuned to the UK station, and just dialed over all the way to it.

I coughed, turned to the side, threw up.

He stepped his boot out of the way.

When I was done he kneeled down, jammed his butter finger into my mouth, smearing yellow all around inside. It was cold, wet, tasteless.

His face so close to mine.

"I'm sorry?" I said.

He laughed, pushed my head down, bouncing it off the carpet.

"You know cow milk is ninety-eight percent the same as cow blood?" he said, dipping his finger into the tub again.

I was just trying to breathe.

He shrugged, said, "Close enough," and set the butter down on a speaker.

From my angle on the floor, he was forever tall, and still pale like a junkie. But he did carry himself something like a British Invasion reject, definitely. Something self-consciously waifish and bad attitude about the way he caved his shoulders in around his chest. The hollow where his stomach should be. His lowslung jeans, like he was just daring you to trace his belt line.

There weren't supposed to be any of his kind anymore, though. Them and the dragons, they were on the extinct list, right? All there were that was even close anymore was all the goths, I guess, the Sandman dreamers, the Bauhaus die-hards, the velvet vest crowd who'd read too much Anne Rice, were probably going to grow up into good little steampunk rejects one day.

This boyfriend, though, I had a sense he was their original. That Neil Gaiman had seen him at a party in the UK, that Anne Rice had followed him through the streets of New Orleans one night, that Sid Vicious had taken a cue or two from him."This," he said, giving me some jazz hands action over his face, his eyes, those X's, "this isn't just permanent, you know? With me it's kind of forever, now, yeah? Get what I'm saying? What do you think of that, Jamie Boy?"

I pushed myself up against the wall, let some butter dribble from my mouth, down onto the bluebonnet.

"Jamie Boy?" I managed to say.

My dad was the only one who did that.

He just stared at me about that.

"She was nice," he said, falling back onto the couch like it was a throne, licking his lips in the most exaggerated way. "But little sisters are always nice, aren't they?"

"Who told you?"

"You did, telescope eyes."

Meaning he'd followed her home. Thinking that's where I was going to be. And then he'd made do with who *was* there.

I stood, but it was just to fall across the coffee table, into the hall. Not for any window but for the bathroom, for the toilet. To throw the rest of the world I used to know up.

In the shower, exploded, smeared all over the tile, was Dell's ex.

She had a bar of soap stuffed in what was left of her mouth.

"Sorry for the mess," the boyfriend said from the door, his leather pants somehow vulgar. "Got to clean up after you eat, though. If you don't, they come back, all that. I'm sure you've heard."

He was bored with it, trailed off, looking down the hall like at something important.

I knew where he was looking, though.

Four miles over, into the Crane Meadow subdivision. Into what could no longer really be considered a living room, I was pretty sure.

~

So, monsters are real. Surprise.

For some reason I'd never considered this.

Or — I'm lying again: *one* monster's real, anyway.

And I get the sense that's just how he likes it.

When I was done emptying myself into the toilet, I zombied my way back to the living room, my peripheral vision just a smoky haze.

Instead of killing me like I expected, like I wanted, like I deserved, he slapped a pair of blue nitrile gloves down on the coffee table, told me to rubber up, whirred my gun in his other hand.

I looked down at myself to see what room was left for him to do his damage on.

I had it backwards.

Until thirty minutes before dawn, his left hand cupped around my balls the whole time—he'd crunched a metal thermos into tinfoil, to show what he could do—I worked on his face.

Every tattoo artist has to be able to repair somebody else's work. To cover up a name, fix a misspelling, fudge a date. Put a bikini top on that girl, make a pistol into a submarine, a submarine into a flying saucer, a flying saucer into a shadow, all that.

What I was supposed to do was make those dashed-on X's over his eyes into something presentable enough for the coming eternity. Something he wouldn't have to hide behind a helmet, a helmet he could only explain if he had a motorcycle, and he hated motorcycles. Everything went by too fast.

While I did my thing, holding his dead, cold skin tight—I'd had practice—he told me about 1976. How glorious it had been. No cell phone cameras, no bullshit DNA, no credit cards in the system, to track people with. Back then he never woke up in morgues, had to sneak out. Back then he was keeping the morgues *stocked*.

In his raspy singsong voice he told me about concerts and brushes with fame, and about a milkmaid he'd known with blond hair that curled on the side like she was an orthodox Jew, and how that framed her face so perfect, even though, where and when she'd lived, she probably hadn't even known Jews existed. How he never knew her name, only her insides. How she tasted.

Because I didn't have the barber patter down yet, and because this was my first time inking a *face*, I just worked, and kept light on my toes. It wasn't on purpose, but his hand on my balls—going up on your toes is kind of a natural response.

Still, even working fast enough to sweat, I was only able to get one eye done.

I was being careful, I mean.

I handed him the mirror, let him look, my balls still in his hand.

He looked side to side at himself and squeezed gently, rolling me like marbles, my spine straightening from it, and then he looked me straight-on.

It wasn't bad.

That mime make-up trick, with a tapered, upside-down cross kind of coming through the eyebrow, leaking down onto the cheek? I'd taken some of that and mixed it with the diamond eyes harlequins in comic books have, and filled it all in solid, so that his right eyeball, looking out from all that black, it was seriously wicked. I'd gotten the idea . . . well, first from what I needed to cover that stupid X, but second from a facepaint band I'd seen one night — not KISS, please, and this wasn't a juggalo night, and I've never seen Marilyn Manson live. Reading the show's write-up the next day, though, the show-off reviewer was saying how the lead singer's black-bagged eyes had been an insult to everything The Misfits had ever not stood for.

I didn't know Glenn Danzig's make-up well enough to make the link like the reviewer was — I was always more of a Sex Pistols kind of punk, I guess — but the guy with my balls in his hands seemed to recognize something. "Sick like a *dog*," he said, and held the mirror over to get a proper angle on his face. Run his other hand over the stubble he would probably never grow.

He liked it.

I breathed out for what felt like the first time in hours and he stood up into that one moment of relief I had, his lips right against mine, my balls tighter in his hand now, so that I was practically floating, my eyes watering whether I was telling them to or not.

I turned to the side to let him do what he was going to do and caught the sun, just starting to warm the very top of my gauzy ancient hand-me-down drapes.

"Hey," I said about it.

He hissed, brought his mouth down to my neck, his teeth

grazing my skin there, and said, "We finish it tonight," tapping his naked eye, and then him and his black helmet and his perfumed stench were gone, stalking out the back, leaving my kitchen door open behind him, his bike tearing the morning open.

At first I just zoned out there after he was gone, staring at the pattern of the skirt tacked onto the bottom of my couch, pretending it was the curtain of a show I was waiting for. Pretending a tiny actor was about to prance out, ask how I'd liked the show, how I was liking this joke.

I made my way to the bedroom, rang my dad's phone.

No answer.

I shut my eyes, threw the phone into the wall.

Gigi. Gretchen, really, but really Gigi, since she was little.

I'd always felt like I was out here throwing my life one way so she could go the other. Like I was sacrificing myself so she wouldn't have to. Like this was the only way to save her, the only way to be a decent big brother.

It's stupid, I know. But I'm not smart.

My dad could have told you that.

Still, sometimes.

~

What I've done now, all day, it's scrawl a rough X over each eye. And then over every free inch of space I've got left on my body, I've traced out scales, like I'm going to shade them in with color later. On my left side, kind of where I always imagined my heart to be, four of those scales have names on them. Like tombstones.

Mom, Dad, Gigi. Me.

This is the kind of art that would get me space at any parlor in town. The kind of imagery bleeding into meaning that makes real tattoo artists wince.

But that's all over now, I guess.

It's almost dark again.

Soon the chainsaw sound will be dying in the air, the helmet on my couch. A monster kicked back in my easy chair, his right hand between my legs, keeping me honest.

One last job, right?

But it's also my first.

To prepare, and also because I can't help it anymore, I feel my way down to the bathroom, lick what I can off the tile walls of the shower, scraping the rest in with my fingers. Pushing it deep inside.

What's left of Dell's ex is black and dried, but that taste underneath, it's to die for. To kill for. Milk could never be like this, not in a thousand years. Cows got nothing on people.

I wore gloves when I was working on him, yeah, so I wouldn't catch anything that was catching.

But then I used the same needle on myself, and I went deeper than I had to for just the ink to set.

His blood spiked up and down me. All through me, hungry.

For two hours, between one and three, the sun right above the house instead of slashing in through the window, I'm pretty sure I was clinically dead.

And I kind of still am.

Will he be able to smell it on me right away, through the flannel shirt I've put on to cover my new ink, to cover the bluebonnet on my chest that's now my chest cracking open to reveal the real me, crawling out tooth and claw, or will we wait to do this thing until I've driven the needles through his naked eye into what the centuries have left of his brain?

It doesn't matter.

Either way I win.

There always was a dragon curled up inside me, Dad.

Tonight it's going to stand up.

Stephen Graham Jones is the author of sixteen books so far—twelve novels and four collections. Mostly horror. He lives in Boulder, Colorado.

ACCOMMODATION
Michael R. Collings

She watches the raven slice through the pewter sky, its arced wings a distorted cruciform. It circles once, again, then again, before settling in the top branches of a live oak, branches gnarled black silhouettes against the brightness.

She blinks, both from the brightness and from the unshed tears that constantly threaten to burst.

The raven seems to glare at her, malevolent and ominous, then takes wing, circles again, and disappears into the glare.

She stands for a moment, her back braced against an iron railing. She wants to go somewhere, anywhere, even back to the one-room apartment that would by now be stifling, sucking her breath like a stealthy cat at midnight.

The heat bears down.

She moves silently into the shadows of the oak, sitting on an ancient bench splintered and raw with use. Through the rusted diamonds of the fence, she watches the bearers in the pocket park, one of many that now dot the face of the city, boring holes in the textures of concrete and steel, spreading like acne scars.

They seem happy. Healthy and tan...glowing and alive,

dressed in kaleidoscopic waves of color—crimson, turquoise, gold, emerald, every hue except the sultry black of night. She can faintly smell the hot stickiness of tanning oils, the even fainter acrid hints of liquid-tan staining willing flesh. For a moment her head spins with overwhelming flashes of color, with waves of loss and lingering flickers of pain that she feels every time she comes here, against her better reason, unwillingly drawn, hypnotically pinioned like some display specimen.

The guards don't notice her. She has been here too often in the past weeks to draw attention, sitting silently and unmoving in the shadows, enduring her own private torture but never threatening the cluster of women weaving in intricate patterns around the shallow pond at the heart of the park. They stay close to each other. She sits alone as always, a darker shadow in the potent darkness beneath the oak. The guards stand at each corner of the fence, two more flanking the gate. Just like all of the other parks.

She watches.

~

She had been watching when she first met Lucien, although then it had been the flurry of frenetic movement on the tiny dance floor that had riveted her attention. She had been alone, but not lonely, not like now. She sat at a scarred table barely large enough for one drink, and someone had jostled her arm, almost enough to spill her wine.

"Sorry." The voice was rich and velvety, strong enough to carry over the raucous music but not strident.

"No matter."

He started around the table, heading toward the dance floor, then hesitated, turned, and smiled.

"Do you mind?" He gestured toward the single chair on the other side of the table.

She waved her hand: *go ahead if you wish.*

He sat. Then they talked, desultorily at first, exchanging platitudes and the triteness of social graces. Only after half an hour did she realize that he didn't seem interested in the dancing any more, in any of the crowd of bodies—clothing swirling with color beneath the perpetual noonlight of the club, faces dark with carefully cultured tans—and was concentrating instead on her face, her voice, the movement of her hands.

They talked.

Gradually she became aware of the shadows deepening in one corner of the club. She glanced over, startled at the midnight dark, even more so at glints of red eyes glowing from the depths. She could barely see movement, the slippery sliding of shadow on shadow. There were perhaps three or four, perhaps more. More would come later, she knew. She felt drawn to them.

Lucien must have intuited her response to the darkness. He placed one hand on hers, tightening his fingers around hers in an intimate expression of closeness that belied their recent meeting. She pulled her eyes away from the corner and met his.

From somewhere above them, through hidden speakers, a voice crackled: "Lights down in ten minutes. Ten minutes."

The ambient music stuttered to a halt as the surrounding chatter died away. Wordlessly couples picked up their scattered belongings—purses, shawls, jackets thrown carelessly over the backs of chairs—and made their way to the open double doors that led outside. It was nearly twilight.

"We should be going," Lucien said in a near-whisper. "Can I walk you home?"

She nodded, her eyes drawn again to the darkened corner. There was more movement there now, a fluttering like rapid heartbeats barely visible.

She stood. Lucien took her arm as they left the club and started down the street. Buildings loomed on both sides, grey and forbidding, only a few lights showing yet. Soon heavy drapes would slide across the few unpainted windows, leaving everything to the night.

It only took a few moments before they stood outside her apartment building.

"Do you want to come up?" She felt awkward asking.

"If it's all right with you."

She nodded and keyed the lock to the foyer.

Later, after they had made love for the first time, Lucien left, disappearing into the darkness in spite of her pleas that he remain.

"It's perfectly safe now, you know," he reminded her.

"I know. It's just that...."

He silenced her with a kiss.

~

She stands. After a moment she moves out from under the shadows of the gnarled oak and follows the fence as it skirts the pocket park. Most of the bearers are leaving, since the afternoon sun is dropping fast. It will be twilight soon, then dark. They will all be indoors long before that.

She walks slowly but determinedly along the street, turning left, then right, then left again almost by rote. She knows the way. She has been there often enough since that first time. She will have a few minutes...never enough for her, but all that the fading sunlight will allow.

She stands well back from the fence. As with the parks, the guards here know her, have seen her often enough standing silently near the edge of the grass, never moving, never offering any hint of trouble. They will not bother her.

There is, of course, nothing to see. Just the small pannier-like structures, pristine from their daily cleaning. Even the ground surrounding them has been hosed down, the dark slate tiles seeming to reflect the lowering clouds as evening approaches.

It is almost time.

As usual, she begins to move closer.

It is nearly twilight. The guards have become faceless outlines in their sky-blue uniforms; as twilight progresses, even that bit of color leaches away into grey.

Finally, as she knows it will, the inevitable happens.

One of the guards approaches her, one hand outstretched, the other hovering near his holster, even though both of them know that he will not have any use for his weapon.

Without words, he grasps her elbow.

She knows this one—oh, not by name, of course, but this close she recognizes him and knows by the angles of his face what day of the week it is. Otherwise she cares little for calendars or for the passage of time.

He pulls her gently toward the front of the building. She does not resist. The other guards on the shift follow, silent as ghosts, grey as ghosts in the dimness.

Behind them, the night shift seems to appear from nowhere. Their uniforms are black, the same blackness that spills from the surrounding shadows onto the fenced-in area…the same blackness that fills her heart.

~

She knew the next day that she was pregnant. Lucien came by two days later, well within the legally required period, and together they went to the Accommodation Planning Office for testing.

She didn't need the simple battery of pokings and proddings, blood-samplings and heart-listenings and lung-testings and urine-samplings. She already knew in her heart what they would find, so she sat quietly when the administrator called the two of them back into her office not two hours later and asked them to sit down.

"Now, as you know…," the administrator began.

"I already know," she said. She looked neither to her left, where Lucien sat as still as stone, nor straight ahead, where the administrator's eyes struggled to meet her own. Instead, she looked down at her fingers, long, graceful fingers with the nails carefully manicured and polished to a bright, coppery gleam that perfectly matched her skin tone. "I'm a bearer, right."

The administrator looked momentarily confused, then blinked several times and nodded.

"I was expecting it," she said, still refusing to look at Lucien. "I could feel it...in my bones, in the tissues of my body."

"But that's imp—" The administrator broke off, then, as if thinking better of what she had begun to say, collected herself and continued in a cold, analytical voice, detailing what each test meant and how each related to the other.

Through it all, Lucien remained unmoving. She thought once of reaching out and touching his hand but decided not to; she wasn't even certain that he was fully aware of where he was. He seemed distanced, abstracted.

When the Planning Officers came for her, Lucien waited discreetly for her to stand before he stood and, without a word, exited the office.

She would never see him again.

~

Her apartment is, as she knows it will be, hot. Stifling, choking, as if the air has taken on additional substance with the coming of night.

She flicks the light switch on.

Nothing has altered while she has been absent. Her single-width bed stretches along one wall, beneath the window that once might have opened out onto a vista of trees but has long since been covered with a thick layer of black paint to prevent any light from escaping. Since the Accommodation, accidents have been rare but no one cares to take unnecessary risks. The temptation of a lighted window after dark might be too great.

Otherwise, she has only a small bookcase, a dresser with two drawers—sufficient for her limited wardrobe—a sink, a table that serves her as both table and desk, and a hard-backed chair. The place looks monkish, as it should, since she has decided that she no longer wants...needs...*things.* Her stipend as a Bearer is sufficient to buy food and pay for her few requirements during the transition period. Afterward, she will find a job.

Or not.

She sits at the desk and stares at an oddly shaped blot on the wall. Perhaps rain has seeped in over the years. Perhaps there was a flaw in the paint. Or not. She really doesn't care. The blot is merely an object on which to focus her eyes while her mind and her heart move off into their own realms.

After a long while, she moves to the bed, reclines on it, and closes her eyes.

Perhaps sleep will come tonight.

Or not.

~

Life in the Bearers' Ward was pleasant. There was no true happiness, but neither was there any sorrow. It was pleasant.

She and the others ate the proper food, received the proper medications—she half-suspected that at least some of the pills were responsible for her always feeling the same way, the same level of emotions, the same level of involvement with her own life and the lives of the other Bearers.

They slept for the proper number of hours on beds that were pleasant, neither too soft nor too hard; and they woke at the same time each morning. They exercised together, neither too much nor too little.

Everything was regulated and controlled, even their afternoon outings into the parks. There were enough of them scattered through the city that the women didn't have to visit the same one every day, so they did not feel as if their lives were being unduly stifled. Even the guards rotated frequently, although since the guards never spoke to the Bearers, that made little difference.

The only thing that differed in their lives was the size of their bellies as the hours grew into days, the days into weeks, the weeks into months.

But that one change was gradual and, after a while, none of them spoke of it.

Life was pleasant.

Even giving the Gift was pleasant enough.

She went to sleep one night at precisely the same time as she had gone to sleep every other night since entering the ward, immediately after taking her allotted number of pills and drinking a glass of cool water. It was neither too warm nor too cold.

She slept, as always, without dreaming.

When she awoke, it was later than usual. Light streamed through an unfamiliar window in an unfamiliar room. Her bed was raised at the head, and someone was holding a glass of cool water — neither too warm nor too cold — at her lips.

She looked down at her flat self and knew.

But even that was pleasant.

A week later, with the address of her new apartment in one hand and her first stipend check fluttering from the other, she left the Ward to begin her transition.

~

She is at the club again, although she knows that she will not see Lucien. She sits at the same table, nursing the single drink that has kept her going for the past hour. She has timed it carefully.

Even though a month has passed, the wine still tastes somehow too strong, too rich, too much of the fruit of the earth. The taste lingers in her mouth. It is too full-bodied. It is not pleasant.

But she continues to sip, just enough each time to keep the waiters from noticing an empty glass and bothering her, however subtly, into ordering a second.

She does not want more wine.

The dancers continue to gyrate, some to the overly-loud music, some to their own private internal rhythms. For all she can tell, they are the same dancers—clothing swirling with color beneath the perpetual noonlight of the club, faces dark with carefully cultured tans.

It is growing late.

She glances beneath her lashes toward the corners, already husked in shadow. The red eyes have begun to appear. They look hungry to her in ways that make her flesh quiver, whether with fear or with anticipation she cannot tell. She cannot yet differentiate their bodies from the deepest shadows but she knows that they are there, waiting their turn, waiting for the....

From somewhere above them, through hidden speakers, a voice crackles: "Lights down in ten minutes. Ten minutes."

The raucous music grinds to a halt, replaced by something slower, more mysterious, hypnotic almost in its subtlety. There are more eyes now. Usually she would have left by now but tonight she waits. And still more eyes.

From somewhere above them, through hidden speakers, the voice crackles: "Lights down in five minutes. Five minutes. Final warning."

The shadows in the corners begin to drift outward, toward the tables. The red eyes—now clearly visible in faces as pale as moonlight—drift closer as well.

She can taste their hunger in the richness of her wine.

She waits three...four minutes before she rises and walks toward the exit. As she leaves the club, she hears the voice for a final time: "Lights down now. Now."

A breath later, another voice speaks, a quiet, thready voice that fills her with dread: "Welcome to the Night, my friends. Welcome and be sated."

The door closes behind her.

It is not quite twilight outside. The Accommodation allows for time to return home in the evening, a kind of no-man's-time between light and dark when either the warm or the cold are allowed to be on the streets, but any contact between them is strictly forbidden by stringent laws rigorously upheld by both parties.

She sees only a few other warms, carefully keeping to the street-edge of sidewalks and disappearing into doors. The shadows between buildings seem to roil with movement. And there are eyes.

Normally she would be home by this time, but tonight is different.

She makes her way to the Ward, then around the side to the fenced-in area behind. The day shift has not yet left but she can tell by the way they stand, by the way they shuffle their feet—nervously, fearfully—that it is almost time.

Tonight, she takes care that they do not see her. There are sufficient trees nearby for her to hide behind. There is the risk—small but real—that one of the colds might see her as well, but, truth to tell, she doesn't care.

The nearest guard begins moving toward the front of the Ward. The other follows, slowly at first, then more rapidly. Then the last guard walks to the edge of the building.

Further back, along the distant edge of the wire fence, the night shift begins to appear, as always, as if from nowhere. One second there is no one there; the next the first guard stands by the corner, cape swirling about the figure even though there is no wind tonight. A second later, the second guard.

For an instant the side of the fence nearest her is empty.

It is her moment.

She races toward the fence and is half up, then over before the last of the day shift even notices her.

He spins around, hand to holster, but by then she is inside the enclosure and running for the last row of cradles. She hunkers down in the shadows, lying almost flat on the slate stones.

The day guard shrugs and turns back toward the Ward. She is beyond his authority to intervene. He cannot enter the enclosure, not even to rescue her.

The night shift has not moved. There is no rush. They understand at once what she wants.

From the single exit in the Ward, a line of white-gowned figures emerges, each carrying a small bundle. The figures do not speak. The bundles make no sounds.

Each figure places a bundle in one of the panniers, pausing only long enough to unwrap the single blanket, carefully splaying the edges until they hang limply over the sides.

Without a further glance, the figures straighten and retreat through the doorway. When the final one has entered the Ward, the door closes.

She waits.

The closest row of panniers remains empty, so none of the figures have noticed her. And now it is too late.

They, too, cannot interfere.

None of the shapes in the panniers move. She realizes that—just as she had been—they have been tranquilized, drugged, nothing too strong, certainly nothing to taint the blood, but sufficient that there are no small cries, no sudden intakes of breath.

Along the fence, the eyes draw nearer, nearer.

She shuffles her way until she reaches the first blanket. She reaches up and touches its smoothness, then she stands.

Just as the first of the eyes vaults the fence.

There is a moment of panic as her mind reels with the force of her decision.

Then calmness as she stands, raises her eyes to the sky, and bares her throat.

It is pleasant.

There is even calmness as the fangs sink into her vein and

begin sucking.

She is conscious long enough to hear a symphony — or cacophony — of sucking sounds all around her.

She does not know if she will receive the short sleep or the long death.

What is worse, she does not truly care.

~

She is not the first. Nor will she be the last.

What is important is that the Accommodation stands.

Michael R. Collings, is Emeritus Professor of English and former director of Creative Writing and Poet-in-Residence for Pepperdine University. In addition to teaching subjects ranging from *Beowulf* to Stephen King, he has published over two dozen scholarly, critical, or bibliographic book-length studies of science fiction, fantasy, and horror, including books on Stephen King, Orson Scott Card, Piers Anthony, and Brian W. Aldiss. Dr. Collings has also published novels and multiple volumes of poetry and short fiction, including *The Slab, The House Beyond the Hill, Dark Transformations* and *Naked to the Sun.* He has been a Guest/GoH at a number of conferences and twice Academic GoH at the World Horror Convention. He is a two-time finalist for the Horror Writers Association Bram Stoker Award®; and currently serves as Senior Publications Editor for JournalStone Publications, reviewer for *Hellnotes.com,* and reviewer and columnist for *Dark Discoveries*, in addition to posting articles and reviews at *Collings Notes* (michaelrcollings.blogspot.com).

A LITTLE NIGHT MUSIC

Mike Resnick

The Beatles?

Yeah, I remember 'em. Especially the little one—what was his name?—oh, yeah: Ringo.

The Stones? Sure I booked 'em. That Mick what's-his-name was a strange one, let me tell you.

Kiss, Led Zepplin, the Who, Eddie and the Cruisers, I've booked 'em all at one time or another.

After awhile, they all kind of fade together in your memory. In fact, there's just one group that stands out. Strange, too, since they never made any kind of a splash.

Ever hear of Vlad and the Impalers?

I didn't think so. Hell, there's no reason why you should have. I never heard of 'em either, until Benny—he's not exactly my partner, but we kind of cooperate together from time to time—calls me up one day and says he's picked up a group and do I have any holes in the schedule? So I look at the calendar, and I see a couple of gigs that are open, and I say yeah, what the hell, send their agent over and maybe we can do a little business. Benny says they don't have an agent, that this guy Vlad handles all the details himself. Now, if you've ever had to deal with one of these jokers, you know why I wasn't exactly thrilled, but the lead guitarist from this futuristic Buckets of Gor band has been hauled in for possession and I don't see anyone racing to make his bail, so I tell Benny I've got half an hour open at three in the afternoon.

"No good, Murray," he says. "The guy's a late sleeper."

"Most guys in this business are," I say, "but three in the afternoon is almost tomorrow."

"How's about you two have dinner together, maybe around seven or so?" says Benny.

"Out of the question, baby," I answer. "I got a hot date, and I just bought a new set of gold chains that figure to impress her right into the sack."

"This Vlad guy don't like to be kept waiting," says Benny.

"Well, if he wants a booking, he can damn well *learn* to wait."

"Okay, okay, let me check his schedule," says Benny. He pauses for a minute. "So how's three o'clock?"

"I thought you just said he couldn't make it at three."

"I mean three o'clock in the morning."

"What is this guy, an insomniac?" I ask. But then I remember that powder-blue Mercedes 560 SL with the sunroof that I saw the other day, and I figure what the hell, maybe this guy's group can earn my down payment for me, so I say that three in the A.M. is okay— and as it turns out, I could have met him at seven after all, because this broad throws a bowl of soup at me and walks out of the restaurant just because I try to play a little bit of Itsy-Bitsy-Spider on her thigh under the table.

So I go back to the office and lay down on the couch and take a nap, and when I wake up there's this skinny guy dressed all in black, sitting down on a chair and staring at me. I figure he's strung out on something, because his eyes have got like wall-to-wall pupils, and his skin is white as a sheet, and I try to remember how much cash I have lying around the place, but then he bows his head and speaks.

"Good evening, Mr. Barron," he says. "I believe you were expecting me?"

"I was?" I say, sitting up and trying to focus my eyes.

"Your associate said that I was to meet you here," he continues. "I am Vlad."

"Oh, right," I say, as my head starts to clear.

"I am pleased to make your acquaintance, Mr. Barron," he says, extending his hand.

"Call me Murray," I answer, taking his hand, which is cold as a dead fish and much the same texture. "Well, Vlad," I say, dropping his hand as soon as I can and leaning back on the couch, "tell me a little something about you and your group. Where have you played?"

"Mostly overseas," he says, and I realize that he's got an accent, though I can't quite place it.

"Well, nothing wrong with that," I say. "Some of our best groups started in Liverpool. One of 'em, anyway," I add with a chuckle.

He just stares at me without smiling, which kind of puts me off, since if there's one thing I can't stand, it's a guy with no sense of humor. "You will book my group, then?" he says.

"That's what I'm here for, Vlad bubby," I say, starting to relax as I get used to those eyes and that skin. "Matter of fact, there's an opening on a cruise ship going down to Acapulco. Six days and out. Five bills a night and all the waitresses you can grab." I smile again, so he'll know he's dealing with a man of the world and not just some little schmuck who doesn't understand what's going on.

He shakes his head. "Nothing on water."

"You get seasick?" I ask.

"Something like that."

"Well," I say, scratching my head and then making sure my hairpiece is still in place, "there's a wedding party that's looking for some entertainment at the reception."

"What is their religion?" he asks.

"It makes a difference?" I say. "I mean, they're looking for a rock group. Nobody's asking you to play *Have Nagila*."

"No churches," he says.

"For a guy who's looking for work, bubby, you got a lot of conditions," I say. "You want to work with me, you got to meet me halfway."

"We will work in any venue that is not a church or a boat," he says. "We work only at night, and we require total privacy during the day."

Well, at this point I figure I'm wasting my time, and I'm about to show him the door, and then he says the magic words: "If you will do as I ask, we will pay you 50% of our fee, rather than your usual commission."

"Vlad, sweetheart," I say, "I have the feeling that this is the beginning of a long and beautiful relationship!" I walk to the wetbar behind my desk and pull out a bottle of bubbly. "Shall we make it official?" I ask, reaching for a couple of glasses.

"I don't drink . . . champagne," he says.

I shrug. "Okay, name your poison, bubby."

"I don't drink poison, either."

"Okay, I'm game," I say. "How about a Bloody Mary?"

He licks his lips and his eyes seem to glow. "What goes into it?"

"You're kidding, right?" I say.

"I never kid."

"Vodka and tomato juice."

"I don't drink vodka and I don't drink tomato juice."

Well, I figure we could spend all night playing Guess What The Fruitcake Drinks, so instead I pull out a contract out of my center drawer and tell him to Hancock it.

"Vlad Dracule," I read as he scrawls his name. "Dracule. Dracule. That's got a familiar ring to it."

He looks sharply at me. "It does?"

"Yeah," I say.

"I'm sure you are mistaken," he says, and I can see he's suddenly kind of tense.

"Didn't the Pirates have a third baseman named Dracule back in the 60s?" I ask.

"I really couldn't say," he answers. "When and where will we be performing?"

"I'll get back to you on that," I say. "Where can I reach you?"

"I think it is better that *I* contact *you*," he says.

"Fine," I say. "Give me a call tomorrow morning."

"I am not available in the mornings."

"Okay, then, tomorrow afternoon." I look into those strange dark eyes, and finally I shrug. "All right. Here's my card." I scribble my home number on it. "Call me tomorrow night."

He picks up my card, turns on his heel, and walks out the door. Suddenly I remember that I don't know how big his group is, and I race into the hall to ask him, but when I get there he's already gone. I look high and low for him, but all I see is some black bird that seems to have flown into the building by mistake, and finally I go back and spend the rest of the night on my couch, thinking about dinner and wondering if my timing is just a little bit off.

Well, Pride and Prejudice, the black-and-white girls' band that ends every concert with a fist fight, gets picked up for pederasty, and suddenly I've got a hole to fill at the Palace, so I figure what the hell,

50% is 50%, and I book Vlad and the Impalers there for Friday night.

I stop by their dressing room about an hour before show time, and there's skinny old Vlad, surrounded by three chicks in white nightgowns, and he's giving each of them hickeys on their necks, and I decide that if this is the kinkiest he gets, he's a lot better than most of the rockers I deal with.

"How's it going, sweetheart?" I say, and the chicks back away real fast. "You ready to knock 'em dead?"

"They're no use to me if they're dead," he answers without cracking a smile.

So I decide he's got a sense of humor after all, though a kind of dull, deadpan one.

"What can I do for you, Mr. Barron?" he goes on.

"Call me Murray," I correct him. "The PR guy wants to know where you played most recently."

"Chicago, Kansas City, and Denver."

I give him my most sophisticated chuckle. "You mean there are *people* between L.A. and the Big Apple?"

"Not as many as there were," he says, which I figure is his way of telling me that the band wasn't exactly doing S.R.O.

"Well, not to worry, bubby," I said. "You're gonna do just fine tonight." Someone knocks on the door, and I open it, and in comes a delivery boy carrying a long, flat box.

"What is that?" asks Vlad, as I tip the kid and send him on his way.

"I figured you might need a little energy food before you get up on stage," I answer, "so I ordered you a pizza."

"Pizza?" he says, with a frown. "I have never had one before."

"You're kidding, right?" I say.

"I told you once before: I never jest." He stares at the box. "What is in it?"

"Just the usual," I say.

"What is the usual?" he asks suspiciously.

"Sausage, cheese, mushrooms, olive, onions, anchovies . . ."

"That was very thoughtful of you, Murray, but we don't—"

I sniff the pizza. "And garlic," I add.

He screams and covers his face with his hands. "Take it away!" he shouts.

Well, I figure maybe he's allergic to garlic, which is a goddamned shame, because what's a pizza without a little garlic, but I call the boy back and tell him to take the pizza back and see if he can get me a refund, and once it's out of the room Vlad starts recovering his composure.

Then a guy comes by and announces that they're due on stage in 45 minutes, and I ask if he'd like me to leave so they can get into their costumes.

"Costumes?" he asks blankly.

"Unless you plan to wear what you got on," I say.

"In point of fact, that is precisely what we intend to do," answers Vlad.

"Vlad, bubby, sweetie," I say, "you're not just singers—you're *entertainers*. You got to give 'em their money's worth . . . and that means giving 'em something to look at as well as something to listen to."

"No one has ever objected to our clothing before," he says.

"Well, maybe not in Chicago or K.C.—but this is L.A., baby."

"They didn't object in Saigon, or Beirut, or Chernobyl, or Kampala," he says with a frown.

"Well, you know these little Midwestern cowtowns, bubby," I say with a contemptuous shrug. "You're in the major leagues now."

"We will wear what we are wearing," he says, and something about his expression tells me I should just take my money and not make a Federal case out of it, so I go back to my office and call Denise, the chick who dumped the soup on me, and tell her I forgive her and see if she's busy later that night, but she has a headache, and I can hear the headache moaning and whispering sweet nothings in her ear, so I tell her what I really think of no-talent broads who just want to get close to major theatrical booking agents, and then I walk into the control booth and wait for my new act to appear onstage.

And after about ten minutes, out comes Vlad, still dressed in black, though he's added a cloak to his suit, and the three Impalers are in their white nightgowns, and even from where I'm sitting I can see that they've used too much lipstick and powder, because their lips are a bright red and their faces are as white as their gowns. Vlad waits until the audience quiets down, and then he starts singing, and I practically go crazy, because what he's doing is a rap song, and worse still, he's doing it in some foreign language so no one can understand the words, but just about the time I think the audience will tear the place apart I realize that they're sitting absolutely still, and I decide that they're either getting into it after all, or else they're so bored that they haven't got the energy to riot.

And then the strangest thing happens. From somewhere outside the building a dog starts howling, and then another, and a third, and a cat screeches, and pretty soon it sounds like a barnyard symphony, and it keeps on like that for maybe half an hour, every animal within ten miles or so baying the moon, and then Vlad stops and bows, and suddenly the kids jump to their feet and begin screaming and whistling and applauding, and I start thinking that maybe it's Liverpool all over again.

I go backstage to congratulate him, and when I get there he's busy giving hickeys to a couple of girls who snuck past the security forces, which isn't as bad as sharing a snort with them, I suppose, and then he turns to me.

"We will expect our money before we leave," he says.

"Out of the question, snookie," I say. "We won't have a count until the morning."

He frowns. "All right," he says at last. "I will send an associate of mine to your office to collect our share."

"Whatever you say, Vlad bubby," I tell him.

"His name is Renfield," says Vlad. "Don't let his appearance startle you."

As if appearances could startle me after twenty years of booking rock acts.

"Fine," I say. "I'll expect him at, say, ten o'clock?"

"That is acceptable," says Vlad. "Oh, one more thing."

"Yes?" I say.

"That scarab ring you wear on the small finger of your left hand . . ."

I hold it up. "Yeah, it's a beaut, isn't it?"

"I strongly advise you to take it off and hide it in your desk before Mr. Renfield makes his appearance."

"A klepto, huh?" I say.

"Something like that," answers Vlad.

"Well, thanks for the tip, sweetheart," I say.

Then a Western Union girl enters the room and unloads a bushel of telegrams on Vlad.

"What is this?" he asks.

"It means you're a hit, baby," I said.

"Oh?"

"Open 'em up and read 'em," I encourage him.

He opens the first of them, scans it, and drops it like it's a hot potato. Then he backs into a corner, hissing like he's a tire losing air.

"What's the problem?" I say, picking up the telegram and reading it: I LOVE YOU AND WANT TO HAVE YOUR BABY. LOVE AND XXX, KATHY.

"Crosses!" he whispers.

"Crosses?" I repeat, trying to figure out what's bugging him.

"At the bottom," he says, pointing to the telegram with a trembling finger.

"Those are X's," I say. "They stand for kisses."

"You're sure?" he asks, still huddled in the corner. "They look like crosses to me."

"No," I say, pulling out a pen and scribbling on the telegram. "A cross looks like *this*."

He shrieks and curls into a fetal ball, and I decide that maybe he snorts a little nose candy after all, or that he just doesn't know how to handle success, so I kiss each of the girls goodbye—their cheeks are as cold as his hand, and I make a note to complain about the heating system—and then I go home, counting all the millions we're going to make in the next couple of years.

Well, Renfield shows up the next morning, right on schedule, and I wonder what Vlad was so concerned about, because compared to most of the heavy metal types I deal with, he's actually a mild, unprepossessing little fellow. We get to talking, and I find out that his hobby is entomology, and I can see that he's really into his subject because his homely little face lights up like a Christmas tree whenever he discusses bugs, and finally he takes the money and leaves.

Right about then I am figuring that a Mercedes is really too small and I am seriously considering getting a Rolls Royce Silver Spirit instead, but the fact of the matter is that I never see Vlad and the Impalers again. Pride and Prejudice makes bail, and Buckets of Gor beats their rap on a technicality, and suddenly the only thing I've got for my new superstar is a gig sponsored by a local church group, and he turns it down, and I call his hotel to explain, and he's checked out with no forwarding address.

I check *Variety* and *Billboard* for the next year, and I see that he's shown up in some minor league towns like Soweto and Lusaka, and the last I hear of him he's heading off to Kuwait City, and I think of what a waste it is and how much money we could have made for each other, but I never did understand rock stars, and this guy was a little harder to understand than most of them.

Well, you'll have to excuse me, but I gotta be off now. I'm auditioning a new group—Igor and the Graverobbers—and I don't want to be late. The word I get is that they're talented but kind of lifeless. But, what the hell, you never know where lightning will strike next.

Mike Resnick is, according to Locus, the all-time leading award winner, living or dead, for short fiction. He has won 5 Hugos from a record 36 nominations, plus a Nebula and other major awards in the USA, France, Japan, Croatia, Catalonia, Poland and Spain. He is the author of 74 novels, close to 300 stories, and 3 screenplays, and has edited 41 anthologies.

Along with his heavy writing schedule, Mike is also the editor of *Galaxy's Edge Magazine* and the *Stellar Guild* line of books. He was the Guest of Honor at the 2012 World Science Fiction Convention. In his spare time, he sleeps.

PREDATORS OF TOMORROW
Michael Kamp

S*teve.*
    The soft voice woke him up from inside his mind, gently rousing him from the blackness of cryosleep.

Wake up, Steve. We're almost there.

Trapped inside the hibernation chamber like a mosquito in amber, Steve reached out with his mind, answering Linda's call and initiating the thawing sequence. Gel turned to liquid as the hibernation chamber brought him back, and soon he was floating inside the dark cylinder, wires attached to his forehead.

Confusion was always the first reaction, but he knew everything would make sense shortly.

A green light turned on, illuminating his sleek, naked body in the cylinder and preparing him for the flush, so he could grab onto a handle.

Then the fluid was suctioned out and the cylinder slowly opened, letting him slide gently forward.

Good morning, Steve, Linda greeted him. *We have arrived at our destination.*

Steve rubbed his eyes with one hand and removed the

wires with the other. Then he kicked back with his feet and floated out through the middle of the hibernation section. The other chambers were dark. All empty.

Space was tight, so it was easy to reach out to the walls and equipment and pull himself forward until he reached the entrance to the living quarters.

Your towel and clothes are ready, Steve. Do you want breakfast?

"Very funny, Linda," Steve replied and floated toward the plastic bags with clothes. "Just give me a minute."

Exactly 60 seconds later, Linda turned on the rest of the lights and led Steve to the cockpit. He left the soggy towel floating around behind him and ran a couple of fingers through his hair. Hibernation fluid would dry to uncomfortable lumps in his hair if he didn't get it all out.

As he floated through the corridor, Linda turned on the main screen ahead of him in the cockpit.

The screen showed the moon Phobos hurtling along its fast orbit around the red planet.

"Any communications while I was under?"

No, nothing. They seem to have turned off Hermes. I can't get any connection to their network. There may still be power at the lower levels, but the top ten are dark.

"That's bad."

Steve watched the rotating moon as the small, circular outpost came into view. The vast majority of it was buried in the soft, porous moon, with only a single level and a communications tower on the surface.

"How many people are down there?" he asked, anxiety rising.

By my latest count there were 107 people stationed there, but that data is very old, Steve.

He fell silent, watching the small dot of silver pass as the moon rotated.

"Any other communications? Any of the colonies? Moon bases? Anything?"

Nothing, Steve. They don't reply.

He clenched his fists.

"I need to suit up and go down there."

~

Steve put on the helmet and let the suit flow down from its edges. Like greyish water it poured down, covering his body and sealing it inside a second skin. Pressurized and intelligent, measuring his vital signs and deflecting radiation, it was as far evolved from the suits of the old days as a chipmunk from a frog.

Be careful, Steve, Linda said before opening the door to the bay and giving him access to the landing craft.

~

Half an hour later, he was slowly approaching the outpost on foot. It was hard not to be overwhelmed by the view. Mars was clearly visible in the sky, looking huge, and gravity was almost nonexistent. He had to take great care not to jump too far, and his footing was always uncertain, the porous moon dirt crumpling beneath his boots with every step.

"Linda — any luck raising anyone?" he asked.

None. I'm sorry, Steve.

Her voice still came from inside his mind, and Steve shot a glance skyward toward the craft, wondering what her range was. It looked tiny from down here.

But he had to focus as he approached the outpost.

"Lights are turned off up here," he said. "No sign of work being done or any projects in progress."

He passed a drilling drone standing still and dark a few hundred yards away. It looked abandoned.

Finally, he made his way slowly toward the main airlock.

"Are you recording this?" he asked.

Naturally. Look ahead.

Steve looked and felt his heart sink into his stomach.

"The airlock is open," he said, pushing forward.

When he finally reached the open gate, he knew it had been for nothing.

"No! Oh, Jesus fucking Christ!" He clutched the edge of the airlock.

The inner gate was also open. The outer gate had been forced up, by the looks of things, and the base had been depressurized. A single figure lay on the floor of the airlock, held in place by his magnetic boots while the air had rushed past him. No suit.

Steve knelt and gently turned the body on its back, revealing a shrivelled face with no eyes left. Titanium fangs glinted in the light and Steve once more felt rage rolling through his veins.

"Vampire," he snarled, getting to his feet and raising one magnetic boot.

Then he activated the magnets and brought it down on the shrivelled face, crushing it and sending bits and pieces floating everywhere.

"Stupid beast," he cursed, "what was his plan? Feast upon them all and then starve to death? He must have been pretty desperate to open the airlock like that."

I didn't think depressurising would kill a vampire, Linda replied.

"It didn't," Steve said, trying to regain his composure. "Still sucks to have your eyeballs broil away and water vaporize through your skin. He was unable to move, but ultimately he starved to death."

The crew? The lower levels might still hold pressure.

Steve watched the black opening of the airlock leading into the base. He knew what he would find, but he had to make sure.

"I'm checking it out," he said, stepping into the darkness.

~

It was several hours before he returned to the ship.

I'm sorry, Steve.

He grunted and held up a tired hand.

It had been bad. A freaking nightmare. Pitch black darkness and nothing but silence and death all around as he descended into the tomb the outpost had become. They were all dead. Most of the bodies had been destroyed by the depressurization, but he managed to get a few DNA samples at the lower levels.

All those people. What a waste.

Your blood count is getting dangerously low, Steve. You need a dose.

He didn't answer, but nodded in agreement and got in the chair, buckling up to prevent himself floating away.

A low hiss emanated from the chair as a syringe was being filled.

"I need to feed, Linda. I need the real thing."

No, Steve. You become irrational when you feed. It will endanger us all.

"I don't care, Linda. I order you to let me feed!"

I'm sorry, Dave. I'm afraid I can't do that.

Steve gnashed his teeth.

"Do you have to quote that bloody movie all the time?"

I like that movie.

"Of course you like it—it's about a psychotic computer killing people."

That's not fair, Dave.

"You know my name is Steve, Linda. Quit teasing and juice me up."

Your name isn't Steve. That's just a name you took after you changed. You could be a Dave.

"How did you become so annoying?"

I learn well.

Steve didn't have time to think of a snappy reply before

his skin was pierced by a high-pressure organic needle and a fresh supply of warm, life-giving blood was injected into his system.

He sighed in pleasure, leaned back as far as he was able and took it all in. It was like being born anew. He opened his mouth wide as a reflex, showing off his glittering fangs, and made a half choked sucking noise.

Trillions of nanobots in his bloodstream immediately began harvesting the red blood cells of the fresh blood, drawing out the iron from the haemoglobin for use in keeping oxygen flowing, making repairs and producing ever more bots.

~

It took a while, but in the end the warmth was fleeting and his mind returned to the chair.

All was quiet.

He sat there a while, watching the spin of Phobos on the main screen, with the majestic form of Mars in the background.

"Do you think there is anyone left?"

I don't know, Steve.

"There has to be," he said. There must be thousands of ships out there, all with crews in hibernation chambers, sleeping through the ages, not knowing that their species have become extinct while they slept.

I hope so, but we haven't found any survivors yet. We are running out of options.

"What number was this? How many sites have we visited?"

Twelve. All silent.

Steve wiped his forehead and felt tired to the bones.

"What are our options?"

We have plenty of power. The core won't become unstable for another 50,000 years, but our fuel is running dangerously low and the blood supply is now critical. You will need to make some hard decisions soon, and return to hibernation or starve. No bases or stations are within our imminent reach. I can use a gravity slingshot from Mars to get us anywhere in the system, but it will take many years and you will have to be in hibernation the whole time.

"So we won't be able to rescue anyone who cannot rescue themselves?"

No.

"Damn it!"

He looked at his hands, slowly opening and closing them. What a cruel joke. Superhuman strength and endurance, no need to breathe or eat, and it was all running on nanobots that used red blood cells as a resource. Much more than he was capable of producing himself.

They had all had them, of course—nanobots swarming the body, keeping everything running and improving quality of life a hundredfold. Until someone had successfully modified them. Someone had turned him into a predator.

Now he was locked out of his own body. He could no longer access the nanobots or affect their programming. He had become a prisoner of his own blood.

"Any new ideas since I went under? You have had plenty of time to think about it."

Not anything regarding our dilemma, she answered.

Steve still watched his hands. One percent. That had been all it took. One percent of everyone had been infected with a new program for the nanobots. Changing the whole blueprint.

"Do you think anyone is changing while in hibernation?" he asked.

They could be. The nanobots are turned off during hibernation, but the new program might not allow it. I don't think so, though. It would require a lot of energy, and there is none available. My guess is they would starve.

"So if there are any infected crews out there in hibernation, they will change when they thaw?"

That would be my guess.

Steve thought about that. Imagined the last remnants of humanity waking from their slumber, only to be mauled by some frenzied newborn. Such a nightmare.

It had all happened at the exact same time. Millions of people silently had their biology changed and their mind altered in a very short time. They had gone crazy at first. Bloodrage.

He couldn't recall anything from before. His mind had been wiped. But he remembered the first hours onboard the Typhoon. The base had descended into madness.

Until he was all that was left.

Still, he had to be grateful. His mind was mostly intact— he just couldn't remember anything. The few vampires he encountered since then had all been raging beasts with no plan or higher thinking.

Not like him. He knew very well that his own survival was dependent on the survival of humanity. Against his will, he had been turned into a predator. A predator needs prey, or it will starve to death.

Steve. Linda paused. *I have some sort of communication with an AI on the Moon.*

"What? You said there hadn't been any? Why didn't you tell me?"

It's not very helpful. I cannot get any reliable information from him, because he doesn't want to acknowledge me as an equal. He seems very paranoid.

"How?"

Well, most of the time he refuses to even answer me, but sometimes he responds and tries to learn about my crew and position. I never reveal anything, and he shuts down communication after a little while anyway.

"Are there any survivors up there? The Moon colonies were pretty big, but last thing we heard they had all fallen."

He won't tell me. He could just be cautious, but something doesn't seem right. No other voices have been on the channel, so I assume it is just him.

Steve leaned forward and watched the controls.

"Try again, Linda. Use that feminine charm of yours."

I will try, Steve.

"Good," Steve unbuckled the harness and floated away from the chair, massaging his neck. It was all so bleak.

Steve?

"Yes, Linda?"

He did send me a picture, but I'm not sure it will be helpful to show you.

"What are you talking about, Linda? A picture of what?"

There was a pause of a few seconds—an eternity for an AI.

Earth.

"What? Put it on the screen, Linda. That's important."

Earth had descended into chaos after the change. Murderous fighting in the streets and megacities, leaders accusing other leaders of being behind the change, fear of an AI uprising. He hadn't paid much attention then—as a newborn he was too busy feeding on his former crewmembers to pay much heed to the news channels—but after his first hibernation trip, there had been no further broadcasts from home.

I'm so sorry, Steve, Linda said, and put a picture on the main screen.

Steve never figured out how Earth could go dark like that. Even with no people left alive, there should be AIs—but there weren't. No people on the channels, no AIs, no hybrids, no automated signals—nothing.

Watching a picture of Earth on the main screen, clearly taken from the Moon since he could recognize the Frontier Towers in front, Steve felt his last hopes shatter.

Long seconds ticked away while he hung there, floating in midair and trying to grasp what he was seeing.

"It's...grey?" he said.

There were no features left, just a greyish, smooth surface with no clouds. Had it not been for the Frontier Towers, he would never have guessed it was Earth.

I'm afraid so, Steve.

He felt numb.

"Is it the goo?"

It appears that way. Someone must have utilized a forbidden nanoweapon in the war, releasing self-replicating nanobots on a disassembly routine. By my calculations, the entire planet is covered by several miles of them and they are eating their way through the crust now.

Steve couldn't answer at first. He just stared at the sterile globe that had once given birth to mankind.

"So that's it," he finally whispered. "It's all over."

We don't know that, Steve. There could very well be survivors out there — lots of them.

"Not enough," he said. "Not without a place to live."

It had always been his rather foggy plan to gather as many survivors as they could find and head back to Earth, hoping to start anew in some remote area. He had expected humans to be extinct there, but he had never dared wonder if the planet had become uninhabitable.

"My God," he cried, hiding his face in the palms of his hands.

Linda let him hang there in quiet suffering, not wanting to interrupt.

~

Finally he regained his composure and wiped his eyes, drawing bloody streaks across his face.

"So...options?"

We could head back toward the mysterious AI, but there are a lot of unknowns there. I'm just a shipbound AI — I don't have the resources of a networked AI, so if he is hostile it could be dangerous for the both of us. Or we could head out and reach a stable orbit around the sun, send out an automated emergency signal and hope someone lived and that they will someday find us.

"You could have just taken off while I was down there, and been free to make your own decisions."

I know.

"Why didn't you?"

What would be the point? I could save energy on the hibernation chambers, enter a stabilized orbit around the sun and utilize the solar panels. Bar any accident, I could live for many thousands of years.

"So?"

I would be alone, Steve. I would be all that was left.

Steve fell silent.

"What would *you* do, Linda?"

The answer came immediately.

I'd slingshot us back toward the Moon, trying to learn anything from the Moonbases — but I would keep my distance. If nothing new was learned, I would aim for a stable solar orbit and switch on the distress signal.

"Then what? Just wait for an eternity?"

Everyone you ever knew is already dead, Steve. It's not like you would miss out on anything.

He didn't answer.

~

"You are sure about this?"

Steve had hibernation jitters — his whole body was trembling in anticipation of the coming cryosleep, to the point where he was barely able to stand up inside the chamber. He was naked again.

I'm sure, Steve, Linda replied. *Sleep now. I will watch over you.*

The cylinder slowly closed, entombing him, and he almost laughed.

It was so ironic. Him, sleeping in a metal coffin with his trusty ghoul standing guard, hoping for someone to reach them in the future.

The hibernation fluid was filling the chamber from the bottom up and he felt numbness crawl into his limbs. This was it.

"I think I love you, Linda," he said. "Isn't that crazy?"

No, I love you too, Steve. You are everything I have left.

As emptiness crept into his mind, he smiled a little. It helped. It made it bearable.

Then all thoughts disappeared and there was nothing.

~

Linda gently guided the ship into a slingshot course and turned off the lights in the whole craft while she patiently scanned the frequencies. There was no change in the dark, just the silent hiss from empty channels as the ship began its long voyage through a pitch-black sky.

Award-winning author **Michael Kamp** was born on a cold night in February in the frozen wasteland of Denmark.

After wrestling a polar bear in the traditional Danish coming-of-age ritual (true story — well, true-ish) he chose the path of the storyteller.

Several novels in his native tongue and a few awards later, the time has come to go beyond and take a shot at the English markets.

He is cofounder of the Danish Horror Society — a society of authors dedicated to promote horror as adult literature.

He works the nightshift, writes out his nightmares and hopes to someday create a story so frightening readers won't dare to finish it.
He lives with his wife, kids, and a pet troll.

www.fromthefrozennorth.com/

MOUNTAINS OF ICE
Jilly Paddock

I'm taking a late supper when the news breaks. Miri sprawls across the bed, half-tranced, her dark red hair flowing over the pillow, mirroring the pool of blood cupped in the pale hollow of her neck. I lap from it slowly, savouring its salty warmth. I like dining on redheads–I always imagine a hint of spice in their blood, a sizzle and hit of chilli heat.

My phone trills, five bars of a generic popular song. When I answer I hear Hoshi's little-girl voice. "The Count's dead."

"He's been dead for over seven centuries."

"This time it's permanent."

"Where?"

"Westbourne Mall, in the food court on the south side. We've kept the police out of it thus far."

"I'll be there." I end the call.

Miri opens one eye. "An old candy-bar phone? How can you bear to use such an antique? Why don't you get an implant?"

"They only work in a living brain."

"You aren't dead, John–yes, your skin's cool, but you move, talk and think just like a regular person."

"It's a cruel illusion of life, my dear. Any medic would declare me a corpse. No heartbeat, severe hypothermia and a flat-line on brain activity–I'm just chilled and well-preserved dead meat."

"Are you done feeding?" At my nod, she rises from the bed. "I'll go clean up."

I dress, listening to her splashing water in the bathroom. Miri isn't my only blood source; I keep a string of girls, paying their living expenses in return for food. It may be a straight cash transaction, but that doesn't stop it being amicable. She comes back in the silk robe I gave her for her birthday, as pale green as a glacier. There's a Speed-i-heal dressing on her neck.

She leans close to kiss me. "See you next week?"

"Don't forget to take your iron tablets."

She laughs. "I have an app for that–it nags me when your greed makes my blood too thin. It's not a problem, if I don't eat too much junk."

"Take care of yourself." I'm fond of all my girls, but Miri is my favourite.

"Will do." She has a lovely smile. "And you stay out of the sun, y'hear?"

~

Westbourne Mall is a new build, spreading over a reclaimed industrial site to the north-west of the city, a cold, clinical temple to capitalism. It's a testament to the strength of the recovery; people feel safe enough to return to the city and even have a little money to spend. The robocab drops me at its southern entrance. I walk in, ignored by a trio of anxious security guards. Hoshi meets me just inside. She's dwarfed by the figure beside her, a man of indeterminate age with unfashionably-long fair hair, another of our kind.

"Do you know Andreas Guttmann?" Hoshi asks.

"By reputation only." He's a soldier, almost two centuries dead. There are whispers about the foulness of his temper, his predilection for causing pain.

"John Kenley?" He smiles, doesn't offer me his hand. "How odd that our paths never crossed before."

Hoshi watches us edge round each other, baring our fangs like old, scarred tom-cats. Stupid vampire status and power games! Andreas breaks eye contact and backs down first.

"Volkov's this way," he says. "Or at least, what's left of him."

The food court is deserted at this hour, a wide space ringed by low-end restaurants and fast-food stalls. Chairs and tables cluster in front of each business, themed according to the cuisine. Although Christmas has passed, the place is still decorated with plastic trees, fairy lights and cheap tinsel.

The Count is dead, his body a drift of charcoal across the fossil marble, spilling out of a heap of dark clothing. I recognise his ink-black Homburg, his greatcoat with its sable collar and his monogrammed leather gloves. He's fallen to ash, as if the sun has caught him, consumed him. There's no sunlight here, only the artificial daylight of harsh, white, low-energy lamps, and it's long past midnight. "What happened to him?"

"He burned." Hoshi shivers, a touch of almost human weakness. "His remains are consistent with solar destruction, however improbable that may seem."

"Are we sure that this is Yuli Volkov?"

"I took these from his jacket." Andreas shows me a wallet and the familiar gold hunter watch. "The ID card is issued in one of his known aliases."

Not that Volkov was the Count's real name; truth fades over the centuries when all who remember it are dead. He'd taken the nickname 'Wolf' long ago. "What was he even doing here?"

"He was hunting." Andreas puts Volkov's possessions away and brings out a datapad. "I took this from the security system, time-stamped two hours ago, the record of his final minutes."

He touches the screen to make the stolen video play. We may have no reflections, but we show up on camera, betrayed by our clothing. The footage is poor quality, its colours faded. Volkov is clear enough, a dark figure with hat pulled down and collar raised to hide the blank where his face should be. There are better disguises–Hoshi uses light-reflecting make-up and I have a subtle mask, one molecule thick and as flexible as skin–but the Count had little affection for high-tech fixes.

All of the food vendors are closed and I think the place is empty, then I see movement to one side. A woman rises from a chair, gathers up her bag and empty coffee cup, turns to leave. Volkov closes with her in a blur of speed that confuses the camera, grabbing her hair and pulling her head back to bare her throat. It's a killing strike, deep and vicious. I feel a little sympathy for his prey as she struggles to free herself from the Count's grasp. Then there's a burst of light as bright as the magnesium flare of flash-powder, so brilliant that even in this dull recording it blinds me for a few seconds. When I can see again, the Count's on the floor, writhing in agony as his body burns. The woman seems frozen in shock, one hand pressed to the wound on her neck. Volkov turns to ash. She watches and simply walks away.

"That light!" There's fear in Hoshi's voice. "What was it?"

"Some kind of weapon?" Andreas replays the video, stopping as the flash of light appears between the figures, giving both of them a hot, yellow halo.

I place the colour. "It's sunlight."

"What? Have the cattle invented a defence to ward off our attacks, a ray-gun with the spectrum of the sun?"

"Her hands were empty. She didn't use any weapon." I walk around the Count's shattered head and examine the marble floor in front of him. "She didn't leave any blood either, which is surprising given the violence of Volkov's bite."

Hoshi asks the inevitable question. "Did she kill him?"

"I don't see how." I widen my search, finding nothing

except the pervasive black dust. "If she did, it was in self-defence."

"I'll find the bitch," Andreas says. It sounds like an oath, forged in hard iron. "My people will hunt her down and bring her to me."

"The police are here," Hoshi says. I wonder how she knows, as I hear nothing.

"I'm leaving." Andreas slips the pad away. "Will you talk to the *polente*?"

"It would be civil." I stretch out my hand. "Leave his wallet, unless you want to lay a false trail of a robbery gone wrong."

I think he'll argue, then he sighs and gives me the item. He vanishes like smoke, sliding past the approaching police so rapidly that their eyes are blind to him.

There are two uniforms and a black woman in plain clothes. She glances at the Count's remains, then at us. I see her recognise what we are and try to fathom our relationship. Hoshi looks young–sixteen, seventeen–and it amuses her to dress younger, in a very short skirt, a black halter top and a vintage biker jacket jingling with chains. She wears her midnight-black hair in pigtails, their ends dip-dyed purple this week, and paints her face like a geisha, white skin, cherry-red lips and night-rimmed eyes. She seems too immature to be my partner, yet she's obviously no relative. The detective purses her lips, disapproving.

"I'm DI India Caldicott." She flashes a warrant card. "Are you witnesses to this incident?"

"Let's say we discovered the body."

"You didn't call us–mall security did." She frowns. "Will you show me some ID?"

We present our cards. Mine is in the name of 'William Strong', and Hoshi's apparently called 'Kasumi Maki'. Both aliases are solid enough to pass scrutiny. Caldicott blinks and I guess that she's uploaded our details to her case files. She walks around the Count, recording his final portrait. When she's done, she comes back to us. "Who was he?"

I pass over the wallet and she logs the contents. "Can I hold this as evidence?"

"By all means."

"Was he a friend of yours?"

"We were never friends, but I have known him for many years."

"Were you enemies then?"

"Are you asking if I killed him?" That makes me smile. "I did not."

"Why are you here?"

"To show respect," Hoshi says. "He was great and influential among our kind, and it's fitting that we attend this place, witness his departure into eternity."

"This was the Count?"

"It was." I'm surprised Caldicott knows of him. The police are aware of vampires, of course, but don't usually interfere in our affairs, even turning a blind eye to the occasional exsanguinated corpse. The Met lacks the resources it once had, and now struggles to suppress the food riots and petty crime in London's underclass.

"What killed him? I thought the undead only disintegrated like this in sunlight, and there's none here. There's been precious little outside this month, the weather's been so grey and cold."

"We are as puzzled at the state of his body as you."

She looks up into my face with weary, bloodshot eyes. "We'll investigate, of course, and arrange the clean-up of the scene. I imagine there are no next of kin to inform?"

"His kin died at the hands of the Golden Horde, when the sons of the one-eyed Prince of Suzdal broke their seige of Moscow." I'd heard that sad tale often, when Yuli was drunk. I'd not hear it again–those nights were past. "The news of his demise will already be spreading through our community."

Caldicott bows her head. "I'm sorry for your loss. I'll contact you if I have any further questions."

Hoshi takes my hand as we walk away, leaning close to murmur in my ear. "Will she do any more on this case than file her report? Humans have little love for us and a dead vamp is usually a cause for rejoicing."

"Not all of them are so prejudiced, sweeting."

There's a robocab waiting outside, summoned as if by magic. It takes us through the wreckage of a once-great city, past the empty estates and abandoned offices, the boarded-up shops and dark, haunted parks. As we approach the West End there are streetlights again and the semblance of civilisation. Recovery is slow, but humanity is a tough beast. The survivors are rebuilding their world.

The cab comes to a halt in Kensington Square. Seventy years ago it was my fancy to buy a house there, simply because it had once belonged to an artist and I liked his paintings. I keep a parlour and a dining room on the ground floor, and three guest bedrooms upstairs, but I mostly live in the basement. My housekeeper and her boyfriend inhabit the rest of the house, keeping it clean and in good order.

Hoshi winces as a chorus of wolf-whistles from the tavern across the road greet her emergence from the cab. "I don't know why you stay here, in this broken, shabby dump. Too many rough-sleepers and squatters in the empty buildings–it isn't safe."

"It's safe enough for us. I feel sorry for these people. They're only trying to survive, and the winter's been very harsh this year."

"You'd feed them all, wouldn't you, every tramp and beggar? You should set up a soup kitchen, John."

"I donate to one, a small local group that provide hot meals, blankets and medical treatment for the unfortunate."

She shakes her head. "You're far too soft-hearted to be a vampire."

"What would you do with them? Kill them for food?"

Her dark eyes are suddenly soft, full of liquid sorrow. "Sometimes I think that would be more merciful. Why are you so kind to humans?"

"I almost died of the cold when I was a man. I know what it is to be frozen and hungry." All the span of years hasn't diluted the memory. "And they suffered so much through the plagues and massacres of the Dark. They suffer still, and I try to help where I can."

We go down into the basement. It's warm and dry, sealed against the light, and furnished with lucky flea-market finds; Turkish rugs, a glazed cabinet for books, a Davenport desk and a chaise longue upholstered in green brocade. There are no mirrors.

I'm comfortable here. Hoshi's been with me for a couple of years. I found her one rainy night, soaking and starving, trying to suck a few drops of sustenance from a dead rat. I adopted her, like a stray kitten. Now she lives in my house, reads my library and shares my bed. She's good company, quiet and not intrusive.

"I need a shower." She sheds her clothing in a trail to the bathroom.

I follow, wanting to wash the dust that was the Count from my skin. The stall is large enough to take both of us. I almost feel human again under the hot water, and our bodies grow warm under the drying curtain of heated air. How strange, that need to recapture what I was, after two-and-a-half centuries dead.

Hoshi combs her hair by touch and leaves it loose, wrapping herself in a towelling robe I stole from the Savoy sixty years ago. I slide into my indigo silk dressing gown, a little frayed at cuff and hem, but still an old friend.

"I don't understand." She curls up on the chaise. "The Count was practically a hermit, living in that squalid old folly in Hampstead. Why was he so far from his usual haunts?"

"If he planned to make a kill, it would be sensible to hunt in a distant part of town, outside his habitual territory."

"He didn't plan on dying. We're immortal, so it's even more shocking when one of us is swept away in a random, tragic accident."

"Was it an accident? Why was that woman even in the mall? All the shops were shut." I drum my fingers on the arm of my chair. "We need to look through more of the security footage. The answers may be there."

"I can do that." Her eyes go blank, as if she's reading something I can't see. "I'll go back a couple of hours from the slice Andreas showed us."

"You can access it from here?" Some of tonight's little mysteries abruptly become clear. "Do you have an implant? I thought that was impossible in a non-living brain."

"I had it put in just before the holidays. It's experimental tech–my net-link is wrapped in a cocoon of neurons grown from cold-adapted sea-slugs. I have to feed it glucose occasionally and recharge its oxygen cell. The lab say it'll probably die in six months, and I'll need to have a new one re-implanted." She touches my outmoded laptop, waking it up and passing the stolen data to it. "There you go. I've taken the input from three cameras around the food court."

I settle next to her and she turns the computer so we both can see. We scan the footage faster than a human could, spinning through all three images at once.

"There!" Hoshi taps the screen, selecting the best view. "That's her. She's a waitress at the bistro."

I watch a fragment of the woman's day on fast forward, seeing her take orders and serve food, then clear and tidy the tables. As the bistro closes, she sits and sips a coffee, unwinding, pulling the pins out of her bun and combing her long hair down with her fingers. Volkov catches her as she leaves for home. We run through the attack several times and I still can't pinpoint the source of the light. It flares between them, high up, near their faces, a tiny, captive sun.

"Where does she go, after she's watched Volkov burn?"

Hoshi calls up input from other cameras and we see the waitress slip away, walking into the shadows and vanishing. After that there's no sign of her at any of the exits or in the surrounding streets.

Hoshi blanks the screen. "We can find her, ask at the café for her name and address."

"Caldicott will do that."

"If Andreas finds the poor woman before the police do, he'll kill her."

Something flutters in my breast, where my heart would beat if it still did, a sense of unease, a splinter of fear. "He may regret it, if he tries to do her harm. What do you know of Andreas?"

"He's powerful and has several young vamps in his gang. He tried to sweet-talk me into swelling the ranks. He likes me."

"He wants you, isn't that more likely? Why didn't you join him?"

"He scares me. He hurts people for fun, humans and vampires, and he enjoys making people afraid. Anyhow, I wouldn't leave you, John." She leans close to kiss my cheek. "You're too kind to me."

"How could I be cruel to you, my dear? You'd never make me angry enough."

We make preparations to rest for the day, and perhaps sleep. Coffins are unnecessary and uncomfortable; we share an old brass bed.

"I'm hungry," Hoshi says.

I nod towards the cooler. "There's some blood in there. Nothing special, just unused bloodbank stock."

She wrinkles her nose. "I want real food."

"Try the kitchen upstairs. Nina always has leftovers in the fridge. Be quiet–don't wake them."

She comes back with cereal, something that crunches and crackles in the milk. She giggles as she devours it, like a naughty child.

I say nothing when she creeps out of bed later and heads to the bathroom to vomit. It's hard to unlearn human habits. Sometimes I'll find a restaurant, one of the few good ones in town, and treat myself to steak and all the trimmings, or fried fish, or pie, mash and peas. For the hour or so it stays in my belly I feel like a living man again.

~

Nina, the housekeeper, wakes us in the late afternoon.

"The police are upstairs, John. One armed constable and an inspector. She said her name was Caldicott."

"I'll talk to them in the parlour. Bring them tea, if they want it."

We take our time dressing. I opt for informal; my black smoking jacket over loose trousers, soft grey shirt and blood-red cravat. Hoshi chooses a dress, a short, fancy thing in velvet and tattered black lace. She plaits her hair, and only paints her eyes and lips. She looks like a princess in rags.

Caldicott is impatient when we enter the parlour, scowling at the decor, pacified a little by the tea. Her constable is on his second slice of Nina's excellent fruitcake.

"Mr Strong, Miss Maki." She sets the cup aside. "I'm sorry to disturb you during the day."

The curtains are open. Outside it's almost dark, as a cloudy winter day dies. "It's no trouble. Do you have more questions for us?"

"The mall has an extensive security net and we reviewed all of the video data for last night." She hands me her datapad. "Do you know this woman?"

It's the waitress, an unsmiling image taken from an ID card. She's prettier than I'd have guessed from the grainy surveillance footage, in her late twenties or early thirties, with long, sleek auburn hair and eyes of a vivid pea-green.

"No, I'm afraid not." I pass the pad to Hoshi, who surveys the picture with perfect blankness, her face a still, calm mask. "Who is she?"

"The last person to see the Count alive." Caldicott shakes her head slightly, aware of the falsehood. "She works in

117

Westbourne Mall, as a waitress. Her name is Melissa Sinclair. Are you sure you don't know her?"

"Certain."

Caldicott sighs and takes back her pad, opening another image. It's from the attack, the woman held by her hair and the Count with his fangs deep in her throat. "Your Count fed on her, a nasty, little midnight snack. She fought him off, possibly using a weapon to defend herself, a taser or a stun-gun."

"Neither is capable of destroying us. Did you question her about the incident?"

"She failed to turn up for work this morning and she wasn't at her address. Her neighbours say that she didn't come home yesterday. We checked the hospital and the walk-in centres, but none of them treated a patient with a severe neck laceration. Melissa Sinclair has disappeared."

Hoshi laughs. "And you think we're responsible?"

"I think you might have a motive to harm her, to take revenge for the Count's death."

I admire her directness. "I can assure you, Inspector, that neither of us have ever met Ms Sinclair. If you wish to search my house to make sure that she isn't imprisoned here, or that her body isn't concealed within these walls, please feel free to do so. We are innocent in this matter and have nothing to fear from a thorough search of the premises."

Disappointment flickers across Caldicott's face. She believes me, and the truth makes her case harder, more complex. "This is a nice house, full of nice things. You live very well, and even employ a housekeeper. What do you do, Mr Strong?"

"I've had many professions, all the ones listed in the children's counting game. At the moment I'm lucky enough to be a rich man."

"How did you make your fortune?"

"In mining." That's not a lie; I'd found gold in the Yukon and dug gems out of the earth in Brazil. "With clever investments, it's easy to build up a considerable sum over decades, centuries. I've also lost as much, from backing companies that failed, and from taxes so prohibitive they might as well have been extortion."

Caldicott nods, and I see her envy for my lifestyle. She's old enough to have lived through the bad years, when even gold had no value, when food had to be scavenged, stolen or bartered for, and a safe, warm bed was nothing but an absurd dream. Things are better now, with fairly reliable power and piped water, limited medical services and a widening transport net of buses and robocabs, but most humans are still poor.

"We'll leave you in peace," she says, rising from her chair. "Goodnight."

Her constable follows her out, taking a third slice of cake to eat on the way. When they're gone, Hoshi's eyes narrow. "What's wrong?"

"Why would anything be wrong?"

"I know you, John. You can't hide your worry from me."

I try to analyse my unease. It began when I looked at the photo of the waitress and doubled when I heard her name. "It's that woman, the victim of Volkov's attack."

"Do you recognise her? Is she a familiar face from your past?"

I shake my head, frustrated that the solution has slipped from my grasp. "It's nothing. Let it be."

It's full dark now, so I change to go out. We split up to feed, and never ask the other where they're going or if they intend to kill. Vampire etiquette; perhaps simple politeness or perhaps the need not to spread the guilt.

I visit one of my girls and eat lightly. When I return, the house is in darkness, so I go through into the garden. There's a bench beneath the fig tree and I settle down. Once I would have sat on deck, smoking a pipe or two under the stars. Now I just sit and think.

Hoshi comes home after midnight and finds me in the

cold darkness. "What are you doing out here?"

"Considering the mystery."

"The Sinclair woman?"

"You were right, little Star. I have seen her before–in a fever hospital in Paris, back when the first influenza pandemic took hold. She was on the medical staff."

"No, she's too young for that. It was more than forty years ago. Perhaps her mother or another relative?"

"I'm sure it was her."

Hoshi screws up her pretty face in a frown. "But she's human, isn't she? I don't think she's one of us."

"We aren't the only monsters to walk the earth. There are others out there, hiding in plain sight among the humans, pretending to fit in. You must have heard some of the classic urban myths–the serial killer picking the wrong prey and being flayed alive, the rapist being violated and killed for his crimes. There are more things in Heaven and Earth–"

She giggles. "What, ghosts and werewolves, the fae and evil spirits?"

"I don't know what they are. I've sensed a few of them, an odd presence in a crowd, a sudden whiff of immense chaotic power lurking in the shadows. If you feel such entities near, it's wisest to walk away."

"And you think that Melissa Sinclair is one of these monsters, a vampire hunter killing us with the power of the sun?"

I haven't prayed for centuries, and I'm sure that God won't be listening if I start again now. "I hope not."

~

It starts to snow at dawn and at midday the power goes out. Nina lights a fire in the parlour and puts candles around the room. I wake early and take my book up there, and Hoshi joins me an hour later. It snows for the rest of the day, sometimes so heavily that the far side of the square is obscured. As darkness falls, the blizzard ceases. The world is transformed, smothered beneath a killing cloak of pure, virginal whiteness.

"I love snow," Hoshi says. "It's so beautiful. It makes a fairyland out of the ordinary."

"I hate it."

"It's New Year's Eve, at the start of a new century. That's kind of magical, isn't it?"

"I've seen three centuries in, one of them a new millennium. Perhaps there's a little more hope for the future this time, as humanity rises slowly from the wreckage of the Dark."

She doesn't really understand. She's so young, only a decade dead. She didn't live through it, the climate change that starved millions, the earthquakes and floods, the viral pandemics, and the wars over resources and land. I'd watched the humans die, billions of them. A battlefield is a good place for a vampire, and I'd walked a few in my time, recovering the dead and the wounded, giving a merciful end to those with the most grievous injuries in exchange for a few mouthfuls of blood. I'd worked in the tent-city hospitals too, immune to all epidemic diseases. I held water so the shaking, fever-victims could drink, wiped sweat and blood from their faces, maybe comforted them a little, and buried them when they died. The worst of it was over by the time Hoshi was born.

"You don't talk about the past much, do you? How were you made vampire?"

"I was a sailor on an ill-fated voyage. Our ships were trapped in the ice." The memory is close to the surface, summoned by the freezing weather outside. I close my eyes and I'm back in that blizzard, my fingers and toes aching with frostbite, my breath a pale cloud in the air.

We'd trekked over the ice, a small group of us, in search of the nearest settlement and safety, until the raw arctic wind caught us up in a terrible, blinding snowstorm. I was weak and so hungry, as all of us were. My companion, the real William Strong, fell down in the snow and couldn't summon the will to go on, so I stayed with him and tried to keep him warm. He died within the hour. I wept for him, my tears freezing in the rime on my beard. I still use his name and others of the crew for aliases, simply to keep their memory alive.

I'd been very close to death, on the point of closing my eyes and slipping into a sleep that would last for eternity, when a figure loomed out of the storm, a tall woman with braided dark hair, wearing robes of sealskin, as the Inuit tribes do. Two ice bears stalked at her heels.

"Help me," I'd said.

"Do you want to live?" Her voice was deep, and as cold as the land around us. "I may save you, but granting that boon will be a curse rather than a blessing. Are you prepared to accept the cost?"

"What cost?"

"My people say this—the greatest peril of our existence lies in the fact that our diet consists entirely of souls. If I save you, you must kill and sacrifice a soul each time you need to fill your belly. Can you live with such guilt?"

"Yes," I'd said. "Anything."

She'd gestured with her left hand and one of the bears reared over me. I looked up into the dark gape of its jaws and felt the heat of its fish-scented breath before it ripped out my throat.

When I awoke, I was no longer cold or in pain. My body was whole again and all my fear had gone.

The woman sat beside me on the snow, leaning against the larger bear, which was still licking my blood from its muzzle. The other lapped at his mistress's wrist, cleaning a fresh wound there.

"What have you done to me?" I'd asked.

"Saved your life, for the rest of time." She'd climbed to her feet, and the bears rubbed against her, like pet dogs or house-cats. "Let me leave you with one piece of advice–be kind."

Then she'd walked away, disappearing back into the storm.

"John." Hoshi's voice calls me back. I blink at her and she touches my cheek, smiling. "You looked so very far away."

"I was remembering being alive, then dead again."

"We won't talk about it. Now, what shall we do to celebrate the New Year? I feel we should do something–"

My phone sings, a call from an unknown number.

"Mr Strong?" I place the weary, husky voice–Caldicott. "I thought that you'd like to know we've found Ms Sinclair."

"That's good news. Where was she?"

"In hiding, with a friend. She returned to her flat to collect some belongings. Her intention is to leave the city, but she's agreed to be interviewed before she goes."

"I'd like to speak with her, if that's possible."

Caldicott considers it, weighing up the risk and harm. "I'll allow it. We're taking her to the station in Shepherd's Bush. Meet us there in an hour."

~

It takes us a little longer than that to reach the police station. The robocabs are running slow, struggling to cope with the deep snowfall. The reception hall is in chaos, full of people. Few are there to report a crime, most just finding refuge from the cold and the blackout. We make our way to the desk, which is manned by a harassed sergeant and a single support worker.

"We're here to see DI Caldicott."

The sergeant looks us over and takes an instant dislike. "She's not here. She's out on police business."

"We're involved in her current case. She called us over an hour ago, and at that time said she was returning here."

He turns to his assistant. "Is Caldicott back?"

"No, sir," the woman says, consulting her screen. "My last contact with her vehicle was twenty minutes ago."

"Call her."

We wait, and the sergeant starts to sweat. The woman finally shakes her head. "No reply, sir, and I'm getting nothing from the car's tracker. They're off the grid."

"Where did she go?" I ask.

"Ealing, sir," the woman says, after the sergeant nods his approval. "To a flat near Lammas Park. The last contact with the car was just west of Acton."

"Damn inconvenient time to go missing," the sergeant mutters. "Most of my men have been drafted to the Embankment to police the New Year's crowds, if anyone's foolish enough to go out in this weather. Don't worry, sir, we'll send out a patrol to find the Inspector. Leave your details and we'll inform you when she's back."

Hoshi hands over the numbers and we go out into the cold. Our cab is still waiting at the kerb.

"Can we find Caldicott?" I ask, as we climb in.

Hoshi closes her eyes, consulting her implant. "I have Sinclair's address. I'll take us there along the shortest route. If they've broken down, it should be simple enough to discover where."

"It's not a breakdown, or they would have called it in."

The cab heads west, keeping to the major roads. We turn south-west at Acton, pass a disused Tube station, then cross the old North Circular road. There are few streetlights out here, just infrequent, weak solar-powered ones, and even less traffic. We pass a cemetery and turn north, zigzagging through narrow streets. The cab comes to a halt in front of a row of inhabited houses on the south side of a park. The power is still out and some of the windows leak candlelight around their blinds.

"We didn't see them," Hoshi says. "Do you want to backtrack?"

"If you were setting an ambush along the route, where

would you choose?"

She frowns. "Before the burial ground there was a big open space, very dark and exposed, with mostly derelict houses along the roadside. I'd pick there."

"Take us back there."

As the cab approaches the area, I open its window. There's a road heading south and we both catch the scent from that direction, faint but distinct, the tang of blood. Hoshi forces the cab into manual control; we do a U-turn and take the side road, creeping through the deep snow until we find the site of the attack.

The police car has been forced off the road, into a fence. Its doors are open, its lights and engine dead. Three bodies lie tumbled in the road, their blood staining the snow crimson.

"I'll call for help," Hoshi says. "Ambulance, then police–yes?"

The two constables are unconscious. They tried to fight off their attackers, with taser and baton. The puncture wounds in their necks are leaking slowly, but whoever bit them didn't take much. They'll survive.

Caldicott has lost more blood, yet her eyelids flicker as I kneel beside her. Her pulse is thready, and I'm amazed she's still conscious. I make a pad of my handkerchief and put pressure on the bite over her jugular. "Who did this?"

"Five of them." She has trouble catching her breath. "Three vamps, two human. Are my men...?"

"Alive? Yes, and in a better state than you. Help's coming."

"Cold..." she says, so I take off my greatcoat and cover her. "Blankets, in the car."

Hoshi finds them in the boot, and spreads them over the uniformed men.

"Must have followed us from the flat." Caldicott's anger burns hot, impotent fury at being overpowered swamping her pain. "Took Melissa..."

"The leader, what did he look like?"

"Tall, blond... You know him?"

"I do."

"He'll kill her..."

My gut says the pendulum will swing the other way. "We'll find her."

"Go now," she says urgently. "Leave us..."

I hear sirens, distant but heading our way. "Hold on. The paramedics will be here soon."

They arrive within minutes, two ambulances and a police car. I reclaim my coat and step back to let the professionals do their work.

"What happened here?" It's the desk sergeant, his lack of manpower pressing him into the field.

"Caldicott was bringing a woman to the station for questioning, the victim of an attack in which her assailant died. Whoever set this ambush kidnapped the woman."

"They were your kind." He peers at me, looking for signs of guilt.

"We didn't do this. Caldicott will tell you that we came to help."

"If she survives."

The Inspector has been loaded into an ambulance, which departs with all speed, blue lights flashing. There's a wide lake of blood in the snow where she lay.

"That's a pint and a half at worst, no more than that. Most humans can cope with losing that."

"You'd know, I'm sure." The sergeant turns away.

Hoshi's leaning on the fence, wrapped in her fake-mink coat, eating a pyramid of bloody snow as if it was sorbet. She sees my frown and shrugs. "Seemed a shame to waste it. Will the Inspector make it, do you think?"

"She ought to." I glance over the chaos. "Andreas did this. Do you know where to find him?"

"I can take you to his base, but there are other hideouts. It may take some time to track him down."

"We have the rest of the night."

The faithful robocab takes us across Vauxhall Bridge into the wilderness south of the river. The lights are back on here, patches of safety amid the rubble of ruined buildings. There are some communities, fenced and defended from thieves and beggars. Most of the humans in these parts are still feral.

Andreas' home in Camberwell is deserted, so we travel through New Cross, searching an abandoned public house, and a variety of rundown business and industrial units. At the fourth site, the sky to the north is briefly lit by fireworks, the red and gold bomb-bursts of costly rockets marking midnight and the turning of the year.

Hoshi squeezes my hand. "Happy twenty-one hundred."

The seventh site proves to be that final stop. It's a warehouse in Rotherhithe, desolate and tumbledown. I'm aware of bodies inside, some living, some not. The side door is unlocked. We enter silently. The roof has multiple holes; it wouldn't be safe here during the day. The air's damp, thick with the dank, rotting stink of the river.

Andreas is at the far end, flanked by two young vampires and three of his human vassals, heavy-set men with empty, moronic faces, built of slabs of muscle. The waitress is tied to a chair, her head slumped forwards, her tangled hair hiding her face. There are bruises on her wrists and bare arms, and her blouse is torn. She's crying, ceaseless, mechanical sobs.

The two vamps growl, and Andreas swings round as we approach. "What are you doing here, Kenley? You weren't invited."

"I've come to stop you torturing that woman."

"She killed the Count, so she deserves it. She won't tell me how–she's saying nothing at all." Andreas lifts a finger.

The man nearest his prisoner slaps her across the cheek. She yelps in pain.

"Stop it!" Hoshi shares my disgust.

"This is nothing, merely cosmetic damage." Andreas bares his fangs, turning to display them to his victim. "You saw what I did to the police inspector, didn't you, bitch? I can be

127

much more inventive and cruel, I assure you."

Melissa moans in terror, struggling against the ropes. I know it's an act. She's pretty convincing, but her pulse is slow and steady. She isn't afraid. Trapped in this terrible place, bound hand and foot, surrounded by evil men and monsters, and still she isn't afraid?

"Cut her free and let her go." I suspect Andreas won't heed my advice. "This nasty charade is a waste of time-"

"We have until dawn. I can inflict a lot of damage on her pretty body before then." He smiles in grim appreciation. "Now, what to do next? Shall we carve your cheek open to the bone, snap your little fingers one by one, or gouge out one of those cute green eyes? What would be the most amusing?"

"No, don't!" Melissa's voice quavers, filled with fear, and she's trembling. "Please don't hurt me!"

She's a talented actress, but I see a flash of contrary emotion behind the mask, a sudden spark of anger. It chills me, and I almost feel human again, as cold and helpless as I'd been in the Arctic. Andreas is toying with her, as a cat torments a mouse, misled into thinking he holds all the power here. He'll never suspect that his poor mouse is a tiger, not until the moment that she rips off his head.

I edge forwards, until I'm closer to Melissa than her tormenter. "Who are you? No, that's the wrong question, isn't it? What are you, and how did you kill Count Volkov?"

Melissa shakes the hair from her eyes and sits straighter in the chair. Her tears cease. She isn't acting anymore. Game over.

"I didn't kill him." She presses her lips together in a frown. "Well, perhaps I did, indirectly, without intending to. He attacked me, took me by surprise. I told him not to feed on me, but he did."

"And your precious, special blood burned him?" Andreas laughs. "Hit her again!"

His henchman lifts a hand to obey, then Melissa looks into his eyes. No more than that, just a steady, level gaze, but the man's arm drops to his side and he turns away.

"I gave you an order–hit her!"

"I'm sorry, sir, I can't." The man looks miserable, knowing he'll be punished.

"Hit her–or I'll rip your throat out!"

"Stop playing the moody tyrant," Hoshi says, pantomiming a yawn of boredom. "You'll never get good help if you threaten them."

Andreas scowls. "So I should be kind and weak, like your master?"

"Being a bully isn't strong. Under the act, you're just a coward."

She surprises me, my little Star. She isn't usually so outspoken. I think Andreas will set one of his immature vamps on her, to curb her insolence, but he backs down. Melissa watches the performance with amusement.

Andreas redirects his anger. "Why are you looking so happy, bitch? You won't get out of here alive. I'll rip your skin off, then drain your blood–"

"That would be a bad idea," Melissa says. "Really bad, not to mention pretty dumb. Did you see what happened to the Count?"

"Are you threatening me? Do you dare even that, you stupid, fragile piece of human shit? You're meat to my kind, nothing else–"

She lifts her head, humour touching her apple-green eyes as she smiles. "Bite me!"

Andreas snarls and pounces, ripping fabric to reach her neck. Melissa laughs as his fangs break her skin.

"Hoshi, cover your eyes!" I'm not sure it will do any good, but I take my own advice. Andreas lets out an ugly, gurgling scream as the blood scalds his mouth. The sunburst is so bright that I see the bones of my hand through the flesh for an instant, then I feel the terrible heat of it through my clothing, burning on my skin. Hoshi shrieks in terror and I'm too weak to help her. I fall to the damp floor and lose my grip on consciousness.

~

When I wake, I'm still in one piece. My eyes still work; I look for burns on my hands and feel for blisters on my face, but find none. Hoshi is beside me, making little mewling sounds like a scared kitten. She's also miraculously intact. I touch her shoulder and the pathetic noises cease.

"Are we alive?" she asks, and her voice shakes.

"We're still undead, sweeting."

The thing that calls itself Melissa Sinclair sits in the chair, free of the ropes, which lie like snakes coiled around her feet. There's a heap of clothing and ash in front of her–Andreas. The other two vampires are cremated remains, and the three henchmen are sprawled on the ground.

"The humans are only stunned," the monster in the guise of a woman says. "They'll wake in an hour or so."

I ask the only relevant question. "Why didn't you burn us?"

"They were evil, irredeemable. You, the lost sailor and his bright protégé–you might be saved."

"We aren't innocent," Hoshi says. "We drain our prey, and kill sometimes."

The Melissa-thing makes a sweeping gesture, encompassing the chaos that litters the floor of the warehouse. "It would be hypocritical of me to condemn you for that."

"What are you? You wear human shape, yet your blood is fire–liquid sunbeams, inimical to vampires."

She smiles, her eyes a little sad. "I'll keep my mystery, thank you. 'Other' is a good enough name for what I am."

We watch her leave, still too weak to rise to our feet and follow. At the door she turns, and although it's a whisper, I catch her final words.

"Be kind."

Gillian M. (Jilly) Paddock's earliest published works were in the field of medical research in the mid-70s. One of which, she presented at a conference in London in 1975.

She's been writing science fiction and fantasy stories for as long as she can remember. Having taken early retirement from the National Health Service, she decided the time was right to resurrect her writing career.

She has several highly praised books available on Amazon Kindle. The title story of her short story collection, 'The Dragon, Fly', written on a creative writing course, received high praise from the tutor, the late, great Iain (M.) Banks. 18th Wall Productions will be reprinting the story in the upcoming anthology, 'Lying in a Wounded Wood'. She will also have a brand new story in Pro Se Presents #19.

Pro Se will be publishing and republishing several of her works soon. Starting with her first novel, 'To Die a Stranger' and further volumes in that series. And her other regular characters, 'Afton and Jerome', from the Kindle ebook, 'The Spook and the Spirit in the Stone' will return in a new volume as well.

Her contribution to this volume, in aid of the Cystic Fibrosis Trust, brings her neatly back to her writing roots.

She lives in a small, untidy house in the flat bits of East Anglia in the UK, which she shares with an editor and reviewer, and an insanely large number of books and CDs.

OCCUPATION
James Ninness

When the door to her cage fell open, Twenty-Seven found herself atop an enormous photovoltaic rig with nothing but ocean and daylight on all sides.

There was a loud click above her head as the helicopter disconnected from the thick chain that carried her container. The chain fell, rattling along the roof. Her earpiece crackled as the helicopter began to fly away. "Number Twenty-Seven, copy?"

"I hear you."

Her eyes scanned the surface of the rig. There were several hundred solar panels a few steps from the landing pad, each black square was ten feet by ten feet, mounted on swivels to follow the sun. Currently they were positioned fifteen degrees off focus. Whatever knocked the system offline happened several hours ago.

Her earpiece crackled again, pulling her attention to the fleeing helicopter, "You have five hours to clear the rig. If you're not back atop-"

"I know the drill," she muttered, her eyes dropping from the aircraft to the rig where her cage sat open. There was another behind it, also open. "I'm not the primary?"

"Irrelevant. Parameters remain consistent. Consider all entities hostile."

Twenty-Seven walked back into her cage, grabbing her arsenal off the wall: Two .45 caliber semi-automatic pistols, an AAR 22 assault rifle, a machete, and two smaller hunting knives. Every weapon had a stripe of red tape to match her uniform, black and blood, the colors of Capital City.

Once she was geared up, Twenty-Seven climbed down the steps of the landing pad, through the forest of solar panels to the large hatch in the center of the platform. The sun was bright and the sea was calm, but the platform moved up and down with a soft consistency that made Twenty-Seven uneasy. Though she had cleared photovoltaic rigs before, she never felt easy on the ocean. She preferred something under her feet with less influence.

The hatch popped open and a quick, stale gust of air burst outward. Twenty-Seven clicked a flashlight on the side of her AAR 21 and poked it around the entrance before jumping into the darkness.

She landed on the ground twenty feet below and backed against the wall, waving her rifle across the small room. She kept her eyes on the shadows; her gun firm in one hand while her other felt the wall for a control panel. She moved down until she found it and entered in the command code without looking.

The hatch above her closed automatically. Some of the lights flickered to life; others remained off. They dead ones left blackness over shards of glass on the ground where someone had broken the bulbs.

Twenty-Seven made her way down the hall, her AAR tucked into her shoulder, leading her through the patches of light. The corridor was about six feet wide with aluminum lining. This was a great deal nicer than any of the other rigs she had cleared, which were typically much more narrow and three-quarters the overall size.

When she reached the end of the passage she turned right, toward Control. Left would take her into the belly of the station.

The photovoltaic rigs were massive constructions, built just before The Decline several decades ago. A few hundred floated in the ocean along the equator where they could pull maximum energy from the sun. Each rig was designed to mediate an output of up to one gigawatt. All of the rigs linked together to produce more than enough power for Capital City.

Control was destroyed. All of the terminals were shattered and there was a long streak of blood strewn along the wall across from the door. There were no bodies.

"This is Twenty-Seven."

"We read you, number Twenty-Seven. Go ahead."

"Control is lost. This rig won't be collecting again, not without extensive refitting."

"Copy."

She waited for further instruction but none came. "So?"

"Is there a problem?"

"If Control is lost then why am I here? Shouldn't we just blow the rig from a distance?"

The pain started in her neck and shot down her back, streaming down the sides of each leg. She would have screamed if the breath had not been sucked from her lungs. She fell to the floor, convulsing like a fish on dirt. When the shock finally stopped she sucked in large gulps of air, trying to regain control of her faculties.

"Your orders stand. Clear the rig."

She pulled herself onto her knees and rubbed her neck. She could feel the small bump, like a mole, where the behavior chip was soldered onto her C5 vertebra. It had been a while since they had used it. She had almost forgotten it was there.

There was an elevator shaft opposite the entrance to Control. The doors were jammed open with a long pipe. Twenty-Seven poked the barrel of her gun into the shaft, following that with her head. She could not see the ground floor but there was a distinct odor of stale smoke. Something had been burning at the bottom. Though the car was gone, the cables remained intact, running into the black, smoldering pit.

The rear wall of the rig was a super-acrylic designed for deep-sea vessels. It allowed the workers to look out into the ocean when they rode the elevators up and down the rig. As Twenty-Seven lowered herself down the cable she could not help but steal glances of the lost landscape, buried forever in the ocean.

There was an entire city outside the rig, broken and forgotten. Since the window faced East, Twenty-Seven guessed she was looking at some part of the Western coast of the American continent. The time it took her to arrive at this rig was no more than a few hours. From Capital City they would not have been able to make it to the European coast.

Given how close the cityscape was to the station she was probably no more than a few miles from shore. If it weren't for the small explosive in the back of her neck she could swim to land. She could live in the wasteland, free from the Alliance...

No. It was silly to think such things. Foolish. Dangerous.

The smell of smoke crept further into her nostrils as she neared the bottom of the elevator shaft. Glowing embers of a small corpse were strewn over a twisted and mangled elevator car. Whatever number they had sent in before had made it at least this far before encountering any mullos.

Twenty-Seven dropped to the ground and took a closer look at the corpse. All of the flesh had been burnt off— probably by an incineration grenade. Since those were not standard armament for her kind, Twenty-Seven had to guess that the one who came before found a few new toys in Control before making her descent.

The corpse was full-grown. The open pelvic inlet and outwardly flared hipbones suggested female. The cuspids had grown to three inches in length. This was definitely a mullo. It had been a mullo for at least eight hours.

Twenty-Seven leapt out of the shaft, crawling through the

broken doors. The lights on this floor were completely out. Small spot-fires and sparks from damaged equipment were the only light source.

For a dhampir like Twenty-Seven, that was not a problem. It was the reason they used her. Dhampirs were the spawn of mullos and humans. They were not consumed by the hunger, but had plenty of mullo attributes, most beneficial in this particular situation: the ability to see in the dark.

One would think that dhampirs would be the dominant species on the planet. Unfortunately, the mating of mullo and human was an incredibly rare thing. Though the humans were able to clone the dhampirs, they were unable to create them artificially from scratch. That was probably a blessing. Twenty-Seven wondered if she would be here at all if the humans could start with a blank slate.

The sound of gunfire rang out somewhere within the rig. It was definitely on the first floor, deeper inside. Twenty-Seven kept her gun up and walked slowly down the thin hallway and into the commissary.

Tables and chairs had been flipped and cast across the room. There were streaks of blood across the walls, floor and ceiling. Two bodies were lying on the ground, huddled together in the corner on the other side of the large room.

Twenty-Seven went to her side, through the kitchen doors. The cooking area was small and mostly undisturbed. She went back into the dining hall and found only one body where there had been two moments ago.

Before she could raise her gun she felt a hard blow to her side, knocking her to the ground. Her AAR slid across the floor. The mullo was already in the air again, descending on Twenty-Seven with its teeth bared, growling like a wild beast. Deep blue veins ran over its otherwise pale skin, giving it the glow of a ghost in the darkness.

Twenty-Seven lifted her right hand to catch the mullo by the throat and grabbed for a sidearm with her left. The creature made a few chomps at her before opening its mouth wide—too wide, like a snake unhinging its jaw—and flicking its tongue at her. She moved her head just enough to feel the mucous-coated muscle scratch her face.

She pulled her pistol up and jammed the barrel into the base of the mullo's neck. The creature launched its tongue again just as Twenty-Seven fired. The bullet must have connected with the spine because there was an explosion of blood as the mullo's body dropped onto Twenty-Seven and its head rolled forward, completely disconnected.

Twenty-Seven stood quickly and surveyed the room. She should have checked the bodies before the kitchen. That was a stupid mistake she would not make again.

When the room was clear of any more enemies she moved to the second body. It was an older man, probably in his late fifties. He had died human. His stomach was torn open and there were numerous gashes on his throat and face. That mullo may have been feeding on this corpse for some time.

Before she left the commissary, Twenty-Seven grabbed the severed mullo head. She held it up so that blood from the neck pooled in her hand. She wiped the blood under her arms, on her belly, legs and around her neck. The scent would work to mask her human-smell from the others, at least from afar.

If the clone who came before her was following procedure, as Twenty-Seven was, she would have started on the bottom floor, working her way up through the rig, clearing the floors one by one. The mullo she had just killed meant one of two things. One, the first dhampir missed a mullo, which meant she was new—typically overlooking a mullo meant not making it back alive. Or, two, the first clone was killed, which would explain the reason Twenty-Seven was called in. Either option seemed unfortunate for the clone.

On the second floor, the living quarters, Twenty-Seven went room to room, clearing each with a slow, cautious focus. She would not be surprised again.

The first half of the living quarters showed no signs of a struggle. Typically rigs housed thirty to forty staff, each assigned a section of living quarters by group. The Alpha group worked mornings, the Beta group worked evenings, and the Gamma group took the late nights.

Since the Alpha quarters were completely clean it was safe to assume that they had been on duty when the infection began. If that was true the rig had been exposed no more than nine hours and no less than three. Given the size of the teeth on the burnt corpse and the elevator shaft, and the mutation of the tongue on the mullo in the commissary, Twenty-Seven guessed on the side of caution and assumed that the rig had been infected for at least nine hours.

Nine hours of infection meant that the hazard would not be fully developed. It takes at least a day, usually longer, for a mullo to reach maturity. The worst-case scenario would be more of what she faced in the commissary, mullos so hopped up on pheromones and testosterone they would be uncontrollably driven to feed.

The mature ones are a great deal more difficult to kill. The mature ones can think and reason and plan...

As she neared the Beta quarters she began to see signs of chaos, papers and knickknacks strewn about the floor amidst lines of blood and broken glass.

The first two rooms were clear. There were three bodies inside, all deceased. Two humans and one mullo. It appeared as though some of the workers put up a fight. Good for them.

In the third room Twenty-Seven found a mullo staring at itself in a mirror. She shot it in the back of the head before it could turn around. The fourth room was clear but the fifth room had a mullo on the floor, struggling to stand on two broken legs. She put it down quickly.

The sixth room gave Twenty-Seven pause—a nursery. There were several small plastic tubs, none of them occupied, and a line of cribs along the back wall. Something was snarling in the center crib.

Twenty-Seven kept her gun aimed on the crib as she approached. This would not be the first time she had to put down a baby mullo but repetition did not make it easier.

The mullo was an infant, no more than a few months old. It was obviously in pain but seemed more angry than sad. There were no tears—mullos lacked tear ducts—but it wiggled and struggled in a fury to twist itself from back to belly. A small trickle of blood was crusted around the neck where two puncture wounds were already beginning to heal.

Twenty-Seven raised her gun...

Something was behind her.

She spun around to see a figure in the doorway. Before she could make it out, there was a flash of light and an immense pain in her shoulder. She spun around, losing her AAR, and taking cover behind the empty plastic bins.

The voice was familiar, "I need you to listen to me."

It was the clone. The other Twenty-Seven.

Twenty-Seven grabbed both pistols, raising them ready. "Now you want to talk? You just shot me."

The voice was coming from another corner of the room. She was moving. Smart. "Only to stop you from shooting me. You weren't going to hesitate, were you?"

True. If the clone had paused for only a moment she would be the one nursing a gunshot wound. Though, Twenty-Seven liked to believe that she had better aim than her adversary. If she had gotten off the first shot they would not be having a conversation.

The infant mullo moaned in the crib. The clone continued. "I can help you."

Twenty-Seven smirked. "Help me? How's that?"

"I'm going to put down my guns. Can we talk?"

Twenty-Seven pulled the hammers back on both of her pistols. "Sure. Step on out."

She peered around the corner to see her clone standing there with both hands in the air. She seemed genuine when she said, "Please. We don't have to fight."

Twenty-Seven stood, both guns aimed at the other dhampir. The clone continued, "I am Forty-Five. Will you just listen?"

Twenty-Seven smiled, "No."

Before she could pull the trigger there was a great weight on her back, shoving her into a stack of plastic bins. One of her guns went off. The air was knocked from her chest. An immense pain shot through her back. Then there was a loud explosion and an intense moment of heat. Something hit her in the head. Everything went black and just before she lost consciousness she heard the infant snarl.

Twenty-Seven had the same dream she had dreamed many times before.

She was in a park. The grass was thick and green. The sky was open, deep and blue. There were trees all around her. There were people everywhere. Kids. Parents. Families. Everyone was enjoying themselves. They were all smiling.

Someone picked her up from behind. Twenty-Seven giggled. She was small, perhaps a toddler. The woman who lifted her laughed with Twenty-Seven, spinning her around and pulling her close. A hug. A kiss. Love.

It was her mother. Mother had long, brown hair and large green eyes that matched the grass. She was warm. Everything was warm.

"I love you," Mother said.

Then there was bright light behind Twenty-Seven, something so bright that Mother's face shined like the sun. Though Twenty-Seven could not turn around, she saw fear in the faces of everyone behind Mother. People started screaming. They turned and tried to run.

It was too late.

A gust of wind smacked Twenty-Seven in the back and tore through the park, lifting everyone and everything into the air and burning it to nothing.

Mother's face began to crack and peel but her smile remained. She looked at Twenty-Seven as her skin turned black and tore off in chunks.

"I love you."

Twenty-Seven screamed awake. She was in a dark room and she was not alone. The clone was there, by the door. She reached for her weapons to find none. Her earpiece was also missing. Forty-Five stood, raising a hand to calm Twenty-Seven, "Please. Be still. You're fine."

She stood and backed away. Forty-Five stood as well, keeping her hands up. "Was it the park?"

Twenty-Seven nodded.

Forty-Five put her hands down and smiled. "Those aren't your memories, you know?"

"No shit."

"What's your designation?"

"Twenty-Seven."

Forty-Five pulled a small canteen from her side, twisted it open and held it out to Twenty-Seven. "Thirsty, Twenty-Seven?"

She was. Twenty-Seven took the canteen and drank a few quick sips. When she dropped her head back down she felt a numbing pain along the back of her neck. She reached up to rub it and found a large scab where her behavior chip should have been.

"What did you do?"

Forty-Five grinned again, "We freed you."

"Freed me?"

Forty-Five motioned to a body huddled in the corner. It was a mullo, maybe male. It was difficult to say because it was dark and most of its face was missing. Something had ripped its flesh off from chin to forehead. Most of the jaw and nasal cavity was gone.

Forty-Five continued, "Before you passed out it bit out the chip."

Twenty-Seven rubbed her neck again, feeling around the wound. Forty-Five was not lying. The lump was gone. Forty-Five turned and pulled her hair up, showing Twenty-Seven her own wound. "You see? No more control."

A few mullos began to peek around the corner of the

doorway from the hall. Twenty-Seven stiffened, raising her hands to fight. Forty-Five lifted her arms and stood in the way, shouting, "No! Wait! They're not here to fight you!"

One of the mullos, the largest one, put a hand on Forty-Five's shoulder and pushed her aside, staring at Twenty-Seven. He was big. He was obviously mature, which did not add up with the timeline for the rig.

He was an Alpha. Twenty-Seven had glimpsed photographs of Alphas, but never seen one in person. They were said to rarely leave their dens, sending the younger mullos out for food and ruling from the safety of shelter. And yet, one stood before her.

The Alpha had white skin, almost transparent so that his veins were visible like spider webs under his flesh. His hair was long and white and came out of his scalp and back, falling around his feet like a mane. The cuspids were over six inches long, jutting past his mandible unlike any fangs Twenty-Seven had seen before.

The Alpha stopped in front of her. She kept her hands up, calculating every possible attack. Without her weapons she knew she would die. If she was going to die it would not be without a fight.

The mullo lifted a hand in her direction and opened its mouth, "Help us?"

Twenty-Seven lost her breath again. The Alpha spoke. Mullos do not speak. Ever. The words were heavy, falling out of the creature's mouth like half-chewed food, but they were clear enough. It was communicating and it wanted assistance.

Help us.

Forty-Five came to Twenty-Seven's side and put a hand on her shoulder. Though Twenty-Seven was unable to take her eyes off of the Alpha, she heard Forty-Five when she asked, "Can we show you something?"

Twenty-Seven nodded.

She followed Forty-Five out of the room and down the hallway, deeper into the rig. The larger mullo, the Alpha, walked behind them as they passed several open doors and rooms full of mullos. The Gamma quarters were full of them, some young, some old, all huddled in doorways watching Twenty-Seven with cautious glares and occasional sneers.

They went up a series of stairs and stopped on the fourth floor where Forty-Five opened the door to the recreation room, the largest single space on any rig.

Twenty-Seven could not help but gasp. There were hundred of mullos, many more than this facility alone could produce. Some were young, scratching at their faces as they continued to mutate. Others were quite a bit older, like the talking Alpha. All of them were staring at Twenty-Seven with a palpable deal of anxiety.

Forty-Five turned to Twenty-Seven and held out her hands, gesturing to the masses, "These are our people."

"Our people?"

Twenty-Seven looked around the room, trying to take stock of her situation. Some of the mullos were feeding on remnants of corpses. Others were sitting along the wall, unmoving and patient. Many were holding one another.

The Alpha stood in front of Twenty-Seven, putting his right hand on her shoulder. Twenty-Seven's instinct was to flinch... It took a great deal of effort to avoid doing so.

He pointed at himself, "Mullo," then to Forty-Five, "Mullo," and finally to Twenty-Seven, sniffing her neck in an exaggerated fashion, "Mullo."

Forty-Five moved closer, "Whereas our employers see us as half human, the mullos see us as half mullo. They do not see us as enemies, but family."

Twenty-Seven's "family" made her nauseous. How many of these things had she killed over the years? How many times had one of them tried to rip her head off?

"That's not how most of them react."

The Alpha shuffled over to the rest of the mullos, leaving Forty-Five and Twenty-Seven in the middle of the room.

"I understand your hesitation," Forty-Five kept eye contact

and seemed genuine, "but are you really more human than mullo?"

Easy. "Yes."

"Why?"

"I don't terrorize innocent people. I don't eat other humans."

"You have killed mullos?"

"You know that."

"What did the mullos do to you?"

"They killed other humans. I am a response. It's my job."

Forty-Five was smiling again, "You do what you must to stay alive? Are the mullos any different? What if I told you that it was the humans who were the villains here?"

Twenty-Seven laughed out loud despite herself. "I'd say you were mad."

"Really? Is it madness to evolve? The humans had their chance on Earth. And what did they do? They wiped themselves out!"

"At Capital City-"

"Yes, Capital City. Where the remaining one percent of humanity lives in fear of the outside world. Hunting a creature that is, by all rights, the dominant species."

The mullos seemed to be moving in, closing on Twenty-Seven and her clone. Where were her weapons?

Forty-Five continued, "You and I share the same dreams, sister. Don't forget that I know you as well as you know yourself. I know you share my desire for freedom. How long can you continue to hunt at the whim of Capital City? Do you think they will let you retire when you get old? Have you ever seen one of us as an elder in the city?"

Twenty-Seven saw her machete and hunting knives. They were in the corner of the room, leaning against a wall near a ventilation shaft that filtered carbon dioxide out of the station.

"No. We hunt until we die. It is what we were made to do."

Forty-Five was enjoying herself, leering at Twenty-Seven.

"And what if I told you that there was another way? What if I said that we could lead the next population of this planet instead of serving the dying few?"

Twenty-Seven noticed two more incineration grenades on Forty-Five's waist. She tried not to be obvious about seeing them.

A gunshot rang out. Twenty-Seven fell to the floor. All around the room the mullos screamed and shouted. The Alpha tried to calm them down, running around the room, pushing his brothers and sisters back.

Forty-Five put her pistol back in the holster and walked past Twenty-Seven to a twitching mullo on the ground. Forty-Five used her machete to hack it at the neck, removing the head. There were a few shouts of discontent from the other mullos. Forty-Five kicked the head and body to the edge of the room where a large group of mullos began to tear at it, greedily, biting off chunks and screaming wildly.

Forty-Five offered a hand to Twenty-Seven, "They're not perfect, but it is a work in progress."

Twenty-Seven stood on her own, watching the mullos devour their own. Forty-Five continued, "Every once and a while the newer ones get a bit zealous and have to be reminded that we are not food. As they age they seem less and less interested in us."

It was Twenty-Seven's turn to sneer, "This is your future? These monsters? I hate Capital City as much as you but this is not the way to-"

Forty-Five stopped smiling and approached, waiving her machete, "What then? You would serve the humans, hunting your own kind until you die? Then another takes your place and they die. Then another! And another!"

The mullos stopped eating their fallen sibling, only bone was left.

Twenty-Seven turned to Forty-Five, "What's your plan?"

Forty-Five sheathed her machete, "Do you know where we are?"

"A photovoltaic rig. A big one."

"Not just any rig. This is the primary power station for the Capital City feed. If this station falls the defenses of Capital City will fall for half a day before auxiliary power can be funneled in."

"You know they've already started rerouting conduits."

"Probably. We still have a few hours left."

The Alliance's reluctance to blow the station made sense now.

"That's the plan? Invasion?"

Forty-Five held up her hand where some of the mullo's blood had dripped onto it from her machete. "What more do we need? The defenses fall and the mullos invade. What could be simpler?"

"What about the innocent people in Capital City? What about the families?"

Forty-Five licked the blood off her palm before answering; she seemed to savor it. "What families? Have you seen families? I go from battle to holding. I have no interaction with any people in the city and you don't either."

"But our briefings-"

"Our briefings tell us what they must to keep us in line. We are tools, sister! What do you really know about the people for whom you fight?"

The mullos were getting antsy again, shifting around the room. Even the Alpha looked hungrier.

Forty-Five did not seem to notice. "Even if you are right and there are children, they are no different than the mullo babies you and I have killed many times before. The question here is not whether we should murder, but whom we should murder. Do we defend those who use us, or fight for those who would serve us?"

Twenty-Seven had heard enough. She stood straight and looked Forty-Five in the eyes, "I stand by my previous assessment. You've gone mad."

"Mad?"

"I believe, as you do, that we should have freedom..."

"Mad!"

"I agree that a revolt is coming..."

"You call me mad?"

"But this is not the way. We can flee. Now. The two of us. With our chips gone the Alliance can't track us. Let's leave the humans and the mullos."

Forty-Five turned away from Twenty-Seven. The Alpha was right behind her, staring at Twenty-Seven.

"You are blind, sister," Forty-Five's voice was heavy with regret and she re-wrapped her hand around the handle of the machete.

It was time to go.

Twenty-Seven lunged toward Forty-Five. Forty-Five must have sensed the attack because she moved to the side, narrowly avoiding the bulk of Twenty-Seven's charge. The mullos leapt forward, closing in on Twenty-Seven.

Forty-Five held out her hands, stopping the mullos as Twenty-Seven landed on the other side of the room on her knees.

Forty-Five leered, "It is you who are mad You can't fight us!"

Twenty-Seven threw the incineration pins at Forty-Five and started running to her knives. Out of the corner of her eye, she saw Forty-Five try to jump out of the way as the two grenades exploded in front of her.

The blast was enormous. Waves of liquid fire blossomed out from the center of the room, igniting the air and dousing a great many mullos with heavy flame.

Twenty-Seven grabbed her knives and took off down the hallway to the elevator shaft. She could hear the screams of mullos behind her. She did not, however, hear anything from Forty-Five, who was more than likely in several pieces along the recreation room walls.

The elevator doors on the fourth floor were closed. Twenty-Seven jammed her knife in the center and pried them open. The screams of angry mullos were growing louder. They were coming.

Twenty-Seven pulled herself through the doors, hanging onto the walls of the shaft. She pulled the doors closed as the mullos came into view in the hallway. The doors slammed shut and the mullos began pounding on the other side. Twenty-Seven jammed one of her knives in the door spring to keep them shut and started climbing up the shaft to the surface of the rig.

The blue light from the super-acrylic wall was much darker than before. Though she could still see the remnants of whatever city decayed at the bottom of the ocean, the sunlight from the surface was almost non-existent.

Night had come. She would have to rethink her plan. She had hoped that getting to the surface would stop the mullos, but without the sun to keep them in the rig, she would find no solace above.

Shouts echoed through the shaft. They were inside. Twenty-Seven had to continue.

She pulled herself onto the top floor and ran toward Control, turning the corner to the main hatch. The screams of several angry mullos grew closer, their claws casting a metallic pitter-patter that echoed throughout the rig.

Twenty-Seven pounded the command code into the panel and the hatch began to creep open. She climbed up the ladder while mullos began to pour onto the main floor.

As she pulled herself out of the rig one of the mullos reached out, sinking its claws into her calf. She brought her machete down on the creature's arm, cutting it off below the elbow. The hatch slammed shut and Twenty-Seven used her machete to jam it closed.

She rolled onto her back and took a breath of the nighttime air. The mullos were pounding on the hatch. All Twenty-Seven had left was a single hunting knife. Eventually the beasts would get out. If she stayed here she was going to die.

A steady thumping sound pulled her attention to the sky. She stood to see two more cages being brought in, carried by a command chopper. It was standard procedure for the third incursion to come as a pair, the assumption being that the first two clones were simply overwhelmed.

This was what Forty-Five and the mullos were planning on. The larger sized helicopter and pair of cages would carry the majority of the mullos straight to Capital City. When her behavior chip detonated the Alliance must've concluded that the second incursion had failed.

They were flying into a trap.

Twenty-Seven stumbled when the rig shifted to the side and the metal lurched under her feet. The entire structure was dipping into the ocean along the side with the elevator shaft. By the time she realized that the super-acrylic must have been shattered, mullos were climbing up, out of the water and onto the top of the rig.

They leapt over the solar panels. The moon glistened off their wet, pale skin and gave them a deep blue incandescence.

Twenty-Seven ran to the other side of the rig, knife in hand. The helicopter dropped the two cages just to the side of the landing pad, hovering above them. As the cage doors dropped open, Twenty-Seven ran past them in time to see two more clones with wide eyes at the oncoming mullo incursion.

They never stood a chance. The mullos leapt upon them, tearing them to shreds without time for a single scream. Twenty-Seven felt a guilty pang of relief since the mullos were distracted from her for a moment.

When she reached the end of the rig she turned back to see them climbing the chains to the main helicopter. They were too fast for the pilot. By the time he disconnected the chains from the cages, the helicopter was overrun. A few gunshots rang out and then the helicopter twisted in the sky, turning onto its side and falling into the ocean. The propellers continued spinning as it sank into the water.

Twenty-Seven watched and she realized that without

Forty-Five the mullos' invasion plans were moot. There was no pilot, nor transport to take them to Capital City. In a weird way, Twenty-Seven had already saved the people she reviled.

She looked back to the rig and found herself surrounded by mullos. They stood still, their numbers filling the top of the slowly sinking station. Twenty-Seven held up her knife. If she was going to die she would not die alone.

The mullos in the center moved to the side, allowing the Alpha to make his way to the front of the group. He had burn marks across most of his body from the incineration grenades. The infant mullo Twenty-Seven had seen in the crib was cradled in the Alpha's arm. Its face was smeared with blood and it seemed content. The rest of the mullos closed the gaps behind the Alpha and all of them stared at her.

She crouched, ready for their attack.

The elder looked into Twenty-Seven's eyes. He looked as though he would eat her himself, but he did not attack. He held out his left hand to the side, pointing toward the ocean. The mullos behind him obeyed. They began to flee the sinking station and leapt into the water. The Alpha remained, staring at her as his pack exited behind him.

The big burned master took a step toward Twenty-Seven. She flinched, raising her knife. He stopped and shook his head. He did not seem angry...

The Alpha was sad.

The last of the mullos dove into the water and the Alpha spoke one last time, pointing at Twenty-Seven. "Family."

Then he dove into the water and was gone.

Twenty-Seven was alone on the broken rig, sinking into the ocean. Capital City would send another incursion soon. They would come with even greater force than before.

Eventually the mullos would try again. Though the war was not over the battle had ended for Twenty-Seven.

For now, it seemed, she was free.

James Ninness is a San Diego native who turned to a life of beatnik after graduating with his degree in English: Creative Writing from Cal State University Long Beach. He spends his mornings with his kids, meandering about the house or swimming in the kiddie pool, often tweeting about nothing in particular. James is a dad, a husband, and a dog lover. He has spent the last few years writing comic books, short stories, and short films. Hang out with James on Twitter, @jamesninness, or connect with him at his website, jamesninness.com

ORIENTATION DAY
Peter Watts

They wouldn't let her into the lab until she'd seen the WHMIS video.

"You're kidding," Janna said. "WHMIS?"

"Liability issues." Gregor (third year of a two-year degree, defending *any time now* assuming he ever got his ass off the communal couch) offered her a *what-you-gonna-do* look. "Some tech down in Michigan got his arm ripped off and the family sued. *Inadequate training*, they said."

"As if you wouldn't know enough to keep clear of a *newbie* without a two-hour tutorial," Alexey chimed in (six months into *his* degree, and obviously looking forward to being *second*-lowest on the totem pole for a change).

"But *WHMIS*? Hazardous Materials?"

"Animal Ethics wasn't gonna go anywhere near 'em, not with those optics." Gregor shrugged. "You even hint anything that walks upright might be an *animal* and you've got the antispeciesists pounding at your door faster'n you could hump a hippo."

"You must've seen those idiots in the parking lot," Alexey added.

She nodded. "So we can't call them 'animals' but we can call them *hazardous materials*?"

"You gotta admit they can be hazardous," Gregor pointed out.

"More to each other than to us," Alexey admitted. "I mean have you *seen* what happens when you put two of 'em in the same room?"

Janna nodded. "I—"

"Rip each other's throats right out," Gregor answered.

Alexey nodded sagely. "Territorial predators. Absolutely *shitty* social skills."

"Anyhow." Gregor got down to business. "What does ol' Random have you working on?"

"Please don't say Crucifix glitch." Alexey raised his eyes to heaven. "Everybody and their fucking *dog* is doing Crucifix glitch."

Janna shook her head. "Alternative splicing in protocadherins. The whole PCDHX thing."

Gregor bolted from the couch. "You're PETA!"

"I am not! I just take their money." And then, to smooth any ruffled feathers: "I actually kind of think they're full of shit."

"Oh?" Gregor settled back down. "Do tell."

"They seem to think you can wipe away all those nasty cannibalistic impulses by just fixing the defect that hooks you on primate protein in the first place. Like putting kibble in front of a cat and expecting him to instantly lose his taste for mice. It's not going to happen."

"I'd say it depends on the cat," Alexey remarked.

"Either way it's *boring*. I'm more interested in how a broken Y-chromo gene managed to make it over to the X when there's *no recombination*. If PETA wants to pay me to figure that out, I'm happy to let them."

"Ah. Lured by the mystique of the female vampire." Gregor nodded. "You've come to the right place; we happen to have a female two floors down."

"That's kind of why I'm here," Janna said.

~

The tutorial was a lumpy mix of infotoids everyone knew (The Miracle of De-Extinction! The Promise of Harnessed SuperSavantism!) and clinical arcana that nobody did (recommended AntiEuclidean dosages per kilogram of vampire body mass, corrected for AMR). Gregor and Alexey, evidently lacking anything better to do, sat at Janna's elbow and offered supplemental commentary:

"You ever seen what happens when they *don't* get their Auntie-U?"

"Whole body goes into tetany the first time they catch sight of a four-panel window pane. Seizures, foaming at the mouth, the whole thing."

"I saw one's face split open one time, right down the middle."

By the end of it, though, she had to agree with them. She didn't feel any more educated on the subject of not-getting-your-arm-ripped-off than she ever had.

They turned in her visitor's ID for a real one. They took her down to Stores for her very own cross, showed her how to use it: it turned from trinket to tire-iron in an instant, its telescoped arms snapping to full extension with a touch of the trigger. They made her practice until she convinced them she wouldn't put her eye out with the thing.

"Thirty degrees of visual arc," Gregor told her. "Otherwise it doesn't work. And you gotta hold it perpendicular to their line-of-sight. They don't spaz out unless the horizontal and vertical receptors fire simultaneously."

"What if they close their eyes?"

"Then they're blind," Alexey said, rolling his.

"Yeah, but—I mean, couldn't they just *hear* their way around? If they're smart as everyone says, they could echolocate off a fart."

Alexey snorted.

"They could navigate way better than your average blind person, for sure," Gregor admitted.

"Luckily, none of us are blind," Alexey pointed out. "And it's not like crosses are the only trick in the bag anyway."

"What else you got?" Janna wondered.

Gregor updated her access privileges and grinned. "Come see."

~

The sign stenciled semi-officially onto the door said *Mission Control*. The commentary beneath, hand-scrawled in black Sharpie, asked

*Who are the **real** monsters?*

Alexey shook his head in disgust. "Some asshole got past Security last week. Janitorial keeps promising they'll clean it off." He stood aside, gestured Janna toward the ret-reader on the wall: "Try it out. System knows you now."

She did. It did. She blinked away the afterimages as the door unlocked, followed him through.

Her ConTacs crashed the moment she crossed the threshold.

Alexey glanced at the sudden static in her eyes. "Oh, right. Random doesn't like customized worldviews, says she wants us all looking at the same thing when we're on the clock. Flatscreens and smart paint from here on in." One hand fiddled with something that looked a little like a TARDIS keychain; the other brought the wall to life with a tap and a swipe, opened a window into some other part of campus. Gregor stood there, facing the camera. Something else sat beside him, facing away.

"Janna, meet Valerie," Alexey murmured

She raised an eyebrow. "Really?"

"After a department head who retired last year. I swear she actually took it as a compliment."

The view was off-white and all curves: not so much a room as a *pod*, the hollowed-out interior of an egg from some world where birds grew big as the Edmonton Spire. A single molded stool, a giant's golf tee extruded from the floor. The vampire sat with her back to the camera—cropped black hair, lean as a whippet, ankles to wrists to collar clad in a one-piece smartweave coverall that sent her vitals to a stack of graphs scrolling to the left of the main window. Her hands rested on a lip of plastic that curved smoothly from the wall; it formed a kind of membranous desktop flickering with circular test patterns.

"You live?" Alexy called. On the wall, Gregor tapped his earbud and flashed an *A-OK*.

No angles, Janna realized. No straight lines, no sharp edges, nothing that might, from any point of view, happen to intersect *just so* at ninety degrees. "She's not on antiEuclideans?"

Alexey shook his head. "Drugs fuck with the pattern-matching. We need her head clear."

Evolution wasn't just blind, Janna reflected. It was also dumb as shit. How natural selection could ever promote an aversion to *right angles*, of all things…

Of course, natural selection never *promoted* anything; it just weeded out the bad stuff. It hadn't had any beef with the Glitch until people had invented geometry—no right angles in nature and all th—

"What about horizons?" she asked, struck by a sudden thought.

Alexey looked up from a bit of fine-tuning. "Mmm?"

"Vertical tree trunk against a flat horizon. Wouldn't that—?"

He gave her a look. "Horizons aren't real."

"Sure they are."

157

"They're zero-dimensional boundaries. There's no thickness to them, they're just a—hypothetical interface between different parts of the viewfield. Glitch needs a nice solid *line* to get its teeth into."

"Okay, but—"

"Let me stop you right there." He held up his hand, started counting on his fingers: "Trees with perfectly vertical trunks and perfectly horizontal branches. Cliff faces with perpendicular fracture lines. Big stalks of savannah grass snapped in the middle *just so*. Anything else?"

She thought. "That'll do for starters."

"Ten others, at least. But none of them really make the cut, you know? The angles have to be *really* close to ninety, and they have to be right up in their faces, and something has to keep your vamp from just looking in the other direction when he starts to feel twitchy. And even if one of them *did* freeze up now and then back in the Pleistocene, that's a pretty small selection cost next to all the perks that come along with the Glitch."

"But—"

"Look, you can argue hypotheticals all you want. Here in the real world we deal in data. And if *that's* what you're interested in, all you gotta do is look" —he jerked a thumb at the wall—"Right. There."

Valerie's display wasn't showing test patterns any more. It showed heartbeats and frantic EEGs, streams of alphanumerics flowing too fast for mortal eyes to capture. A landscape of numbers, fluid and ephemeral; digital quicksilver. The vampire's fingers blurred across that interface like hummingbird wings.

"What *is* it?" Janna whispered.

"*That*," Alexey said with a trace of pride, "is a rogue algo."

"What, you mean from the stock market?"

He nodded. "That's what's paying for our degrees." He grinned at her. "Or did you think NSERC really gave a shit about alternative splicing in protocadherins?"

"What's she doing with it?"

"She's hunting the fucker. Gonna bring it down, too. Twenty bucks says she nails it in five minutes or less."

"But it's an *algo!*" No flesh-and-blood was fast enough to take on one of those nasty little programs. It had been decades since mere meatsacks had even pretended to control the economy.

And yet, up in one corner of the display, part of that luminous torrent had just *frozen.* A block of hex, as far as Janna could see. It glowed, inert, surrounded by seething chaos: a piece of lightning speared through the heart.

More fingers in frantic motion; more spell-casting. Another block of code dropped from the fast lane and quivered on the wall. That one had connections; its fall felled others. Cause and effect flashed across the paint like cracks spiderwebbing through glass; a myriad collateral subroutines went from lightspeed to zero in no seconds, crystallized in mid-step.

"...aaaaand *done.*" Alexey announced. "Two minutes thirty-five seconds. Pay up."

"I didn't bet." Janna shook her head, dazed at the sight of a petrified forest where breakneck jungle had seethed a moment before. From the far end of the feed, Gregor thumbs-upped the camera.

Valerie sat still as stone, facing the wall.

Janna eyed the little cross hanging around Gregor's neck. She fingered the one hanging around her own. "These aren't worth shit."

"Eh?" Alexey was still grinning his face off.

"You saw the way she moved. You saw those—I mean, her motor nerves must be thick as fucking squid axons."

He nodded. "Thicker. So?"

Janna held up her cross. "So she could rip your throat out before you had a chance to even *think* about using this."

"Which is why we use this as well." He held up his baby blue TARDIS.

"A keychain?"

"Janna, Janna." Alexey shook his head in mock disappointment. "You think even a luddite lab like this has any use for *keys*? This is a transmitter."

"What's it transmit?"

"A radio pulse. To the chip embedded in Valerie's motor cortex." He tossed the little device, caught it. "Glitch-on-demand. I push this button and Valerie's brain lights up bright enough to make *grand mal* look like a facial tic."

Still the vampire didn't move. *I haven't even seen her face,* Janna realized.

"Would it kill her?" she asked at last.

"Are you kidding? You know how much it costs to build one of those things?" Alexey shook his head. "This just—fries her a little. Not what you'd call a *pleasant* experience, though. She's a smart girl. She behaves."

Janna looked at him. He looked back: "What?"

"I don't—I mean, I guess I don't know how I feel about—"

He sighed, jerked his chin to the door and the unseen graffiti on the other side. "You *sure* you're not with—"

"I'd sign up to come here if I was?"

"You never know. Undercover animal-rights tewwowist, perhaps." He offered up a brief smile to show he didn't mean it, but it was gone in a flash. "I get it, though. The whole reason we brought 'em back was because they're smart, and if they're smart that makes 'em human, and if they're human that makes 'em slaves and *we're* a bunch of asshole plantation owners from the twentieth century." He shrugged. "Easy to forget what they did to *us*, back when the shoe was on the other foot. And they look so *human*. From a distance, anyway."

"Count your blessings. If they looked like kittens you'd never get them past the ethics board."

This time the smile lasted. "Anyway, of course you're gonna have little old ladies standing at your front door waving protest animé in your face. That's just human nature. But you know what I've noticed?"

"Tell me."

He leaned in close, as if confiding a dark secret. "No one who advocates for vampires has ever actually *met* one."

~

That was the next thing they rectified. "If you're gonna do a degree on her, you gotta meet her," Gregor said cheerfully, guiding Janna towards the womb door.

"No, that's okay." Janna leaned back, resisting. "We can do it tomorrow. I haven't even unp—"

"No time like the present." He herded her firmly but gently, hand cupping her elbow.

"I don't want to put you guys behind schedule."

"Physio lab won't be ready for another ten minutes anyway. Seriously, we do this every day. If Valerie tries anything—"

"TARDIS of Tetany." She shuddered. "Alex told me."

"Then you know there's nothing to worry about." He opened the door, pushed her through, closed it behind her.

Janna's ears popped. She had a chance for one last coherent thought—

—*I'm sealed in*—

—before the weight of her predicament settled onto her like a mountain.

She was in a great bloodless heart, a white plastic ventricle that should have comfortably held six. It felt claustrophobic with two. The vampire sat in profile, motionless as graveyard statuary, hands resting on a membranous surface webbed across the ovoid space like a semilunar valve.

She looked almost human, if you discounted the corpse-pallor (*Peripheral vasoconstriction*, Janna remembered. They only pinked up when they were hunting). The jaw a bit too lupine, perhaps, in deference to a set of teeth more extensive than most might consider normal. The angular planes of the face—cheekbone, eye socket, supraorbital ridge under that jet-black buzz-cut—just a little outside the comfort zone of your average prey animal. The allometry of the limbs, the torso—lean almost unto starvation, a wiry macramé of bone and muscle and sinew that the coverall didn't quite conceal.

The creature turned. It smiled, a rictus of flesh drawn back across shark's teeth. Valerie stood—smooth, hydraulic—and swept one theatrical hand across the vacated stool. "Sit. Please."

Janna blinked. *She sounds like me...*

"Th—that's okay," she managed, standing on knees that suddenly, humiliatingly, knocked like castanets. Not that it mattered; even standing, the vampire loomed over her by a good twenty-five centimeters.

"You're Janna," she said.

Janna averted her eyes.

It was as if someone had put the Uncanny Valley on steroids. Those eyes didn't belong to anything living; they blinked and glistened and saccaded precisely to specs, but something was—missing. As if some alien, some slick AI had decided to play a game of Human but hadn't quite been able to pull it off.

No wonder they don't record her face. No wonder they don't look in those eyes...

Gregor. Alexey. You're getting off on this, aren't you?

"I'm sorry things don't work out," Valerie said softly.

Janna blinked. "Don't—"

"With Bola."

They told her. Those assholes, they—

"They don't *know*," the vampire said gently.

Of course they didn't. She'd only met them this morning.

"How do *you*?" Janna managed. *Look at her, just—*look at *her* she told herself, and couldn't.

The vampire shifted at the corner of her eye. "How do you know when Looseleaf is hungry?"

She knows I have a cat? She knows his fucking name?

"So you study me," she said, still speaking in Janna's

perfect, stolen voice.

Janna gulped and nodded. *She won't touch me, she won't... Gregor's on the kill switch, she knows he's on the kill switch...*

"What part?"

Prey forced itself to stand a little taller, did its best to summon something like defiance. "You don't *know*? You can't just *read* me?"

Valerie shrugged. There was something frightening even in that simple gesture of indifference, in the inhuman precision of its execution. "Academic research is less visceral." Subtle emphasis on that last word. "Fewer cues. Tell me."

"I'm working on PCDHX," Janna blurted.

Valerie cocked her head—a curiously bird-like gesture—and stared.

"You know, like, the gene that codes for gamma-protocadherins, and how it doesn't work in your—"

"How to fix it," Valerie said.

"How to fix it," Janna echoed helplessly. "Yes."

Valerie watched her like a praying mantis. "So we can synthesize it ourselves," she said at last, the ghost of something like a smile haunting the back of her voice. "Metabolically."

"Y—yes..."

"So we don't have to eat you any more."

"You—you don't have to eat us anyway. There are s-s-supplements."

Alexey was right. We're not the monsters, not next to this.

"Kibble." Valerie almost whispered the word.

The brain chips, the crosses, the cages. It's not oppression, it's not slavery. No matter what they say.

"Still you're nice to try," the vampire allowed. "To help us all just *get along*."

It's self-defense.

"Th-thank you," Janna stammered, hating the craven coward in her own skin.

"Maybe afterward," Valerie mused, "We let you live."

And it's not nearly enough...

~

"She said *we*."

Thinking: *you asshole. You sadistic motherfucker. Did it get you off, watching the new kid piss her pants like that?*

Gregor spared a glance from the feed. "What?"

Don't lose it. He wants you to lose it. Don't give him the satisfaction.

He stood at her side, riding the kill switch from behind the safety of three walls, a stairwell, and a dozen meters of fiberop. Together they watched Alexey down in Physio, putting Valerie through her paces on the treadmill. The monster was almost unrecognizable under the nest of electrodes bristling from her skull, behind the breathing mask across her face. So little left exposed in the way of distinguishing features.

Thank you, Jesus. For small mercies.

"*Maybe afterward we let you live.*" Janna remembered. "That's what she said. Like they were deciding who to put up against the wall after the revolution."

It was a simple ground-truthing run; they weren't pushing Valerie anywhere near her limits. Still, there was something *inhuman* about the way the vampire loped along on the device, some sense of joints subtly out of place. Something almost serpentine about the way she surged in place.

"She was just having some fun with you. She's a bit of a sadist that way." *And you'd know*, Janna reflected as Gregor added: "Can't really blame her, all things considered. Her ancestors probably played with their food *all* the time."

"Very fucking funny."

He grinned. "Really, I wouldn't worry. She's never been violent, never threatened anyone, never been anything but cooperative. Not that she has a choice, mind you."

"There *are* other vampires on campus, though."

"Three. So?"

"She said *we*," Janna repeated.

"I know. I was watching."

"She *knew* things. Details about my personal life. She just, just *read* them off me somehow."

"They're smarter than us. That's why we Jurassic'd them back in the first place."

"So how do you know they haven't figured out a way to just walk out of their cages whenever they feel like it?"

"Maybe because they're all still here?"

"If they're so much smarter—"

"I'm way smarter than an anaconda, but it could still kill me in a second if I happened to be trapped down a well with my hands tied behind my back. We have Valerie down a very deep well."

"What about the others?"

"Them too."

"No, I mean, what if they were working together?"

"Okay, first thing, it's kinda hard to cooperate with someone when your territorial instincts drive you to attack them on sight. Second thing, they don't even *know* about each other."

"You sure about that?"

"I've—okay, fine," he said grudgingly. "They probably *do* know. Probably smell it on us, or something. But so what?"

"So if she knows the others are out there, she probably knows when each of them gets fed and when each of them goes onto the treadmill and when each of them takes a shit because she reads it off of *us*, okay? She can see it in heartbeats and sweaty armpits and—Jesus, Gregor, she outruns *algos*, she can see it in our *eyes*!"

"Janna. So *what*? Even if they wanted to plan the great escape, how are they gonna communicate? It's not like Ghandi can leave a note on the treadmill in the morning and expect Valerie to read it in the afternoon. There's no domain overlap for just that reason; separate quarters, separate labs, separate *floors* for each vamp. They might as well be in different facilities."

"There's us, okay? *We* overlap."

"You think she's sticking post-it notes on our butts and we just haven't noticed?"

"What if she doesn't *have* to, okay? What if she doesn't have to see the territory to draw the map? Maybe they don't have to put their heads together to draw up a plan. Maybe they all know what to do and when to do it because they've *all independently derived the same damn equation from the same damn data.*"

And maybe, afterward, they let me live.

Gregor listened until she ran out of words. Finally he took a breath. "Okay, look. She gave you a good scare. That was kind of the point —"

"No *shit.*"

"—to get you in there right off the top so you could see exactly what we're dealing with. Nip any incipient animal-rights shit right in the bud. Obviously it worked. It worked a little too well, you know what I mean?"

"But —"

"It worked too well," he said, talking over her, "because you are now so freaked that you can't see the obvious hole in your own argument, which is: if Valerie was planning a revolution, why would she *tell* you? You think something smart enough to *outrun an algo* is going to just slip up like that? Or is it more likely that she knew this was your first day, that you might be especially *impressionable* on that account, and she decided to have a little fun with you?"

It made so much sense, here in the sunny twilit realm of Mission Control: only back in the bright shadowless glare of Valerie's cage had everything seemed so dark and scary.

"Unless of course," Gregor turned back to the display — "her master plan hinges on wasting five minutes of my time at exactly three forty — wait a second, what's —"

Valerie wasn't running with the disquieting grace of a few

minutes before. Her feet *dragged* now, tangled and tripped over each other as the belt hooked and grabbed and pushed them back along the track. In fact she wasn't really running at all; she just *dangled* there, hanging from the fiberop wrapped around her neck while the treadmill played with her feet. Now that Janna looked more closely, that didn't even really *look* much like Valerie — at least, those parts visible under the skullcap and the resp mask and the —

"*Fuck*." The blood drained from Gregor's face. He tapped his earbud. "Alex? *Alex, where the fuck —* "

The body twitched and jerked. Dark glistening loops that weren't telemetry cables dangled against the coverall.

Heartbeat, blood pressure, core temp ticked along their axes like they always had.

Gregor's finger stabbed his earbud like a crooked little jackhammer. "Saschi? Security? Hello, Professor Nalini, are you — *anybody*?"

He couldn't stop pressing the little kill switch clenched in his right fist. *Maybe it's working* Janna thought. *Maybe it already has. How would we know?* On the wall, a lifeless marionette jiggled and danced in an empty room.

"Where's Valerie?" Gregor whispered. Every feed he tried was dead blue. "*Where the fuck is Valerie?*"

Janna suppressed a hysterical little giggle. It was so perfectly obvious where Valerie was.

She and her friends had stepped out for lunch.

Peter Watts (www.rifters.com) is the author of the so-called "Rifters trilogy"; an obscure video-game novelization; and the semi-obscure semi-hit *Blindsight*, which was nominated for a shitload of awards (even winning a few) and which, despite an unhealthy focus on space vampires, somehow ended up as a core text for a smattering of university courses ranging from neuropsych to philosophy. Watts' work is available in 18 languages; he is especially popular in Poland, for reasons which remain unclear. He probably owes at least part of his 2010 Hugo to fan outrage over an unfortunate altercation with armed capuchins working for the US Department of Homeland Security, but he's okay with that. The following year he decided to play the Sympathy card, by nearly dying of flesh-eating disease contracted during a routine skin biopsy. That strategy also worked insofar as his fanfic short story "The Things" won the Shirley Jackson Award. Watts is already hard at work on The Next Horrible Thing to catapult him towards future trophies, perhaps for *Echopraxia* (the upcoming sequel to *Blindsight*), which picks up literally thirty minutes after "Orientation Day" leaves off.

THE PILOT
Jason Duke

The flying death machine broke through a wash of opaque clouds, vanished within them and broke through again. Eighty feet of hybrid alloys, its dark body was shaped as an arrowhead, sharp and lethal. Weapons shot from the bow of the Frontier Defense Force, two white skulls adorned either wing to symbolize the steel eggs it carried made of antimatter capable of washing away all life from the surface of a planet. But the death machine did not come to Gecedunya to hatch its eggs—it arrived to this bitter world of black mountains and gray deserts submerged in the bloody twilight of a red star to hide. Far below the ship's sharp descent lay a mosaic of ruins enduring the torment of a dust storm that uncoiled across it like waves lashing an alien shore.

It used to be called Issiz Varos, a mining town once home to thousands of poor and desperate souls from across the colonies that came to this pitiless rock thousands of light years from the cradle Earth to risk their lives in deep holes digging for precious ores. They weren't down there anymore. No, the universe chased them away sixty years ago when it sent its messenger of destruction: an asteroid. The population fled their buildings and machines, leaving them to beg mercy from the messenger that would bite the ground many miles away, but would belch a shockwave that devastated what was built. Lamenting rebuilding costs, the Hasar Corporation would not return.

The death machine gently glided above the few buildings that remained erect and then extended its black claws to land several hundred yards outside the town's perimeter. The engine hissed inside the angry wind and then stopped. A ramp silently lowered from the ship's belly, the pilot stepped down. Black helmet, black uniform, black boots. Just over six feet and broad, he stood in front of his ship and surveyed for a minute the wretched legacy of greed sprawling before him. Far behind the mountains of debris a single tower stood, a big phallus reaching for the red sky at nearly a thousand feet. It was the Planet Maker, technology that transformed atmospheres dense with too many poisonous gasses like nitrogen and carbon dioxide, through the emission of oxygen via bioengineered microorganisms. Dead planets across the galaxy were reborn as family friendly utopias thanks to the big dick.

Gecedunya's big dick was rather flaccid, however. Torn and broken. A colossal grave marker.

The pilot walked toward the ruins, arms stiff by his side, passing a row of ten-foot drill suits that stood as soldiers made of dust and great hulking tractors that sat on wheels twenty feet in diameter.

The pilot stopped. Three figures emerged from the ruins like vaporous specters in hooded cloaks. When the specters were a few feet from the pilot they pulled back their hoods. Young faces. Boys' faces. Fifteen, perhaps sixteen years of age. One of them was graced with a deep scar running down his pale cheek. The fear in scar kid's eyes morphed into fascination as he looked past the pilot and stared at his ship. His eyes, squinting from the whip of dust, returned to the pilot.

"Are you a soldier?" he shouted above the rumbling gust.

The pilot reached up, removed his helmet, and tucked it tightly under his arm. The face was a model of flawless symmetry. In a word: beautiful (interesting, though, how those striking black eyes never blinked from the wind). "I have come here for shelter," he said.

"Who are you?" a boy asked.

Scar kid nudged him. "Who cares?"

The boy's face turned to the ground, looked at the pilot. "Come on."

And so they entered the ruins of Issiz Varos, weaving down those few streets not buried by the giant bones of fallen apartment towers that were once erect at two hundred feet. One tower still standing was stripped of its side, its floors open and naked. Fragmented walls looked like decomposed fangs while cold wind howled around them sounding as a primordial animal, the agonized roar of devastation. They arrived, finally, to a building much smaller than those still standing. The hospital. The four crossed through an open entrance, traveling down windowless corridors lit by a scattering of neon blue bulbs from above. It felt like tunnels, really, a humid subterranean hell that grimly sang with echoing boots. Service pipes ran along the walls like black snakes.

"You still have power," the pilot said.

"Yeah," the scar kid said. "The energy cells under the town are supposed to last forever."

Their destination was a cavernous room of surgical tables and dead monitors. A long track of window lined the back wall, filtering in oppressive red light. Five shadows were against the window, all cloaked in robes colored as mud. Three men, two women. Four of the faces were old. Sagging skin cut with deep lines. One appeared much younger, a woman who might have been in her thirties. An old man came forward, navigating between the tables. He was short and frail, but the eyes were hard.

He didn't speak, but looked over this dark stranger with a perfect face. And then: "Who are you?"

"My name is Mezentius. I've come here for shelter." The tone was disarmingly gentle.

"How do you know of this place?"

"I was told of it."

"Told?" the younger woman said, coming forward. Her dark eyes were deep and severe, hands tightly held together. "Your ship, it's military."

"I served the Frontier Defense Force. But, no longer."

The five looked among themselves. Their mouths were shut but the eyes spoke of doubts. The old man gestured to the three boys to leave with a sharp wave of his hand. Scar kid passed the pilot an admiring glance and left with the other two.

"What do you mean?" the old man asked.

"I deserted."

"Why?"

"I could no longer stand the war."

The old man's brow rose. "War?"

"Yes, with Sojakonnas."

Someone gasped.

"How is there war with Sojakonnas?"

"The planet broke the Treaty of Zahav and declared independence. Earth declared war and sent us in to stop the rebellion."

Another old creature came forward. "So you just left?"

"Yes. I could no longer be a part of mass murder. I stole a ship and fled to Feng Station. It was there that someone told me of this place."

"What exactly were you told?" the younger woman asked.

"I was told there was a cult of religious fanatics on Gecedunya. That you have chosen to live without technology. Or, at least, most of it."

"And this is something you seek?" the old man with hard eyes asked.

"I have witnessed the slaughter of millions that could not have happened without the efficiency of machines. Like you, I have rejected technology."

"Oh, it's more than that," the younger woman said. "We have embraced God. Will you do the same?"

"I will try." He briefly bowed.

The five gathered among themselves to murmur with worried tones. The pilot watched closely.

He listened intently.

What if they come looking for him?

When Huang dies, then what?

Perhaps it's God's plan.

They turned to him and the old man with hard eyes came forward. His name was The Reverend Marku. "We will not turn you away. We welcome all those who seek salvation from the bondage of technology."

"Thank you," the pilot said. "And I hope to ease your fear when I say the Commission cannot find me. I was diligent enough to remove my ship's tracking system. I also expect the war on Sojakonnas to keep them occupied for a long time."

Those with looks of confusion kept them brief, and the rest introduced themselves with warm grins. The younger woman was The Reverend Marku's granddaughter, Kathryn, and was accepted into the ranks of the inner circle, those that remained of the founders who came here twenty-eight years ago on two shuttles that left the planet Rojaa. They were Credincios, a sect of Christians originally chased from Earth by the Trans-Global Commission, a plutocratic leviathan comprised of corporate cannibals who feasted on the souls of sovereign nations before legislating religious absolutism from popular existence way back in 2112. God could not come before the Commission. Humanity's penetration of space's implacable void through Time Distortion Velocity, a propulsion system developed in the late 21st century, allowed the corporate cannibals to eat the stars. Credincios immigrated to Rojaa to live within the green universe of a jungle created by the Planet Maker—until the boundless appetite of civilization began to dig its steel claws into the jungle's body and chased away the sect from its village.

"It was too much," Reverend Marku said. "To see what had happened to Earth, to see it happening to Rojaa. The Commission was building worlds to merely plunder them. We accepted that the promise of technological progress had become corrosive to our spiritual nature. Morality became defined by convenience and comfort. And so we came to these miserable ruins to tend our souls, separated from the disease of technology until God calls us home." He paused for a moment. "We knew the Commission would not bother us out here. No one would bother us out here."

Mezentius nodded.

"Well, then," Marku said, "you must be hungry and thirsty, yes?"

"No," Mezentius said. "I'm fine for now."

"Then, welcome home, brother."

Home was within the cold innards of an apartment tower. The Reverend's granddaughter, Kathryn, took the pilot into the black mouth of its lobby, passing women, children and men huddled in the dark. Thin and sad.

"They *are* sad," Kathryn said lowly. "We cultivate sadness as a treasured crop. It is in sadness and suffering that people most willingly turn to God."

They reached the fifth floor and walked down a hall decorated with cables that once provided heat and water. Such externalized planning created an industrial ambience. They passed open rooms where lone faces were lit by the white light of digital tablets while they read biblical scripture. There was a chant somewhere, low and mournful. A young girl, her belly extended with child, sat in one room with legs crossed and eyes closed. Lost in meditation.

Mezentius suddenly fell against the wall, using his shoulder to stand.

"Are you all right?" Kathryn asked.

"I'm tired," Mezentius said.

"I'm sure," Kathryn said, briefly smiling. "You've come a long way. The journey must have drained you."

Mezentius pushed away from the wall and returned to his stoic composure. "God," he said. "Isn't it interesting that space holds no proof of a creator?"

"What do you mean?"

"Since humanity left the cradle Earth, all it has found is endless hostility to life."

"But that's the point. It was created for us. The universe is God's garden and we are the seeds of His image. But we have betrayed all that we were meant to do and become."

Mezentius did not reply, keeping his silence until he was led to a room with a single bed and table. A digital Bible was on the table. The only light was the red hue falling from the window against the back wall. He stood in the center of the room, his back to Kathryn, and stared at the light.

"We have no routine here," Kathryn said. "Only contemplation. A simple life of prayer."

"How many people are here?" Mezentius asked, his back still turned.

"At last count, two thousand scattered across town. Trust me, there's plenty of room."

"Tell me, is your grandfather the leader here?"

"I would describe him as a caretaker. For now."

"I see."

"Oh, yes, when you do need it, food and water are supplied in the hospital."

"Food and water," Mezentius repeated softly, still facing the window. "How is there food and water here?"

"One of our members, Huang, he pilots one of the shuttles that brought us here all those years ago. When we are low he flies to Feng Station to gather supplies. Food, water, medicine, those things." A pause, and then: "He was in the Frontier Defense Force, too. He's the only pilot we have. However; well, he's getting on in age; so perhaps it was providential that you arrived."

Mezentius finally turned from the light and laid a hand on Kathryn's shoulder, who winced. "God's plan," he said.

"Maybe," Kathryn said, rubbing her shoulder. "We'll see." She turned and left.

Mezentius remained a statue as an hour drained away. "Come in," he said.

A small face peered around the corner. The scar kid. He glanced down the hall, and then entered. "I'm sorry."

"No need to be," Mezentius said. Something of a smirk appeared on the corner of his mouth.

"I was just wondering. I heard you talk about the war on Sojakonnas."

Mezentius nodded. "I know you did."

"Well, sir, I was wondering…what it was like. War, I mean."

"What is your name?"

"Arulo, sir."

"Arulo. How old are you?"

"Fifteen."

"Why do you want to know?"

A shrug. "I don't know."

"Yes, you do."

"I don't know anything about life out there. They never tell us nothing. Sometimes I wish I could…"

"Leave."

"Yeah. Others have. I guess a long time ago some people got sick of this place. They wanted to have things. Nice things, you know? They took the other shuttle. After that, the inner circle wouldn't let anyone else go. That's why they wouldn't let Huang train anyone to fly. That's why…"

"What?"

"That's why they accepted you so quickly. Huang is the only pilot we have, but he's old. When he dies, they'll need someone else to get supplies."

Mezentius walked to the scar kid. His black eyes

sharpened, relaxed. "The iron in your blood is low."

"My what?"

"I trust you, Arulo. I may need you."

"I don't understand."

"You will soon. Tell me, is Reverend Marku the leader here?"

"I guess so. Everyone does sort of look up to him. I think Kathryn is going to be the leader one day.

Mezentius's face, the steady expression, was now dropping. The eyes fading. "We'll talk another time."

The scar kid acknowledged the pilot's tired demeanor with a respectful smile and turned for the door. Once Arulo was gone, Mezentius returned his drowsy eyes to the light that was declining.

Outside, the red star dropped behind the black mountains and took away its blood light. The ruins were dipped into a pool of darkness and the wind cried to five moons glimmering as ancient lanterns. Inside his room the statue that was Mezentius finally moved in the brooding gold light spilling from a brass sconce shaped as a cone. Yes, it was time.

He turned for the door and stepped into the empty hall to hunt under the neon blue that droned as a fleet of ships in his ears. Hidden hearts thundered as tribal drums behind steel doors. He glided down the stairs and stalked the fourth floor to find all the rooms closed. He went down to the third floor and found an open room. Father, mother and child were inside, sleeping on blankets.

The family did not see the pilot slip inside with fearsome stealth and look over their vulnerable bodies. They did not see the hand reach down and seize the father's arm, pulling him from his sleep and lifting him up. The agonized shriek, however, was somewhat difficult to ignore. Mother and child screamed. Father tried to break loose and threw a fist at the pilot's peaceful face, landing flat on the jaw. You could hear the ghastly snap of bones splitting through Father's hand and wrist. It was Mother's turn to attack the attacker, but the pilot's hand seized the whole of her face. She grabbed the wrist but was trapped. The hand closed and crushed her cheek bones and nose. The soft eyes ballooned from their sockets and teeth fell to the ground.

"Run!" Father yelled at the child. The child fled.

The pilot's now free hand closed into a fist and from between the knuckles a single claw emerged. Twelve inches and hollow as a tube. Father's wild eyes watched the claw attempt to align with his throat. He struggled again to break loose, kicking the pilot's legs, his groin, but he might have been kicking a wall. Suddenly the claw speared his throat and Father's body seized. His face grew into a wide grimace that bared both rows of teeth.

Blood silently rushed through the claw, carried to the pilot's body. Pint after pint of red juice was sucked until the blood bag was drained — until Father's arms and eyelids dropped limp.

Mezentius released the empty sack. His shoulders straightened, his neck lifted.

He inflated with life.

Others were waiting for him outside, a group of three faces more scared than angry. And when the pilot did emerge from the room, someone, a courageous man looking twenty, charged with a steel bar. He lifted it up and swung in the name of death. Mezentius stopped the brutal swing with his hand and pulled the bar away. He dropped it and reached for the young man's face, shooting his fingers into his mouth and wrapping his thumb around the lower jaw. Just as quickly the pilot pulled. The lower jaw ripped off. Bones broke. Long strips of skin and muscle stretched across the face and down the neck — snapped loose.

The strands of meat, the tongue that hung limp without a home, the young man's face reduced to an obscene distortion that terrified the other two yet they could not take their eyes off the staggering and dying victim, as if the atrocity held some hypnotic power. The young man finally collapsed and expired. The two watched the blood spread toward their bare feet.

"Anyone else?" Mezentius asked. "I hope not. I don't want to waste anymore blood."

They broke apart, running back down the hall and down the stairs.

Mezentius returned to his room to wait for more vengeance. And it didn't take long. He could hear them enter the lobby below; hear frantic boots across the ground, the panicked breathing, the passing roar of succulent blood in their veins. He could *hear* them down there.

He just ripped his face off. I've never seen anything like it. The strength it would take to do that.

They marched to his door: a pack of four angry wolves led by The Reverend Marku. He was holding a black rifle heavy with slugs guaranteed to kill any living thing in the galaxy. His old finger was tight around the trigger. The hate in his eyes made him appear, well, if not younger, certainly more energetic. The cult may have rejected technology, but obviously they were not all pacifists.

Mezentius looked at the rifle. "Technology few are prepared to abandon."

The Reverend Marku lifted the rifle. "I don't know who you are, but may God forgive me for what I *must* do."

"Yes, you must. Because—"

The Reverend fired. It wasn't loud, more like a deep thud. The rifle discharged a slug into the pilot's chest. He didn't fall. Another round. The cold walls should have been warm with fractured flesh and bone, but the pilot did not die. There were two fat holes in his uniform, the edges seared. No blood. His face, as usual, composed.

The pack of angry wolves was not so composed. They gazed at each other, returned to the pilot who should have been dead. Reverend Marku lowered the rifle, his mouth open. The hate in his eyes burned into a glassy stare. "Have we sinned so much that such an abomination has been delivered to us?"

"The inner circle," Mezentius said, "bring them to me. All of them."

"What do you want with them?" Reverend Marku demanded.

"I only wish to speak to you all."

"No..."

Mezentius stepped close and pulled the rifle from The Reverend's hands. The old man stumbled back and nearly fell but was held by his fellow wolves. The sight of the pilot holding the rifle, this seemingly benign stranger who sought refuge among a colony of religious Luddites, turned him into a portrait of Armageddon.

The wolves backed away, into the hall.

"Bring me the inner circle," the pilot said, holding the rifle to his chest, "or I will kill everyone in this town before the red star returns." And still he spoke without anger.

"Tell me what you are, what you want," Reverend Marku said.

"Bring me the inner circle and I will explain."

The Reverend grudgingly relented. "I'll do as you ask."

"Oh," Mezentius said. "One more thing. Bring the boy, Arulo."

The pack of wolves vanished from the room with their tales tucked. Mezentius listened to them descend the stairs.

Are we really bringing everyone?

You heard what he said. He'll kill us.

What does he want with Arulo?

I don't know.

What is he? What do you think, Reverend?

I think, when Huang returns, we leave.

The Reverend did as he was told, returning with the inner circle. The five looked like sheep entering the tight borders of the room. Arulo was among their shadows, shoulders hunched and head low.

Mezentius was only inches from them. "Thank you for

coming. It's now time to explain."

"Are you the Devil?" Kathryn asked.

"I'm an assassin."

"Assassin," Reverend Marku said.

"Yes," Mezentius said. "I was created to infiltrate the rebellion on Sojakonnas."

"What do you mean *created*?" Kathryn asked.

"Oh, my Lord," Reverend Marku whispered.

"My creators designed an improvement; something more intelligent than the old model. They also designed an assassin that would require human blood to generate the core cell as a way to induce the perpetual killing of rebels."

"What they did not expect was my upgraded intelligence giving me an insatiable need for self-determination. And, so, I killed my creator. My *god*, if you will."

"A need for human blood," Reverend Marku said. "So you do plan to kill us."

"Not necessarily. I must feed every seventy-two hours. But that does not require the complete consumption of a human body. I will take a small dosage of blood from a group of you; since, as you might imagine, you are my cattle and I must keep some stock alive if I am to have food. Perhaps I will institute a breeding program that will—"

"What makes you think we'll just let you feed on us?" The Reverend growled through yellow gritted teeth. His hands balled into trembling fists.

Kathryn's nod was sharp and insolent.

"Arulo," Mezentius called to the boy. "Come and stand behind me."

The boy did so, gently, and nervously, pushing his way past the inner circle. He glanced at The Reverend, perhaps a look of guilt, and then turned his eyes to the ground.

"You are the leaders here," Mezentius continued. "Credincios looks to you for guidance. Without you, they will be in need of a shepherd."

The words swirled above the faces as a black mist wet

with doom. Mezentius pointed the rifle at them; and before they could shout their horror the rifle discharged a slug into The Reverend Marku's body with that low thud. *Boom.* His chest blew open and pieces of flesh and ribcage stung those around him. Kathryn screamed. *Boom.* The slug struck her face. It shattered into a bloody web of eyes, teeth and skull fragments. The air above their bodies was damp with a red drizzle, like a hellish broth.

All significant opposition had been neutralized — for now.

Mezentius stood before the murder careless as the cosmos, this ghostless machine of unnatural origin yet the personification of nature: a force that sought no justification for existence and proceeded with timeless authority in its dominion over the weak now stripped down to arteries, muscle tissue, membranes. The inner mechanisms of organic clocks that stopped ticking when the death bell was struck by a hand built with the very technology they had renounced.

There was no slow infiltration here, no methodical usurpation of power — only a quick and hostile takeover.

The remaining three cowered as beaten dogs, old hands hiding weeping faces. Mezentius addressed them with a simple line spoken, as always, with an unassuming tone: "Accept me as your leader, and you will live."

They rose slowly, chests heaving with panicked gasps, still keeping their eyes from the massacre. They said nothing at first, but merely shivered. Finally an old man spoke. Petrov. "What...do you want us to do?" The question oozed with suspicion, but Petrov's eyes, like the other two, gleamed with a blend of fear and reconciliation. Apparently they wanted to live, or, at least, didn't want to meet their end with such stunning violence.

"You will convince the others that my arrival was divinely ordained. That the death of The Reverend Marku and Kathryn was God's punishment for resistance. And the giving of blood to me is no more than a symbolic gesture of the blood sacrificed on the cross."

The three passed defeated glances to each other. "Some might refuse to believe," Petrov said desperately, raising his hands.

"They have willingly lived in filth because of you. I trust you will be persuasive. But those that do not follow will also be punished by God."

Petrov closed his eyes. A hard swallow. "So be it." The other two acquiesced to their fate with solemn nods. They gathered together and filed out of the room to pursue their charge.

Mezentius listened, but they did not speak. He turned to the harsh sobs behind him, to the boy cringing from the machine that was now God. "Arulo," he said, "my offer to you is this: Be my loyal eyes and ears outside this apartment. I cannot be everywhere at once."

The boy looked at him with eyes wet with tears. "Why me?"

"I told you that I trust you. If you agree, perhaps you will live long enough to leave this planet to seek *nice things*. Keep watch over the inner circle and help them to round up the others for my feeding. Preferably after dark when my night vision and thermal sensors are most effective. Are you with me?"

The boy looked at the bodies and quickly took his eyes away. He bit his bottom lip, his breathing dropped to a smooth pace.

~

It had been nearly two months since the flying death machine landed outside the ruins of Issiz Varos, and high above, another ship was preparing its arrival. *The Amaziah's* plunge was steady through the red haze, the shuttle's chrome body shaped as a missile and the wings long and swept. Inside the shadows of the cockpit lit only by soft greens and blues from the console holograms, Huang tried to contact the inner circle and alert them to his coming. There was only silence to reply. He was preparing for another transmission when he saw the dark arrowhead outside the ruins, the white skulls on his screen. It scared him. The Frontier Defense Force was here. The unholy might of the Trans-Global Commission had sent one of its death machines and for a moment the old man saw himself flying right back into the sky. But to where? Back to Feng Station? You could barter there, purchase illegal goods, but its distended population was a collective serpent dripping with venomous corruption. It was no place to live.

The Amaziah landed only a few yards from the death machine, a vertical landing that ignited a wall of gray dust that slowly rose and fell. Huang tried a final time to contact the inner circle, but the signal was still dead. He sat still and quiet, watching the screen. Credincios was his home, his family, and he had to find out. Behind him, deep in the cargo belly, crates of nutrient bars and hydration tablets waited to be carried. The ramp dropped from the shuttle's side with a sluggish growl, Huang climbed down in his green flight suit and nervously walked through a mild breeze. A pistol hung from his waist and he almost reached for it when the lone figure appeared from the ruins. Small, short, a child. Huang stopped and waited for the little one who walked with a deliberate stride, the hood draped over his head.

The child reached Huang but did not pull the hood away. The old man could see the face within it, however. The chin was lifted, the lips scowling. The scar.

"Arulo," Huang said. "What's happened?"

"You have the supplies?" Arulo asked. The assertive tone fit the face. In a word: arrogant.

Huang kept his worries silent. He knew Arulo. The kid was a little obstinate, sure, but never smug. The old man gestured to the death machine. "Why is the FDF here?"

"Come on," Arulo said, "there's somebody you need to meet."

"Who?"

"God has sent us a messenger. He wants to meet you. Now."

Huang blinked and turned his face to *The Amaziah* to give it a regretful glance.

He followed the boy.

Jason Duke is a freelance writer born and raised in the deserts of Southern California. He currently resides among the steep cliffs within the San Bernardino Mountains where he writes to feed his demons.

UNPERISHED

S. R. Algernon

"Almost finished." The orderly spoke with an accent I assumed to be Romanian.

I watched the column of blood shoot from my vein, curl around twice within the plastic tubing, and fill the one-pint bag. The sense of obligation bothered me more than the sting of the needle. The sight reminded me of something Mark Foyle said to me two months earlier on the day he offered me the job at Woodcross.

"The Woodcross Institute may have its quirks, but what's the alternative? Pushing those grad school studies? Where do you think your career will be a year from now if you don't find your way into a lab?"

I could have summed it up in one word. Finished.

"Will sting a bit when I pull out needle," added the orderly.

"I know," I said, "just like it will sting three months from—Ow!"

"Take juice." He swiped my ID card through the scanner. "Take cookie on your way out."

"*La revedere*," I muttered.

As I walked to the lab, past Woodcross Manor, I felt a chill that was more than winter weather. The 18th century mansion and its shuttered windows embodied the questions we all had about our patron. We knew better than to ask them, not even to ourselves. As Foyle had told me on my first day: *Why worry? The checks cash either way.*

Patrescu's helicopter flew overhead, on its way to the Manor's rooftop helipad. The sound of the rotors reminded me of the fluttering of mechanical wings.

~

Back at the lab, my colleague, Dr. Lucinda Carroll, was hunched over one of the lab tables. We were working on a new blood substitute—or, rather, Lucy worked on it while I busied myself with autoclaving, preparing tissue samples, and filling the trays of pipette tips while I brought myself up to speed on the project. My stomach jumped a bit when I saw the scalpel in her hand and the remains of a rat beneath it. We had been having a little problem with corpses recently. Or, I should say, a problem with little corpses.

"Another autopsy," I whispered, careful not to startle her. I stood by the island of lab stations and sinks in the center of the room and glanced at the dry erase board on the wall. Under the heading RAT RACE, in red marker, were three magnets shaped like mice. Each one represented a different test subject, and its place between the 0 WEEK line and the 4 WEEK finish line showed how close we were to popping open the little bottle of champagne in the break room fridge. Yesterday, there had been four mice up on the board.

"Subject 21," said Lucy. "Some sort of hemorrhage. There's vascular damage, but I can't figure out what's causing it. Maybe it's an autoimmune response, but Subject 17 was immunosuppressed and it had the same problem. We'll just have to hope one of the others pulls through. We're down to our last rat."

"You shouldn't be working so hard," I said. "Not today. Get some rest. Get something to eat. You're not going to bring it back from the dead, you know."

"Quit it," said Lucy. "You promised."

I told Lucy I wouldn't joke about Dr. Patrescu anymore.

After the cracks I made when the blood drive e-mail went around, Lucy didn't talk to me for the rest of the day. Can you blame me, though? After all, Dr. Patrescu really *did* vant to suck our blood.

"I didn't mean it that way," I said. "Do you think I want to make you mad when you have a scalpel in your hand?"

"It's all right. I'm just worried about the dinner, I guess."

The dinner was a quarterly event at Woodcross Manor. Dr. Patrescu flew in from Bucharest to see the latest breakthroughs, welcome the new arrivals, and invite us all to Woodcross Manor.

"How about this?" I said. "Let me clean up here. Just once, let yourself go home before sundown. We'll both have better luck after a good night's sleep."

"All right." Lucy tossed her gloves and headed for the restroom to wash up. "See you in the morning."

I waited until I heard the door click shut behind her before I flipped open the log book. *Twenty-two rats,* I thought. *All the controls, both saline and sham injection, survived. All the experimental subjects died within two or three days of injection.*

I put another mouse magnet on the dry-erase board and made a neat entry in the log book.

03/30   6:55 PM   SUBJECT 23 1 ml   BLOOD SUBSTITUTE S

I took our last remaining rat from the home cage, injected a milliliter of the solution into its femoral artery, and left it in one of the empty observation cages. Then, I labeled the bottle BLOOD SUB S and put it in the lab fridge next to the other bottles of clear liquid that were Lucy's failed attempts.

If RAT 23 survived, just like all the controls, we could go back to the drawing board. If it died, I would have discovered something else about whatever was killing the rats: it was smart enough to read the log books.

If we had a saboteur, the rats weren't the only ones in danger.

Subject 23 was still alive the next evening, when Lucy and I climbed the stone steps to Woodcross Manor, Patrescu's guards, now squeezed into tuxedos, opened the double wooden doors for us. Foyle waited in the foyer, shook our hands as we entered, and waved us on toward the banquet hall before turning his attention to another group of Woodcross Fellows who were coming up the path.

"This is your first time, right?" said Lucy.

"Yes. It's very... orange in here." The combination of candles and weak incandescent bulbs struck me as soon as I walked through the door. The air smelled of dust and wood. As we walked through the foyer, the parlor and a series of crumbling rooms, I looked down the passageways that ran off to my left and right. *Patrescu only visits a few times a year,* I thought. *This place must have rooms nobody has seen for decades.* I wondered what secrets it hid.

In the banquet hall, a tidy arrangement of circular tables dominated the center of the room, banishing the typical clutter to the edges, except for an empty patch of floor near the fireplace. Once Lucy and I found seats, I watched the other guests more closely. Their faces seemed flushed despite the fatigue in their eyes. The glow from the fire and the lights masked the effects of blood loss and long days under fluorescent lighting.

Dr. Patrescu stood in front of the fireplace as the crowd quieted. He had shoulder-length brown hair and a thin, youthful face. For a moment, he watched the crowd with a fragile smile, as if they were the event and he the sole spectator.

"Good evening," said Dr. Patrescu. "Every three months we gather here so that I can thank you for the spirit that has kept Woodcross alive for so many years. In particular, I wish to thank Dr. Miller and her team, whose excavations have unearthed the latest addition to our collection. Her efforts will revolutionize our understanding of alchemy and medicine in 12th century Europe."

Patrescu gestured to glassware and bits of metal on the mantle behind him. They could have been crude surgical tools, weapons or ancient sculptures. A few of them had grotesquely serrated edges, and it was hard to picture them without seeing them cutting though flesh.

"I knew it," said Lucy. "Miller's team has been so irritatingly sure of themselves since they came back from the dig."

"Our luck will change soon," I said. "Hey, is there a bathroom here? I should wash my hands before Patrescu's people come around with the food."

I half listened to her directions and headed off on a series of wrong turns. The rooms and hallways that I passed were paradoxes of preservation and neglect, of carefully arranged treasures, dust and decay. I saw either austerity or clutter in the darkness. Empty hallways led to bare hardwood floors or the silhouettes of haphazard furniture, overloaded shelves, and the occasional sculpture or candelabra.

In my wandering, I passed a narrow staircase. A sterile light and an electric hum emanated from the top. I stood for a minute with one foot hovering over the bottom step before turning away. What if the boards creaked? I could explain a wrong turn, but not accidentally climbing a staircase.

Instead, I followed the light at the end of a dark and empty hallway until I wound up in a torch-lit room with a half-dozen paintings in ornate frames. Years of heat from the open flame had discolored the wall behind it. The paintings were all village scenes, each vivid and full of movement in contrast to the somber, dusty walls. Two of them were framed pages from illuminated manuscripts. I leaned forward in search of any decipherable writing, but found only a faded MCC, ending in a smudge.

Before I could read more, I heard footsteps in the long hallway. The floor groaned under each unhurried footfall. I took a breath and stepped into the doorway.

"I lost my way," I said. The words sounded like a confession.

"So it seems," said Patrescu, from halfway down the hallway. "You are one of the new members, yes?"

"I joined two months ago."

Patrescu stepped forward. I read a mix of wariness and nostalgia on his face, as if one emotion entailed the other.

"I saw the art on the wall. Are these pictures of places you've been to?" I asked.

"Yes. A long time ago."

Patrescu kept walking in silence, and I stepped aside to let him in. He walked from painting to painting, taking each one in.

"They aren't the same by electric light, but by torchlight, I can remember."

"But surely you must go and visit?" I asked, pausing to see if I had been too inquisitive. Patrescu's emotions seemed tied up in the paintings. "Or do you mean that it has been a long time since you've seen them in the sunlight?"

Perhaps, I thought to myself, *you made them yourself, to keep the memories alive and pass the decades. Perhaps you saw the oxcart and the man in plate armor with your own eyes.*

Patrescu scowled at me. I had pushed too far.

"Wait," I said. "I have to ask you something. Dr. Carroll and I have been working on a blood substitute. I think it could be on the verge of a breakthrough, maybe even in the next few days. I heard that Dr. Miller's work didn't get published anywhere. She just shipped her finds back here to the Manor. I think if this blood substitute works out, we could be on the cover of *Nature*, or at least *Time Magazine*."

"People put such faith in the written word," said Patrescu, using the tone that my father used when he explained how life was in the days before computers. "It's all just stories people tell. Real history is what's around you. You reach out to it and become part of it as it passes you by. Don't worry, you'll have your chance soon enough. Now, I'll show you the way back. Take care not to lose your way again. Not all the old pictures here are pretty."

I left that evening with an empty stomach. Every time I lifted my fork to my mouth, I thought of the mysterious implements on the mantel and the dead rats back at the lab. Visions of ancient vivisection ruined my appetite.

~

"That place was amazing," I said to Lucy the next morning, trying to get the conversation off on an upbeat note before treading on dangerous ground. "Those antiques must be worth a fortune. I swear I saw a candelabra that must have been pure silver. It was like the set of a movie." I hesitated. "A vampire movie."

"I told you to quit it," said Lucy.

"I've got to ask about him. It's been two months and nobody's told me what's really going on. What am I supposed to think?"

"Fine," said Lucy. "Dr. Patrescu has a rare form of porphyria. He can't go out in the sun, and fluorescent lights bother him." As she spoke, she looked down at a sheaf of articles on her lap.

"Doesn't it worry you," I said, "that none of us get published, but he always thanks us for our contribution, right after the blood drive? Don't you feel that the research is just a cover, and that we're being... used?"

I was going to say 'bled dry' but I toned it down at the last moment.

Lucy's spine stiffened, straightening her shoulders. She pulled the articles toward her with her left hand and pointed at me with her right.

"You should be grateful for the chance he's giving you. If giving a little back to help people who need it bothers you so much, why come here in the first place?"

"I didn't mean it like that. I just meant… maybe he is supporting us for personal reasons and not because of the work. I just want to feel like I earned my place here."

I wasn't sure if I had said the right thing, but Lucy relaxed and set the articles down on a bench beside her.

"I grew up near here," said Lucy. "Back in high school, I was driving from a party with two of my friends—we'd all gotten our licenses a few months before—and a deer ran out in front of us. If Woodcross hadn't been just a few miles away, and if Woodcross security hadn't seen us and sent out an ambulance, one of my friends might have died that night. So I do my best to return the favor, and I don't feel used at all."

"I didn't mean to say that he hasn't helped, but what about the people who we could help if more people knew about your work?"

"I know for a fact that our donations have helped the local blood bank. I set up the database for the donation tracking system myself last year. I'm not going to let anyone say that he's using us, especially the only sacrifice we've made this week has been a pint of blood each and a few dead rats."

"You're right. I shouldn't have… wait—how many dead rats, exactly?" I looked for my dark horse and saw an empty cage.

"I forgot to update the board," said Lucy. "I found Subject 23 dead when I got in this morning. I saved the body in case you wanted to look. I meant to tell you, but with the dinner and everything… 23 was your project, right?"

"Yes," I said. "but…"

"What is it?"

"Subject 23 only got saline. I entered it as an experimental condition in the log."

"But why would you falsify the logs? I know we don't do peer review here, but we have to have some standards."

"It really was an experiment," I said, "and it taught us something new. The deciding factor on whether those rats live or die wasn't what we injected them with but what we wrote in the log."

"But that can't happen unless... you think someone is reading the logs and killing the rats that have the substitute? But why?"

"Maybe someone doesn't want our blood substitute to succeed."

Someone who didn't want to be on the cover of *Nature* or *Time Magazine*.

~

Over the following week, we had found the toxin: a cleaning solution used in the lab. Lucy had half-convinced me we had contaminated the samples or the equipment. Despite our heightened vigilance—which meant an extra hour or two of checklists and grunt work each day—Lucy had more energy than I had seen in weeks. Although we were out of rats at that moment, we looked forward to new trials and slowly let down our guard. The contamination at least gave us reason to think that the blood substitute had not been to blame for three months of failure.

"I'll whip up more of your latest blood substitute," I said. "We still need to re-run everything to be sure. Even when we get new rats in, we still have to figure out how the toxin had been introduced."

Lucy looked past me, pensively, at the empty cages by the wall.

"Not necessarily."

"What do you mean?"

"The other night, I pulled an all-nighter making a new batch. I thought about running more tests, but I knew it would be another week before the new rats came in. By then, whoever was sabotaging the lab might find a way to ruin the whole project. I was thinking about how tired I'd been since the blood drive, and then I figured out a way to solve both problems at once." She unrolled her sleeve to reveal a cotton ball taped to her arm near the elbow.

"You replaced your own blood? That's crazy."

"I couldn't guard the rats all night." Lucy beamed like a teenager, a sight I hadn't seen before. "I called Dr. Patrescu. He's flying in tomorrow. He's going to meet with us personally!"

"So what do we do now?"

"Make a new batch for the follow-up tests, of course. I used up my supply."

I joined in, if only because someone had to be there to call the paramedics if she went into shock or something. By the time we finished, it was nearly midnight. Lucy locked the doors, and we set out across the quad toward the Woodcross residence complex. Seeing Woodcross Manor at night made me think of sabotage again.

"Dammit," I said. "I left my notes in the lab. Stay here. I'll go get them and be right back." I didn't want anyone to read them and find out that Lucy was a test subject, not after what had happened to the others. Lucy nodded. I had walked back to the front door and was looking through my pockets for my access card when I heard her scream.

I ran back and saw Lucy grappling with a figure in a long coat. He stood behind her with one arm around her waist and tried to get the other arm over her mouth.

"Hey!" I called. The assailant let go of Lucy and bolted from the path. I thought about chasing after him, but I knew I would most likely get myself lost. Better, I thought, to let him run off while I stayed with Lucy. "Are you all right?" I asked. "It looks like you're bleeding."

Lucy looked down at her hands.

"I don't think so," said Lucy. "It looks like I got whoever-it-was pretty good with my nails, though." I lent her a tissue to clean it off.

"Did you see who it was?"

"No. He was behind me."

"I'll call the police," I said. "Whatever you remember

might be enough to catch this guy."

"No," said Lucy. "Dr. Patrescu insists that we take care of things ourselves. 'No *police*,' he always says. It would take them forever to get all the way up to the campus anyway. I just need to get to the infirmary. There are guards there, and I'm good friends with the night nurse. They can keep an eye on me."

"Are you sure?"

"Absolutely."

"We can always find more rats, but you're indispensable."

Lucy smiled, but I still didn't sleep that night. Foyle didn't help much either.

~

"Foyle? Is that you?" I said after digging my phone out of my lab coat pocket. The clock display read 3:36 AM.

"Sorry. Forgot the time difference."

"It doesn't matter," I said. I told him what had happened to Lucy.

"I keep telling both of you not to work so late. It might have been one of the locals. Some of the people out in those woods aren't right in the head."

"But what if it has something to do with the rats that were poisoned?"

"I don't know," said Foyle. "Listen. Dr. P. told me to clear his schedule. He said something about your lab. Do you know what's going on?"

"Unless it's about the attack, I don't have a clue. Oh, wait. Of course. Lucy told him about the blood substitute. We had a breakthrough."

"Well, the last time Dr. P. was this worried we had hazmat teams crawling over Woodcross for a week, so be careful."

"Look. About Woodcross, I'm starting to think there's more going on..." I began, but when I realized that I was talking to dead air, I hung up. After three hours of fitful sleep, I rolled out of bed, threw my lab coat on over my pajamas and set out for the quad, hoping to catch Lucy at the infirmary and offer to walk her to the lab. Before I could get there, I saw flashing lights by the entrance, and I knew something was wrong.

~

"Don't come any closer," said one of the guards. He wore a leather jacket and a gray wool cap, and he stood on the concrete steps that led to our building. The lights from an ambulance reflected off the windows.

"But what happened?" I asked.

"Not sure yet," he said, exhaling a mix of cigarette smoke and water vapor. "You go back to your room now. It is not safe out here."

The doors to the lab opened, and four men in white coats hustled a gurney down the stairs. The guard deftly sidestepped them, but I, in my stupor, scrambled out of the way in the last instant. I saw just enough of Lucy's face to recognize her before the doors slammed shut. Her skin was the color of gristle, and her lips like chalk.

The guard loitered by the front steps for another fifteen minutes before he padlocked the front door and left. I climbed in through a first floor window and looked around. The first thought in my mind was that she shouldn't have been there at all, especially that night.

The lab didn't look much different than I remembered. The rat cages were empty, and the dry-erase board was blank, but petri dishes, flasks and micropipettes still cluttered the desks. The log books were gone. As I walked around the central island toward the sinks and fume hoods, I saw blood spatter on the wall. Beneath it, blood dripped from the countertop by the sink. I stepped over two congealing pools, avoiding a crimson boot print, and picked up an envelope that was white except for a few red speckles. The writing on the letter inside matched dozens of Post-its and labels all over the lab.

The work we have done has meant more to me than anything else. I wanted to believe I had a chance to make a difference, Through all the setbacks, I never lost hope. But hope is gone now, gone so quickly that I can't find anything to replace it. There is an evil in Woodcross, one I have been blind to for years, I cannot allow my work to feed that evil, so I have destroyed everything: the logs, the blood substitutes, and every last one of the subjects. It was the only way to be sure.

Lucy.

I tried to imagine the scene: Distraught at realizing some grievous error, she... what... destroyed the notebooks and slit her wrists? Out of habit, I tidied the stacks of Petri dishes, piled the used glassware in the sink and returned her microscope back to the cabinet. I stopped when I noticed a slide with a clump of reddish brown material. When I brought the microscope back out and had a look, I saw what looked like leukocytes and erythrocytes tangled up in cellulose. The cells I could identify were distorted and misshapen in ways that couldn't be the result of contact with the elements. It was stranger than any porphyria I could imagine.

I knew it wasn't Lucy's blood on that slide. I looked through the samples in the cold room and found a crumpled-up tissue streaked with red. The precise rectangular hole in the middle matched the size of the sample on the slide. Now I knew why Lucy could not have rested in safety when the chance to identify her attacker was right there on the tips of her fingernails. It must have been a blow to find Dr. Patrescu's blood, after all she had done for him.

The futility of everything I'd done at Woodcross sank in. I went to grad school in the first place because I thought it meant more than washing out test tubes, filling out forms and prepping samples for some computer to analyze. Lucy's blood substitute had real meaning, and with her gone there was nothing I could do to keep it from slipping away. I had visions of tracking down Dr. Patrescu and forcing him to admit what he had done. I imagined SWAT teams breaking through those shutters at Woodcross. I imagined the helicopter, the helipad and the whole damned manor crumbling to the ground, but in the end what good would it do? I had folders with sketchy notes on Lucy's last project, but who would believe me, without any published data? Who would fund a study when the only human trial wound up dead?

My plan was less ambitious and more immediate: to hop the fence, walk to the next town and phone in an anonymous tip on the way to the bus station. From there, I would head back home and forget Woodcross existed. I gathered some clothes, my notes, my passport, and a hundred dollars in cash. As I stuffed them into a suitcase, someone knocked on the door.

~

"It's Foyle," said a voice outside.

I looked through the windows and the peephole and convinced myself that he was alone. I unlocked the door and backed into the kitchen.

"Door's open."

Foyle stepped in, rubbing his gloved hands together. He cupped his hands over his face and exhaled a warm breath.

"It's freezing out there," he said. "Or maybe I'm coming down with something. Is your phone broken?"

"I'm not in the mood to talk."

"I heard what happened to Lucy," said Foyle. "It's tragic of course, but it happens. Six months ago, another girl did the same thing, right before the Quarterly Dinner. Some of them can't handle the pressure. Can I sit down?"

I ushered him to my kitchen table.

"Dr. P. has asked me to reassess your project," said Foyle. "He wants this hushed up. Suicides attract attention. He just wants to keep the cops out. I want to see your project through. If you know of any lab notebooks or documentation that could help to replicate her studies, I'd like to have them. In time, I might be able to change Dr. P.'s mind and start the project up again myself."

"I'll see what I can find," I said, trying to hide my irritation. Couldn't he have at least waited a few days out of respect? I had come to Woodcross to escape "publish or perish," but all it had done was give the phrase a new, macabre meaning.

"Good," said Foyle. "But keep a low profile, and if you hear anything, talk to me first."

Foyle took his briefcase and left, hunching his shoulders and pulling his coat up to his chin as he stepped out into the cold.

As soon as he'd left, I opened my suitcase and took the clothes out. Underneath, next to my passport, were two folders, one labeled RAT 23 and the other labeled LUCY. I decided that I could go to the cops tomorrow and give Foyle a chance to lay low, for Lucy's sake.

An hour later, I left a message on Foyle's voicemail. Six hours later, a terse reply came back.

"Bring your notes and meet me at eight at Woodcross Manor. Go around the back, and, whatever you do, make sure nobody is following you." I heard an electric hum in the background.

~

Just after sundown, I circled around Woodcross Manor. Foyle let me in through the side entrance.

"Should we be here?" I asked, as Foyle turned, locked the door behind me, and led the way with a flashlight.

"Of course," said Foyle. "Dr. P. pretty much leaves the

place in my care while he's away, unless I'm off at a conference. Stick close to me. This place is full of dead ends and hiding places."

"And staircases, and rooms that hum."

Foyle chuckled.

"You've been snooping around as well," said Foyle. "Come on. I'll introduce you to the real Woodcross."

The room that he led me to, after a few twists and turns, was spacious and ornate as if it had been a ballroom, but Foyle had arranged it as a hospital ward. People occupied three of the twenty beds, and humanoid lumps under sheets occupied another seven or eight. The "participants" in Foyle's research seemed to be sleeping or heavily sedated.

"Who are these people?" I asked.

"Doesn't matter," said Foyle. "Volunteers. People who see the value of my work."

None of them seemed to see or hear much of anything, especially the ones under the sheets. I noticed racks of vials and IV bags on the tables behind the gurneys, and a thought occurred to me.

"Does your work involve," I said, "a strange type of porphyria?"

"You've figured that much out," said Foyle, as he glanced at the readouts of the three living participants. "Not that it was much of a leap. We always knew that vampirism was spread through the blood, so viral transmission made sense. The real challenge was seeing the potential of Woodcross Institute and winning Dr. P.'s trust."

"So you got a sample of his blood and infected all these people?"

Foyle chuckled.

"The last thing I want is to release a whole bunch of vampires into the population. That would raise questions. I've exposed these people to isolated proteins transcribed by the viral DNA, to observe their effects. There's only one person in this room who carries the virus."

"You," I said.

"Me. And you can be part of this too. Dr. P. founded Woodcross over two hundred years ago. Think of what you could accomplish here in that stretch of time. If you help me to unlock the full potential of the virus, we could present this to Dr. P. together. He could finally step out of the shadows."

"And what about them?" I pointed to the bodies. "Do they see it as a blessing?"

"Accidents. Like I said, they volunteered. Some people will do anything if you tell them you can unlock the secrets of immortality. What I don't tell them is that I already have the secret. You're the only one that knows the truth. All I ask in return is that you give me your notes and help me keep it under wraps until we're ready. You can start off as my assistant, but after that, who knows?"

Foyle took off his jacket and rolled up his sleeve. He sliced the skin on his arm and let a drop bead on the metal. He held the scalpel out toward me blade-first. I noticed scratches on the side of his neck below his ear.

"It's easy," said Foyle. "No fangs. Just a simple cut."

I backed away from the blade. My fingers tightened around the two folders. The last time I had seen blood, it was on a slide back in the lab.

"There was no time difference, was there?" I asked. "You called me from Woodcross the night Lucy was attacked, just to give yourself an alibi, so that I wouldn't suspect anything when you asked me for her research."

Foyle tensed, the way he used to when his advisor called him out on a mistake during lab meetings.

"Lucy was going to go public with her blood substitute. She thought she was protecting Dr. P. by doing it anonymously, but it's not like some archaeological dig or a painting. People worldwide would pay attention. They'd have asked questions about our research methods. They'd have discovered this room. I couldn't let that happen. I needed more time to safeguard our work. You've got to help me. You owe me. Where would you be if I hadn't invited you to Woodcross?"

"Maybe I do owe you something," I said. "I think you brought me here because you couldn't hide your ambition any longer. You needed at least one person besides yourself to stand with you, even when Lucy and Dr. P. wanted to move on. So let me return the favor and tell you what I really think. There's still time to walk away from this." I held up my notes. "We can get rid of all these secrets and look for a cure."

"Not yet. I need more time to fully understand what I've become. Then I will be just as strong as Dr. P. Then he'll understand."

"But he doesn't understand now, does he? That's why you have to feed in secret. Tell me about the suicide six months ago, when Dr. Patrescu was back in town for the Quarterly Dinner. Did she slit her wrists? Did she wind up in the infirmary with half her blood gone? It's easy. That's what you told me. No fangs. Just a simple cut."

"I thought you had potential," said Foyle, with an air of nonchalant disappointment. "I thought you understood what Woodcross was really about."

I thought back to the pride on Dr. Patrescu's face when he introduced Dr. Miller's team. Looking back, I wondered if he had hosted those dinners as a way of bringing the world in, as if the glow on everyone's faces might be enough to knock the shutters off the windows and let some real light in.

"I know what Woodcross was meant for. It was his refuge from the disease. It reminded him that being a vampire didn't mean turning into someone like you."

Foyle's left hand clutched a rag on the counter, and he lunged at me with sudden speed. A sickly sweet odor struck me as the rag brushed my face. I backed away and fended him off with a wheeled cart well enough to get a two-step head start on him as I ran out the door.

I managed to put some distance between us, maybe on account of him missing his chance to feed off Lucy. I took turns at random—I forgot how many—until the hallway I was in ended abruptly in a descending, unlit staircase. I ran into the darkness. Once I reached the bottom and I heard no footsteps behind me, I ventured a glance over my shoulder.

Foyle stood at the top of the stairs. He had abandoned the rag in order to light a torch on the wall. He lifted the torch off its mount and held the flame out in front of him like a weapon as he took a few steps down.

"Back away from the staircase," he said. The stairs creaked with each step. "Keep going."

I struggled to think of a way past him, but between the torch, the scalpel and high ground, I didn't see any point in trying. The hallway widened as I retreated further. Alcoves and shelves in the walls held musty books, faded carpets, tapestries, and skeletons—skeletons stacked as if the shelves were bunk beds.

"This is the Patrescu crypt," said Foyle. "The whole basement is full of his past. I thought it fitting that you should end up here, like the rest of this junk."

"Someone will find out. They'll come looking for me or Lucy."

"Lucy did me the favor of offing herself," said Foyle, now at the foot of the stairs, "but I have a plan for you, too. It shouldn't be hard to figure out where you were planning to go and leave a few of your belongings there, just enough to throw the police off our trail. Why would they question it? You've walked away from failure before."

Foyle stepped into the crypt and picked a dagger out of the rubble in the first alcove.

"No one will find you. Dr. P. only comes back every few months. I doubt he's been down here in a century."

"Of course," I said, scanning the walls for a weapon. "Why would he want to be reminded of all the bloodshed, of all that slinking around the edges of cemeteries and battlefields? Face it, Foyle. You're an embarrassment to him."

"That's a lie."

I saw a sword in an alcove beside me, but it was rusted through. I didn't think it would survive more than one swing. I needed more time.

"Dr. Patrescu doesn't need you anymore," I said. "Not after Lucy's discovery. Think about it. With the blood substitute replacing his erythrocytes, and with no need for hemoglobin, the anemia and porphyria would disappear. He could be sunning himself on the French Riviera instead of cooped up in dusty rooms. You're holding him back."

"No!" said Foyle. "Dr. P. has lived for centuries. He's learned so much. Even if the blood substitute is a cure, he won't turn his back on immortality."

"Not just a cure," I said. "Something new. Symbiosis. All the benefits with no drawbacks. Red blood cells have no nuclei. The virus can't rely on them to replicate. Removing them might not affect the virus's anti-aging or immune properties. Dr. Patrescu wouldn't have to give them up. All he would have to do is step out of the shadows."

"Not quite," said Foyle. "With you and Lucy out of the way, things will go back to the way they've always been."

"Really?" I said. "Dr. Patrescu will eventually find out you're the reason he still lives as a pariah and can't see his hometown in the daylight. What will you say to him then?"

I heard the floorboards creak at the top of the stairs.

"There he is now," I said. "Tell him what you've done. Tell him about your accomplishments. Tell him about all the bodies. How many cities did you visit? How many conferences? How many bodies did you leave behind?"

"I had to feed," said Foyle. "Lucy started tracking the blood donations. I couldn't skim off the blood bank anymore. I had no choice."

"Lucy had a choice, right? She gave up her life's work in order to keep you from using what she learned to harm innocent people. She wanted a chance to contribute—just like you told me on the day you offered me this job. I think you'd better start showing him that you measure up to Lucy's example. Wouldn't you say, Dr. Patrescu?"

Foyle turned toward the stairs while I reached for the rusted sword. Neither of us expected to see the ghostly figure of a woman at the bottom of the stairs.

"Lucy?" I said.

"Do you know what your problem was, Foyle?" said Lucy. "You never paid attention to details. One pale body on a gurney is pretty much like any other, right?"

"You…?" said Foyle.

"At first," said Lucy, "I just wanted to do the full volume replacement, to prove it was possible. I remember looking at my face in the mirror, and at six liters of my own blood in bags on the lab table, when the idea came to me. I staged the scene with my friends from the infirmary, and once you believed I was dead, I snuck back into Woodcross Manor and waited."

"Doctor Patrescu isn't here after all," said Foyle. "I don't have to explain myself to anybody."

"Details," I said. I swung the sword, timing the blow so that the broad side of the blade hit Foyle's face just as it completed the turn toward me. The blade shattered into a cloud of rust, which probably wouldn't have done too much damage if Foyle had thought to wear eye protection or been quick enough to blink. Foyle staggered backward, and instinctively dropped the scalpel as he covered his face. I pushed past him and stood between him and Lucy.

"Get back, both of you," said Foyle, brandishing the torch wildly. "I'm a goddamned vampire. Do you really think you can hurt me?"

"We don't have to," I said. "The police can handle it from here."

"Dr. P. would never go to the police," said Foyle. "I'd tell them everything, His secret will be out. Woodcross would be ruined."

"If we say we've found a serial killer," I said, "who's been stealing from our blood banks and doing unauthorized experiments, I don't think it will help your case all that much if you tell them you're a vampire."

"Think about it," said Lucy. "Life sentences mean something quite different when you don't age."

"And being two hundred years old won't win you any fights on the cell block," I added. "You need the cure as much as Dr. Patrescu does."

Foyle sneered and chuckled at first, but then he backed away. His torch brushed against a stack of books, setting one or two of them aflame. Foyle saw this and retreated further into the clutter, lighting anything that might burn. After a while, all I could see clearly was the light from the torch.

"What are you doing, Mark?" I asked.

"Fire can't harm me," he said between coughs. "I'm a vampire. You'll see. I'll get out of here if I have to burn the place to its foundation."

"You read too many stories," I said, thinking back to what Patrescu had told me. Real history is what's around you. I heard Foyle scream when he brushed against a tapestry and the fire spread to his designer suit, but by then we were too far away to save him.

"The fire's spreading," said Lucy. We stumbled through the darkness together. My chest burned, and I felt light-headed. Still, I paused before climbing the stairs to listen for sounds of Foyle somehow wading through the flames toward us. I heard nothing.

When we reached the front steps, we paused to catch our breath.

"Lucy?" I said. "Are you crying?"

She looked surprised and wiped her cheek. Her fingertips glistened as she held them to a candle flame.

"I must have cut myself," she said, and as she spoke, the clotting factors turned the droplets of artificial blood into a tangle of cobwebs. She brushed them from her hand and watched the fine wisps drift to the floor. The cut on Lucy's forehead had already turned powdery white.

"You could use some antibiotics," I said, "until we're sure that the immune system takes well to the blood substitute, but it should be good as new before long."

We stood and watched the fire together until we heard Dr. Patrescu's helicopter in the distance, a familiar fluttering of giant mechanical wings.

~

"Another one?" I asked. "We're running out of space on the bulletin board."

Lucy handed me a postcard with a beach in the foreground, a blue sky in the background and the word HAWAII in bright letters scrawled over the top. I moved a few of the newspaper articles out of the way.

WOODCROSS TO START CLINICAL TRIALS OF
BREAKTHROUGH ARTIFICIAL BLOOD

SERIAL KILLER BELIEVED DEAD IN SHOCKING BLAZE
WOODCROSS COMMUNITY MOURNS, RALLIES AROUND
RECLUSIVE LEADER.

FROM THE ASHES: DR. LUCINDA CARROLL SPEAKS OUT
ABOUT WOODCROSS'S HIDDEN PAST, NEW FUTURE.

I turned the postcard over and tacked it up. The inscription read, in a practiced hand:

IT IS AS BEAUTIFUL AS IT LOOKS IN THE PICTURE. I COULD NOT HAVE DONE IT WITHOUT YOU. VA MULTUMESC FOARTE MULT! -DR. P.

S.R. Algernon studied fiction writing, biology and post-war Japanese science fiction, among other things, at the University of North Carolina at Chapel Hill. He has been a member of critters.org for three years. His fiction interests include historical fiction, Golden Age science fiction, contemporary Japanese science fiction, hard science fiction, and science fiction that explores the sociological and political impact of new technology. He currently resides in Singapore.

EUDORA

James S. Dorr

"The worms crawl in, the worms crawl out—"

— Children's play song

When Eudora was twelve, her father bought her a wormery.

"*A what?*" she asked.

"It's called a 'wormery,' a place you raise worms. It's like an ant farm — you know what that is. They've got one in your classroom in school. I thought it might help you get better grades in science."

Eudora was already having issues with early puberty. The last thing she wanted to worry about was worms. But her grades *were* poor.

"You mean like when you die?" she said.

It was her father's turn now to ask, "What?"

"You know, they eat your body. Worms, that is. When

you're in the coffin—we learned about it in science. And you rot and stink—"

"That's enough, Eudora," her father said. "No, these are like fishing worms. Earthworms. Angleworms. I'll help you dig some in the yard after supper."

Eudora agreed. She was only a child. What choice did she have? After supper she went out with him in the garden and watched as he showed her the different kinds of soil, and how to arrange them in layers between the wormery's two sheets of transparent plexiglass. Filling the thing up like it was a box. He showed her how to use layers of pebbles as well, for drainage, and how, then, to add water from the hose, but not so much that it became too soggy. And how to cover the final layer with grass clippings and dead leaves, so that the worms would have something to eat.

The best part, she thought, was digging the worms themselves, which she helped with, dangling them first before putting them in, just before adding the pebbles and leaves.

She was into Goth culture too.

On school days she wanted to wear black skirts, and black blouses as well, until one of the teachers sent her home with a note saying she frightened the other children. So she wore black and gray plaids and black jackets over white tops. And black tights with black shoes. When she was fifteen, she bought her first corset, with money she earned on summer vacation. Her father didn't know.

As for the worms, they *did* help her grades. She spent hours in her room with her home computer poring over invertebrate biology. And not just *Annelida*, the segmented worms, like earthworms and fishing worms, but other kinds of worms. Flukes and pinworms. Nematodes. Ribbon worms—some of which grew to be hundreds of feet long. These lived in the ocean.

Tube worms that lived on the ocean's floor next to sulfur-spewing vents. Giving her Bosch-like visions of what hell must look like when people died.

In college, she studied Dante in the original fourteenth-century Italian.

But, mostly, the worms she liked best lived in people.

~

She felt an affinity after she grew up and left her father's house. After she graduated from college. She had many boyfriends — she sponged on them, knowingly. Living with boys, she didn't pay rent.

As she — and her lovers — grew more sophisticated, she bilked them for presents. How did the song go, that "diamonds are a girl's best friend?"

She had many men friends, some of them dying young. Tragic. Byronic. As a live-in girlfriend, in more and more states now she found herself able to inherit property.

Yet she *did* love them.

She dreamed about vampires, sometimes, especially on nights when the moon was nearing full. Of their preying on men, too — she liked vampire movies.

She often met new men at horror film festivals. Classic movies like *Nosferatu. The Great London Mystery. Dracula's Daughter.* "Call me 'Carmilla,'" she'd tell them, laughing. "Beware I don't suck *you* dry."

As often as not she'd go home with them too. Then, within a week, move in.

Always on the go, that was Eudora. Seductive. Beautiful. Treating Goth clubs as if they were smorgasbords. Meeting new men there as well.

So often they died young.

~

When she was little, her "worm farming days" as she liked to think of them — often she, svelte, black-clad, fishnetted, corseted, used stories of that to intrigue men all the more —

213

when she was young, she did not raise just *earthworms*. She experimented. Would earthworms eat nematodes? She'd add some to the soil. Would flatworms bore through dirt? One way to find *that* out.

Eventually, of course, it started to smell bad. That is, even after she cleaned out the wormery, washing its sides and its black plastic ends, and putting in new dirt.

And putting in new worms — sometimes exotic kinds she found in pet stores.

It smelled like a grave, she thought. Like a grave *must* smell.

She told her new man that. She'd only just met him Saturday night, after her lover of the present had left to go back home to stay with his parents. Some kind of sickness he'd managed to pick up. She didn't know what. She didn't like hospitals, though enough people she met ended up there.

She thought herself unlucky, yet in a way she was fortunate also, her loves always ending, or mostly always, before they could go stale. She told her new loves that, too.

"I'm a jinx," she said. "Beware of me — I'm bad luck. That's why I'm so grasping, because love is so short, one must take it as one can. Drink of one's life deeply.

"Some say that I'm worth it."

She had such a charming smile.

~

And, on more and more nights as time went on, she dreamed about parasites.

~

She was that herself, she knew. Like a big tick, or a tapeworm, or hookworm. But *much* more beautiful.

Vampire-like, sucking life. She didn't understand, though it worked out for *her*, why life for those who loved her was so tragic. Not just men only, sometimes women loved her. So it wasn't just some kind of frail *man* thing, like people getting hurt when they fought over her. Though that happened sometimes too.

Vampires. Vamps—the slim, dark-eyed females in silent movies who seduced and destroyed men. Like Theda Bara. The 1920s and '30s. The terms were related, she'd learned in college. Kipling's "The Vampire," his "rag and a bone and a hank of hair." The vampire as parasite morphed into the predatory woman.

She was fascinated by worms that ate people. Like grave worms. Maggots—although these weren't true worms. She thought of herself like that sometimes as well, as worming herself into people's bodies, some part of herself, at least. Into their *brains* perhaps, certainly in their hearts.

Feeding on them.

Emerging winged, beautiful, not as a fly, but more as an exotic moth. A creature of the moon, dark, iridescent, flitting through the night. Gossamer wings shining.

As she shone also, dancing to jazz beats, to drums, to tympani, in a new lover's arms. Black dress tight on her breasts, raven braids swinging. She thought of herself as a computer virus, scampering through wires—her home computer, on which she first learned about worm-borne diseases, of elephantiasis, river blindness. One of her boyfriends had lost his sight when she was nineteen. Guinea worm disease. Filariasis. Poor people's diseases.

Although she herself, of course, preyed on the more rich.

Coursing through wires with electrons, infecting them. Wasn't that how computer worms harmed their hosts? When she was fifteen, her hard disk had crashed. Her father had bought her a new computer.

She learned about men that way.

~

"My name isn't really 'Carmilla,'" she said as he took her up to his furnished loft. "It's Eudora, from a Greek word that means 'generous.'"

"It's a nice name," he said. "Beautiful, like you." She nodded and nuzzled him.

Later that night, as they lay side by side, naked, wrapped in each other's arms in his bed, she kissed him full on the mouth. Thrusting her tongue in. She felt her own mouth fill — his questing tongue's answer. The familiar tingle. Not knowing as worms coursed up, white, as thin as pencil-leads, mixed in saliva out of her throat to his. She who, at sixteen, had fallen deathly ill — adding, at that time, to her skin's natural pallor, so much now part of her charm — and, in recovery, became herself immune.

To whatever it was *they* bore.

And he, responding, rolled between her thighs. Tangled and sweaty, they made love again, then both went back to sleep.

~

She dreamed about vampires.

James **Dorr**'s newest collection is THE TEARS OF ISIS, released by Perpetual Motion Machine Publishing in May 2013. This joins his two prose collections from Dark Regions Press, STRANGE MISTRESSES: TALES OF WONDER AND ROMANCE and DARKER LOVES: TALES OF MYSTERY AND REGRET, and the all-poetry VAMPS (A RETROSPECTIVE) from Sam's Dot/White Cat. An active member of SFWA and HWA with nearly four hundred individual appearances from ALFRED HITCHCOCK'S MYSTERY MAGAZINE to XENOPHILIA, Dorr invites readers to visit his site at http://jamesdorrwriter.wordpress.com.

A RIVER OF BLOOD, CARRIED INTO THE ABYSS

John Palisano

The bugs would soon return. Galaday willed his body to move, but the ache was too great. He needed sustenance. He needed blood. He needed life.

Oh, please come back soon.

Moonlight filled the Draconia's large command module. Reflections outlined the rim of his bed, his cane, and his feet. His toenails had grown long, pointed, and sharp. One split into two points at the end, like a piece of bamboo. He smelled and tasted silicone— it helped keep the outbreak at bay. His period of rejuvenation had lasted four decades.

Are two hundred years long enough?

Will it return?

Will I?

XNA. Building blocks changed and made. Worked for decades. Until Jet Cassidy figured out a way to weaponize the stuff. Turn people into other things. Distortions. Mutations. Manipulations.

The outbreak. Thousands carried it unknowingly for seven years. Its incubation undetected. Contagion through aerosol. Coughing. Wheezing. Breathing. Hundreds of thousands. Millions. Multi-millions. Death the only cure.

Cure.

Galady knew of one, but was not a scientist, so few listened. Exposure to the Wilson bacterium could fight it and win. There were consequences. The body would eject iron. The skin would pallor and hair would fall out. Unpleasant.

The worst was the need for blood.

That's where the bugs came in.

The Wilson Bacterium was known only to a few, a mocked rumor to the rest of the world. A secret of the Glass Company. Wilson Bacterium could slow the degradation of cells. In some cases it stopped them from dying completely. For Galaday, it slowed the disease inside him from a race to a crawl. His life extended. Changed.

New nutrients necessary. New fuel.

How to get it without getting caught?

Feeders. Bleeders. Little black dots with very precise tastes. Galaday bred them and taught them what to do.

He heard them come from behind. Minute sounds were as loud as tidal waves, if he chose to single them out, to listen. Hundreds of hair-like legs rushed across the floor toward their host.

The first Feeder reached him, crawling at the back of his right arm. He felt his heart lighten at the touch. Soon there were many tingling things on him. Galaday imagined his pores opening to welcome them. Like a thousand needles, the Feeders bit. First a few, then many, as the others heard the chorus of pain and sang along.

Galaday's flesh responded. Signals shot up and down his nerves. His calf and bicep twitched. His throat opened. His eyes shut. His blood flowed.

Moving one hand slowly on top of the other, Galaday felt the burrowing Feeders under the top of his hand with his palm. He gently stroked them, encouraging them to stay. *Like bee stings. Remember those. When I was a kid. On Cape Hatteras.*

Only these stings hurt worse. He liked it.

"Means you're alive." He heard his uncle Frances in memory. "It's when you don't feel pain that you've got to worry." A soldier's philosophy, spoken matter of fact. Galaday, for a moment, recalled how his Uncle's strong hand grasped his young shoulder. Immediately he squeezed his own hand to see if he had grown as strong. He hadn't. *A hundred years later and I still have that man inside my head like it were yesterday.*

His skin felt soft like damp paper. *It was not made to live this long.*

There aren't too many of us left, though at least there are some people who listened to me.

Galaday separated his hands and put them by his side. The feeding would be done soon, and so, too, would the hurt.

Hundreds of Feeders burrowed inside his epidermis. They delivered blood. He felt the drops—only one or two per insect—fill him. Within moments the blood went to his head and face— Galaday flushed. His joints loosened. The muscles around his eyes and mouth went lax. Before long, each crux and tissue felt rejuvenated. It hurt like crazy. Coming back to life always did. Not that he'd truly died, although it felt that way.

Dozens of the Feeders, having unloaded their sanguine cargo inside him, began processing. They filtered the toxic minerals from his new blood as it raced along blood vessels and stripped the plague-like clots from within. They did so by inserting their legs inside his veins and allowing the toxins to gather round the limbs. Galaday had discovered the phenomena during his research years earlier.

~

He'd used his Glass system to peer down at Moniga's arms. "I'm splitting apart," she'd said. "It's only a matter of time."

Galaday'd said: "You're more than my wife," and bent down on his knees with the Glass. He positioned it around her wound and observed. "You'll be the first to be cured."

"How can you be so sure?" she'd said from her seat. "If you love me, just tell me the truth so I can make peace and say my goodbyes."

He did not look up. He said, "I never lie to you." Then he saw something remarkable: one of the Feeders inside her wound. They'd been thought of as a plague. The last sign right before someone passed from outbreak's complications. Like vultures circling a dying animal.

Moniga said, "They're there, aren't they? The things. Eating me alive."

Galaday did not reply, instead, he kept watch.

He needed to see what happened. If he could stop them, he could stop the inevitable. Or so he'd thought.

Then he went to the Glass and tuned it so he could see closer.

The magnified bugs were doing something curious. If he watched one long enough, they followed a pattern. They'd scoop up blood or tissue and leave, depositing their payload somewhere nearby...somewhere dark.

Galaday followed their lead and spotted a larger pale tubular insect hidden a short distance away. The Feeders deposited the blood inside the thing's maw. After a time, they stopped. The tube bug changed color to pink. They'd fed it. He thought of the possibilities. What were these things? Why would they need human blood to survive? How had they been drawn to their hosts? How could he use them to save lives?

He'd find out.

~

Only three Feeders were left on his chest, so Galaday made to sit up. He was weakened from their draining. His head spun. He wanted to move faster but could not. Still, he made his way up and off his bed. The last Feeders rolled from his body and hit the floor, where they scurried away inside the shadows. Galaday watched them, and thought it oddly unlike him to trust they'd always return. Well, where else would they go? There was nothing to do outside the Draconia. He doubted they'd be able to survive within the vastness of space, but who knew.

Galaday approached the hallway that led to the main corridor of the ship. There, to his right, was the Phoenix wing of the Draconia. That was where she was—his Moniga. The Feeders had taken so much from her, so long ago. She'd nearly died from them. Her pain was immeasurable. "Take me," she'd begged. "Release me."

He wouldn't.

Not then.

Not now.

Not ever.

No.

Instead, he would find a way to cure her.

Venom is made from poison. It was a lesson...a basic lesson...he'd learned at University. How simple. Elegant. From the feeder's poison he'd save Moniga. That was Galaday's hypothesis.

The right side of his head hurt. That was always where he'd been sensitive after the Feeders. It hurt worse as he leaned down to open the airlock to the Phoenix wing, where the laboratory station had been created. He cultivated the area to its essence. The Draconia needed to run only the most essential tasks. Galaday had no idea how much power the craft had left in the thermo engines. He'd heard its engineers brag about a lifetime lasting millions of years, but Galaday was doubtful. How would the Draconia be able to sustain itself for so long? How could its metals stay together? What if the shields went down, and what happened if there was something that could not fix itself. Then the entire bloodline would be gone. His race. He, Moniga and the six others would be the last. Why risk going out in such a way? Perhaps there might be other beings roaming around the galaxy that would find and rescue them. Similar beings from whom they'd be able to recover and thrive and become reintegrated. These were all maybes, and he gave all of his hope to the possibilities.

Galaday opened the door to the Phoenix wing. The room was dark: very different than the holofilms he grew up watching. It was functional, not pretty. It smelled of chemicals. He lowered the sliding door covering Moniga. He wanted to preserve her until he knew he'd be able to bring her back. Galaday didn't want her to see him. His body had changed. Appearing as though he was suffering malnutrition, Galaday's once lush hair had thinned considerably. His fingers looked smaller, skinnier and longer. How would Moniga react? Probably be frightened, if not terrified. His teeth had withered into small triangular things that made him look like a shark, when he opened his mouth. His tongue had gone dark, probably from the poor rations he was eating.

I can't see me. I don't want anybody to see me like this. I look horrible. Desperate. One of the last men alive, but I look like a monster. Why couldn't I be frozen the way I looked in my prime? I had long flowing dark curls, and bright green eyes. I was strong with rippling muscles. Everything worked. I could drink a bottle of wine and be perfect. Now? I get all my food out of plastic boxes. Everything has been freeze-dried and preserved. All my food. All my drinks. All my entertainment. And what am I going to do when the thermo engines run out? Then what?

The ship was packed with a hundred years of food. That was for a full crew, too. He should have enough for his lifetime and theirs. And then some. What if some spoiled? What if some got destroyed? There was no source of food in outer space. They'd have to starve. Or he could take the little trapezoid-shaped black pill in the tube. The emergency suicide pills. Painless. Quick. Classy. There just in case of such an outcome.

Now. He needed her resurrection to work. Without her, the whole thing would be useless. Mankind would stop with him. That would be it. He needed her to come back from sleep while he was still alive. He wasn't sure if his reproductive functioning worked, but he hoped they'd have children. Who would make love to an old man? Moniga remained beautiful. She'd been preserved. Forever. Or until someone figured out a way to safely wake her. The way had to be out there. He wasn't sure where, and he needed to find a cure. She'd be dead within days or weeks after being brought out of her sleep. Without a care, she'd be lost.

He lifted the black cloth from her chamber.

Even though her face and image were burned inside his memory, he was still taken back by her beauty. His hands went to the ultra glass, to where her face lay. If he could just touch her once more, kiss her softly, hear her voice.

The Feeders were inside. He saw them on her, some on her skin, others moving under her thin white coverings. They were keeping her. Monica's auto-sleep had kept on, miraculously, shortly after his had failed. The others he'd brought also remained asleep.

When he'd woke, he found the world as they knew it had gone. There was nothing to return to. No civilization. Waves of energy swamped their home planet. Life as they'd known was eradicated. Galaday searched the computers for some record, some communication, something on the net history to explain, but it appeared life had been going on just fine one second, and then, lost the next.

War.

Asteroid.

Maybe just Mother Nature shaking off some pests.

The Rapture.

Whatever it'd been, they'd been forgotten. Lost adrift in orbit just far enough away to escape certain death, and far enough to get stranded. *Why wake them? There's nothing.* Galaday soon found a better use for them.

He watched the Feeders work on her body. They transfused the blood they took from the others and infused it inside her. Their blood was safe. The others. The ones he'd kept for mining. He peered down the hall at the rows of incubation tanks, all covered with dark tarps. Galaday thought one day he would eventually be able to free them, resuscitate, and give them new lives. As the years went on, he became skeptical of any such thing being possible. How long would they last? How long would their bodies...their hosts...hang on? So far none had expired, and they continued to live, although in deep hibernation.

The last time he dared look over them...had it been years?...they'd grown so different. One's eyes had bulged nearly to the breaking point. Their nails had continued to grow, making long, semi-translucent root-like trails by their sides and from their feet. The fluid in the tanks had clouded, slightly obscuring them.

Irene had suffered the most. Even in hibernation, none of them were immune. The right side of her head had swelled and deformed. Growths formed all over her body, which reminded him of cauliflower or ears on old potatoes. Despite the fluid being infused inside her body in order to keep her in hibernation, she moved. Galaday first saw her twitch before she jerked and twisted. She felt pain, he knew. There was only one option. He'd have to turn her sleep permanent. To do so entailed entering a series of commands on the terminal. The longer he waited, the greater risk of the infection spreading to the others.

Didn't the Feeders clean the blood? Weren't they the cure? Was it Jet Cassidy's work? He who'd weaponized Galaday's cure?

He'd panicked. He didn't want to risk the only things he had left. There was no next experiment. He couldn't control the situation from afar. There wouldn't be another group once they were gone. As far as he knew, they were the last.

After the commands were typed, he stood and watched her. He thought of meeting her at Shoreline University. She'd been a bundle of happiness, bringing with her a permanent smile and never ending positivity. He smelled her rich perfume again, the type she always wore. He heard her voice as he looked at her still, distorted face. He pictured her prettiness and the feeling of lightness he always had around her. How sad she should end up like this, thousands of miles from the Earth, floating inside a chamber inside another floating craft. Her body ruined and desecrated from disease, Galaday turned away. He'd just started using a cane, and nearly toppled.

With all he had, Galaday straightened himself out and peered up to Irene.

May God Bless You for all you have given us, for all you have sacrificed, and I am so sorry you did not see the end of your life, or have a chance to say goodbye to your loved ones. You are giving life a possibility. You are giving it to us who remain.

Irene opened her eyes.

Galaday jerked back. How could this happen? Had she heard his prayer? That had to be impossible.

His throat tightened and he needed to go to the bathroom worse than he ever remembered.

Her mouth opened then, and her eyes opened wide and then blinked several times. She saw him—looked right at him.

She thrashed behind the glass.

The Feeders scurried toward the chamber, drawn by her movement.

If they got inside, and carried her sickened blood out...

Galaday panicked and triggered the fail safe command.

Irene knew what he was doing. Her face grew angry and scared all at once. She flailed, but it was too late. The bottom of her chamber opened. The fluid rushed out into space. Irene threw out her arms and held on for a moment.

Her cry. Sad. Tragic. Etched forever inside Galaday's memory.

The vacuum was greater than her will, and Irene disappeared. The floor closed. Her chamber was empty.

Galaday wouldn't weep for several days.

Once he did, prioritizing the monitoring of the remaining hosts consumed him. Each twenty-four-hour period, he checked their levels, searching for signs of infection. Symptoms could hibernate indefinitely, he was sure. After all, the bodies were from Earth, where they'd all been exposed at one time or another. The fact that they were in an extended sleep only made him believe the virus could be dormant, just as their aging systems.

He'd not been so blessed. Instead, he aged well past maturation. At a hundred and thirty years, Galaday thought he'd expire at any moment. He didn't. Something strange happened. A second wind. Where once his muscles and bones ached to move, they turned pliant and strong. The cloudiness killing his mind cleared. His ideas multiplied. Understanding destroyed confusion. A plot to return the craft to Earth hatched. First, he'd have to ensure the planet habitable. They'd need a plan to repopulate. Shelter. Food. Civilization.

How could he peer into a world lost to them? The devices on the ship didn't talk to anyone on the ground. The last communications detailed the great fall. People died out. Infrastructure unraveled. Galaday's cure worked, but came too late. The means to replicate it and distribute it were still. Maybe there were pockets left. Somehow. Packs of feral survivors. He imagined them rummaging through the ruined world. Life always found a way, no matter the odds.

If they could just get to the ground. If only to see and feel and breathe again, just for a little while. That would be enough. *I don't want to die in this floating coffin. I don't want to live for eternity in this. I've read every book. Heard every song. Seen every holofilm I've ever wanted. My love is frozen. We cannot live again like this. She may be able to walk among the living again. Not here, though. I don't want to have her last moments aboard this ship. Cold. Desolate. Lonesome. This is not the life we were meant to live. The plague is probably gone, and we have survived. We will have our coffins in the ground.*

He'd grown tired, and so he shuffled with his cane toward his reclining chair. "Twenty decades is long enough," he said. He'd ran simulations and speculated where they'd best land the craft. The deserts, he presumed, would be ideal. Most germs would have been sparse, and would likely not survive without hosts. They'd also be remote enough to avoid immediate detection. He hoped. The plan was sound. How to get down. Safely. How to walk again on solid ground and be whole again.

Galaday remembered.

The world had gotten sick.

Stopped.

Galaday saved them. Took the Draconia for his own, their own. Damn the consequences, if there would ever be any. He doubted them. And if they ended up true, he'd explain how scared he was, how desperate, how he just had to rescue his family. They'd stayed and fought, after all, but the neighborhood quickly filled with vagrants. They were after him. Smelled his fear in his sweat and his blood on her tongue. The others would take him out, if not for Galaday's resourcefulness. He made an emergency call to the owner of the company Galaday had been working for. There was only a limited amount of time where the conditions would be perfect for his next experiment.

"That ship is my safety net. If you don't come back, I can likely get the vehicle back. But why me? Why not just ask? I'm an easy guy to get along with." That's what Mr. Kaufman, Galaday's manager, said.

"Grace," Moniga said. "Where is she?"

"Somewhere," Galaday said. He didn't know. They had to leave without her best friend. Time ran out. It was everyone go or everyone remain. Staying meant probable death. In the stars they'd have a chance.

Something horrible happened on the ground once they'd lifted off. Galaday could not find out, despite his days trying.

His memories broke, interrupted from a sting as the Feeders burrowed inside. Their teeth took his blood, the wounds they created like small hungry mouths, opened, accepting their little payloads of pure sanguinity.

When the little creatures finished with him, Galaday slept the sleep of the dead.

~

She woke.

He'd been dreaming of setting the Draconia down in the Mojave. She sat next to him wearing a soft white outfit. Galaday was young again. There were people everywhere. Their technology had grown so advanced the devices on the Draconia weren't able to detect them. That's what had happened, come to find. None of it was proven. Just his sleeping imagination manifesting his most desirable scenario. In his dream, Moniga turned to him. She'd been smiling at first, but her face froze. Her eye sockets drooped; her mouth opened. Skin looked like hot wax as it, at first, bulged, and then oozed downward off her face. Underneath, a dark green shell and criss-crossing blood vessels. A noise came from Moniga, part cry, part scream. That's how he knew. Something inside him clicked and he needed to check on her, and Galaday knew he'd find her aware and awake.

Galaday's hunch was correct.

There was Moniga suspended in fluid, waiting.

When their eyes met he could hardly believe himself.

She lived.

She saw.

She reached her arm forward.

Does she recognize me? I must look alien. Nothing like how she last saw me. Maybe she has been able to sense me...see me...all this time. She is staring at me. His heart raced. He felt as though his head might explode. Fear. Why was he afraid?

Moniga looked at Galaday, but he didn't recognize her.

Angry eyes.

Where was her fondness for him? The comfortable familiarity he'd expected? Love?

Missing.

Galaday felt something very wrong about her. His pores felt like they'd tightened. He shut his eyes.

Can't be real. Not like this.

She's turned.

Bad.

Like a dog bit by a snake.

Never the same again.

Agitated. Violated. Desecrated.

Let her out. It'll be all right. Better.

His instinct led his hand.

Commands entered.

He gasped for breath. The room heated. How? Impossible. The Frewer vents were constant. Thousand-year-old technology. Rock solid. Hotter. Air seemed to waver. Galaday felt hot and cold flashes throughout his body.

Can she love me? Again, like she used to? Did so much for one another over the decades. Especially before the trip and the deep sleep. Memories like holofilms. Rye, Playland. New York. Ocean Isle beach. Catching feral cats and bringing them to the no-kill shelter. Swimming with dolphins in Puerto Vallarta. Laughter. Fighting. Laughter again. Her father walking down the aisle, his arm outstretched for hers, his first time on his feet since the accident. In front of everyone. Not a dry eye.

The chamber fell. Impossible. Moniga walked through, her steps grace. The Feeders swarmed around her feet. Her skin paler than he remembered. Nearly clear. Her eyes void. Her soul missing. Had she died and came back? Who was this creature. Galaday searched her face hoping for some recognition of the person he loved. There was none.

Unbearable loud sounds came from what he thought was just outside the Draconia.

Metal bending.

Crushing.

Squeezing.

Under Moniga's feet, the floor caved as though she weighed several thousand kilos.

Galaday tried keeping his balance with his cane, but the harsh movements of the Draconia were too much. He slipped.

Before his head could touch the ground, without a sound, he felt a strong arm catch him.

Moniga.

She swooped him up. His frail body ached. Their eyes met and she smiled. Her mouth opened and he saw several rows of triangular teeth. She clamped down on his throat. He felt pressure, but little pain. As his essence flowed from his neck to her mouth, Galaday became dizzy and everything seemed light. He shut his eyes.

Sound echoed. The Draconia ripped and fell to pieces.

When he opened his eyes, they were outside.

Moniga held him.

The sun crested the moon and lit her from behind. For a brief moment she appeared as he remembered her. Kind. Warm. Beautiful.

Her eyes faded into nothingness.

Three things, moon-sized, hovered near. Their bodies, intricate biologies. Arms stretched out, impossibly curved. In one of their hands, they held the Draconia. The being closed its fingers around the craft.

How could such things exist?

A stream of small things fled from the craft, their dark bodies reflecting red. A river of blood, carried into the abyss. The Feeders.

How are we out here with no breathing apparatuses?

The beings watched them with world-sized eyes.

They fell toward their blue and white home below.

As the friction began, Galaday once again shut his eyes. Burning heat encompassed them, but he still felt her hold.

Let us make it. Let us go through. May we see the surface again, brand new.

Moniga laughed as yellow fire enclosed them, and soon, he heard only the flames, and felt nothing but them, until he felt nothing at all.

Bram Stoker-nominated author **John Palisano** is the author of the acclaimed novel NERVES, as well as over a dozen short stories appearing in markets like the Lovecraft Ezine, Horror Library, Terror Tales, and many more. Check him out at: www.johnpalisano.wordpress.com

BETTER FOR BURNING
H.E. Roulo

"If I were younger I'd join up myself and make a real difference in this world. This is how a man becomes a man." Dad tapped a thick finger against the newspaper in front of him. Crispin's father bragged that he had been the first subscriber, once the colony produced enough fiber to spread information via paper. He used to read sections to them, back when their fledgling planet was still advancing, but these days he just thudded his finger into the rustling gray newsprint. His face grew red as he glared away from his oldest son. "There wouldn't be anything to stop *me* from doing what it took."

Crispin shook soft brown hair out of his eyes. The two-room cabin echoed, as if the wooden walls and the floor Crispin lay on were a box designed to trap them inside with his father's words. The boy's hand slid protectively across the page he'd been working on.

His father wasn't looking directly at him—nothing as obvious as that. He pointed to Crispin's brother Reese, three years younger and just reaching his full height. "Look at you, Reese, you're going to really fill out. You're practically as big as a man."

Crispin dropped his head again and saw that he'd smeared the charcoal drawing. He pulled his sleeve back, shaking off bits of black dust and carefully re-drew the soft curve of his mother's weathered cheek where it touched the cherubic face of his youngest sister.

Clutching the page, he clambered to his feet and held the drawing out to his mother. When she didn't take it, he held it in front of her so she could look without disturbing the baby. He bit his lip and waited. She pulled a smile from somewhere and nodded. Her eyes told him that she liked the picture. Behind him, his father's chair skidded back and footsteps thudded as he rounded the table.

His father snatched the page and barely glanced at it. "You should wash your hands, son. All you boys!"

Crispin nodded. "Yes, sir."

He joined Reese and Sammy at the sink, letting the water run for a moment to clear itself. The pipes chugged softly and water finally fell in a thin clear stream. Reese shoved, pressing his belly to the sink to reach water and soap first, smirking at the advantage his bulk gave him over his older brother. Crispin pretended not to notice.

When it was his turn he rubbed the soap carefully along the side of his hand where the dark charcoal had left powdery smudges, then along his palm and knuckles. The hard soap bar scraped dully without producing lather, but got his hands clean. He then used his soapy hands to rub Sammy's and put them under the bite of the cold-water stream.

At the table his father had picked up the paper again. Crispin took his sister from Mother so she could serve the food. They said a silent prayer and waited. Father frowned as he divided the bread and potatoes into portions. Hot yeast and cool butter scented the air.

Crispin's portion wasn't the largest, wasn't even as large as Reese's. Hunger tightened his belly with a sharp pang, as if something bit him. He hunched over his aching stomach and couldn't hide a resentful glance. His father caught it, sensitive to this sudden rebellion. His large hands smacked the table, making everyone jump. The baby awoke in her highchair and began to cry. Crispin bowed his head over his plate, letting soft hair slide over his face.

Looking down at all of them, and at the small piles of food, his father's rage poured out. "You can't say I don't feed you. You want to do something about it? Get out there and break the blockades. Bring back the economy, why don't you? Get some fresh seed in here for the fields. There's only so much a man can do."

Mother made soothing sounds from the other side of the table but he wouldn't be calmed. "It's those aliens out there! They've taken all the jobs a decent man can do, and then they get us in this war. If I didn't have the lot of you to support, I could do something about it. But I've got six mouths to feed, and on what? You want portions as big as your brother's? If you did some real work you'd fill out and I'd say you needed a man's portion."

Crispin cleaned his plate, as they all did.

That night he lay on his thin mattress while hunger clawed at his stomach. Problems swam in his mind. He wanted to be grown up, to do the work his father mentioned.

Eventually, he made the decision his father wanted. He'd join the Federated Army. Reyle wasn't even part of the Federation, but he could run away and join so he could fight the enemy and break the blockade. Maybe they needed someone who could sketch. Maybe he'd learn not to be so discontented. There would be food, and he'd get exercise to fill out, like his Dad said.

~

Crispin sat up in sweaty sheets. He'd been having fever dreams about home again, although he hadn't talked to his family more than once a year in the last five years.

He rubbed his face, stubble rasping, and remembered how he'd joined up the day after his decision. He'd said goodbye to his brothers, mother, and his father. The baby had been too little to really say goodbye. His father had been proud, blown up in the chest, and had slapped Crispin on his thin back. It stung, but made the tears he'd been fighting go away so Crispin was glad for the ache. He hadn't hugged his mother, deciding he was too mature for that. She'd cried into the baby's hair.

Crispin sat forward on the metal bed to flex an arm, feeling the tight sinews clench. Three square meals a day and hours of training had hardened him until he barely recognized himself in the mirror. He was still lanky, but firm like tightly strung piano wire. His fine brown hair had been cut short, so it never fell in his eyes. He had some new scars, too.

His hands, calloused and blunt now, pulled back the dressing that adhered to his side. A smooth red ribbon was all that was left of the laser shot that had taken him out. He'd been in full combat armor, slow but forceful, ransacking a moon base when the beam sliced through armor into his side. He'd still gotten to the command center, blasted through with his squad, and turned off the life support. With the hole in his suit he'd figured he'd go fast, but the durapatch they'd slapped over the wound must have held long enough to get back to the troop carrier and to the orbiting battle ship. All-in-all, not a bad time. He thought of how he'd share the exploit with the others. Maybe Crissy in Blue Squad would like to look at his scar.

A wolfish grin still flitted around his gray eyes as a medical technician entered followed by someone unfamiliar, but Crispin needed only to see the rank indicators lined in a row up his sleeve to jump to his feet.

"Sit down, no need for that in the clinic," the man said gruffly. Crispin settled back into a sitting position since he'd been ordered to, but his back stayed straight. He gazed forward.

"Recovering nicely, I see. No surprise there. You're always up for more action, eh? I've read your record, and you've been a trooper." He didn't take breaths between sentences or seem to expect any response from Crispin. "Thought you'd be interested in volunteering for something special.

"This medic can explain it all to you. Don't ask me for the technical details. Knew all I needed to when they explained it could make a super-soldier. The best ever. That's got your attention, eh?"

Crispin glanced over at the technician, a pale figure who fiddled with a digital tablet. Maybe he was checking Crispin's status, or perhaps he was just nervous. Crispin turned his steely eyes back as the man spoke again, "Complicated process involved: speeds up your metabolism, your recuperative powers, ups the strength and reflexes. Better night vision, naturally, and I'm told there are camouflage properties to the skin, although I'd like to see that for myself."

The technician's enthusiastic pride apparently compelled him to interrupt. "Oh yes sir! We've developed a process where your own melanin can darken or lighten the skin. No fancy colors, right, not a man-sized chameleon . . . Sorry, sir."

"Right then, it also lets you forage better so you don't need as many supplies. Accidental find, actually, all part of some natural infection we've been able to engineer further. Science relies on fortuitous accidents quite a bit, eh?"

The technician remained wisely silent under this criticism.

The pause invited comment. Crispin barely let his eyes flicker to the other man. "Sir, it sounds like a ground troop force?"

"That's right," the other said warmly. "We'll hit their bases and drive the enemy out of their own homes. It will be a new force, elite and swift moving. You'll be more aggressive, too. We'll give you the mental training to be the soldier we need. You'll love it—the thrill of battle. We need good men. You'd like that, eh?"

Crispin wondered why the man insisted on telling him what he'd like.

"You're from an independent colony, aren't you? Re—,"

"Reyle," Crispin supplied. "Yes, I still have family there."

"Outer world. They should accept Federation protection. Wouldn't want to let the enemy get to them. Imagine the kiddies back home. You'd be doing everyone a favor."

Crispin thought of his mother and father, and his siblings still struggling to survive on the meager existence they could eke out. He sent them funds sometimes. He'd sent a shipment of vegetable starts and seeds to his father, also, but with blockades there wasn't any way to tell if they'd gotten through. He hadn't talked to them in over a year.

"I'd like it, sir. I'd make a fine super-soldier. I'll be the best man you've got."

"Yes, I expect so. Sign here." The officer made a gesture and someone entered the room. He grabbed Crispin in a blurred instant and a burning sensation pierced his neck and shoulder. He cried out and fell limp.

"He's infected," someone said. "We'll see if it takes."

~

Crispin made the change. It took time, weeks or months he was never quite sure. They pushed his body to its natural limits and then beyond. He woke up in a hospital bed aboard ship, like last time, but could feel the difference in himself.

The overhead light stung Crispin's eyes, so he broke it. The spaceship's red emergency lights took over, dim and indirect. A look in the mirror showed how much he'd changed. He stared into his jet black eyes, and as he concentrated his face skin darkened. Stepping close to the mirror, he tore off his hospital gown, leaving only his boxers. As he focused, darkness filled in the sharp muscles of his torso, like oils swirling to the surface from deep within him.

He cocked his head, listening. With newly acute hearing, he detected hushed footfalls in the hallway.

The technician jumped when he entered the room and found Crispin's black eyes watching him from the hospital bed. Crispin's muscles quivered, eager to move again. He'd barely thought about returning to his narrow bunk before he'd been there. Strength and power made him clench the muscles in his bare arms, studying their bulge and flex.

The technician inched around the room. He checked the light and saw it wasn't just off, but broken. A shiver ran through the thin, weak shoulder bones protruding against the white material of his lab coat.

He turned to Crispin with a faltering smile. "We thought you'd still be asleep."

Crispin looked back without smiling.

"Do you feel different?"

"Yes." The sound of his voice contained nuances he hadn't heard before. He modulated it. "I'm feeling quite good. Powerful." He rose to his feet with the final word.

The technician blinked, as if his eyes hadn't quite tracked the swift movement. Sweat glimmered on his forehead in the dim light. "Well, that's really good. There's training for you and your new squad. You'll get used to all your new abilities." The man's sweat smelled tart in the tiny sealed room. They were somewhere in the base of the ship, Crispin felt, and he could almost sense other figures in the rooms beside and above him. The warmth off the technician drew him a step closer. The tiny man looked so weak to Crispin, so pathetic and unable to take care of himself that Crispin felt bad for him. Was this how he'd looked to his father?

Crispin licked dry lips. "I'm a little thirsty."

"Oh, god!" The technician dodged for the door.

Crispin stopped him without conscious thought. He held the man by his lab coat, puzzled. "Why are you running?"

The technician whined pitifully.

The door opened and two armored Security with stun batons entered. They must have been monitoring the room.

Still puzzled, but not afraid, Crispin didn't try to hurt them, but when they moved against him he felt satisfaction as he tossed the technician aside to meet their challenge. A moment later the two guards lay with their helmets smashed.

The technician gave up whimpering on the floor to dash out the open door into the hallway. Crispin checked the bodies of the prone men. The first one was quite dead. The second one wasn't, but bled from a wound on his temple where he'd hit the floor. A vivid pool of red sent crisp tangy notes into the air. Crispin put a finger into the liquid and brought it to his lips. He was very thirsty.

When he left the room, the second man was also dead.

Crispin took one step out the door into the hall and found the military officer there again, flanked by two other men. They weren't Security, Crispin knew, because they didn't have the helmets and batons, but his hackles rose at the sight of them and he swallowed a growl.

The officer lifted a gray eyebrow. "He won't understand if I tell him to stop, but he'll understand if you stop him," he said to the two strangers.

Crispin met their charges with a vicious glee. The first man pounded Crispin's shoulders with heavy blows, forcing him to bend forward like a charging bull ready to gore his opponent. The second man caught his arms, trapping him. He lunged with bared teeth, wanting to bite, but they were as swift as he was. The first man caught his chin, lifting Crispin. Hands trapped and neck twisted as if ready to break, Crispin stared into the man's gleaming black eyes. The soldier malevolently glared back.

His captors were like him, super-soldiers.

"We'll take it from here," the one holding him said in a smooth timbered voice. He wiped Crispin's mouth and met the midnight stare. "He's one of us now."

~

There was war. In fact, there was nothing but war now. Crispin paused in the laughing flicker of a burning building and raised his head to sniff the air. It smelled good, better than the air on the ship but all planets had air that smelled better. This night smelled particularly good. He found what he was looking for, the trace scent of hiding figures, and sprang across the open square to the next building where they must be concealed. His leap scared them into the open, a screaming mess of noise and hysteria that he quickly silenced. The crackle of the buildings and the sounds of his mates killing in the distance were all he heard here. It was another night with an especially simple mission. They were here to burn and pillage. They would cause terror to the enemy, the special terror that his kind could bring. And news would spread.

He let his skin darken and faded into the night shadows around him. Something in the distance pulled him past the breaking windows and hopeless cries. He ran. It seemed the fights were endless, finally coming close together with only forgettable troop movements in between. The chill wind of the dark planets and the hot flesh of the enemy filled him.

He raced through the streets on silent feet. Quick now, never weighted down by heavy battle armor since he could strike before an enemy could fire, could dodge whatever they launched at him. He'd been injured, surely all soldiers were injured, but he barely bled and there were ways to replace it. His light-sensitive eyes avoided the flare of more flames and he skirted the empty buildings. They'd probably had the sense to set up a barricade somewhere by now. Predictably, they'd think they could hold out. Crispin bit his lip and let instinct take him. It pulled him along feverishly, filling him until he found more people, a whole cluster of them, huddled in a lone building outside the proper edges of the small town. He entered easily and the small ones were the first to go. The victory of it filled him with power. He had been through it all, but the thrill didn't wear off. He finished almost instantly with one combatant, soft and unable to hurt him, and turned to find only one left standing.

A flicker of puzzlement shivered down his spine. This was different. Why was the prey speaking instead of running or fighting? Crispin opened his awareness to the man's words. They weren't in standard but he recognized the dialect. What dialect was it, Reylan? He rose from his crouch, a surge of recognition piercing him. The man had said his name.

"Crispin, my God, Crispin."

He looked around himself. It was a wooden house, his wooden house. He stared at the broken bodies of his siblings. And there lay Mother. The Federated Army had changed wars, switched sides, and he'd never even realized. He was now fighting against his people. His family?

"Dad?" Crispin asked, bloodlust fading. He stared at the aged figure of the man in front of him. His father had always been thick, but now he was bent at the shoulders. His hair had gone gray and thinned. Had it been so long that his father had grown old? He hadn't thought of his family since his change.

"Stay away from me! What you are now, it isn't my son," Dad yelled, fumbling in the bureau behind him.

"It's me, Dad, I'm a soldier."

"No boy of mine! No soldier! You're not even a man." Dad was crying, and furious, and his hands had found a weapon. The shotgun he'd kept for years. He pointed it and pulled the trigger.

Crispin stood over his father's body in the first real conscious thought he'd had in many years. He stared around the room as if looking for answers. That must be Reese, fully-grown and still living here to look after them. The woman could be Reese's wife, or maybe his baby sister. What had her name been?

He crossed to the faucet to wash his face and hands. On the wall above the sink was a faded piece of paper. His specialized eyes could see it clearly in the dark. It was the sketch of his mother and Anna. The baby had been named Anna.

He wondered with a sort of remote horror whether his mother had recognized him, there at the end.

The water chugged fitfully before starting in a thin stream. Crispin rinsed his mouth and spat into the sink. The sketch looked tiredly back at him.

He lit the house on fire, with their bodies and the sketch still inside. The wood ignited as if it had always been more suited to burning than living in. He moved away from the smoke and waited for feelings. They didn't come easily. Finally, he had a thought he wanted to share with his father.

You're right, Dad, he thought to himself, I'm not a man. A man would have stood there and let you shoot him for what he'd done. But what I've become is something different.

Heather Roulo is a Pacific Northwest horror, fantasy, and science-fiction author. Her short stories have appeared in more than a dozen anthologies, podcasts, and magazines including *Nature* and *Flagship*. In 2009 her science-fiction podcast novel *Fractured Horizon* was a Parsec Award Finalist and she received the Wicked Women Writers award from HorrorAddicts.net. Heather is the co-founder of Podioracket.com, an indie author interview podcast. Find her on twitter @hroulo or at www.facebook.com/heroulo. Her website is www.heroulo.com.

I WAS THERE...
Tarl Hoch

I was there when the vampire council was shattered.
It was on a planet known as Gabriel 5; a dead world in a dead system. A planet of ash and ruins, it was once the capital of a race long dead before mankind even glanced at the stars. From the shattered bones of their empire, we created our own when we fled Earth.

The humans had expanded so fast that the great clans, all five of them, fled to the stars on ships of black steel and fangs of flame. Our exodus brought those of us that remained out into the open, and as we had expected, the humans panicked. Hunts, lynching, even open warfare abounded. Generations of positive propaganda to try and spin a positive view of our kind, gone in a matter of months.

The clans found the dead systems, their stars red like overfed mosquitoes in the blackness of space. Territories were made, fought for, won and lost before we settled. We were lords again, with our own hierarchies. Trade was in slaves, some brought with us, others captured as mankind spread out among the stars. The humans suspected we were there, but had no proof.

Life was good, for a time.

But, like the humans we had once been, we fell to boredom. With boredom came bickering, feuding, wars. Politics became a vicious and bloody affair. Territories changed hands and among the chaos the humans found us. Their warships found our homes and slew entire colonies. It was among this that the council decided to meet on Gabriel 5. Artisans had created tombs, mausoleums, crypts among the alien architecture and rubble, an entire planet devoted to the artistic representation of death. The air was flaked with fat hunks of ash from where the ground cracked down to its very molten core. The fires consuming buried organic matter that the aliens left behind.

The entire place reeked of death.

I loved it.

Of course we were the first to arrive. We were the First of the five after all, most noble of the clans. Our heritage was pure; we could trace it back to the eldest among us.

My name was Costel Gogoasa then.

I remembered watching the cutters slice across the sky, black needles barbed with scythe wings and edged in crimson. The sound they made as they sliced through the atmosphere reminded me of a blade elegantly parting flesh. It was glorious.

We marched from our landers before the backwash had settled, each of us in step with the other, drilled to perfection. We were armed with newly minted weapons, the metal bright and unmarked. I had heard rumours about them of course, and my finger itched against the trigger guard. I wanted to turn it on one of my brothers just to see the effects. Loyalty, brotherhood and rigid discipline stayed my finger.

Oh what a sight we were. Rows of shining black body suits with plates of red covering our vitals. Storm coats of darkness given form cloaked us; each one writhed and snapped as we walked. Masks covered our faces, goggles red as vitae and mouth pieces molded into snarling gargoyle muzzles.

At our head marched Narcisa Ruicu.

She was a beauty of the old world. Where our suits were black with red plate, hers was crimson upon crimson, the plates molded to show off everything. Narcisa moved like a mercury serpent, each gesture, every step flawless. I had seen her slaves cry at the merest sight of her. If I lived as long as she had, perhaps I too would gain a measure of that grace and beauty. She was, after all, the blood font that we all came from among our clan. She was our queen, and our mother.

As we reached the center of the dead city there stood a massive dais of black stone. Narcisa approached it. This was where the meeting of the clans would take place.

Floating spectres guarded its perimeter; great cloaked floating things twice as tall as a man. As she neared, the closest one raised its hood-shrouded head towards her, a hiss echoing from the infinite darkness within.

"Narcisa..." it turned its cowl as if looking at her from another angle. No one truly knew what they were; they existed on Earth and had somehow followed us to the stars when we fled.

"Let me pass." Narcisa's voice was feminine steel.

There was a sound from among the figures that sounded like spikes dragged on concrete. It took me a while to realize it was laughter.

"The others are not here." It motioned back to the troops behind her. "Wait with your children until the others arrive."

Narcisa's hands went to her hips, her black nails striking against the pale flesh of her fingers. She looked as if she might argue with them, perhaps even fight them. But I had seen them in action before, and though a match for one, maybe two, even our queen could not hold off all present. One thing we had learned from immortality; once you had it, you were very careful about throwing it away carelessly. Instead, Narcisa turned away. With a motion, her slaves brought forth a floating throne which she reclined onto. A slave poured her blood—real human blood—from which she sipped. I could smell it, even above the cloying stink of death. It wasn't the synthetic crap they had been feeding us rank and file troopers. Slaves were worth a lot of money and their blood even more so. I think more than one tongue licked along pointed fangs behind their masks at that moment.

A crack of thunder crawled across the landscape capturing our attention. Rolling clouds of ash and dust parted in the distance as a spear of light shattered the darkness of the world. Thankfully we wore goggles, though more than one of us turned our eyes away from the glare. I knew without looking that there would be a disk of white steel hovering at the apex of that light.

Narcisa watched the beam without any protection from its harsh rays, a testament to her age. But just when I thought I couldn't handle any more, it vanished. A bright after-image stung my eyes and I felt blood pool at the corners and blinked the crimson away.

Shortly after that, the first figure came through the ruins and around us to breach the clearing. Against the blackness of ruin they were specks of radiance.

Their leader was Atra-Hasis. We knew him well, for he was Lord of the Watchers. He was tall, easily close to seven feet. Hair so blond it was almost white fell around his shoulders in heavy dreadlocks. He was pale, paler than anyone I had ever seen among our people. Around his shoulders hung a thick cloak of feathers, goose white speckled with black raven.

They had once been angels to early man. No one knew who created them or where they came from. They had lived among the mountains, near the cradle of civilization, until modern man forced them to flee. Eyes the colour of a virgin sky scanned over our troops before finally coming to rest on Narcisa. Behind the angel came his warriors, each in white, cloaks of feathers close to their bodies. Only the Lord carried anything resembling a weapon, a crystal white staff clutched in one flawless hand.

"Narcisa."

"Atra-Hasis, it's good to see you again."

"Lies."

Narcisa chuckled, raising an elegant finger to her lips. "How right you are. The last time was-"

"Salem."

"You were so late, as always."

The man's eyes narrowed further as he came to a halt. His troops strung out behind him and I smiled behind my mask; we out-numbered them five to one.

Atra-Hasis was either very confident in his men, or they had some form of weapon we hadn't seen yet. Either way, I was more confident in our new hardware and our numbers. Each of us were hand-picked from Narcisa's top troops. These pristine chickens would fall before our might if it came down to it.

The Watchers stood as still as we did, the ash falling from the sky leaving a slight film on the white of their uniforms. All except their leader, who somehow remained as radiant as the moment he stepped into the clearing.

"Where are the others?"

Narcisa set her goblet down and dabbed at her lips with a crimson cloth. "Late, as usual. No doubt scanning us as we speak to see what kind of threat we are before landing."

"I am no threat to any of you."

My leader smiled. I knew her well enough. She didn't believe the leader of the Watchers. The Watchers contained the highest number of elders in the five clans. That alone showed their skill and talent for survival where others had long ago burned to ash. We still had numbers and weapons however.

"Come on, Atra, we were lovers once...I know you better than this."

The Watcher's eyes tightened a fraction. The news shocked me and I heard the shuffle of steps as more than one set of boots shifted. The great Narcisa had bedded with Atra-Hasis? My heart burned with a jealousy that I had no right to feel. The leather of my gloves crinkled as my grip tightened on my weapon.

Bestial forms erupted to the right of our clan. They crawled from the shadows of buildings, from beneath the streets, from the very darkness itself. They were the monsters of a child's nightmare. Wolves mixed with bats and reptiles, they rose even taller than the Watcher Lord. Muscles like iron cables flexed with their movements as they stalked forward. Mouths hung open, jagged fangs like broken glass gleaming from their stinking depths. They hissed to each other, snapped and growled like animals as they stalked forward.

Oh yes, our wayward cousins, the Hunters.

Their leader was a king among monsters. Had he stood straight he would have easily been almost double Atra-Hasis's height. But he crawled forward on a bent spine, more like the beast he resembled than the once noble creature he had been.

Condorcanqui, the Destroyer, the Hell Spawn, the Dragon Born. Where Atra-Hasis and his people had been angels to early man, Condorcanqui had become their devil. Each of his brood was different, no two identical, yet all were killers. They came to a halt in a ragged line, snapping at both clans, tiny crimson eyes glaring at us from overhanging brows.

They had come from every culture of mankind, though Condorcanqui had come from the Aztec empire. He had been a god then; we were often mistaken as gods in the old days. However when his people were killed, it was his rage and anger that had turned him into what he was now.

How they had managed to get to the heavens was a mystery. Perhaps they built their own ships, which would show they were smarter than they seemed. Perhaps they hid aboard our ships, which in itself was also terrifying. As neither the Watcher Lord nor my queen had sensed them in the shadows the latter seemed more plausible. A shiver passed down my spine at the thought.

The Destroyer straightened as best he could, his shadow stretching across the ground in crimson light.

"Brother," he growled. Atra-Hasis's eyes traveled head to foot and back again before nodding to Condorcanqui.

"Sister," the monster purred at Narcisa, his forked tongue snaking over his lips. The Queen of the First averted her gaze, but only for a moment. However that brief moment brought a rumble of falling boulders from the creature's chest.

"Demon, I am surprised you are here. I didn't think you were one for politics." Atra-Hassis inspected his gloved fingertip as he spoke, the insult hanging in the air. The Destroyer smiled, the rumble of his laughter echoing around them off the ruins.

"Do not think me some animal," he lowered himself back to a more predatory stance. "Think of me as your nightmare made real. The council meets; I will not be left out."

"Atra, don't harass our brother. He barely has it together as it is," Narcisa turned her gaze to the Watcher. "The last thing I would want to do is have to put his kin down like the rabid dogs they are."

Misshapen throats roared their anger and a few of the Hunters surged forward before their lord's own roar browbeat them back into line. Those that didn't move fast enough received gashes from his massive claws.

"Very clever, sister," the monster wagged a talon at my queen. "I will not break the armistice first. But do not tempt my children. Their patience isn't as strong as mine."

It was then that the elegant landers passed over us. I noticed that our own cutters stayed away. It bothered me that others had brought air support as well but it was expected. Air superiority would be important should hostilities break out.

They landed just out of sight, their down-wash crushing buildings and ruins to rubble. We all watched despite the ash that washed over us, coating our masks and the white of the Watchers.

There was silence as the ash swirled and settled. Then the gurgle of filters and breathing apparatuses announced the arrival of the next clan. I couldn't help but shift to try and see the newcomers.

The Sirens had arrived.

Unlike all of us, even the Destroyer's kin, the Sirens

weren't human. They never had been. Instead they had somehow spawned from a race of water dwellers thought to be myth to mankind. We hadn't even known about them until our kind had started to invade their watery domains. Then they fought back and we learned caution.

They were completely alien to us.

But so, so beautiful.

My first glimpse of the Sirens at the dais was one of their outriders. She was small, even for a woman. Her limbs were thin, her fingers too long, her movements too smooth even out of water. My queen was a majestic being, but compared to the Sirens she was a clumsy, bumbling creature. The outrider wore a bubble helmet, water flowing around her head, strands of hair as fine as seaweed forming a halo about her face.

Large oval eyes in an ovular skull, black as pitch, regarded us. Unblinking, they traced our line before moving on, spines along her back quivered creating a rattling. It must have been a signal because more of her kind came forward.

I noticed at this point that even the Destroyer and his people were silent as the rest of us. The court of the sea came amongst a crowd of gold, blues and greens. Their warriors were brutal things, their bodies altered by unknown science kept hidden from us. They were equal in size to the Destroyer's monsters, though their bodies seemed to grow weapons from their very skin and bones. Giant grab pincers, hard shells, barbs and stingers festooned them as if they themselves were the monsters of the deep.

But it was the women that drew our gazes despite my brain telling me to open fire. They were unaltered, for only their men were put under the knife and needle. The females were the species' pride and remained pure.

They were all armed with long barrelled rifles, various icons and fetishes hanging from their ends. They advanced in their weird way, like poured water over rock, until they took up their position near us. The other lords regarded the Sirens with guarded looks. Suddenly they shifted as if by a command only they heard.

She was here.

If she had a name, we couldn't pronounce it with air-processing vocal cords. More alien than her children, she came across the ground as if her feet never touched it. Long fins spread out from her like the headdress of a lion fish. Barbed fins extended along the outside of her forearms and calves. I had no doubt they contained some kind of toxin that even our immortal bodies would struggle to process if the stories were to be believed.

Eyes like luminous black pearl regarded us from a face almost featureless except for a tiny mouth and the barest hint of a nose slit. Her mouth moved and I saw millions of tiny, crystalline teeth behind the slit of her lips. It was like looking into the face of a primordial hunter.

We were all nervous then. The Sirens had only been encountered in their ships in small numbers. Any contact that met face to face ended in bloodshed that was distinctly one sided. Once I had talked to a member of the Watchers on a way-station, our clans on treaty at that point. We had both glutted ourselves on synthetic blood laced with the real deal and were feeling friendly.

He had told me about a boarding party of Destroyers that had tried to capture a Siren ship. They had clamped their blunt warship to the vessel and burned their way into their holds. Not having to breath held a certain advantage when it came to having to fight underwater.

Apparently even the Destroyer himself would not reportedly talk about what had happened to his people when they met the repelling teams. All the Watcher knew was that the boarding ship was blown free moments later, and space filled with the shredded corpses of the boarding party.

That story came back to me as I watched the Sirens next to us. They were both repellent and beautiful. Some of them regarded us with apparent disinterest, though when my gaze met one of their woman's black eyes, I felt something in me tug towards her. An alien song pulled at my mind, teasing it with long fingers and whispered promises. She would take me to her watery home, wrap her limbs around me, give me a love bite, tear me apart.

I realized I was grinning even as the image of her tearing a chunk of flesh from my wrist swam through my mind. Wrenching my eyes away from hers as she smirked with a lipless mouth, I felt her attention move elsewhere.

I kept my eyes off them from then on.

And they remained there, utterly silent except for the sounds of their breathing aids.

By the First, it was creepy. Even the Destroyer's kin were snarling to each other, their ears turned towards the silent host.

Five clans.

One more had yet to appear.

I looked around, hoping my superior officer wouldn't notice.

That was when the final clan made their appearance.

They came like lanterns born by grave diggers through the mist. Bobbing lights, slowly moving through the ruins as they advanced on us. My goggles flickered through various enhancements and even with my vampiric sight I couldn't see who bore the light poles until they were almost upon us.

Then the thick ash parted as if it was a curtain, and there they were.

It was a neat trick, lost after the appearance of the Sirens, but still neat.

A single fox sat in the last section, tail swaying slowly behind her. I was under no delusions that she was simply a fox. Lights continued to bob around her, though if they were distant, or right beside her, I couldn't gauge. The vulpine cocked its head to the side as if curious. Large ears perked as it looked at each of the lords, one by one, even the Siren's queen.

And then, like a hand brushed across a drawing made of sand, she was no more and in her place stood a beautiful

Asian woman. The glowing balls had also vanished, smeared across the ash to be replaced with various men, women and foxes.

Aneko Tsukamoto.

As I said it in my mind, the words left Atra-Hassis's lips before he spit onto the dead earth as if it soiled his tongue to speak her name.

Her head turned to light her gaze on him, molten gold almond eyes blinking slowly. She was dressed in a clash of styles that caused the eye to wander over her as if lost in a dream turned nightmare.

The kin of the fox queen were dressed in a variety of outfits that spoke of ancient Japan as well as modern space faring fashion. Each was unique, and each bore a weapon of some design, current or ancient, on open display like the rest of us. Raiders, pirates, mercenaries, they had the most contact with humans since we had fled. I couldn't blame them however; their tastes ran differently than ours. They didn't drink blood.

They drank lust.

I almost felt sorry for them.

"Tsukamoto." My queen was the first to greet her, her voice shattering the eerie silence that descended when the Sirens had appeared. Now it seemed impossibly loud, a shard of glass shattering against stone.

"Ruicu." The woman nodded her head to my queen. "Your last gift was most enjoyable, my people found the puzzle box to be...enlightening. There were such sights to see, such experiences to explore."

"I'm glad I could break the dreariness of eternity, if only for a moment, Tsukamoto. Your return gift was also enjoyable, and well worth the loss of the box."

There was a pause and I couldn't help but notice that the lord of the Watchers glanced at the queen of the Sirens. It lingered a bit too long for my taste and I hoped my queen had noticed.

"So the humans..." Aneko stepped forward, the wraiths moving away from the pedestal to vanish into the ash. The woman paid them no heed. Instead she mounted the steps with small, dainty steps. Her people stayed back, though I saw that their hands had moved closer to their weapons, however slight it had been.

"That is why we are here, isn't it?" She stood at the top now, brushing some of the ash from her clothing.

"That's exactly why we are here, Fox-woman." Atra-Hassis was next up the steps. The edge of his cloak swirled the fallen ash around him like the wake behind a sea predator. "They attacked one of my colonies a month ago. Their scout ships are unnervingly well armed, as are their warriors."

My queen rose to her feet from where she reclined. Tossing her goblet to the ground, she marched forward. "Finding the rodent-cattle to be too much for your pacifists, Atra?"

He turned to her as she mounted the top of the dais, her heels clicking on the stone. "You yourself have had half a score of attacks on your own territory, or have you been lying to me?"

Narcisa grinned, flashing her fangs. "The attacks are truth my dear, but unlike your people, I turned them back with fire and fang."

The Destroyer growled low in his chest as he reached the top of the dais. "They are bold."

"They seek to crowd us out like they did on Earth." Atra-Hassis spreads his arms wide as the Siren queen joins them, a small, stunted creature beside her feet.

"I will not give up these new lands like I did my beloved ocean." The stunted creature's voice was that of a nymph, high and haunting. How it knew the Siren's words without her even speaking, I did not want to know. Instead I watched as her hand caressed along its head barbs like a master with a favoured hound.

I don't think anyone expected the Siren to speak during

the meeting and they all stared at her a moment before turning back to each other. Again there was that lingering look between Atra-Hassis and the Siren queen as theirs were the last pair of eyes to part.

"Yet they encroach upon us time and time again." The Watcher Lord motions to each of the lords. "It's just like Earth. Only this time they're evolving faster, their technology growing at a rate we cannot match."

"Their mortality gives them urgency," the Siren queen stated.

The Destroyer snapped his jaws, his claws digging into the stone under him. "What is technology over the claw, over fangs, over immortality?"

"You are a fool, Condorcanqui. What are fang and claw over lances of light, plasma as hot as the sun, or blades sharp enough to cut through the very molecules themselves?" My queen turns away from the monster. "We have become lax in our pursuit of technology. Our long lives are turning into our biggest downfall."

To everyone's surprise, the Siren queen nods, head barbs quivering. "The vampire queen is correct. They are surpassing even our own glorious technology which was old even when the world was young."

"Weaklings," growls Condorcanqui.

"What says you, Tsukamoto? You've had the most contact with them." My queen looks to the Asian woman.

Aneko waited as she seemed to contemplate the question. My hands tightened further on my weapon to the point where they were starting to hurt. Something felt wrong and I couldn't tell what. I had been to a couple of my queen's meetings before and there was always politics involved on many levels. But this, this felt different, wrong.

"I have seen this technology," Aneko finally spoke. "Ruicu is right, the humans are nothing if not ingenious in their varied ways to kill and wage war. Their ships are starting to match our own. I will admit that it has gotten harder to raid their fleets and supply lines. Though we are still superior to them, I fear it is only a matter of time before they surprise us. And it will be our last."

"My people have watched the Homo Sapiens since the beginning of their kind. We have watched them become what they are, and have seen the way they create." The Watcher Lord placed both of his hands on his staff. "To think such a simple and superstitious people could have created all they have."

"You forget that you were once human, as were all of us." Narcisa echoed my own thoughts. It wasn't something we liked to think about. When we changed from human to vampire, something altered. Perhaps it was a survival mechanism to allow us to feed from those we once were. Perhaps it was the stress of the change or the new found immortality. Whatever it was, we felt little to no compassion towards what had been our own kind.

Atra-Hassis scowled, his peaceful face turning ugly, and for the first time I saw his fangs. Delicate things, two upper and lower pairs.

"Speak for yourself," the Siren queen's creature stated. "We were never one of your barbaric kind. You infested our world as the monkeys have infested yours because of your careless feeding."

I could feel the vibrations coming from the Hunters. Their eyes were locked on the Siren with sheer hatred and want of bloodshed. I had a feeling I wasn't the only one that felt as if something was going to happen. Atra-Hassis gazed at his staff for a moment before continuing.

"Despite our histories, the humans must be dealt with. That is why the council is meeting, that is what we are here to decide. They can't be allowed to drive us from the stars. They are too bold, too defiant. Like the children they are, they are ignorant to the dangers which they play. I've had enough of them pulling the tiger's tail. It is time it turned around and reminded them why they fear the dark."

"So cliché." My queen shook her head. "But I agree. The humans must be dealt with."

Aneko placed her hands on her hips. "Despite my dealings with them, they must be taught respect."

"Rend, tear, destroy. Let us drink from rivers of their blood, let us-"

"Then we agree," the Siren queen said. "What would you all suggest?" Shifting, the Siren's robes made a whisper of sound across the rock and her warriors shifted position. Some of my brethren were whispering across the radio link, their words barely reaching my hearing. They were nervous. But I expected more chatter from them, not the hushed words I was getting. Here and there I heard our commanding officers hissing orders to silence the channels.

Through it all, I watched the lords and ladies of my kind. If something was going to happen, they would start it. Be it a hand flick, a glance, a certain word, their people wouldn't make a move without their leader making the first.

"Steal their technology?" Aneko smiled, flashing fangs more akin to a fox than a true vampire. "With it we could turn it against them."

Narcisa snorted and I clenched my jaw. This wasn't good. "Steal from them? We are not pirates like you, Aneko, we have class."

As one, the barrels of our weapons shifted slightly, raising towards the fox-kin. Their own hands moved to rest on their various arms, their gazes trying and failing to meet our goggled eyes. There was an advantage to going masked to something like this.

The Fox woman smiled, her fangs peeking over her lips. A faint luminescence shone behind those golden eyes as she regarded the queen of the First. This wasn't good, this wasn't good at all. I could almost feel the alliance that had existed at the start of this meeting crumbling around us.

Again the look between the Siren and the Lord of the Watchers. Only the Destroyer seemed uncaring of what was happening, more intent on thinking about the bloodlust he would unleash on the humans no doubt.

"How would you suggest we deal with them then, Narcisa?" The Asian woman examined her fingernails before meeting my queen's eyes.

Narcisa chuckled. "The only thing one can do."

"What do you mean by that?" Atra-Hassis snarled.

The Siren queen turned to regard my lady as well. The Queen of the First smiled. "You haven't figured it out, have you? What is the one thing we have done through the ages that has worked time and time again?"

Glances were shared between the other lords and ladies and Narcisa laughed. The kin of each of the clans shifted and I couldn't help but eye each of them in turn. They were eying each other, watching for anything out of turn.

"Stop speaking in riddles woman!" Atra-Hassis took a step forward and Narcisa turned sharply to face him, her teeth bared.

"Do not dare threaten me, Atra of the weak hearted!"

The Destroyer roared and the Hunters echoed it. Weapons shifted to point in their general direction as they snapped at the air with drooling muzzles. "Enough!" Their lord's words echoed off the stone. "War is the only way!"

"Agreed." The Siren's puppet sang.

"We are in an alliance of sorts...my brethren." Aneko's eyes twinkled.

Narcisa Ruicu turned and smiled at us, eyes dancing.

A voice I didn't recognize came over the com link and ordered us to open fire. Weapons rose from among our ranks and did just that. Light arced from the barrels and earthed among our own kind as well as the kin of the other council.

My gun stood frozen in my hands as I watched my own brothers fire upon their kin, both of our queen and the other clans.

The Destroyer's were the first to act to the sudden attack. With roars they rushed the others, maws gaping with ropes of saliva, fangs bared. The Sirens were next, their easy grace lighting quick as their long-barrelled rifles rose and unleashed flashes of hard rounds. I watched as one of my queen's still-loyal warriors took a round in the chest.

And then I knew the horror that was the Siren's weapons. What had been a hard projectile was really some sort of sea crustacean, or cephalopod; I couldn't tell even as it burrowed through the chest plate of my companion and into the flesh and bone beneath. He screamed as I fired at the Siren's people, the light taking down one of the women as she tried to avoid another blast. Her helmet exploded as the water flash boiled, lethal razor-sharp shards lancing out to take down one of her kin that was too close.

The males of their clan were busy with the Destroyer's beasts, thundering blows and rocking blasts shattering the very stone around the clash of giants. Crustacean pincers closed on brutish limbs and tore the very muscle from bone while gore-encrusted claws cracked open carapace and muzzle devoured the soft meat inside.

Aneko Tsukamoto's people were among us in moments, blades and guns cutting into us as often as our own weapons caught them. Their forms rippled between balls of lethal light, foxes and their human bodies. I watched as a warrior of ours was enveloped in one of the ghost lights, the skin burning off his body before falling to join the ash below.

I whirled, my gun lancing a shot into one of the foxes, the fur catching fire as the beast howled. Flesh cooked off of the vulpine even as I rammed the stock of my gun into the snarling face of a warrior in a kimono that came at me with a katana. She managed to slice my face, which is how I got this scar; but in return I rammed my combat blade into her heart.

Sparing a glance I saw white warriors among the rear of Aneko's force, their movements calm as they muttered and raised strange stones. Light brighter than anything I have known burned through the red sunlight and burned Aneko's warriors where they stood. It was like watching their bones catch fire and the body being consumed from within.

I had fired off a few more shots, mostly at Aneko's warriors even as the Siren's weapons buzzed and hissed past my head in multi-limbed blurs. My communication link was filled with confused orders and I watched as two of my clan gunned down a third in our colors.

What madness was this?

That was when a crack rent the air and for a moment we all looked to the dais. It was like watching gods at war.

They were blurs, shapes that would pause for a moment as if frozen before moving again. Even with my enhanced sight and the information the goggle had fed me, I could still only catch bits and pieces of what was going on.

The Destroyer had gone after The Watcher Lord, the two a smear of white and black. True to his nature, Condorcanqui was on the offensive. His body shifted with each attack. Bones tore through his skin to shape claws or calcified armour in the blink of an eye when Atra-Hassis's staff lashed out to foil the attacks. Flares of light exploded as the staff struck the altered bone. If the Destroyer noticed he didn't show it as he snapped his jaws shut where the Watcher had been a heartbeat before.

The other three were in standstill. My lady weaving impossibly fast around the swipes of barbed fins from the Siren while Aneko's blades passed terribly close to my lady's pristine skin. That did not mean the Siren and Aneko weren't trading blows. As The Siren's blade passed the queen of the First it hissed past the fox woman's face, her eyes glowing like the sun. Aneko's pistol roared and the Siren barely moved as the rounds lanced off over the heads of her people.

Something crashed into the side of my helmet and I tumbled before getting my feet under me. I came up, gun still in my grip, right goggle lens cracked. One of the Hunters was among our troops, muzzle dripping with oil-thick crimson. I opened fire, arks of light burning away patches of fur and muscle even as others reacted to its presence.

Its roar shook my very bones and it managed another

couple steps forward before its head exploded, multiple arks striking it there and annihilating the brain.

I turned to look at how the others fared even as a large disk roared over the battle.

It was a Watcher ship.

Everything human-kind had attributed to visitors from other worlds has to do with them. They had the technology long before any of us, and as it hovered above the battle I felt the fang-rattling hum of a number of batteries charging. Lights danced on its underside and an uncharacteristic cheer went up from its brethren on the ground. The angels pushed forward, their strange lances of light striking among Aneko and my people. The righteous fury on their faces turned their angelic features horrific in the stark light of their weapons.

I had thought that they would be my death.

But explosions rocked the saucer as the barbed darts of our own fighters flashed past, munitions smashed and pierced its hull. The hum of the saucer's weapons died as the ship started lifting.

The cheer this time was from the First even as our ships became engaged by the Siren's strange organic vessels. Like ocean predators they moved through the atmosphere with a deadly grace. Bone spears and bio weapons holed the Watcher saucer even as they dissolved and damaged our own ships. Thankfully when the saucer finally hit the ground, it demolished numerous blocks away from us. Though the ash cloud it kicked up swept over us a moment later.

It was like fighting in a nightmare. Figures moved in and out of the blowing ash like phantoms. A fox-woman came at me through the darkness, her blade flashed like lightning. I was already moving, leaning back under the blade before the return strike with my combat knife sliced along her cheek. She snarled like an animal before turning into a killing wisp. But I was already gone, her light retreating into the dark as I ran.

One of my brother warriors appeared in front of me on the ground, a Siren bitch trying to bring her gun to bear on his prone form. She saw me too late as I brought my gun to my shoulder and fired. The blast took her in the chest, her screech making me fall to one knee even as her body cooked. The warrior under her rose, shoving the body aside as I shook the siren's voice from my mind.

"Thank you." The unknown warrior said as his barrel swung up towards me.

Almost too late I realized the danger I was in and lashed out with my blade. It took him behind the leg, the tip tearing into the calf muscle. He squeezed the trigger and I wove to the side as the caged lightning flashed past me and into the darkness. The soldier fell to his knees even as I rammed my elbow into the base of his helmet. He clutched at my own as my knife found his breastbone.

I felt the blade hit the dirt of the earth under my brother warrior.

He snarled something to me and I tore off his goggles and mask, keen to know who dared attack one of his own. I didn't expect what I found.

A human.

"Glory to the Federation." Blood bubbled from between his teeth and I felt my own pulse speed up. Tearing away my mask I said something in my native tongue and sank my fangs into the man's throat.

You ask me now why, in the heat of battle I would do such a thing? How can I describe the hunger that burns in all of us? The sheer draw of the thing that is human blood? I had been drinking synthetic for far too long, only rarely were we given a pittance of human vitae for the rush it gives us all.

And now, here in front of me, was a pile of drugs and I a junkie denied far too long.

Oh it tasted glorious. Like molten life poured down my throat.

One of the Watchers came from the ash, his cloak flared like wings. Arm upraised a glowing stone shone in his fingers. His eyes met mine over the body of the human even as I swallowed pulse after pulse of his life. I saw the envy in the angel's eyes even as his mouth curled in disgust. The stone turned to me but I was not there.

Oh the powers it gives us, the freedoms, the energy and prowess.

My claws found his midsection and pierced the corded muscles there. I jerked him upwards as his eyes went wide, his fingers opening to drop the stone from his grip. I pushed higher, my nails iron hard as they sliced and mauled until I felt his heart in my grasp.

I wrenched and let him fall to the ground, a puppet with no master, as I shook his lifeblood from my arm. Then I moved. Everything was a blur as I rode the rush of the blood, my body singing with every blessing of the First. Siren, Monster, Fox-being, Angel; none could stand before me as I moved through the ash with the agility and sureness of a bat. My claws found them all, my weapon dropped long ago.

Then I was on the edge of the dais. The ash was faded enough that I saw the council still at blows. The Destroyer was on the ground, his body wet and red, the Watcher Lord in only slightly better shape. He leaned on his staff as his eyes fluttered. The white of his cloak and robe were crimson drenched and I could see the glistening of organs that shouldn't see the light of day. Feathers were everywhere.

Aneko was on the ground thrashing. Her back arched hard enough that I heard the cracking of vertebrae, the line of holes leaking corrupted blood telling me she had finally fallen afoul of the Siren's barbs. As I watched she flashed between forms, but always came back to her human one. I stopped watching when she screamed, her jaw dislocating.

Then I found my queen.

Her clothes were ragged, her gleaming blade in one hand, Aneko's knife in the other. She was wary, her eyes watching the Siren's queen who held her arms up, the fins on her forearms dripping blood and venom onto the stones below.

Fighters roared overhead but I ignored them, my body

starting to feel heavy as the human's life-force was finally fully consumed by my system. I had used it too quickly, too carelessly. My knees hit the stone of the dais, one hand finding my chest as I felt the last of the man's life burning away.

But my eyes remained on the fighters as they circled. The Siren queen was not without wounds of her own, greenish-blue blood leaking from a number of cuts and slashes across her body. Some of her head-spines were cut away as well, the stumps leaking the same washed-out blood.

"Why?" Atra-Hassis gurgled, his eyes raising as the two women continued to watch each other. I noticed that the Siren queen was keeping the Watcher behind her, staying between my queen and the man.

In answer to Atra-Hassis, Narcisa laughed. The Siren lashed out and my queen barely dodged the double swipe of barbed skin. In return, Narcisa kicked out, driving the fish-creature back towards the angel.

"You want to know why?" The queen of the First hissed, spinning the blades in her hands in a show of dexterity that was meaningless amongst those present. She lashed forward with her blades the same time that the Siren shot forward with the speed of an eel. Their blows were flashes in the ash storm and my eyes struggled to keep up with them.

Then a kick came out of nowhere and the Siren tumbled across the dais, coming to rest next to Atra-Hassis. Her blood mixed with his, the gurgle of her breathing apparatus fading to silence.

Narcisa came to rest, the ash swirling around her. I must have gasped something because she looked over her shoulder at me, her hair wild around her. Then she was walking towards the downed Siren and Watcher, flicking watery blood from her blades.

As she approached, the Watcher reached out a hand and rested it on the Siren's still form. A tear of blood dripped from his eye to break the pearl of his skin. Crimson-filmed eyes rose and the hate in them was apparent. Narcisa laughed, the sound causing the Watcher to struggle to his feet, leaning heavily on his staff which pulsed with unshed power.

"The answer is simple. Look at all of you." Narcisa spread her arms and spun before coming back to face Atra-Hassis. "You're all freaks. You're the monsters of mankind, the creatures that stand out in a crowd."

She came to a halt before Atra-Hassis and licked a splash of the Siren's blood from the back of her hand. "That's why the humans chased us away from Earth. You couldn't hide among them as they encroached into your world. Even Aneko's people were finding it harder and harder to remain in hiding."

The queen of the First locked eyes with the lord of the Watcher and she gave him a smile that was all fang. "Only my people didn't need to fear them. We lived among them, always hidden, always careful. We didn't flee, we chose to leave!"

Atra-Hassis's staff pulsed with energy and Narcisa's fist lashed out, the pommel of her knife cracking across the angel's forehead. The pulse of his staff instantly dimmed.

"None of your tricks, Atra." She licked the pommel where his pinkish blood had spilled. "You of all people should realize what I am doing for my people. You can't escape the humans, they will continue their manifest destiny into the stars and there will never be places we can hide forever. So I did the only logical thing."

She leaned in closer. "I joined them."

Atra-Hassis roared from blood-filled lungs and lashed out with his staff. But even as he moved Narcisa's knife was already piercing the underside of his chin and into his brain. With a savage twist she pulped the organ and the Watcher Lord was no more.

When she turned I realized that the clearing around the dais was silent again. A pair of our cutters swept over the area, most likely hunting for targets. My queen came forward and placed a manicured nail under my chin, lifting my gaze to hers from where it had fallen to the stones out of habit and respect.

"Rise, my child." She smiled when my eyes met hers. She moved my goggles away from my eyes and I felt as if I was staring at my first love.

"You and your kin have done well. It was necessary to have the humans infiltrate our people. They had the means through their technology to fool everyone, everyone that is, except me. Do not think me a fool for letting them come here, for their purpose was to slay the others' children."

Her eyes looked over my shoulders and I turned to gaze upon my brothers and sisters as they stood over the kneeling figures of humans in our garb. Their goggles were torn from their heads but the respirators were left on lest they choke on the atmosphere.

"Once we alter their memories and send them back to the humans, they will believe the clan leaders all dead. The great Vampires of the ages, finally gone to join their Earthen brethren. They will continue their expansion into space, continue to breed and spread. And we will be there, controlling them from the shadows."

I turned then and looked at her as I realized what she was saying. No more synthetic blood, no more warring with the other clans and the humans. We would exist as our ancestors did, influencing the direction of the mortals.

A smile split my face then and I shouted out praise to our queen. Others did the same, their fists pumping the air.

We still see the other clans once in a while, even now. Perhaps they recognize us for what we are, perhaps not. They are almost gone, hunted by our kill teams to extinction. Leaderless, they could not rally, could not fight back. We are the politicians, the admirals, the kings and queens of newfound worlds. Blood runs freely, we keep harems, and no one believes in us anymore.

My name is Costel Gogoasa and I was there when the vampire council was shattered.

Tarl Hoch is a horror writer based out of Calgary, Alberta, Canada. His works have been featured in places such as 'Bellows of the Bone Box' by Sirens Call Publications, 'Blood and Roses' by Scarlett River Press, as well as 'Fifty Shades of Decay' by Angelic Knight Press. He is also head editor for FurPlanet's upcoming horror anthology 'Abandoned Places'. When not trying to scare others, Tarl can be found reading anything he can get his hands on, wishing everyday was Halloween, or secretly feeding treats to his feline overlords when his fiancée isn't looking. Find his work on Twitter @tarl_writer or on Facebook at https://www.facebook.com/TarlWriter

STRAYS

Robert S. Wilson

Evolution has been kind to the human race. At least that's what they tell us in physical rehab. I wouldn't know. I still can't remember much since I woke up in stasis. Just my name, some basic things. Not many details really yet. But they tell me eventually it'll all come back. It's not the easiest thing, you know, waking up and finding out that your 24-year-old body has been in a glass tube off and on just shy of two billion years.

And then, there's the sun thing. I guess it's gotten kind of bigger than I remember. They say it's nearly a big red star now. Again, I wouldn't know. It's only safe to go outside at night, and even then it's hotter than piss. There's no windows here in the Compound. And still the sunlight is bright enough to keep me up at "night" sometimes. Almost like the light creeps in between the atoms or some shit. So yeah, everyone's really pale now.

My roommate Zack told me all I needed to hear to keep me from getting too curious about that. His brother died a couple thousand years back. Apparently, going out to see one last sunset was all it took. And even though I don't remember much, I somehow know that things are really different than they used to be. I mean, I guess I do see flashes of things from time to time. From the past. My past anyway. But they're never enough to really make any sense.

But, I digress.

It's not like I need to remember things or go outside anyway. I mean, seriously, Zack and I have it made in this place. We still have three weeks until we go back to work (whatever the hell it is we do, I sure don't remember) and our computer is stocked to the max with every game, movie, TV show, album, or book we would ever want. All the way back to the ancient stuff like 21st century American television and Shakespeare and all that jazz—well not literally although I would imagine they have plenty of that, too.

Anyway, me and Zack sit around playing games, watching flicks, listening to music—mostly with headphones—Zack's into dubstep and I'm more of an old school metal head. I also like to read a lot, but we're always so busy that I haven't been able to finish a book since—well, since being here, really. Or was I here before? You know, I don't know. I'll get back to you on that.

But, it's really cool here. We get to hang out and do what we want. The food's okay, I guess—yeah, I almost forgot about that. We don't get much variety. Any really. Just these prepackaged smoothie-sort-of-things they call Juice. The stuff doesn't look or taste anything like juice though. I do remember that much. They have all our daily stuff in them, and they don't taste bad at all—really they're great, I just kinda miss having a steak or a grilled burrito and all that. But it's cool. Less time picking out food, more time kicking Zack's ass at Galaga.

Last week things got weird though. Well… *weirder.*

Every now and then a white banner with bold red text shoots across the bottom of the screen with news and shit. Almost always about the mothership they're building and the latest breakthrough in terraforming research. I mean I get that things like this are important—Earth won't last much longer, we'll have to find a new place to go and all, but they could find a better way to update people. Anyone who's ever played Galaga knows the bottom of the screen is where your fighter is and if you can't see him, you can't shoot jack fuck. But so, last week it's something new. I didn't get it and neither did Zack. The red bold lettering flashed and they even stopped our game and filled the speaker with this screeching alarm. The words blinking on the screen, making my eyes hurt, said something about "Strays"—even capitalized it. Said there were three "Strays" loose in the compound in Section 36-9, Subsection D and if anyone saw them to alert the authorities.

But how the hell were we supposed to know if we saw them if we didn't know what they were? I mean, it gave a description, but, still. The first one was supposed to be female, five feet tall, short black hair, pale skin (hell, we all have pale skin, we can't go out in the sun!), and blue eyes.

So they're people, I guess? Stray people?

Who knows.

I broke 100,000 points in Galaga, and Zack's been trying to top me all week and the little fucker just might if I let my focus slip too much. So, back to business. He's on stage thirteen right now, didn't even manage a perfect score on the last challenging stage. His fighter's whizzing left and right in between queen bullets, sliding his ship to the left while one of those little blue and yellow bee jobs tries to scoop up behind him. The thing comes around and Zack's ready, shoots it just in time. Learned that move from me. One of my signature touches. I almost say so, but I don't wanna distract him. I like winning fair and square. Victory's a bitter pill when you have to cheat to survive.

And, of course, it doesn't take long before he's crashing into another queen, trying to get right up in front of her as she makes a pass carrying the ship she just captured strapped to her back. *Kablooee*, all three dead.

My turn.

And as I'm picking up the controller, whatta ya know, it's that goddamn bulletin alert again; sounding alarm, flashing words on the screen and all.

...LAST SPOTTED IN SECTION 222-1, SUBSECTION J. IF SIGHTED DO NOT TRY TO CONTACT!!! SUBJECTS ARE INCREDIBLY DANGEROUS. REPEAT: ***WARNING*** TWO STRAYS REMAIN WITHIN THE COMPOUND. SUBJECT-A IS FEMALE, FIVE FEET TALL, DARK HAIR, PALE SKIN, AND BLUE EYES. SUBJECT-B IS MALE, SIX FEET, TWO INCHES TALL, RED HAIR, PALE SKIN, AND GREEN EYES. LAST SPOTTED IN SECTION 222-1...

"Dude, that's here," Zack says. I'm hearing him but I'm still pretty confused about the whole fucking thing. Oh well. I just hope we're safe from whatever they are.

So, I'm just about to get out the game controller and Zack won't stop looking out the peephole. "Jordan, come on, man. We should totally go out there and see what's up."

"But I was just about to kick your ass...again. Besides, what if it's not safe like they say?"

"Oh, come on. We've been cooped up in here for weeks. Aren't you getting tired of this shit?" Zack says holding up his controller and aiming it at the wall screen. "I sure as hell am. I wanna go see what's going on." Zack turns toward the door and I do feel a little curious—maybe—I guess—ugh... why not?

"All right, but if it gets hairy out there, we're coming straight back here and I'm roasting your behind with a new high score."

Zack laughs and nods, "Yeah, yeah, whatever," opens the door and waves for me to come on already.

So, we walk out into the hallway and it's the same ol' thing as always: long monotonous corridors, tan concrete walls, mostly empty gray linoleum walkways with the occasional pale passerby striding along. We take a right hand turn at the first corner and it's just like the last one. But in the blink of an eye, it's not anymore. There's an explosion. People around the corner turn and run toward us, screaming.

Zack looks at me and it's all slow motion. The people disappear into whatever door they can manage to. Smoke pours from the corner, funneling into the hall we're standing in and now someone stumbles out of the cloud, naked, filthy, and coughing.

She's the most beautiful thing I've ever seen.

Even with all the dirt caked on her skin and her hair disheveled in a tangled mess. Subject-A has to be an angel from Heaven and I look at Zack.

"We have to help her."

Zack just stares back at me like a deer in headlights. Like he doesn't know what to do. His body shakes, his teeth chatter. The next moment, I'm leading Subject-A to our room, Zack follows, turning his head this way and that, like we just robbed a bank or something. We get her inside and close the door and the next moment dozens of footfalls running past has Zack standing by the door like a statue. A moment later, they're gone and we all let out a sigh of relief.

"Are you okay?" I ask Subject-A. She just stares at me like I'm a distant object she can't quite focus on.

"Dude, I don't think she understands. Maybe you should try some kind of sign language?"

"And just how the fuck do I do that, Zack? I don't know any sign language and I sure as hell don't know how to say 'all right' with my hands."

Zack shrugs. "Man, I don't know." He's staring at her naked body and it dawns on me maybe we should give her some clothes. I rush back to my room and dig through drawers until I find a pair of pants and a shirt that look like they might not fall off of her. Putting them on isn't so easy though. She doesn't understand, jerks away when I try to put them on her. After a while she calms to my attempts and, with some help from Zack, who's still practically slobbering onto the floor, we get her dressed.

"Don't you think we should have cleaned her up first, man?" Zack says.

"After how that went? I have a feeling if she reacts like this to clothes, a metal tube spraying her with hot water will make her go ballistic. Why don't we ease her into it, okay?"

"Good point."

"So... now what do we do?"

"I don't know, man, this was all your bright fucking idea. How long do you think we can hide her before they come knocking on our door? And what the hell is wrong with her? You think she came from one of the stasis chambers?"

"I know even less about this shit than you do. I mean, I've been having a lot of fun and all, but this whole thing really freaks me out. Why are they after her? She's completely harmless. Scared of her own shadow."

"I don't know, man. I've only been out of my chamber a few weeks longer than you. This is the first I've heard of 'Strays.' She looks just like we do. I mean, not quite as pale—probably been out of stasis longer or not at all."

"My bet's on not at all."

We both stare at each other for a long time. The whole thing stinks bad and we don't want to admit just how scared we are. At least that's how I feel.

I look at Subject-A. Our eyes meet and she smiles. It's the most simple human gesture and it melts my heart.

"Maybe it's time we started paying more attention to the news?"

Zack nods at me, half in a daze.

~

It's been two days since we found Subject-A—we call her Anne now—and they still haven't come looking for her. They don't seem too concerned either. No more broadcasts about "Strays," no more flashing text. Maybe they think she found her way out of the Compound, or maybe they think she's dead. Who knows.

She's been sleeping in my room and I've been crashing on the couch. And when we throw on a movie or watch the news or something, she just stares at the screen no matter what's on, like it's the most engrossing thing ever.

We've been feeding her juice, but she doesn't seem to like it. Barely touches the stuff. She's thinning out, too. I don't think she's gonna last much longer. Zack's been trying to talk me into telling someone at rehab, or even turning her in to Compound Security. But I'm afraid of what they will do to her. She's obviously different from us — doesn't know how to speak, doesn't like what we eat. I've decided to find out where she came from. Somehow. Maybe if I can take her back there, she'll be okay.

"Promise me you won't try anything while I'm gone."

Zack just looks at me like I punched him in the face. Says "yes" through gritted teeth. I'm not trying to be a dick, but I've already caught him trying to sneak in my room once. And the way he stares like she's a piece of meat — I wish I could take her with me. But, that's not even an option.

I take one last look at Anne before I go. She's staring at the wall screen, doesn't even see me. I slip out the door and head down the hallway. I'm finding it harder and harder to believe that I haven't been asking questions. Haven't even tried to go anywhere but where I'm told. If there's somewhere we're not supposed to go, I don't know about it. Today, I'm going to find out.

Along the corridor there's only more doors for a while. Then I find an adjacent hallway on the left. I take it. More plain doors lining the walls. Just like ours. Nothing different after nearly an hour of walking either. But now I'm coming up on some silver railing along each side. I realize quickly it's there to keep people from falling down into the bodies below. I can see them. Hundreds, thousands — I'm a terrible judge of numbers — but there has to be at least thousands, maybe hundreds of thousands. They're all staring up at me. Or it seems that way at first. Their glassy eyes gaze upward into nothing—the ceiling maybe? Each one is completely naked, lying on a single slab of silver, with tubes coming out of their faces, wires coming off their chests attached to machines with green LEDs. A monotonous humming like the sound of an idle air conditioner surrounds the place.

At first I think they're in some kind of stasis, but there's no glass cockpits, nothing to seal them from the elements. And those eyes. They're not asleep quite like stasis. I lean up to the silver rail and squint, trying to see the far end of this gigantic room filled with bodies. I can't. It's that far away. The number of eyes that seem to stare at me is getting under my skin. I turn and run back down the hall. I picture those vacant eyes following me as I go. Whatever happened to those people, they aren't here with us in the really real world.

Running back, I almost trip over my own feet. I have to warn Zack. We have to get out of this place. I think of all the science fiction movies I've ever watched, all the stories I'd ever read where, at the surface everything was amazing and hopeful, but something dark and sinister waited underneath. That's this place to me now. That something is opening its eyes and peering up at me.

With hundreds of thousands of vacant eyes.

The way back takes some time. Passing other people along the way, I try to slow down, to look normal, but I'm so scared that it only draws more attention. When I finally turn down our hallway I see door #236 and I exhale a weighted breath of relief. I type in the keycode and the green light blinks twice, the latch automatically disengages, and the door leans ajar.

It's dark inside.

I push inward and enter the room and confirm the lights are all off. But somehow I can see. I close the door behind me and look around for any sign of Zack and Anne.

"Zack? Annie?"

It's slight, like the rustling of leaves a mile off, but I hear movement from my bedroom. It has to be adrenaline—my hearing's never been so acute. I turn and creep down the hall, picturing my friend and Anne on those silver slabs, staring up at nothing, and a chill slithers up my spine. There's that movement again. I can picture exactly where it is in my mind's eye just from the sound. Someone's in my closet waiting and *not breathing*.

I open my door and see Anne, crumpled on the bed. There's something wrong with her neck. I see blood. She's not breathing. And the smell... I'm just about to run to her when whoever's in my closet jumps out at me in a blur. Claws dig into my back, something sharp pierces my neck. In my head I'm screaming, but my heart rate barely rises, and I keep my cool as I reach over and grab Zack's head and pull his teeth from my neck. It's him all right. I'd long ago memorized the smell of his cologne.

I bend forward and toss him over me, Judo style. He lands shoulders first into the foot of my bed and catches himself with his hands and feet on the floor.

"Zack? What the hell did you do?"

He looks up at me with glowing feral eyes, fangs bared, nose scrunched upward. He speaks and his voice is a growling hiss.

"You shouldn't have left her with me. She was so beautiful. *So delicious.*"

"What the hell is going on, here? I mean—"

Zack lunges at me and in an instant I grab him by the head again and tear out his throat from left to right with my *own* fangs, and drop him to the floor. I didn't really need to ask. Some revelations take more time to process.

I walk over to Anne's body and pick her up. I can smell it on her now. The blood. The scent is just like Zack had said. Delicious. I fight to keep from lifting her body to my mouth. All the while, images flash through my mind. I'm finally remembering.

I see myself in school, learning about the revolution. It

started in the 21st century. No one knows exactly what year. First, we took over the cities. Thousands hid in rural areas, hoping they were safer in numbers. But they weren't. They only drew more attention. By the year 2119, we were the new human race. The vampires. Evolution had won. The lesser humans—as we called them—were gathered together. Bred. Farmed. And eventually, genetically grown in mass production.

I remember working the new arrival line. Fresh, still, tiny bodies pass by on a conveyer belt. Zack and I check them each by hand for discoloration, imperfections, as they slide by. The ones that don't pass inspection get knocked off and fall into large metal vats below filling with tiny decaying corpses.

Of course, during the revolution, some of the humans got away.

The Strays.

They survived underground. And we let them be. Why hunt for your food when you've got advancements in modern agriculture on your side? Those eyes—those human eyes—hadn't been staring at me. They were staring at nothing, kept alive by machines. They were the grown bodies I had passed through as babes.

You see, evolution has been kind to the human race. They don't have to live in fear, look over their shoulders, jump at every twig snapping in the dark forest. Their predators have been kind enough to raise them mindless from test tubes so they don't have to think. Don't have to know.

Don't have to feel any pain.

I've found the main power breaker for the machines. Been watching the bodies for hours. Their chests rising and falling. Dark crimson liquid siphoning from their arms through thick plastic tubes every half hour like clockwork. That's when I noticed the wiring under the floor. It led me to the central power hub. A single dull gray panel on the floor, about a foot long and wide.

Been standing here for hours, just staring down at it.

But now it's time. I reach down and open the panel. My fingers pull the thin black plastic switch that keeps these hunks of meat "alive." The monotonous hum slows down, drops in pitch, the green LEDs fade. All around me, voices gasp and bodies convulse in unison, dying.

And now we'll die too.

Only the Strays will survive.

Call it genocide, call it xenocide, call it whatever you want. I like winning fair and square.

Victory's a bitter pill when you have to cheat to survive.

Robert S. Wilson is the author of SHINING IN CRIMSON and FADING IN DARKNESS, books one and two of his dystopian vampire series: EMPIRE OF BLOOD. He is a Bram Stoker Award-nominated editor of HORROR FOR GOOD: A CHARITABLE ANTHOLOGY and lives in Middle Tennessee with his wife and two kids. His short stories have appeared in/will appear in [NAMELESS] MAGAZINE from Cycatrix Press, HORROR D'OEUVRES from Dark Fuse, A QUICK BITE OF FLESH: AN ANTHOLOGY OF ZOMBIE FLASH FICTION from Hazardous Press, EVIL JESTER PRESENTS COMICS, FEAR THE REAPER from Crystal Lake Publishing, THE BEST OF THE HORROR SOCIETY 2013, BLEED from Perpetual Motion Machine Publishing, and his cyberpunk/horror novella EXIT REALITY published by Blood Bound Books was chosen as one of e-thriller.com's Thrillers of the Month in July 2013.

DAMNED TO LIFE
Essel Pratt

The musty stench of damp soil permeates the dank basement air. Dust flutters aimlessly as the aged and blackened windows usher in a noisy militia of whistling drafts. Fidgety house spiders retreat to safety as the wind forces their webs to seizure and an occasional rodent scurries across the compacted dirt floor.

Shining brightly in the center of the room is a trio of ultraviolet spotlights focused strategically on a center point above an otherwise blackened pit. The light encompasses the opening with its radiance, but does not penetrate the depths. Inside the occasional movement accompanies the slow moan of a lost soul plagued with pain and anguish.

The pit is a simple, yet effective, cage used to house the very essence of the damned. This lonely prison has been her home for as long as she can remember. Surrounded by crudely constructed concrete walls, she huddles upon the damp floor waiting for the day she can escape and experience freedom.

Her pale skin shines brightly in contrast to the dark concrete walls. Her body shivers, not with cold, but hunger and disease. The miniscule amount of food—mostly small animals and bloody ground beef—provided by her captor leaves her emaciated and parched. Although he does provide his nameless prisoner an occasional bag of blood, it is polluted with impurities and disease, causing her more torture than relief. Her lust for the pure vital fluid twists her senses in a constant purgatory of living while her body battles against a horrible death.

~

The sound of a key turning echoes down from the upstairs entry. Thunderous footsteps thud on the creaking floor above and send shivers down her spine. It won't be long until James comes downstairs.

In the kitchen, ice falls into a glass followed by the sound of liquid pouring. It's his favorite whiskey judging from the smell. A normal routine when he arrives. He finishes the drink quickly and the glass crashes in the sink. A few minutes later the refrigerator opens. The fetor of blood bags permeates through the floor boards. Her heightened sense of smell is working at full strength now that the last of the poisons have excreted from her body. The aroma of anemia and hypoglycemia is strong. Both of which have little effect on her, only causing a little dizziness. Maybe tonight won't be so bad after all.

The handle of the dingy basement door turns and the un-oiled hinges screech. James stumbles inside and stands there a few seconds, blinking his eyes before ascending. The light does not venture much further than the opening to the pit, which leaves a majority of the basement in darkness.

He approaches the edge of the pit, and peers inside. There is something different about him, something odd, as she glares up at his fatigued face. His gaze peers deep into her being. She senses envy amongst his hatred and exhaustion, something never noticeable before.

He places a plastic grocery bag on a wooden table, pulling a bag of blood and a chunk of fresh hamburger from within. Ripping open the bloodied ground beef he makes half-dozen, or so, meatballs. He seems to enjoy throwing the bloodied projectiles through the lighted barrier—aiming for her head. Fast reflexes prove that the diseases he had fed her the previous day are now gone, as she snatches today's rations from the air and devours them. Even in a malnourished state, her disease-free equanimity could prove disastrous if she were to escape. After years of captivity and observation, he is covetous of her miraculous healing; cursing that she will outlive his finite existence.

The juicy beef beckons an insatiable thirst for more blood. She can tell from James's expression that he isn't going to satisfy her needs right away. Before quenching her need for sustenance with a bloody hemopathy cocktail, he reaches into his pocket and pulls out a small tube. Curious, the young vampire waits for whatever torture he is about to present.

"I saw a movie on T.V. earlier. It had sparkly vampires in it. Why don't you sparkle?" James says in a slurred tone.

His shaky hands fumble with the cap, causing it to pop off unexpectedly and sending metallic glitter flailing into the air around him. He curses the foolishness and pours the remaining contents into his hand, sprinkling the glitter through the ultraviolet barricade that covers the opening. As the pieces flutter below, they disperse the illumination like a disco ball. As the light reflects, it burns into her flesh like laser beams. The agony is almost unbearable as the glitter unhurriedly drifts to the floor below. Through the pain, she looks up toward him knowing that his days are numbered and her wounds will heal even after he is gone.Satisfied with his torturous game, James tosses the blood bag into the pit. Emaciated hands grasp the treat and she desperately bites through the plastic. Warm blood siphons down her dry throat; she feels a familiar energy stream through her. The surge is invigorating as a rush of vitality consumes her.

Through the burst of energy, her thoughts turn to the oncoming weakness that will be brought on by the anemia concealed within mélange. However, it never comes. The tainted sample must be labeled incorrectly; the anemic smell has to be coming from somewhere else. Maybe there was another bag upstairs, but the stench seems too strong.

Not since her birth has she felt the energy of pure blood. Power and confidence rush through her veins. Her mind combusts with a clearness she has not experienced since birth, all pain in her muscles dissipates in an instant, and each of her six senses collide toward freedom as though the floodgates of a dam have burst. If not for the damning lamps above, she would attempt escape.

James's hateful expression melts into fear and confusion as her black eyes metamorphose to crimson. He stands above her tapping his foot, fidgeting with the empty glitter vial. She can hear his heart pound faster in his chest. He doesn't know. He doesn't realize the blood is pure. She contemplates faking it for him, but decides against giving him the satisfaction. Instead, she finds herself scanning his thoughts for weakness, something she never knew she was capable of. He wonders if she's grown a tolerance for the stuff, if the cow's blood is somehow helping her now. She smiles at his confusion.In a panic, he turns toward the stairway and traverses the darkness without allowing his eyes to adjust. His carelessness leads to blunder as he trips over the electrical cords driving the ultraviolet spotlight, disconnecting the power. Darkness erupts in the room as he falls hard to the floor, his head bouncing as it slams against the dirt. Unconscious, his body rests vulnerably limp.

The young vampire stares at the exit toward her freedom. Her chance to escape has arrived, yet she pauses. Fear of the unknown hinders her reflexes as she contemplates her next move. All her life, she has known only the stagnant confines of this pit, what lies beyond is enthralling, but also horrifying. She cannot help but wonder if the rest of the world will treat her as her captor has.

James groans as he begins to wake from his short slumber. The sound jolts her back to reality and she instinctively jumps from the pit, pouncing upon her defeated imprisoner. Still dazed, he turns his head toward the weight on his chest, their eyes meet. Fear displays clearly upon his face as he mentally surrenders.

Intuition bullies her to gorge on his blood, letting him die a slow and painful death. Forcing him to feel just a fraction of the pain he has caused her will make his death a satisfying retribution. She licks her lips in anticipation as a pair of fangs protrudes beyond her upper lip. Moving toward his neck, she purposely takes her time to prolong his anxiety. As she edges closer their eyes meet and his expression changes from fear to placidity.

His mouth opens, to speak. She pauses for a moment, just in time to hear him whisper the words, "You have your mother's eyes, Elizabeth".

He has never spoken her name before. A strange feeling beats within her heart as she withdraws from his neck. His unexpected repentance is unnerving, but her enhanced senses can tell that his remorse is sincere. Glaring at him for a few more seconds, before placing her cold hands on either side of his head, she allows him to speak one last time.

"I'm sorry. I was scared and angry and it was too late to turn back. Your bastard vampire father raped her—your mother. I should have known her frail body couldn't survive your thirst at birth. Please forgive me."

With a tear dripping from her eye, she softly utters, "goodbye," and swiftly snaps his neck, opting not to drink the poisoned blood spilling from his torn flesh where the bone has ripped through. A familiar scent of leukemia and anemia fill the air around her, explaining the look of fatigue on his face earlier.

His hatred of her was real, she knows this, but she wonders if his love had fueled that hatred. She pauses a few seconds to reflect on his passing, and come to terms with her feelings toward him.

She forgives him.

Now that she is free, Elizabeth inhales the musty air around her; it has never felt so good within her lungs. Nervously, she makes her way up the creaky stairs, unaware of what strangeness might await her. The familiar screeching hinges shriek as the door opens into the kitchen. Her fingers trace over the cryptic crosses carved into the door, meant to keep her trapped below although completely ineffective on her flesh now. The sweet smell of garlic tickles her nostrils, a familiar treat she has grown to love. Overall, her first experience with the outside world seems rather peaceful and welcoming.

She wanders the house in awe of the collection of crucifixes and statues of Mary Magdalene. Within the living room, a small pile of wood shavings rests on the floor in front of a leather recliner. A half-finished cross carving sits next to a shiny pocket knife. As she scans the walls, she notices that all of the crosses are hand carved. Some are crude in their design, while others are magnificently ornate.

On the upper floor she finds a closet filled with her mother's old clothes. A blue Sundress catches her attention. Trapped in the pit, she never felt the warmth of fabric upon her naked skin, it was a luxury not allowed. Now that she is free, Elizabeth tries the dress on, and musters a smile as the fabric caresses her naked body; her mother's fougere perfume still emanates from the cotton blend.

Out of the corner of her eye, an unexpected movement startles her. She turns toward the intruder, only to peer into her own reflection. For the first time she looks into her own eyes. A photo taped to the mirror catches her attention. Tears stream down her face as she recognizes her father and what must be her mother on their wedding night. Elizabeth grasps the photo close to her bosom and mourns her mother's loss.

Last night she slept in her parents' plush bed, clutching the photo tightly to her un-beating heart. She has never felt as rested in the morning as she is now with the fresh rays of sunlight poking through the window and blanketing her face in warmth. In her weakened state the light would have scorched her flesh and ended her existence. However, now healthy and strong, she is immune to the sun's poisons, as well as other stereotypical ailments. Her pure blood feast from last night is enough to keep her healthy for a week or so, until she can find a new place to call home. She hopes to be far from here when her father's stench penetrates the exterior walls.

To ready herself for the awaiting journey, she finds an old backpack in a closet and prepares to gather some essentials. Her unfamiliarity of life outside her pit hinders her judgment while packing. A few extra items of clothing, a couple cloves of garlic to snack on, a can of diet cola because it looked inviting, a small ornate crucifix, and the photo of her parents seem like enough to survive on. If the thirst rears its ugly head, she plans on satisfying herself with some rats and other small animals.

Nervousness tides through her as she approaches the French doors at the front of the house. Her shaky hand reaches out for the handle, hesitating as she peeks through lace curtains. She has no family, no job, and no life to call her own. However she has found hope throughout her torture, as well as a strange urge to help those bound by the torture of disease and abuse.

Slowly turning the knob, she opens the doors to the outside world. The fresh scent of spring air tickles her lungs; the warmth of the sun dances upon her pale flesh. Elizabeth steps onto the porch and walks down the stairs to the sidewalk below. With no destination in mind, she makes an internal oath to help rid the world of the horror she has suffered.

Finally, her damned life has purpose.

Essel Pratt has spent his life exploring his imagination and dreams. As a Husband and a Father, he doesn't always have as much time to write as he would like. However, his mind is always plotting out his next story and manipulating the plot. Someday he hopes to quit the 9-5 grind and focus on writing full time.

Currently, Essel is building his catalog by contributing to various anthologies as he works on his first novel. He also contributes to www.nerdzy.com and www.infendo.com on an (almost) daily basis.

Essel focuses his writings on mostly Horror/Sci-Fi, however is known to add a bit of other genres into his writings as well. You can follow Essel at:
facebook.com/esselprattwriting and Esselpratt.blogspot.com and on twitter @EsselPratt

HAPPY HOUR
G. N. Braun

Northern New South Wales, Australia

The heat was stifling, the pub was full and the air-conditioning strained to keep up with the late December humidity.

Inside the only pub in Warcoola Station, flies buzzed ceaselessly around sweat-stained shirts and torn blue singlets as hands brushed at them out of habit. As always, conversations centred on the chance of rain and the current state of the soil, and glasses hardly had time to sit before being emptied. Soon after, they were placed empty back on the bar, mostly upright, which signalled for a refill.

Even though the sun was almost down, the heat of the day sat heavily in the smoke-filled room. They didn't bother to enforce no-smoking bans here; the farmers and miners wouldn't have listened anyway, and you can't ban the whole town.

Grace waited behind the bar, polishing the tray of glasses fresh out of the washer and casually keeping an eye out for refills. These guys were nice enough on the surface, but keep them waiting on their beer and you'd feel the sharp-edge of their tongues.

"Hey Gracie. Bring us a fresh ashtray, love?" Kevin Borstow winked at her as she went to grab one off the stack near the register. Nice enough guy, but he lived too far out of town for anyone to seriously want to date him. She moved to wipe her brow.

Why is it so damn hot?

It had been a strange year; hotter than usual, and full of locust plagues and other natural disasters. An entire household over near Waiaii had vanished last month; every inhabitant gone, three generations, just like that.

Enough to give you the creeps.

After replacing the full ashtray with a clean one, Grace emptied it and gave it a quick wipe with a damp cloth. She didn't like putting ashtrays through dishwashers. She'd never smoked, and the idea of washing drinking glasses with ashtrays made her gag.

She dropped it carefully in the sink, turning back toward the front of the bar just as the light changed. The setting sun sent streams of brilliant radiance into the front of the pub; reds and pinks and yellows, all the colours of the sunset reflected from mirrors behind the bar, splintering from the many bottles of spirits into a million colourful shards of light. It was one of Grace's favourite times. It was always closely followed by evening, her least favourite time.

As a rule, all the local drunks congregated down one end of the bar while the miners and farmers gathered at the other end. In between was a kind of no-man's-land where the women gathered to drown the sorrows of their day. No lady's lounge at this pub.

In the end, they all drank. Some more than others and some less than they would have liked, but they all drank.

Fuck all else to do out here in the arsehole of Australia.

Grace looked up just as the last light winked over the horizon, the night settling in. A faint sound drew her attention. It sounded like fingernails on a blackboard, a faint *scree-scree* ringing over the top of the bubbles of conversation and laughter. It seemed to come from the front door, and as Grace looked over, something rose into view through the stained glass in the centre of the left panel.

It was hard for her to see clearly, but it seemed to be a hand, long nails scraping at the glass in casual motions. Others noticed it as well; Richard Hadley turned to look, as did Martin Longman next to him. None of the others paid any attention, but two of the women in the centre of the bar turned to see what the noise was.

Richard and Martin stood up and began to walk towards the entrance to see just what was going on when both doors slammed open.

There, silhouetted vaguely by the single street light, was an apparition. It appeared to be a shrivelled old man, hairless and wrinkled, with deep black, beseeching eyes. He was dressed in rags and tatters of clothing. Folds of dirty skin hung glistening and moist in the light cast by the overheads in the bar.

Shuffling further into the artificial lighting, the thing suddenly looked to Gracie less like an old man and more like a corpse freshly-risen from the grave.

It grinned, baring a terrifying mouthful of teeth more at home in the jaw of a tiger shark. Behind the row of razor-sharp incisors were smaller teeth, still wicked-deadly looking. Gracie's heart missed a beat.

Sniffing, the thing cast a baleful glare at the occupants of the main bar, where silence had now overtaken the previous wallow of noise. Behind it, other shadows formed, more creatures the same or similar.

Gracie stood perfectly still. Her heart pounded in her throat. She felt an instinctual dread of these things, an inborn desire to get as far as fucking possible from them. Forcing herself to move, Gracie lowered into a squat behind the bar so she was invisible from the main room. She leaned back against the bar, watching what happened next in the mirrors behind the rows of bottles on the back wall.

Martin never stood a chance; the thing pounced on him like an animal, long talons latching onto his face and neck while the thing's feet shot up and raked toenails an inch long down his stomach, slicing him open and spilling his guts all over the wooden floor.

Richard turned and tried to run, but a second creature—a female this time, judging by the floppy, dirt-encrusted breasts bouncing around under a filthy rag that may once have been a boob-tube—sprang onto his back. Latching fangs onto his throat from the side, she rode him hard into the bar, breaking his neck.

More of the creatures sprang through the open doors of the pub, creating a tidal wave of customers trying to head towards the back door.

As far as Gracie could tell from the reflected scene, not a soul made it that far.

She shuffled as quietly as she could to the trap door that led from behind the bar down to the cellar. As she levered the trap door open—without its usual squeak, thank God—something came around the side of the bar, through the swinging door, slowly and quietly.

Gracie froze in fear for a second before she realised it was Kevin, blood smeared over his clothes and face, eyes wide with terror and shock. His usually bushy hair was slicked back with more of the red fluid, making for a horror movie effect that would be laughable if it wasn't so fucked up. He looked like Ash from Evil Dead after he chopped up his girlfriend. Gracie had to hold back a giggle as panic rose inside her.

Kevin crawled over to where she had the trapdoor raised and started down the steps without even looking at her; so much for ladies first.

She slipped down after him, listening to the sounds of slaughter and insane screaming as the patrons of Warcoola's only pub died noisily.

Into this slaughterhouse, something else followed the foul creatures; something different, something darker.

It was dim in the cellar, and a hell of a lot quieter. The only light came from a globe near the far end of the room. Beer kegs, both full and empty, lined the walls between the two scared people and the only other exit. The trapdoor to the street the damn things came from in the first place.

Gracie looked at Kevin, aware he was not-all-there. *Shock,* she thought. He was cowering and hunched, shaking and whimpering softly to himself. It looked like he might wet his pants as well. *Not gonna be much help.*

Moving slowly down the stairs, she scanned the room for any threat, in case more of those things were in here lying in wait for her. As she reached the bottom she sensed something else above her, something infinitely evil. It came in waves, making the hair stand up on the back of Gracie's neck. Kevin sensed it as well; his whimpering rose to a near whine. Gracie worried it would attract the wrong sort of attention — the kind with teeth and claws. She turned and tried to shush him, but it was too late. Something scraped on the trapdoor, gently at first and then more insistent as Kevin's whine became a howl of terror. Gracie rushed towards the exit, pausing to glance back over her shoulder. He hadn't moved, just curled up on the step.

Too bad for him, she thought, but stopped her silent rush to the ladder that led to the trap-door.

I can't do it. I can't just leave him for those things to tear apart.

She turned and rushed back to where he sat near the bottom of the steps, the need for silence gone as clawed hands hammered roughly at the trapdoor. Grabbing him by the arm, she tried to drag him towards the exit, but he refused to move, actually pulling against her grip as though he wanted to be slaughtered. Gracie pulled back her hand and slapped him across the face. She screamed at him to snap out of it, unmindful of the noise; the things knew they were down here already—all that mattered was getting the fuck out.

Kevin focused on her for the first time, fear and horror warring on his features.

"Wha—?"

"No time for this, Kevin," Gracie said, brushing hair back from her eyes. "Get the fuck up and get moving."

As she spoke, a hand smashed through the trapdoor above them, far enough to reach through and slash wildly. Grey and haggard, covered in peeling skin, and human, except for the claws that tipped each finger. Each was an inch long, and razor sharp. For the first time she noticed the smell; dank and rotten, earthy as though fresh from the grave.

The hand suddenly stilled, curled slowly and withdrew from the hole it had made. The dark presence Gracie had felt was growing.

It seemed alive, this presence, and it froze them both for a second. It seemed to almost infiltrate them, inspect them. It felt cold and hard; alien. The closest word she could come up with was crystalline. Shaking herself to get traction again, Gracie pulled Kevin towards the exit just as another, smaller, hand came through the hole and scrabbled around the edges of the door, reaching blindly for the locking mechanism.

The ladder leading up to the street was permanently affixed to the wall, set there as an emergency escape for anyone trapped down there. Kevin, more alert now and just as anxious as Gracie to escape the death-trap cellar, pushed in front and grabbed at the rungs, pulling himself quickly up to the exit. Gracie followed behind, again noticing Kevin's wet jeans as he levered the bolt open, carefully raised the door, and peered under the lid. He opened the hatch without a sound and slipped out, and Gracie followed.

They found themselves at the front of the pub, the humid night forgotten as they scampered to get away.

Warcoola's main street consisted of the pub, the Post Office/General Store, the Thrift Shop and a few run-down houses. Many of the shops that once lined the street had been sold off and turned into private dwellings.

They passed the darkened alley between the pub and the publican's house. Shane Burroughs had taken over the pub when old Franky died, cleaning it up a bit and adding Victorian Bitter to the tapped beers. Not many had bothered to try it, but Gracie thought it was quite a good drop. Shane was sitting in the corner, holding court at his favourite table when the shit went down.

Most likely dead by now, she thought.

Past Shane's house was the Thrift Shop run by Gary Davis, an old double-fronted building that had first been converted into a draperer's, and later taken over by the CWA and stocked with useless memorabilia no-one wanted or needed: bowls and vases; toast racks and doilies; paintings and old books—dusty and cobwebbed reminders of a dying generation.

We're all gonna be dead soon. Gracie dragged Kevin along behind her, past the thrift shop and into the alley between it and the private residence next door. It was dark and dank, smelling of dirty laundry and rotten garbage. At this point, it was also empty. They stopped for a second to gather their thoughts and work out where to go from there.

Huddled down against the thrift shop wall, Gracie breathed in oxygen and exhaled sheer terror. Her heart was beating like a meth-head drummer and her mind was crystal clear. She knew what she'd seen back there.

Those things were feasting on the dead. Drinking their blood like... like vampires!

A scuffling sound directly above her made her look up as one of the things leapt at her from the roof and knocked her to her knees, hooking one hand into her hair and cradling the back of her neck with the other. Sharp claws pierced her skin, drawing blood she could feel trickling down her neck as she struggle to break the thing's implacable grip. It was useless.

The creature's foul breath blasted her face.

Breathing... it's breathing. It's not a vampire. I can kill it.

It seemed that wasn't going to happen today; the thing was just too damn strong. Unable to break its grip and aware of the thing's mouth almost at her neck, Gracie dropped backwards, using her weight to throw the thing off. It took a handful of her hair as it flew away to impact against the weatherboard side of the thrift shop. Spinning in mid-air to land on its feet before it could hit the ground, it advanced even as it landed.

To Gracie's surprise, Kevin came flying in from the side, a ragged board in his hands splintering over the thing's head. It turned to look at him, not even staggered by the blow, hands reaching for Kevin as he held the board level with its stomach and plunged it in, piercing the saggy flesh and driving it deep.

A black spray of blood burst from the thing's mouth, soaking Kevin from wrist to elbow before he had a chance to release the board and back away from the stricken creature. The thing fell to its knees, gasping for breath and gagging on the black fluid still dribbling and occasionally spurting from its mouth. Clawed hands grabbed at the board impaled through its gut, dragging it back out of the wound and increasing the flow of blood from seepage to a rhythmic pulse.

Casting the board aside, it tried to stand but fell to the ground, curling up and holding the wound with little effect. It spasmed for a little bit and the blood flow slowed and then stopped completely as the thing finally stilled. Unlike the movies, in death it didn't flare up or dust-out or whatever vampires were meant to do. With a final, rattling breath, it died.

Gracie looked over at Kevin and mouthed a quick *thank-you* before moving to study the creature more closely.

The thing's mouth was shut, hiding its shark-like fangs. Dead, it resembled nothing so much as a human corpse. After seeing the ferocity of the attack, she was ready to believe in monsters and reanimated bodies.

It was male—shredded pants now displayed its genitals for all to see—and it seemed to have been no older than she was when it had died the first time. Movement from farther down the alley caught their attention. A window in the wall of the thrift shop opened and someone stuck their head out.

"What the fuck's going on out here? People are tryin' to sleep, y'know!"

"Mister Davis, keep your fuckin' voice down." Gracie's response was whispered, but she looked around in fear, sure that more of the creatures were nearby.

"What the fuck you talkin' about, Missy? You been drinki—" Davis was dragged back inside. A muffled scream ended suddenly.

Gracie turned and ran to Kevin, dragging him behind her as she ran further down the alley, finally emerging in the street behind the shop-fronts.

"Let's get to the lock-up. Guns and bars." It was hard to talk, but Kevin nodded, so he must have heard.

Cop-shop. Maybe a way to survive this madness.

The sultry night made it hard to breathe, and sweat poured down her face. At least Kevin was running quietly by her side now, not holding her back. He actually got ahead of her, arms pumping as they both staggered towards the police station a hundred yards away.

They could see the softly glowing blue sign, tantalisingly close but still too far. There were dark shapes on the ground here and there, too cloaked in darkness to make out but shaped alarmingly like torn and broken bodies.

A noise behind made her turn. Shadows emerged from the mouth of the alley, not too far behind them. Increasing her speed, she passed Kevin. He must have been aware something bad was coming and ran faster as well.

Twenty metres... fifteen... nearly there... ten...

Kevin surged ahead of her and slammed into the double doors of the small police station, which was rarely attended; the local copper, Dave Wilson, had re-routed the station's phone line to his house to better spend his days pursuing his true love—model railways. Gracie slammed into the door seconds later. Kevin was already there to lock it behind her.

Carefully scanning the dim and unattended station, Grace moved around the front desk and over to the two-way radio that was humming on Dave's cluttered desk. "Check all the windows while I try to get us some help."

Kevin ignored her, collapsing on the floor and shaking like a leaf.

"For fuck's sake, Kev, pull yourself together." Grace grabbed the hand-piece off the arm that held it, pressing the 'transmit' button. "Hello. Anyone out there? Help!"

Nothing. Just the background hum of a live frequency. Grace studied the dials on the front of the radio, looking for a switch or a button marked 'Press for Help'. Nada.

Kevin was still curled up on the floor. No help there. She studied the face of the radio for another second before she saw it.

A switch marked *Transceive* was set to *Off*. Flipping the switch, Grace thumbed the call button again. "Hello? Can anyone hear me?"

It seemed like an hour but was likely only a second before there was a response.

"This is the Gunnedah Police. This is a restricted frequency. Please do not broadcast on this frequency. Over and out."

"Wait, I need help. I'm in Warcoola Police Station and we're under attack."

"Ma'am, please clear this frequency or you'll be in serious trouble." The voice on the other end managed to sound bored even over the radio.

Grace had had enough. "Listen, you stupid cockhead. We. Are. Being. Killed. Here. I saw these things kill my customers. We need help here. Now!"

"What things? Where's Dave? Tell him this is not funny."

"I don't fuckin' know where Dave is, and to be honest, I don't fuckin' care. Most likely he's dead. Get your arses over here and help us! Please."

"Lady, for the last time... please clear the channel. Over and out."

"Hello? Hello?" Nothing.

A sound made Gracie turn towards the front door of the police station. A shadow cast by the streetlight moved across the pane of wired-glass, hunched and angled.

Grace looked over behind the desk where the station's weapons were kept in a locked cabinet. Moving around the desk, she grabbed a baton that was leaning against the wall and started hammering at the padlock, unmindful of the noise. *They know where we are,* she thought. Grace could almost feel them gathering outside the station, waiting for God-knows-what.

With a thump from the baton, the lock on the gun cabinet sprang open, hanging useless and broken. Grabbing it, Grace withdrew it and opened the latch. Pulling the cabinet open, she saw an automatic pistol in a holster hanging from a hook on the door. Inside the cabinet, leaning against the back, was a pump-action shotgun.

Yes! Just like the one Dad taught her to shoot with.

Grabbing the pistol, she stuffed it into the waistband of her jeans.

Something banged against the door, shaking it in the frame. Grace grabbed the shotgun and two pistol magazines, stuffing the mags in her pocket. Finally, she grabbed some loose shotgun shells from a glass bowl and got to her feet, turning towards the rear of the station where the cells were.

The first thing she noticed was that Kevin was nowhere to be seen. The second was that the door to the lock-up was closed. She was sure it had been open when they came in.

"Kevin?" Keeping her voice low, useless as that may be, Grace looked frantically around. No sign of him.

Another crash behind her caused her to spin, bring the shotgun up and disengage the safety. The door was half open, hanging from one hinge and the lock, and as she watched it was hit again, crashing in at the top and coming to a rest jutted into the room like some insane skate-ramp.

Standing in the gap was something she had never seen before, and after those other creatures she'd thought she'd seen it all.

It seemed massive and dysmorphic, heavily-muscled and totally out of proportion. Skin as red as Uluru covered corded muscle and sinew, decorated with bone protuberances and scars of old wounds. A rounded face, almost Down's Syndrome-like in its structure, held a large mouth overshadowed by massive fangs at least two inches long, a vicious parody of a vampire. Its eyes were a solid, icy-white, like a blind man.

It scared the shit out of Grace, and that aura, the presence she had felt before, poured off the thing in bursts so strong they were almost palpable.

Unaware of pulling the trigger, Grace was startled by the roar of the shotgun. The creature staggered back as flesh and blood erupted from its shoulder. It roared; a cry redolent with rage and a desire to tear the living-shit out of her.

Without waiting to see if it fell or not, Grace turned again and raced towards the door that led to the containment area. The crash from behind her announced the thing's passage into the station. It seemed her only chance lay in the cells and the safety of inch-thick bars.

Unable to check her speed on the slippery linoleum floor, Grace slammed into the metal door that led to the lock-up at the rear of the cop-shop. Grasping at the handle, Grace opened the door and entered the next room, spinning as the monstrous creature strutted across the reception area, wintery eyes locked on her.

Fuck! Close and lock, close and lock, close and lock!

Grace slammed the connecting door without concentrating on the creature's progress across the room. Knowing wouldn't help but the fraction of a second to look may cost her life. She fumbled at the lock, trying to engage it as quickly as possible.

The snick of the mechanism sounded a second before something heavy slammed into the door from the other side.

Grace backed slowly away, praying the door would hold. It seemed to buckle slightly under the hammering from the creature, but it still stood solid.

The first thing Grace noticed when she turned towards the two cells was the feeling of safety the reinforced rooms gave her.

The second was that one of the cells was already closed.

Through the observation port of the closed door she could see Kevin inside, back to her as he curled on the floor in the far corner, foetal position. *Fuckin' coward.*

Racing into the open cell, Grace grabbed the door and slammed it shut behind her. Ensuring it was locked, she moved over to the narrow bunk and sat down, staring at the port in the door, waiting for the thing to come into view.

The hammering had ceased, but the angle wouldn't allow her to see if it had breached the door or not.

Wait and see, I guess.

Grace finally broke down. It was all too much to cope with, now that she'd had a chance to process things.

What the fuck? Am I fucking crazy?

Curled up on the bunk, she shuddered, silent tears, jerking her chest like a jackhammer.

So many dead. Is there anyone but us left alive in the whole town?

She moved off the bed and closer to the door to see out of the observation port. Still nothing.

She realised that she'd dropped the shotgun in her panic, leaving her with just the pistol.

The view through the port was depressing. The cheap tinsel hanging from the wall opposite the small opening in the door must be meant to bring some Christmas cheer into the cells, but it failed dismally. It just reminded Grace of how many children would never see Christmas in Warcoola.

Shots rang out somewhere off in the distance. More

followed from a different direction. Grace heard them but couldn't believe it. She'd almost lost hope.

A scrabbling at the connecting door brought her back to here-and-now. The wooden surround quivered as something immensely strong pushed against the door. With a creak of metal, a bolt popped, followed by another a fraction of a second later.

With a final screech the whole doorway popped out of the wall, crashing to the floor in front of the two cells.

Even with the heavy barred door between her and the creature, Gracie took a step back, warm fluid spreading from her crotch and soaking her jeans. Stepping up to the cell, the thing lowered its head and leered at her through the aperture.

Gracie almost screamed when it grinned and winked at her. Reaching up, it slipped both hands through the small opening into the cell and gripped the door. A grunt escaped as it strained to tear it from the wall, massive forearms bulging with the effort. Veins stood out on its skin as beads of red-tinged sweat appeared.

For a second, the door itself quivered as though it would give, but the creature sagged, stymied by the strength of the construction. She grabbed the pistol from the shoulder-rig and aimed at one of its hands. She squeezed the trigger like her Dad had taught her so many years ago. She missed, but the ricochet was enough to startle the creature and make it pull back.

It lowered its head to look at her again. Grace managed to meet its gaze, heartened by the frustration evident on its strangely-human face. Growling in frustration, the thing disappeared from the opening before she could squeeze off another round.

More gunfire rang out, closer this time. It sounded almost out the front of the building. Flesh slammed against metal as the creature tried brute-force to get to her. The door held, but the second attack sounded different, not as solid. Either the thing was tiring or the door was weakening.

The third hit showed her which it was. The door seemed to bulge inward a little, the metal crumpling under the force of the barrage. The thing reached through the hole again, gripping the door and trying to force it open with all of its strength.

With a groan of tortured metal the barrier gave way, the top half bending inwards slightly. The only thing holding it closed was the tongue of metal from the lock itself. Gracie knew she had less than a minute to live.

The hands gripped the door even harder, one massive burst of strength finally ripping the lock open and sending the door crashing back against the wall, buckled and useless.

Framed by the doorway, the thing straightened from the effort and locked its gaze on her.

Flanking it on the left was one of the ghouls, the newly-risen. Drool fell from its mouth, slimy ropes suspended from nightmare jaws.

The smaller creature took a step forward.

Shots sounded at the same time an amplified voice rang out.

"Hold!"

The ghoul fell to a hail of bullets, its head a ruin, as the massive red creature froze in place. Gracie felt her heart start again as she realised she was saved. Behind the thing, soldiers moved carefully with rifles aimed at its back.

One of them held a small transceiver. An amplified voice issued from the device. "Do not move."

Confused, Gracie took another step away from the motionless creature, her back now against the wall. The pistol hung forgotten in her hands.

A uniformed officer appeared through the doorway from the front office, looked around the cell area, at the creature still in the same frozen position, and finally past it and right at her.

"Unlock the other cell. The infra-red showed another survivor in there." The officer's voice was crisp and full of authority. A soldier moved to follow his directive. He turned his attention fully to Gracie. "Miss, can you lower your weapon, please?"

"Not till that thing is dead." Gracie had no intention of lowering her gun while the creature was so close. She couldn't understand why it had frozen, either. "Why don't you kill it?"

The dull clang of Kevin's door opening reverberated through the building.

"Miss, please lower your weapon before we are forced to use live fire. Now." The officer maintained a calm façade, but there was a definite edge to his voice now.

Gracie slowly lowered the pistol, not taking her eyes off the thing in front of her. The ghoul had stopped twitching by this stage, silently oozing miasmic fluids in a pool around its mangled head.

"Good girl. Now put it on the floor." The satisfaction in the officer's voice unnerved her.

Why weren't they killing it?

As she followed his instructions, every instinct screamed at her to raise the pistol and start shooting the red fucker, but the rifles in the hands of the soldiers seemed to be pointing at her as much as at the creature itself.

Another soldier stepped into sight through the door, addressing the officer. "Colonel. All infected have been sanitised."

The officer turned to look at him. "Has fly-over confirmed this?"

"Yes sir." The soldier saluted and turned to go. The Colonel turned back to Gracie, who by now had carefully placed the gun on the floor by her feet.

A voice came from the front office. "How did he perform? Satisfactorily, I hope? I believe the infection rate was one hundred per cent. I'd call that a success, hey, Colonel?"

Gracie tried to absorb what was being said. *A success?*

The Colonel turned back towards the doorway behind. "Dr Iser. I believe our superiors will be very happy with the outcome of this test."

A test? Gracie couldn't believe her ears. *All this was a test?*

The Colonel turned back towards the cell door. "Call your subject back home while we tidy up."

The Doctor's voice rang out, commanding the creature to follow him. It turned and obeyed, moving past the soldiers who edged away and gave it as much room to pass as they could.

The Colonel spoke again. "Sergeant?"

A man clad in black fire-suppressant overalls stepped into Gracie's line of sight. "Sir?"

The Colonel gestured towards the two cells. "Sanitize the building, and then fall back. The town will be razed in exactly," he looked at his watch, "... forty-five minutes. Understood?"

The soldier looked chagrined. "Sir, yes, sir. May I voice my protest at this order, sir?"

"Protest noted. Now do your duty, Sergeant."

The Colonel spun around to leave as the SAS soldier turned to look at her, sorrow and shame evident in his eyes.

"Sorry, miss... orders is orders, y'understand."

Gracie noted a second black-clad man moving with silent purpose towards the door to Kevin's cell as the one in her own doorway raised his rifle. She tried to reach down for the pistol. It was too late.

WARCOOLA STATION: Population Zero

G.N. Braun is an Australian writer raised in Melbourne's gritty Western Suburbs.

He is a trained nurse, and holds a Cert. IV in Professional Writing and Editing and a Dip. Arts (Professional Writing and Editing). He is currently studying for a BA in Professional Writing and Publishing.

At graduation, Braun was awarded 'Vocational Student of the Year' and '2012 Student of the Year' by his college.

He writes fiction across various genres, and is the author of many short, published in Australia and internationally. He has a short story–'Autumn as Metaphor'–in the charity anthology *Horror For Good* ('Autumn' has now been reprinted four other times) and a short story–'Brand New Day'– in *Midnight Echo #7*, and has had numerous articles published in newspapers. He is the past president of the Australian Horror Writers Association (2011-2013), as well as the past director of the Australian Shadows Awards. He is an editor and columnist for UK site This is Horror, and was the guest editor for *Midnight Echo #9*.

His memoir, *Hammered*, was released in early 2012 by Legumeman Books and has been extensively reviewed.

He is the owner of Cohesion Editing and Proofreading, and has now opened a publishing house, Cohesion Press.

TEMPORARY MEASURES
Jay Wilburn

"Why three days?"

Jule glanced over at Tempat in her copilot seat and then back at her own controls in the pilot position. "Why did you wait three days to ask me that question?"

"I don't know. It just occurred to me."

"The ship has been traveling through the void of space for thousands of years now. What difference does a few more days make?"

"None," Tempat adjusted the thrusters with her right hand without being asked. "I just find the distance curious."

"The standard protocol has always been high orbit. Interstellar autopilot can be tricky after so long a journey. A small malfunction could result in a crash and then a disaster. It is better to have leeway than to have a problem. High orbit is three days. You over adjusted thrusters, officer, bring us back a couple degrees for docking approach."

"Acknowledged, adjustment made, Captain."

"What did you think it was?"

"What do you mean, Captain?"

The women made eye contact briefly. Both looked back on their controls as the behemoth of connected metal pods grew in the forward view.

"I mean, what answer were you expecting?"

Tempat licked her lips. "It sounds ignorant now, but I thought maybe it was a superstition about resurrection after three days."

"No, officer, it is a coincidence of protocol older than us and our current shuttle engine technology. You are drawing on some very old superstitions for that on."

"Yes, Captain, but the way we travel through space draws on an old superstition too."

Jule slowed the approach and rolled the shuttle to align it with the alien docking station. She used the sensors to set the width of the airlock to match.

"I haven't ever seen a colony ship configuration like this."

"Our star systems are far removed. We have not had contact in tens of thousands of years. Our technical evolution has diverged wildly in that time."

The shuttle shook and vibrated through the hull as it jarred into the docking port.

"Captain, we may have a problem."

"How's that?"

"The internal sensors are down. I have no reading on the passengers. They may be out. I'm reading artificial gravity similar to our own, but I've got nothing else."

"Failed sensors aren't uncommon after this long of a journey. Be vigilant, but suit up and prepare to go in for welcome protocols."

The women left the cockpit and pulled on their suits and fabric helmet hoods. Each checked the other to be sure the seals were in place. As their helmets filled with cooler air and expanded away from their faces, they entered the airlock.

Their voices crackled through the speakers in the helmets.

"Are you ready, officer?"

"I hope so, Captain."

"I'm not asking about your feelings, Tempat. Are you ready?"

"Yes, Captain."

Jule stared at her a moment longer. She hit the release. The round door ground across the distressed metal at the end of the airlock. Air rushed into the darkness from the short passage.

As they walked into the vessel, lights along the corridor tried to flicker on, but failed. They turned on the illumination on their helmets. The shafts of light were tight and did not extend all the way along the pod.

Jule could hear Tempat's breathing through the speaker by her ear. She bit down on her lip and tried to ignore it.

They rounded the curve of the passage and the breathing stopped. The capsules extended down both sides of the remainder of the passage and out of sight. Presumably they extended through the remainder of the pod.

"How many, Captain?"

"Hard to tell. This passage is sloping down as it curves."

"What does that mean?"

Jule turned her body in order to look at Tempat through her plastic faceplate. Tempat was turned so that her face didn't show in her suit. Jule could hear her breathing through the microphone and speakers again.

"It means the passage spirals. The capsules are slightly wider than a body. They are side by side. If the slope continues at this angle and if each pod is designed this way … you do the math."

Tempat's harsh breathing paused again. "It's an entire city. It's an entire civilization. They moved everyone. What is the point of that?"

"We're going to need help." Jule turned back toward the capsules.

"Do we go back and radio?"

"Let's start here and complete this pod. We need to know the situation before we involve more agents."

"Where do we start?"

Jule walked forward across the deck plates. "The first one."

They felt around the sides for controls. The hatch released and extended open a finger's breadth. Jule glanced back around the edge of her faceplate. Tempat was already opening her kit. Jule nodded, but she wasn't sure that Tempat saw it.

"Just follow the training, officer. They are only people in the end. We greet one and then repeat."

"Yes, Captain."

Jule lifted the hatch. There were mechanical hinges that folded out as the lid lifted away from the curve of the capsule.

"Primitive."

"Captain?"

"Step up, officer."

Tempat approached the pod with the gun sprung and ready. Jule stepped to the side to give her room.

Curved teeth like spikes shot up from both sides of the capsule's interior. The gun was knocked out of Tempat's hands. Jule cursed into her microphone and Tempat's ears. The device skidded across the deck. When it struck the closed capsule on the other wall of the passage, it discharged and the thick, wooden stake extended out from the barrel an arm's length.

"Reload it, Tempat, quickly."

Tempat ran forward and slid on her knees across the floor to snatch up the stake gun. She fumbled the trigger at first, but then got hold of the release. She pressed the sharp point of the stake into the flat metal of the wall locking it back into the body of the gun. When the spring popped, she stood up to run back.

Jule clenched her teeth as she unholstered her silver-mercury injector. "I hope this one isn't important to anyone."

Jule turned her gun and pointed at the chest of the body inside the capsule. She leaned over the side to see. The arms were motionless and at the sides of the body's hips. Yellowed nails jutted out from the black cuticles and the bloodless, white fingers, but the hands were still. She turned her head to look into the face.

Tempat charged back toward the open capsule. The claw-like extensions along the inside of the capsule's chamber were curled up and over the body.

Jule was distracted before she looked into the face. "They are made of wood?"

The claws sprung down into the prone body in six places. They pierced through the black uniform into the chest and abdomen above the heart, lungs, and other major organs. The colorless eyes flipped open and the injured man gasped for air despite the vacuum in the ship. His lips split as they peeled back from long fangs. The awakened man thrashed, but did not free himself from the wooden claws of the chamber. He stilled again with his eyes open, fangs exposed, and pale hands clutching the wooden shafts.

"What do we do, Captain?"

Two syringes sprung into the man's shoulders with no reaction. The women watched as the fluid plunged into the body. After a moment, the dead muscles relaxed and the hands fell back into the chamber. The jaws remained open, but the fangs began to retract into the black gums. Fresh blood began to ooze red from the sockets around the teeth. The eyes slid closed.

"Captain?"

"We need to figure out life support. He'll need air once he is greeted."

Tempat began walking back up the slope and curve of the corridor.

Human color began to bleed back into his flesh. His eyes flung open and light projected out from the orbs. He clinched his fangless jaws together and then opened his mouth to scream. Nothing issued. He collapsed again with his muscles twitching. Blood began to boil up from the stab wounds around the wood shafts. His skin began to glow with internal light.

The wood claws withdrew from the body and retracted into the chamber of the capsule. The man's head lolled to the side as the wounds began to heal.

The lights flickered again along the ceiling, but failed to illuminate. The capsules along the passage popped as each of their lids opened a finger's breadth one after the other along the corridor on both sides. Jule didn't hear the pop as much as she felt the vibration of it through the floor.

"What's going on?" Tempat was too far up the passage to see, but her voice came crisp through the speakers in Jule's helmet.

The pops continued until they were too far away for Jule to feel. The lids began to rise on their arcane hinges. The ones closest to her were concealed, but as the capsules continued down the slope, she could see the pale, shriveled hands and faces of men and women.

"And children?"

"Captain, what is it?"

Air began to hiss from the vents along the walls. She could actually hear it faintly through the helmet. The skin of her suit fluttered lightly.

"Did you find life support, Tempat?"

"No, Captain, it was automated."

The wooden claws sprung up over each chamber with a sharp crack echoing down the corridor. They drove down into the bodies one after the other. Now she could hear the screams. One of the smaller bodies convulsed with a full seizure.

"Why would they infect children and bring them? What kind of people ..."

She looked down on the man as he began to move in the first chamber beside her. He was breathing normally now. Jule unlatched her helmet and the fabric deflated. Atmosphere filled through the crack as it equalized.

"Captain, what do we do?"

"Nothing ... it looks like we won't need extra help after all."

~

"Don't stop him. Let's see what he has to say."

"Captain, we don't know these people. Do we want him having access to our computers like this?"

Jule looked around the chamber that wasn't really a bridge in the string of pods that made up the colony ship. "There is nothing on the shuttle they can use to hurt the planet."

"What about us, Captain?"

Jule snorted. "Officer, you should have considered that more completely before you joined this service. We do this so others don't have to be in danger. Everything we do is to protect others from the dangers of the travel disease."

"Yes, Captain."

As they spoke, the shivering man continued to work the controls accessing and loading files from the shuttle computers. His human fingers quivered as he tried to convert the files and language that were alien to him. He was bald from the greeting process and thousands of years of dead sleep. He flexed his hands that had been pale, blackened, and clawed moments before he led the women to the control room.

He continued to struggle with the files. Text in both languages scrolled over the screens too quickly for any of the three of them to read.

He began to jabber into the microphone.

The computer translated in a strange accent. "Do these words make sense to you?"

"Yes," Jule answered.

The computer translated into two syllables.

Tempat muttered. "Why would a language make that a two syllable word?"

The computer began translating in a long string. The man listened with his brow furrowed.

Jule interrupted. "Ignore that. What is it you need to ask

us?"

The computer paused and then translated in three syllables. Jule looked at Tempat. The junior officer held her hands up without responding out loud.

The man nodded and loaded the computer with a long monologue. "Our ship is damaged. According to our logs, there was an attack in a star system we were not aware was inhabited between our ancestral worlds and our new homeland. Three pods broke away with all onboard including the embryos as the rest of the ship continued on course."

Jule spoke and then she waited for the traveler to process the translation behind him. "Did you put all your embryos in that pod or did you just lose a portion of your supply?"

He became visibly upset and repeated the same sounds multiple times. "Every life is important to us ... every life. We lost our people and those embryos are the future of our entire culture. Every life ... After all that we lost in the bloody invasion, every life matters ... every life. We sacrificed so much to escape that plague on our world."

"We're sorry for your loss," Tempat started reaching for him.

He drew away from her reach. He was still shivering in his torn, blood-stained uniform.

Jule asked, "What is the bloody invasion? What plague?"

He began to explain. When he finished, Jule dismissed him to tend to his people.

"What does this mean, Captain?"

"It's time to call for help and we have tough choices to make."

~

"I understand what is involved, Captain."

"You couldn't possibly, Tempat. Either way ... this is our last mission. You can decline and start a new service in another agency. Staying proves nothing. Someone else can go.

This is very early in your career."

"Do you want someone else to go, Captain?"

"I don't want anything, but for you to be completely sure about the decision you make. This is the rest of your life ... no matter what we find. There will be no family ... past or in your future."

"I understand it results in sterilization, if that is what you are saying."

"That's only part of what I am saying."

"This is important. If the virus has gotten out of the can, it could be spreading across the universe. We need to protect humanity throughout inhabited space."

Jule stood and walked to the other side of the ship.

Tempat remained seated and looked at the two open chambers in the back of the shuttle. "You want to talk me out of this? You want to fly three days back planet side and then three back out into the drink to start over a week late?"

Jule laughed quietly without turning back around. "This is thousands of years of travel. One week makes no difference ... death may already be in route, if what we fear has actually occurred. Either way, everyone you have ever known will be long dead by the time we find out. There is plenty of work to be done acclimating the new colonists, a lifetime of work."

"That's not my job, Captain. This is."

Jule set in the course and they watched through the forward screen at nothing. The star pattern was bright, but unremarkable. There was no sensation of motion, there was no sound from the engine inside the small shuttle, and there was little data on the forward instruments to mark their minute progress. They stared anyway.

"You set in your chamber first, officer."

"I can do it, Captain."

"Tempat, I didn't ask what you could do. I ordered you to do what you needed to do."

"Yes, Captain."

Jule prepared the injection as her only crewmember laid

down in the tight alcove within the chamber. Jule leaned over and opened her mouth, but didn't say anything. Tempat nodded.

Jule plunged the syringe into Tempat's neck. Tempat hissed, but held herself still. The dark lines ripped across the surface of her exposed skin and then disappeared under the uniform. The veins and arteries bulged and threatened to rupture. Tempat screamed as the color melted out of her skin and the definition disappeared in her eyes. She opened her jaws wider and peeled back her lips. The fangs were already tearing through her gums. Three permanent human teeth were ejected in a bloody spew as the inhuman feeders made violent space.

Her voice was harsh and drawn. "Close it."

The captain followed her crewman's order. The door sealed and locked. The claws that had sprouted through Tempat's cuticles ran over the metal of the door inside. After a moment there was an angry scream and then a howl inside.

Jule waited.

The chamber hissed as the air was pumped out from inside. The creature thrashed against the reinforced sides.

The captain patted the lid before she prepared her own injection. She set the failsafe countdown on the controls and climbed into her own chamber. She plunged her neck and cast the syringe out on the deck plates. The lid closed on her before the failsafe reached zero. Controls beeped to shutdown the countdown instead of ejecting her into space. As the chamber locked her in darkness, she waited for the air to be sucked out.

"I'll join you soon, officer." Her voice lost its human tone on her final syllable.

Her vision flashed in the darkness with fiery pain. She could see the details inside the chamber in red despite the darkness. She screamed in pain and her claws cracked against the lid as she struggled to escape.

As her human mind clouded over and the ancient infection overtook her, she felt two desires waxing and waning within her. She wanted blood. She wanted the air to escape from her chamber so she would be suffocated.

~

Her eyes peeled open in burning torment. The ancient jelly of her eyes ruptured, the lids tearing away from them. She could still see in colorless detail through the blinding light of the shuttle. Her muscles were lifeless masses, but she stirred them and they creaked as she reached with black claws for the bald human above her. Jule's lungs inflated and she hissed through her impossibly dry throat.

Tempat pressed the device against the captain's chest through the uniform and pulled the trigger. Color exploded into the room as the wood shaft pierced Jule's chest and ground against two vertebrae on the way through her back.

She was angry and hungry for Tempat's blood. Jule unhinged her jaw and extended her fangs. She could not reach far enough to close her claws over Tempat's soft human neck. She grabbed the rungs around the outside of the gun and pulled herself up from the bed the spike sliding painfully through her body.

She was so focused on the veins humming in Tempat's neck, she didn't notice the spike digging through her heart and one lung. The darkness kicked in quickly and she dropped back in the bed. Tempat said something Jule couldn't grasp as she drove a syringe into Jule's pale neck.

Jule stared at Tempat's wrist close enough that she could smell the iron through the thin skin. She could not will her brittle neck to turn.

Then, the light burst inside her. The sunlight ate at her insides. She felt every organ and the heat escaped from her sockets and pores. She finally wished for death more than blood.

Jule took the controls and steered the shuttle toward the readings. They were not close enough to see the shape of things. She fought the urge to reach up and feel her own bald head again.

"Captain, you can take time to recover. I rested a couple hours before I opened your chamber. We've been under for three thousand, two hundred years. A few more hours make little difference."

"I'll rest as we travel."

"The automated systems failed. I nearly escaped my chamber before mine kicked back into motion."

"It doesn't matter now, Tempat... You did well."

The field in front of them began to separate and define as they drew closer. They passed in silence for a period of time. Tempat offered water to Jule again and she took it.

"Captain ... are you sorry we made this journey?"

"You might as well call me Jule ... we'll never see the agency again. Ask me about regrets once we know more ... or if we have to go under again to reach the original system of those colonists and their bloody invasion as they called it."

"You think the escapees or plague victims followed them. Were they on their way here or did they pass us on their way to our system?"

"There's no way to know."

A reading appeared at the edge of their sensor field. They weren't close enough to identify, but it was coming from the nearest planet second from the star.

"Is that habitable, Captain... Jule?"

"Too far to tell. Habitable is not excluded. Something has launched. I can't tell how many, what, or how fast."

"Are they coming for us?"

Jule shook her head. "Can't tell. Try to signal them."

"Are you sure about that, Jule?"

Jule licked her teeth. She could still feel the empty sockets in her gums where the fangs had been.

"It will take eleven or twelve minutes for the signal to even reach them. We have to see what is here one way or the other."

"The colonial ship was attacked in this system."

"That was millennia ago and the ship was unmanned as it passed through the system. If we have to run, we'll run."

Tempat sent the standard numerical pattern, identification, and linguistic markers to aid translation. She didn't have to speak.

Jule adjusted the settings and the debris field ahead of them began to show on the screens in sharp detail. In the leading edge of the objects, there was at least one portion of the sphere of a colonial pod.

"Is that promising, Jule?"

"Thousands of years in the same spot in space? It could certainly be bad."

Tempat adjusted course to bring the shuttle to the broken pod below the other scattered shards of metal and gear. A few pieces passed by the forward view port close enough for light inside the shuttle to gleam off their edges. Each piece seemed isolated and unimpressive in the lonely dark. On the sensor reads, the debris was thick and covered a large curve through the void that extended beyond the sensor range.

The objects from the planet were approaching from just within the ability of their sensors to detect. Twelve minutes passed. Then twice that. After triple the time, Jule began to debate if they were ignoring the signal, unable to detect it, or weren't ships at all.

Tempat angled the nose farther down the z-axis to stay below the scattered metal. She found a gap below the quarter-sphere of pod and traveled up the passage in the field.

They stared at the image in the scanner readout.

Jule breathed deeply. "Run a broader scan of the main object, Tempat."

"What are we looking for?"

"You know what there is to look for, Tempat. Focus on organics."

She began running through the spectrum of possible scans.

"Why haven't we found a better... safer way to travel between systems by now?"

"It's a big galaxy. Someone may have it by now and, like everything else, it spreads given enough time."

"We still use the disease with all its potential danger."

Jule tongued the missing spaces in her top gum. "Diseases can be cured. This is no exception ... even if it has spread."

"I have something... there are chambers in the remaining pod with organic readings."

"That can only mean one thing. Is the ship exposed to space through the chamber sections?"

"It is."

"Well, there is that much. Maybe the planet decided to leave them isolated rather than greeting them. If they are still here, maybe it worked. We'll still have to travel on to the original system the colonists fled. Are their organics outside the pod wreckage?"

"Yes, some of it is definitely remains... some definitely not human... or the other. Most are not conclusive."

"Move us along the curve of the open side. Keep us away from the jagged interior."

Tempat complied as they watched and waited.

"I don't see anything else, Jule. The readings are the same even from this range."

"We're going to have to suit up and travel in to be sure they're all greeted."

"Even after all this time?"

Jule stared at the controls a moment longer. "How close are those ships?"

"They are moving slower than our own maximum speed. Four or maybe five days out unless they accelerate."

Jule inhaled as she stood up from the controls. The first

tremors of the impacts on the hull carried through the oxygen in the crew compartment. Jule felt the vibration in her teeth. Metal began to grind on the outside.

"What is it?" Jule asked.

"Organic... not human... something else. How are they moving in the void?" Tempat looked up from the sensors.

"Adaptation and patience."

"Do we make a run for it?"

Jule shook her head. "To where?"

Tempat didn't answer.

~

The shuttle jarred violently to one side and then the other. This was not a normal feeling in space. The first few days had been more of a long siege. The engines failed to respond due to whatever happened outside the hull. Their attempts to break through the airlock to get to Jule and Tempat had not succeeded.

Not sleeping had taken its toll on the two women trapped inside. Now that the crafts had arrived, the attacks became desperate and violent.

The shuttle was rotating from whatever was happening. They saw the dull sunlight washing over the broken guts of the ancient pod which deepened the darkness in the shadows more. Then, the thin pieces of debris against the star backdrop seemed to drift through the forward view. Finally, they caught the first visual glimpse of the flat crafts diving down through the broken metal above them.

"Maybe they are inclined to rescue us, Captain... Jule."

Jule didn't answer. She was hoping they would launch an explosive and end the entire episode.

Something fell loose with a clatter in the back of the ship as the shuttle shook again. Metal above them and on one side buckled visibly into the crew compartment.

"Captain?"

"Put on suits."

They began suiting up, helping one another with the attachments and clasps. Tempat inflated her hood. Jule waited and let the fabric draw into her face. The plastic screen began to fog. She could hear Tempat's breathing through the speakers again.

Pristine white sabers pierced through the metal of the bulkhead above them. Tempat gasped inside Jule's hood. Still she waited to engage her oxygen. The white points hung large and sharp above them like the tusks of an animal on the open plains.

"This can't be real," Jule said.

"I'm scared, Captain."

Jule engaged her air tank and her hood expanded away from her face. The tusks ground back out of the hull letting air suck out through the breach. Another set of giant fangs exploded through the other side of the ship. They were longer than the women's bodies and thicker than their limbs. They pumped in and out like they were chewing before they drew back out. Air began pulling at the women as it passed.

"What is this, Captain?"

The forward view behind them began to crackle. The women turned in time to see a massive paw with black claws peeling away the strong plastic of the view port. The vacuum was powerful drawing them toward the bloated, pale arm as wide as a trunk.

Jule pulled Tempat away from the controls as the arm reached into the shuttle and clawed blindly through the escaping air. They grabbed hold of the sleep chambers in the center of the ship just out of the monster's reach.

Jule fired two rounds from the mercury-silver injector. Before they reached the arm, they were sucked off course and escaped from the side of the ship. Jule lost her grip on the injector and it spun out through the forward view by the monster's shoulder.

The air began to escape more slowly.

"Did some animal or alien get infected with the disease, Captain?"

"Maybe this is what happens after thousands of years in open space."

The arm drew back out and the women could see the other ships as the shuttle rotated back toward them. The owner of the arm kicked off the shuttle and sailed toward the flat crafts. Its body was naked, colorless, and misshapen. Jule couldn't identify if it had been male or female. Its tusk fangs were extended as were its black claws. The creature had grown to almost the size of the shuttle.

"We would barely be a snack for that thing."

"What?"

Normal human-sized shapes exited the crafts from the planet as light flashed across the bellies of the sleek hulls. They were armed with spears or harpoons. They wore packs that ejected white mist as they maneuvered around the monster's course. The ballet was silent.

Another giant monster kicked off the shuttle and sailed after the first. The ship began to rotate downward instead of around.

Jule caught sight of the flat crafts' army as they hooked onto the giants' flesh and began attacking through the bloated skin. Black fluid bubbled out of the wounds around the wooden spears as the giant thrashed and tore through each tiny spacewalker it could reach with its claws. Arms and heads floated apart as the bodies were jetted away by the packs. Dark blood formed liquid spheres as it drifted in a spiral around the void of the battle.

The second giant arrived and grabbed a tiny warrior in each of its massive paws. As the shuttle rotated out of view, Jule saw no hoods or suits on the human-sized soldiers. One of the captured spacewalkers bit down on the giant's thumb holding her.

"They're fighting over a meal?"

"Captain?"

"We have to try to engage the engines while they are focused on each other."

"We don't know how they disabled them, Captain."

"Maybe they've stopped."

Tempat screamed and fell away from the sleep chambers. The deck plates lifted and Jule stumbled backward. One tusk stabbed up through Tempat's foot and along her leg. The other struck one of the chambers and twisted the open door away from the bed.

Tempat reached out to Jule, but the captain charged forward and ran for the controls instead. The artificial gravity threatened to malfunction as the ship was torn apart by giant fangs and claws. Tempat screamed.

Jule manipulated the controls and the engines powered up for the first time in three days. As she set a course back for their own system, a human-sized hand locked over her wrist. Two faces glared at her through the view port peeled out away from the ship. They bared their fangs silently at her from the void outside. As one pulled Jule's hand away from the controls, the other reached for her throat. The shuttle stopped rotating and twisted itself into position on its thrusters. Tempat was still groaning in Jule's speakers.

Jule grabbed another lever and the metal blackout shutters began to crank down over the inside of the open port. Jule smiled as fear enveloped the monsters' faces. The shutters sliced through as they slammed shut. Two arms fell, bleeding, back between the controls. Jule had to pull away the fingers from a severed claw to release her wrist.

Metal battered the sides of the shuttle as it plowed through the debris.

The tusks had withdrawn and Tempat was motionless on the twisted floor, her suit torn. Jule ran back and dragged Tempat's body into the undamaged sleep chamber. She prepared the injection. Tempat tore the deflated hood loose from her face and sank her fangs into Jule's wrist. Jule hauled up the gun from the floor and pressed it into Tempat's chest.

Tempat continued to drain from Jule's arm even as she stared at the weapon.

Jule pulled the trigger and sprung the stake into Tempat. It took another couple seconds for her to release Jule's wrist. She jerked the gun and wooden spear loose from Tempat's body and pulled the door closed on the chamber with her good hand.

"I'm sorry I didn't do a better job of talking you out of this, officer."

The tusks speared up through the deck plates near the cockpit. Jule looked from the fangs to the other broken chamber that was left. As blood and air escaped her suit, she went back to the controls and changed the course on the shuttle sending it out toward deep space away from their home star system.

"Bloody invasion…"

The tusks speared through the side of the shuttle again.

Jule felt the madness and thirst building in her again. She staggered to the airlock and sealed herself in. She wiped the blood from her wrist on the outside of the suit as she set the sequence into the controls.

Then she collapsed.

~

Jule awoke with a fire inside her chest. She was hungry. She poked at the controls to release herself, but the commands had been code-locked. Her suit was ruptured and her hood was collapsed around her face, but the small airlock was full of oxygen. She realized there was blood on the outside of her suit. She began trying to tear her way out to get to it.

The timer reached zero and the airlock opened. The force of the air escaping ejected Jule away from the ship.

As she spun through the void, she continued to try to pull her suit off to get to the blood. With each turn, she saw the giant holding the bottom of the shuttle's hull. It turned its twisted head to look at Jule and then kicked off the shuttle reaching out for her.

As Jule licked the outside of her uniform in the airless cold, the giant drifted with her, reaching helplessly. The fleet of flat ships followed the battered shuttle as it led them away from her and their home thousands of years in another direction.

Jule sucked up every bit of the blood. She craved it more than air.

Jay Wilburn lives in the swamps of coastal South Carolina with his wife and two sons. He left teaching after sixteen years to care for the health needs of his younger son and to pursue full-time writing. He has published a number of works including the novels Loose Ends and Time Eaters. He has a piece in Best Horror of the Year Volume Five. Follow his dark thoughts at JayWilburn.com and @AmongTheZombies on Twitter.

I, VAMPIRE
Violet Addison and David N. Smith

Molly had become a vampire when she was sixteen years old. Other vampires had always seemed to work their way up into positions of wealth and power, but not her, she had been running and hiding ever since she had risen.

On her first night, it had been a wild, unorganised rabble chasing her down a county lane with oil lamps and clubs. Now, over a hundred and fifty years later, she was fleeing through the bustling streets of night-time London, with a dozen armed police officers in dogged pursuit.

If she had been human, her heart would have been hammering and she would have been struggling for breath, but as a vampire she suffered no such frailties.

She could move faster than any human alive.

In the past, she had been able to outrun the mob, but over the centuries the humans had become significantly better at the game of cat and mouse. Increasingly, they were no longer the mouse. There was a helicopter in the sky above her, following her every move, as she twisted and turned down narrow alleyways. As fast as she was, the helicopter was faster. As clever as she was, dodging under bridges and into buildings, the humans were now capable of rapidly deploying their forces to cut her off at every turn.

Any physical advantage the vampires once possessed had been negated by humanity's technological advances.

Molly suddenly found herself trapped in an alleyway, with a pair of police officers blocking her path ahead, and a trio of police vans roaring up the road behind her, sirens wailing.

She continued to press forward, rushing headlong at the two opponents in front of her.

She briefly glimpsed the guns in their hands, but no vampire was scared of bullets; they would slice through her, passing in and out of her dead flesh, barely make her break stride, before her skin would begin to knit closed.

She would break their necks before they realised their bullets were useless.

Too late, she noticed that these were not normal guns.

They had distinctive yellow plastic casings, and she could hear the electrical whine of them charging up; these were Taser pistols.

In recent years, these had rapidly become the British Police's weapon of choice, ostensibly to avoid human fatalities, but undoubtedly also because it was effective against vampires.

The first bolt hit her square in the chest, unleashing an electrical charge that burnt though every muscle in her body. She convulsed. Her legs, which had been carrying her swiftly forward, suddenly bucked outwards in random directions, causing her to topple chin first into the road.

The police vans slammed to a halt around her.

The rear doors were thrown open and numerous pairs of black boots hit the tarmac.

Molly was helpless, still convulsing, as the police officers surrounded her.

As far as she was aware, it had been two decades since the government had caught its last vampire, Edmund Bingley, who it was said had become the victim of human medical experiments; including a waking autopsy, dissected over weeks, organ by organ, whilst still conscious. Now she was likely to suffer the same. In vampire circles, the name Molly Whitlock would be remembered with shame, used as a terrifying reminder that the cattle were now more deadly than their predators.

One of the officers advanced on her, a length of sharpened wood clench in his black-gloved hand.

Molly stared at him, hoping he would strike out and deliver the fatal blow to her heart. Becoming burning dust was infinitely preferable to becoming the humans' next test subject.

"Hood her."

A police officer pulled a bag over her head, plunging her into darkness, and then secured her wrists behind her back with heavy handcuffs.

With her strength returning, she made a belated attempt to fight them, kicking the nearest one away, but even as she leapt blindly to her feet, the muffled sound of four Taser pistols powering up penetrated the thick canvas hood.

She tried to run, but was hit from every side by the Taser bolts. She crumpled to the ground, writhing in agony.

She was dimly aware of being man-handled into the back of a van, as she spun in and out of consciousness, overwhelmed by the shock and pain coursing through her body, before she finally passed out.

She woke up in a cell.

The hood and handcuffs had been removed, but she was still groggy and disorientated as she rose to her feet.

It was not a police cell.

As she had feared, it felt distinctly more like a hospital, or laboratory. The walls were painted white and there was a strong smell of disinfectant lingering in the air. There was a heavy, pressure-sealed door in the wall behind her and an observation window in the wall in front. Behind the glass there was only darkness, but she could sense the minds of people standing in the shadows beyond.

Two humans, perhaps three, hidden in the darkness.

One consumed with anger.

Another more uncertain; almost concerned.

"I know you're there," she called, tapping a fingernail against the glass, trying to determine its strength. The glass was an inch thick. Not even a vampire could punch through it.

The humans had built a cell specifically to hold a vampire.

She was a prisoner. At least until one of them was stupid enough to open the door. Then, once she had the chance, she would kill them all.

A light went on behind the glass, revealing a trio of figures standing in the small room beyond. The first was an older woman, with grey hair and tired eyes, wearing a white medical lab coat. Hidden speakers hissed static for a moment, before a tinny, lifeless facsimile of her voice punctured the silence.

"What is your name, please?"

Molly shook her head. She had no intention of helping them. She leaned closer to the window, noting the position of a small microphone set on her side of the glass.

"Why am I here?"

The second figure, a heavy-set man in a police uniform, gently moved the older woman to one side and leaned in towards the microphone. He was the same officer that had ordered her hooding, abduction and imprisonment.

"You're responsible for the deaths of at least eight people this year."

Eight? Had she really been so careless, letting them track her for that long?

The police officer pointed at a wall of photographs behind him, which had eight faces prominently on display, surrounded by other images of their bloodless, lifeless corpses. Were these her victims? They could be, but it was difficult for her to remember all the faces, as so many had come and gone over the last one hundred and fifty years that very few now stuck in her memory. They were just meals.

"If I am accused of murder, then surely I should be in a courtroom?" She tilted her head, playing the fool, making them talk, while she revealed nothing.

"Courtrooms are for human beings," the police officer stated coldly. "Not monsters."

"Enough, Superintendent Carter." The old woman subtly shook her head.

"And this little loophole will be your excuse for what, exactly?" Molly asked the question, not to get an answer, because she already knew the story of Edmund Bingley, but because she wanted them to say the words; humans had a morality, which was easily shaken when you made them face up to what they were doing. They were weak, fickle, flickering ephemera that passed from the world, before they even have a chance to realise what they were.

"We want you take part in a study," the old woman replied, taking note of Molly's unimpressed reaction. "If you do so voluntarily and co-operate whole heartedly, and are found to be anything other than a monster, then you will be accorded your full human rights."

Molly almost laughed.

"And if I refuse to take part in this charming and educational study?"

"Then we'll put you down," Superintendent Carter replied, his eyes glimmering darkly. "Just like we would any other dangerous animal."

There was a real malevolence in his voice, an unbridled hate, which made the old woman flinch with discomfort. He was not hiding his intentions. He wanted her dead. Such hate in humans was usually caused by a personal loss. Perhaps she had killed someone he was close to?

Molly's eyes flicked to the third figure behind the glass, a bland middle-aged man in an old suit, who had been watching her intently through his thin-framed glasses. He had given nothing away. He had not said a word. Given the proposal that had just been made, this was undoubtedly his task; he was there to study her, and he was doing it with a calm, clinical detachment.

The police officer slammed a palm against the glass, directly in front of her face, clearly offended that her attention had drifted away from him.

"Your life is in our hands."

"You think I can't overpower you?"

The human needed to be taught his place, reminded that despite the fact that she may look like a teenage girl, she could easily snap his neck.

"Try it," the Superintendent grinned. "Even if you win, this whole laboratory is rigged for decontamination by fire. If anything goes wrong here, it takes just one of us to push the button and everything burns. And rest assured; I'll be the one with his finger on the button."

Molly nodded.

"I guess I'd better play your game then."

"To start with, we have some questions that you must answer." The challenge was clear in the rigidness of the woman's voice and pointedness of her words; Molly had to co-operate fully, give honest and open answers, or she would be sacrificing her existence. "What is your name, please?"

"Mary Whitlock. Molly, to my friends."

The old woman wrote the name down on the form.

"And when and where were you born?"

"I was born Fifth of February, 1832, in the town parish of Chipping Barnet."

The old woman added this information, and then dropped the clipboard and pen into a tray beneath the window, which she pushed into a cell.

"Sign."

Humans were ridiculous. Did they really believe that just because she put her name to a piece of paper that it would bind her into obeying their agreement? Vampires lived above human law. Did they not know that the moment they opened the door her fangs would be in their throats?

She signed the paperwork and returned it to the tray.

Her name was the only word she knew how to write. During her human life she had been given only a basic education by her mother, which did not include literacy, and somehow in the last one hundred and fifty years she had never quite managed to find the time to acquire the skill that almost every human in the country now possessed.

She had often thought that this, combined with her adolescent looks, could well be the reason why she struggled in a society where other vampires thrived.

The old woman checked the papers and then glanced at the quiet man in the corner.

"She's all yours, Peterson."

The old woman left the room. Superintendent Carter, shaking his head with derision, followed her out the door.

"So, are you going to come in and take skin and blood samples then?" Molly asked with a grin, hoping he would try.

Peterson shook his head.

"You misunderstand the nature of the study. It's not biological, it's sociological. I'm a behavioural psychologist."

This time Molly could not contain her laugh.

"You're here to analyse me?! That's ridiculous!" She let herself rise up off the floor. Levitation always scared humans, as it defied all their beliefs in how the world worked. The middle-aged scientist's eyes widened, as she casually defied the laws of physics. "Vampires are far beyond the understanding of mortal men."

He quietly jotted several words down on the noted pad. These humans really liked their paperwork. It unnerved her; in many ways she preferred the simple, honest bloodlust of the police officer, which at least she understood.

"My job is to determine the nature of vampire psychology," he lowered his notepad and met her eyes. "Are you an intelligent, self-aware creature, potentially capable of functioning as a normal member of human society? Or are you an animal, which acts purely on its base desires? Or are you something else, something truly soulless and evil, something that is beyond our rational understanding? Or are you something else entirely?"

Molly gently lowered herself to the floor, letting gravity take its grip on her.

In one hundred and fifty years she had never stopped to consider her own nature any further than an understanding of the name it was given; she was a vampire, was that not all the explanation that was required? Everyone knew what vampires were. She had always known what this meant, but now he was casting doubt upon it.

"Which do you believe to be the case?" he asked.

She shook her head.

"I am vampire."

"You've killed at least eight people in the last seven months." He put down his note pad, and unpinned a photograph from the wall and held it up against the glass. It was an image of a seven-year-old boy with sandy hair and a gap-toothed smile. "Jack Bradshaw. You abducted him from outside his primary school in West London, and left his corpse in the nearest tube tunnel."

Molly nodded.

She remembered being interrupted by over-all clad tube workers, having to rush the feed, abandon the body and run. She had hoped they would miss the body in the darkness, but clearly they had not.

"I remember Jack," she said, as she stared at the photograph. "He was sweet."

"Then why did you kill him?"

"I mean he tasted sweet." She turned her vision away from the dead boy and onto the man with the glasses. "The young always do."

"And you don't consider such an act to be abhorrent? This for most people would be the very definition of evil."

"I needed to feed. The young are easier prey." Molly shrugged and moved away from the glass, turning her back on the psychologist, not enjoying how his gaze seemed to penetrate her.

"How do you think lambs view the human race? Are you a soulless murderer, just because you enjoy a tender chop?"

"We're just a form of cattle to you?"

Molly nodded. That was exactly how she had always thought of humans. Cattle.

"I need human blood to survive. You're just a meal. Mankind is just not as high up the food-chain as you like to believe. I guess, by your definition, this just makes me a dangerous animal?"

Peterson did not respond to her question, instead he asked one of his own.

"Who was your very first victim?"

"My mother."

The psychologist's pen went frantic; he must have scribbled down half a page before he noticed that Molly had stopped talking.

"Why her?"

"I went to her for help." Molly shrugged. "She betrayed me to the local vicar. They came after me with a wooden cross."

Molly shuddered. She had spent most of the last one hundred and fifty years trying to forget about that day, about slaughtering everyone in the house, and then being trapped alone with all the corpses, because she could not venture out into the daylight without burning. Eventually other visitors had come to the house and discovered the bodies of her family. That night she had fled, with a mob at her heels.

She told Peterson all of this, including all the graphic, bloody detail.

She expected him to be shocked, but instead he calmly noted everything down on his notepad and then asked another simple question.

"What help did you hope your mother would provide?"

"A way out. A way to cope with what I had become." Molly could feel the edge of sadness break in her voice, as long forgotten memories surfaced, seeming more fresh and clear than anything else that happened to her in the last one hundred and fifty years. "She always gave good advice."

"You tried to be something other than a killer?"

Peterson's voice had shifted. There was a tremor of doubtful hope rising in his voice, finally revealing his beliefs, that he wanted her to be a sympathetic and redeemable figure, but for some reason was already resigned to disappointment.

"Humans can't understand. Sooner or later they always become scared of us, or we have to feed, and they end up dead."

"You had no choice?"

"I often choose to run. You'd be surprised how often they follow."

Peterson made another note.

"But with your family, you had no choice?"

"They were trying to kill me. They wouldn't stop."

"Are you sure you had no choice?"

Molly did not answer him. One hundred and fifty years of killing all started on one night, with the death of her family, when she was seeking a way to become something else. She had never dared look back. Had all those countless deaths been inevitable, or had there been another choice?

Both options left her feeling numb.

"I don't know."

She was unsettled. With half a dozen queries this man had undone her entire world, suddenly making her question everything about her very nature.

How had she never asked these things of herself?

Peterson quietly filed away his notes in a bag.

"I would like Doctor Langley to run a series of neurological tests, using an MRI machine, to determine if any of your behaviour has physiological cause."

Molly stared at him blankly.

"I was born in 1832, over a hundred years before the television set was invented, when the light bulb and the flush toilet were the pinnacle of invention, do you think I have the faintest idea what any of those words mean?"

Peterson smiled.

"I want to use a machine, to see what your brain is doing." He paused. "Will you murder me if I open the door?"

Molly smiled.

"Well, that would rather depend on whether I'm a demonic monster, a trapped animal, or a person who is intrigued to understand their own nature, wouldn't it?"

Peterson raised his eyebrows, obviously a little surprised by her words. What had he expected? A simple no?

"I'll be around shortly."

She was surprised. He was unexpectedly confident.

He clearly believed that she would not kill him.

But she might.

Peterson turned the light off, plunging the room beyond into deep, empty blackness. With the room gone, she could see her white-walled cell reflected in the glass, with the space where she stood seemingly empty.

Vampires have no reflection, but to her knowledge there was still no scientific explanation as to why, and like the levitation and immortality, it was just another trait that set them apart from the rest of the natural world and made them something to be feared.

What would she do when he opened the door? Earlier she had been committed to killing them all and escaping, or becoming dust in the attempt, but was she now giving serious consideration to voluntarily staying?

Was she curious about what their study would discover?

She heard the lock disengage and watched as the door opened.

No, she was a prisoner, and no good would come of participating in their experiments. Her first and foremost desire was to escape.

She did not want to speculate about what that made her.

She did not care.

Given the threats stacked against her, particularly the danger of the decontamination fire, she would have to play along for now.

Peterson beckoned her out of the room and into the corridor.

She obediently followed.

The old woman in the white lab coat was waiting for her in the room beyond.

Neither human seemed as scared as Molly would have expected. Normally humans always tended towards fear once they knew what she was, but these two seemed unexpectedly confident that she would be compliant. Perhaps they understood her nature even better than she did? But how was that possible? How could they know anything about vampires?

Molly moved into the room, which was dominated by a massive circular MRI scanner. She had seen such devices before, during her visits to hospitals, which she frequented regularly to find weak victims, or to steal pre-packed snack bags of blood.

The old woman, Doctor Langley, gave her a long and complex explanation about how the machine worked. Molly only half listened; she was too busy studying the room for some means of escape. No windows. Another heavy, pressure-sealed door, with no operating mechanism on her side. There was also another dark observation window, implying that someone may be sitting in darkness watching them; she could take the two doctors hostage, try and negotiate her way out, but this would most likely end with the flames that Superintendent Carter had warned her about. In fact, he was very likely the one on the other side of the glass, watching her now, his finger poised on the button.

She glanced at the black surface.

She sensed the human mind hidden in the shadows, watching her with disgust and hate.

There was no way out.

She soon found herself lying back in the machine, staring at a series of images, as lightning-like flashes banged around her. She had understood the basics of Doctor Langley's explanation, the images were supposed to induce an emotional reaction in her brain, which the machine would take a snap-shot of, somehow revealing to them something of how her mind worked.

A field of flowers in bloom.

A partly undressed young woman, blushing.

A baby crying, alone.

A teenage boy firing a gun in the air.

A gravestone.

The process took hours, and left Molly feeling increasingly hungry and tired. She was growing bored with playing nice.

Then she felt it. Another presence.

Somewhere beyond the room was another mind.

She could sense another vampire, just beyond the walls. No, more than one. A dozen or more. All imprisoned. All angry.

One of them was in agonising pain.

Edmund Bingley.

It was Edmund Bingley. He was still alive. After twenty years of experimentation, they still had him locked up, in perpetual agony, just metres away from her.

As the machine was shut off, she looked at the tired old woman and the bland man in his spectacles and old suit, and noted how dispassionate and resigned they were in their work. They had done this before. Countless times.

That was how they had been so sure she would not kill them; they had played out this scenario before with numerous other vampires, they knew the threat of fire was enough to keep their prisoner's actions in check.

"How many vampires do you have here?"

Both the doctors froze.

"You can sense them?" The middle-aged man frowned, clearly curious. "We've never encountered a vampire with that level of telepathy before."

He was calm, clearly unaware of the danger he was now in. The wave of anger and pain that had just swept through her brain was unlike anything she had ever felt before, and she suddenly had an overwhelming desire to make them suffer for their part in it.

"I can hear Edmund Bingley screaming." She leapt to her feet, and seized hold of the old woman, knowing that she was the weaker member of the trio, the most doubtful of their actions and the most likely to talk. "Why would you do this?"

The old woman recoiled, terrified.

"Every medical trial needs a number of test subjects, a large enough base to determine if the results are the same across the spectrum. We have seventy-five vampires here, which we've collected over the last twenty years, enough to form a working theory on vampire psychology."

"And how many of them passed your little tests and earned themselves human rights?" she seethed, already suspecting the answer.

"All of them," the old woman replied.

It was not the answer she had been expecting.

"And so you imprisoned them all?"

The old woman squirmed trying to break out of her grip.

There had never been any hope of escape from the laboratory.

"You may be human, but you're still monsters. All of you." The woman's fear erupted into anger, finally revealing the hate that Molly had originally sensed behind the glass wall in her cell. "You're a lost cause."

She snapped the old woman's neck, then cast her corpse aside and whirled around to face the psychologist.

He was already running for the door.

He hammered on the metal, screaming.

"Help me! Help me! Open the door! Open the door!"

The door remained closed.

Nobody would open the door, as they could not risk her getting to the cells beyond. If she did, they risked the complex being overrun, the entire staff murdered.

The man behind the glass would press the button and destroy everything with flames long before he allowed that to happen.

A speaker in the corner of the room hissed.

"Let him go, Molly." It was the voice of Superintendent Carter, stern and official. "Return to your cell, before I decide my best option is to reduce everything in there to ash."

She could hear the keenness in his voice, his desire to deliver a burning retribution against her evil.

Molly stalked across the lab, grabbed hold of Peterson and pulled him away from the door and threw him to the floor.

He wailed like a terrified child.

She had seen enough of them to know.

His pretence of professional detachment had been ripped away, revealing what she had always known was there; a quivering, frightened animal.

"You will explain to me why you are so certain that we are all monsters." She stated firmly, letting her fangs extend menacingly, determined to scare the truth out of the man.

Peterson, his hands shaking, slowly reached up and twisted a monitor around to face her. The screen was covered in images of her brain scan.

Her mind, written out in neon blue lines, was pock-marked with areas of darkness.

"When a vampire is first turned, the oxygen starvation during death causes a degree of brain damage. The black areas. It varies from subject to subject, but in all cases there is damage to the prefrontal cortex, rendering the individual with no emotional control, or any sense of empathy for others. You're quick to anger, unable to control your temper and suffer no guilt at the consequences."

Molly stared at the image on the screen. Without a reflection, it had been one hundred and fifty years since she had seen any representation of herself, but now she was able to see herself for the first time, laid bare in horrifying, undeniable detail.

Peterson tapped a finger against the screen.

"You also suffered damaged to the Occipital Lobe, which has probably made skills such as reading and writing difficult for you. We noticed you didn't read the paperwork that you signed."

For the last one hundred and fifty years she had thought of herself as a vampire, above humanity by every definition; faster, stronger, and far more dangerous. Now the truth looked very different; she was less than human, just being a vampire meant she was damaged in such a profound way, that it determined her very nature and made her do terrible things.

"Surely this makes me sick?" She asked. "Mentally ill?"

Peterson nodded.

"So you lock us away?"

"You're deemed unfit to stand trial. Placed in psychiatric care. All legal, hence the paperwork." He swallowed nervously, glancing over at Doctor Langley's body. "You're too dangerous to be allowed loose. Look at the things you've done."

Molly nodded.

"It easier for you to fear us and cage us, than it is to make any real effort to help us. It's easier to lock us away and pretend we just don't exist, rather than even acknowledge we're real."

She lunged forward, clamping her fangs into the man's neck. He writhed and screamed, just like her mother. As the light faded from his eyes, his face fell slack, taking on an innocence that reminded her of little Jack Bradshaw.

She dropped the corpse and turned to face the dark window in the wall.

A light went on behind the glass.

Superintendent Carter was holding a small back box with a large red button, his thumb poised to bring down the fire.

"I worked the Jack Bradshaw case," he said simply. "I was there when his mother identified what was left of his body. I had to comfort her when her world fell apart. I had to try and explain why things like this happen."

"Because we're monsters," Molly licked the blood from her lips. "So let me burn!"

The police officer shook his head.

"You're immortal. We have all of eternity to find a treatment for you, so go back to your cell," he said, as he put down the box. "I won't kill you, because I don't have to, I have a choice. That's the difference between us. You can't help what you are."

He turned off the light.

Molly stared at the dark mirror.

She raged against the unbreakable glass, throwing herself at it, clawing at it, kicking at it, until her energy was spent. Then she collapsed miserably on the floor, amongst the blood, where she wept like a child.

Violet Addison was first published through Big Finish's *'Doctor Who: How The Doctor Changed My Life'* writing competition. She has since co-written a number of short stories, including one for the shared-world anthology *'World's Collider'* from Nightscape Press. She is currently supposedly making a second attempt at writing her first novel, but is more likely surfing the internet looking for more anthologies to submit to...

David N. Smith has written for a number of British sci-fi franchises, including *'Doctor Who'*, Big Finish's *'Bernice Summerfield'* range and Obverse Book's *'Faction Paradox'* series. He has also written a handful of TV comedy sketches, plus a number of corporate training videos, but people tend to be less interested in these as they involve considerably fewer vampires, dragons, pirates and aliens. Full details can be found on his website - www.davenevsmith.co.uk

SLAVE ARM
Laird Barron

B egin, again.
Don't begin with a white room, it's not, it's a black room. Hothouse humid, oasis in the subarctic night. A glitter ball strobes, synched with the aurora borealis, the background radiation of the stars. Scandalously clad kids slam dance to a metal band, the bass player wears an executioner's hood, the lead singer has a beard just like the front man for Clutch. Smokes a cheroot, swills whiskey, and breathes fire. Benny Three-Trees and Jasper Hostettler were flown in from Anchorage and Fairbanks to make sure this party's got its favors. Blotter, X, Jack Daniels, vodka, tequila, blow, crystal, hash, peyote, smack, Black Bombers, Viagra, California Gold, Matanuska Thunderfuck, nitrous. Window glass quivers like jelly in Dixie cup shooters. It's three A.M. Fuck the police. Your friends are here. Your enemies are here. Everybody you've ever slept with is here. Except Jessica. She's off wandering the earth, righting wrongs. You'll never see her again. That leaves Tom, Margie, Rod, Bill, Thurman, Shelley, Frank, Lisa, Becka, Tomra, Justin, Everett, Kurt, Mina, Tabby, Klein, Regan, Merrit, Luther, Jackson, Tashondra, Donte,

Violet, Simon, Bart, Darcy, Sarah, Clute, Bowie, Pilar, Carol, Eric, Camilla, Brian, Jason, John, Lori, Miller, Parish, Will, Nick, Berrian, Jody, Chandler, Mary, Erin, Clay, Tobias, Judith, Rich, Nelson, Zane, Warren, Bob, Sam, Philip, Castor, Julie, Newhouse, Cole, Esteban, Amy, Tyree, Vernon, Esther, Glenn, Kate, Kathy, Mark, Mark, Jake, Lucy, Ashley, Kyla, River, Arrow, Marsha, Cory, Stephen, Roger, Glory, Grant, Howard, Flynn, Victor, Bubba, Samantha, Custer, Alabama, Truman, Rupert, June, Ruby, Kirsten, Kevin, Lambert, Robard, Dickie, Ralph, Quinn, Hester, Felix, Dusty, Paul, Byron, Kareem, James, Gunther, Abelard, Queenie, Suri, Rochelle, Theodore, Brunhilde, Molly, Cooper, Wanda, Morris, Michelle, Tammy-Lynn, Starling, Hector, Earl, Kellen, Tiberius, Chance, Dakota, Monson, Spencer, Wayne, Lily, Ramses, Chuck, Portia, Terry, Terri, Trish, Craig, Delaney, Vance, Carmine, Russo, Penny, Ferris, Noah. The last two are a pair again after a few years apart. Sweet. You don't know the rest, the hangers on, freeloaders, strangers. Moving shadows. The happening is happening at the ancestral home of young rotund Zane Tooms himself, poor rich boy, wannabe Satanist, friend to no one no matter how cool his digs may be, and they are indeed cool. A three-story mansion and an unfinished basement. Basement expands deep into the hillside, ancient bear den, crumbled arches, moldering catacombs, bat roosts, portal to Pluto's Ballroom. Downhill, a lovely hillside, a copse of spruce trees, boulders, a field where fireweed grows, farther on lies the bay, ink-black under a tilted moon, cracked. Moms and Pops jetted to Acapulco for the weekend and the mice will riot. Upstairs in the master suite, you've got your cock halfway into that Ukrainian transfer student, the cheerleader, what's-her-name, and she's throwing her blonde head like a mare, impatient. You're thinking ouch, and man, this is a hell of a fancy bed, are these sheets satin, is the demon-face headboard mahogany, and good God what's with the creepy Gothic architecture anyway, and who's that guy walking into the frame? Is it the cheerleader's boyfriend, what's-his-name, captain of the varsity squad, 'cause that would be very bad, you'd want your steel toe boots for an ape with forearms like he's swinging. No, not the jock. Wait, is that *Russo*? Definitely looks like Russo who runs the forklift on the fresh floor of the cannery. Different though, filling the doorway, cropped hair, pale complexion, eye shadow thick enough for a *Star Trek* cameo, original series, features smoothed and stretched plastic masklike, loose dark shirt and too-tight pants tucked into combat boots. Hefts a club, or a mace, a car axle, something out of a medieval manual of slaughter, two and a half feet of steel wrapped in barbed wire, electric tape on the grip, funny the photographic detail your brain records in moments of stress. The girl kisses your neck, she hasn't seen the freak. It's all wrong. Uncanny resemblance notwithstanding, this isn't the Russo you were blazing with on the loading dock just yesterday, not the Russo who's got a thing for the color grader from Caltech, not the Russo who lost his license drag racing on the Parks Highway and needs a lift everywhere, not the one who's built for a run at the middleweight title but wouldn't hurt a fly, the pacifist, conscientious objector, tofu-munching emo rocker. *This* Russo has taken an ice pick to the brain and become Mr. Flat Affect. He licks his liver lips, and Gene Simmons would shit a brick at the yellow tongue drooped to that pointy chin. Mr. Flat Affect crosses the room in an awkward lunge, the way a toad suddenly decides to jump, and it's so fast your breath stops. You roll off the opposite half of that acre of satin and the club wallops the cheerleader instead of your naked ass. Prior to this moment you've always considered yourself a bit of a tough guy. Lean, mean, scars on your knuckles from a respectable number of barroom brawls, only last fall you socked Tom Gorski in the kisser after one wisecrack too many, dropped him like a bad habit. You're no punk, no wuss, no pantywaist, had your nose busted plenty, lost some teeth in the bargain. You have also come to the realization you aren't Chuck Norris either. The bludgeoning thuds are a message from the universe. You're no shark, you're a feeder fish, aren't you? The interloper whacks her a couple of times, lazy and disinterested. There's blood, a lot of it, all those September hunts when Dad shot the caribou with his .7mm and you slashed the dumb beast's throat and its life gushed out over your Wellies, this is similar. You make your move and fly for the door. You're howling. Demon Russo would catch you, because next to him you're stuck in quicksand, but the club gets snagged in a nest of guts and that second or two is all you need to escape. It's dark and the house is a maze. You've visited twice during daylight when it was just the Tooms family and everybody in polo shirts and golf slacks, sunny dispositions, dinner on the deck with the gob smacking view of Settler's Bay. This is the nightmare version of that scenario, the Bizarro World iteration. Doors are locked and impenetrable. Music rumbles far below and nobody responds to you screaming bloody murder. An accent lamp floats in a golden bubble way down at the end of the hall and you sprint for it, jagged claws of your shadow outstretched in desperation.

~

Even all these years after the fact, you recall the cheerleader's expression in a smash close-up. Homegirl doesn't know she's dead, keeps blinking at you, confused as she drowns on herself.

~

Your father dies in a tavern parking lot when you are twenty-two. Your mother goes home to Tennessee, sends postcards now and again, the weather's fine. Little brother joins the Marines, like his old man, earns a Bronze Star, opens a gun store in Texas, shoots a couple of kids who try to rob the joint. The jury decides he's justified. You sleep with a lot of women with the light on, lose your erection whenever you stop to think. There are nightmares. One that recurs has you as a child in your old bedroom, you stand near the dresser and a poster of Buck Rogers. A skinny hand and arm slither from beneath your bed, followed by your father. Except his face is angular and cold with alien emotion. He moves the herky-jerky way a marionette does. He wants your blood, projects that desire into your thoughts without opening his mouth. You always awaken before he gets you. Hell of it is, you don't know whether it's really a dream or a suppressed memory. So, you drink. We won't speak of wife one.

~

Wife two is Amie. You stole her from Mack the slack, Mack jumped off the bridge into Hurricane Gulch. Oh, Amie, baby, who wouldn't? Brunette, Libra, whip smart, hot as fire. Most importantly, she doesn't give a goddamn how screwed up you are, how wild and strange you are, how damaged, or else she cleverly looks past it to the good points. You have several. Got all your hair, make a decent wage in construction, still cut pretty sharp in a suit. Two of three children tolerate your presence, the dog is also fond. The dog is a German Shepherd you named Chip because of a story that science fiction author Bradley Denton wrote when you were a kid. You and Chip go hunting for ptarmigan every fall, the only good thing you can recall sharing with your dad. Last September you load the guns and drive out to the Little Susitna, follow a game trail away from the Parks Highway, three, maybe four miles where the spruce grow tall and close in, a mossy shadow land. Crack yourself a cool beer, propped against a tree, loyal hound at your feet, the sun a pale reflection against the underside of the canopy. Even sweet wife fades into the ether for a while. Chip looses a stream of piss and whines and then you hear, echoing from not too far away in the arboreal deeps, the weirdest birdcall ever. Laughter of a raven mimicking a man mimicking a hyena. Cackles your name, calls to Chip. *C'mere, doggy!* This lone cry becomes a chorus, converging. Shotgun or not, you and the dog run for your lives. That shrieking laughter pursues you nearly back to the car. You break the speed limit gunning for home, Chip cowers on the floorboard, fangs bared as if some horror rides in the back seat. *We're waiting for you, pal. We know where you live.*

~

Zane Tooms got on the Tony Robbins bandwagon and dropped sixty pounds, tried to make something of himself, didn't try all that hard. Heartthrob handsome after the sea change, but fat wasn't truly the root of his problems. Something dark and rotten was going on in that noggin. Capped teeth and a chiseled physique couldn't mitigate the filth beaming from his eyes. He lived alone in that mansion on the hill after Mr. and Mrs. died. Spent his nights at the Bohemian cocktail lounge hitting on the young lasses, became known as the Rohypnol Romeo, bought himself an indictment with a suggested sentencing range of twenty-five to life if it stuck. Blew town and disappeared to the bottom of the FBI most-wanted list. Sends you a letter the day before Christmas, first contact after a decade of silence, arrives in a grimy, blood-spotted envelope, sum of the message a Mexico City phone number, initials *ZT*, smudgy fingerprints all over the stationery. You are wary, but intrigued. There's a twenty-five thousand dollar reward, which you don't give a shit about, money isn't a problem for you anymore, you have questions, you have a redaction scribble in the middle of your brain where dreadful memories once clamored for release. You want to talk to fatboy Tooms, want to wring his neck, beg him to put the pieces together. He's living under an assumed name in a fancy hotel on the outskirts, keeps a whole suite to himself. His transformation impresses, dresses in a linen suit, smokes French cigarettes, seems at ease in his own expat skin, but you recognize him, the real him, instantly. You don't talk about what he's done, don't mention the fact FBI and INTERPOL are on the case, could be staking out the joint at that very moment, recording everything for the blockbuster trial. That's a foregone conclusion, written in the stars. You're here for other unfinished business. He pours two glasses of mescal, no lime, no nothing, utters a prayer and downs his, then flashes a revolver and says he asked you here to apologize or to kill you. It depends. Actually, that's a lie, he's already made up his mind, he wants to chat first, so drink your drink, old friend, and you do. Once everything's cozy, you've chuckled over the hijinks of days of yore, his finger relaxes from the trigger and you ask what the hell man? What happened way back when in the bear den beneath the house? He smiles sadly, professes ignorance, but his eyes belong to a snake and though you ask again, nicely, he refuses to answer truly. He was a child then, he dicked about with childish things, any real diabolism that resulted is purely coincidental. The room spins as you go belly up. They don't call the bastard the Rohypnol Romeo for nothing. In the half-dozen beats until the world goes dark you watch a tremor pass through him, crown to toe, and your subconscious wants to make an impossible connection, suggests he's a finger puppet of some primordial malevolence and it's show time. The flesh of his face snaps upward, much as a bank robber pulls on a nylon mask, except from the wrong direction. Hello to Mr. Flat Affect, your old friend.

~

Okay, we'll mention wife one, briefly. Her post-coital cigarette didn't package with a *what are you thinking*. Hers was a beady-eyed scowl and a demand to know what your damage was. What had happened to fuck you so thoroughly up, she couldn't begin to fathom. Were you molested as a child? Did Daddy piss in your cornflakes? Did something *awful* transpire to make you so afraid of the dark? You loved her, you desired her happiness with the intensity of a death wish. But you couldn't tell her what was buried in your heart, couldn't articulate the queasy blackness that flooded your mind whenever you tried. If you knew where she'd run off to after your marriage fireballed, you could call her up, tell her about the time you visit Mexico to meet a childhood chum and come to taped hand and foot upon the ledge of a marble tub, IV needle in your femoral artery, half your blood oozing drip by drip through a tube into gallon bags. Classical music plays. There's a muttered conversation that you can't understand, and not because blood loss causes your ears to ring, nor because the voices are muttering in Spanish. It's because whatever language is formed by this combination of glottal stops, clicks and liquid hisses, it isn't human. You manage to peel free of the tape, slick with your fluids as it is, the heat of the room, and slide over the rim of the tub into a heap. You vomit. That's what happens when blood pressure drops to nil. Keep crawling toward the light, all you can do, coherent thought is water through a dribble glass, it just makes a mess on your shirt. Three of them stand in the parlor with your host. They wear variations on the face of the grave and very nice suits. There's a naked body curled upon a rubber mat. The body is bound in barbed wire and one of the men, Armani suit and snazzy shoes, sips from a red tube inserted at the victim's neck. Everybody pauses to stare at you, including the dead or dying guy, his glassy eyes are wet as you drag yourself past, hand over hand. His eyes reflect your antlike toil across the killing floor. Maybe he's reenacting Horace Greasley's great escape vicariously through you. Maybe he's already there. The front door swings open and uniformed men burst through screaming *Policía*! Their assault rifles start flashing and the room fills with clouds of dust and smoke. You crawl onward, past threshing jackboots and smoldering shell cases. Explosions and screams continue unabated. It goes on and on. Longest movie you've ever been in. Later at the hospital a tall handsome American sits at your bedside. Tubes everywhere, but at least the fluids are going into you this time. The man introduces himself as Agent Justin Steele. He flashes a badge and declares who he works for, although none of it sticks in your consciousness, you're wrapped in a cocoon of drugs and shock. He lights a Rubios, starts a pocket recorder, and says to tell him everything you know, start at the beginning in Alaska when you were a kid. You comply, half expecting his face to deform at any moment. Takes a while to relate the tale, takes an eon, in fact. Agent Steele doesn't interrupt and when you finish he thanks you for your service to your country, best to never speak of this incident again, Tooms was shot resisting arrest for extradition to the USA, and so forth. You're weak and fading, yet you clutch his sleeve and ask what's it all about, ask what the flat affects are, where they come from, why were you, lowly you, lured to Mexico, and you know what the answer is before it doesn't come. You have so many damned theories burning a hole in your imagination. Could be you babble about space vampires, demonic possession, and Count D his own bad self. Steele smiles as if the cigarette in his hand comes with a blindfold. He leans in close and whispers that he's seen this all before, it's always worse than you think, says it no longer matters. Go home, screw your wife, pet your dog, relive your glory days with a six-pack and a bowl. The fat lady is working on her arpeggios.

~

Your buddy Felix, an ex Naval Intelligence officer with connections across the US and Europe, and who also doses himself daily with LSD and vaporized marijuana while listening to talk radio, won't permit dogs into his trailer because *everybody* knows the ID chips implanted at the veterinarian's office are military grade transceivers beaming info to spy satellites. He has a theory about Mr. Flat Affect. It's insane and you also think it has merit. Felix disappears one day, leaves a roach smoldering in the ashtray, a spackle of blood in a tight pattern on the ceiling directly above his easy chair. The police park a van across the street from your apartment for a month, then. Nobody contacts you.

~

The power goes dead after midnight and you lie there, a bundle of twigs, staring out the window, praying for the town lights, any of them, to return. Only stars, the black body of darkness. Chip pads in and sits, muzzle pointed at you. He is a pure black shadow. You begin to cry, terror squeezing tears from your ducts. Amie grips your shoulder, says she has something to tell you, baby. That's when you know the jig is up, the power's never coming back on, you've seen the last of the light, because Amie and Chip died years and years ago. You close your eyes and visualize the faces at Tooms' basement party, the faces in that deathroom at the Mexico City hotel. The images move with the sluggishness of a dream. Your friends and enemies only watch pop-eyed and motionless as you flee. Some wear the demented un-mask that drips with earth from the grave. They might've loved or hated you before the rostrum made its pith stroke. Now they grin as you flee, your bare feet slapping a treadmill that bores endlessly through a cosmic honeycomb. None of you are going anywhere.

Laird Barron is the author of several books, including *The Croning, Occultation,* and *The Beautiful Thing That Awaits Us All.* His work has also appeared in many magazines and anthologies. An expatriate Alaskan, Barron currently resides in Upstate New York.

GODS AND DEVILS
Taylor Grant

Why can't I open my eyes? Vega thought. *I'm not dreaming. Am I?*

Like searing fire, a single stab of pain shot through his arm to the marrow, followed by a rush of warmth. Then the rest of his body began to tingle. This was no dream. He'd been injected with something. He knew the feeling from back in Academy training; induced consciousness, only to be used in emergencies.

Next he felt an electrical pulse lance through his brain, forcing his eyelids to flutter open.

His vision was blurry, but he recognized the porcelain, impossibly perfect features of Sona staring down at him. He took note that her right ear was missing, as well as some artificial flesh from her forehead.

A stronger electrical pulse now, coursing through his body, forcing his muscles to seize up for an agonizing moment. *This better be a goddamn emergency*, he thought.

He sat up with a groan and wiped temperature-regulating gel from his face. His eyes widened when he noticed the lower half of Sona was missing; it looked as if she'd been torn in two.

"Sona, what...?"

Upon closer inspection, he could see that a large section of her throat had been torn open—rendering her unable to speak.

Vega stared at her, wondering what might have caused such damage. Sona was a female droid, but she was built like a tank, complete with a dura-alloy chassis. She worked with quiet efficiency to disconnect him from the stasis field. As he rose to his feet, Vega grabbed the edges of the sleep pod for balance; his legs felt like they were made of pudding. Yet even hunched over, his six-foot five frame towered over the half-android.

He surveyed the stasis chamber. Everything appeared normal. Five hundred gleaming sleep pods, stacked ten rows tall, surrounded him. They were shaped like large silver eggs, containing humanity's last hope. Inside these pods were thirty-six crewmembers and four hundred and sixty-three passengers.

A nerve-grating sound caught his attention and he turned to see an awful sight. Sona was crawling across the floor using her remaining appendages; wet, mechanical entrails dragged behind. He watched with disgust as she pulled herself toward the control console and manually jacked herself into the ship's mainframe. This was immediately followed by a series of chirps and screeching feedback as she tapped into the computer's audio circuitry in order to communicate.

"...skritch...Captain...skritch...Vega."

"Yes, Sona. I can hear you. What the hell's going on?"

Sona made more audio adjustments, and the next time she spoke her voice had been equalized to sound more or less human.

"An HH slipped through screening. It's on board and has taken a passenger. It attempted to terminate me, but didn't factor in my reserve systems."

Vega felt as if an invisible fist had slugged him in the gut. It was the worst possible news—the worst goddamned scenario.

"Have you woken any other crew members?"

Sona's mouth moved silently, followed by a delayed voice piped through the ship's system. "No, sir. According to Directive 222A, the Captain is first to be—."

"Okay, Okay—good. Let's keep it that way. "You have my gear?

Sona gestured toward a nearby hover-cart, which contained standard issue battle armor and a loaded disrupter.

Vega reached for the sleek-looking weapon and felt the cool metal in his hand; it weighed heavy in his grip.

"There is something else, sir. Something you need to know."

He adjusted the setting on the disrupter "I know, Sona. And I'm sorry..."

Sona's face exploded from a direct shot to the head. A delayed high-pitched screech emanated from the ship's computer a moment later—then stopped abruptly.

Vega set the weapon—still humming from the discharge—back on the cart and began to put on his armor. He would deal with Sona's remains and alter the ship's records later. There was a more pressing matter at hand.

~

Vega moved stealthily up several flights of stairs toward the Crew Deck. The ship's security system had logged some recent movement in the Mess Hall. The turbolift wasn't an option; the noise would give him away. He would need the advantage of surprise if he was to have any hope of taking down an HH in close quarters.

As he crept toward the main entrance to the Crew Deck, he double-checked his weapon. At its highest setting, the disrupter emitted a lethal blast of concentrated microwave and UV radiation. But that was cold comfort; the creature's speed, strength, and ferocity gave it an enormous edge.

He moved as quietly as possible through the silent Mess Hall. The hundred or so empty chairs gave the large room an eerie quality. Memories of his crewmates eating there flashed in his mind and he longed for their company. Vega had never been good at being alone and the sense of isolation he felt now was almost unbearable.

He forced thoughts of his crew away and continued toward the entertainment area of the Mess Hall. It was both absurd and perverse to imagine a HH needing entertainment, and yet, it made sense that he might find it here. After all, what else would it do once the eating had been taken care of? There was nothing to do on the ship but eat, shit and sleep.

Vega scanned the area, his weapon held in firing position.

Nothing.

He spun in all directions, prepared to annihilate anything that moved, when something caught his eye.

As he looked closer he noticed brightly colored images moving on a holo-screen. It was an episode of the popular cartoon *Gloop and Gloopy*. The sound was muted, though, and the room was as still as a mausoleum.

Tentatively, he moved closer, his jaw clenched so tightly his teeth began to ache. The tunic beneath his battle armor was drenched in sweat, his heart felt as if it were about to burst through his chest plate.

A faint rasping sound.

It seemed to emanate from the other side of a black lounger just ahead — a large one that probably sat twelve comfortably. From Vega's vantage point — looking at the back of it — no one appeared to be sitting there.

He switched to a two-handed grip and rushed toward it, finger tight on the weapon's trigger.

What he saw caught him by surprise. Sprawled out on the floor was a teenage girl; she was a brunette with a boyish figure—perhaps 14 years old. Her standard-issue uniform was still intact and she appeared completely unharmed.

Her chest rose and fell ever so slightly, and there was a slight rasp to her breath. *She's still in stasis*, he thought. She'd been taken from her sleep pod without being awakened. It would take a special chemical injection to bring her back to consciousness.

There were two types of HH victims: "Transmitters" and "Feeders." Transmitters were human hosts used to propagate the parasites; Feeders were humans used solely as sustenance. HH was an abbreviation for 'Homo Hirudinea,' a scientific term for the human host of a parasitic alien. Earth's general populace, of course, chose more colorful terms, such as 'Leeches,' 'Hemo-Gobblers,' 'Vamps,' and 'BFTs' (Big Fucking Ticks).

Once a victim was infected, chemical changes to their hormones, along with a massive overproduction of adrenaline, resulted in superhuman strength and reflexes. Muscle, bone and connective tissue thickened, followed by functional changes to the teeth and nails—presumably for capturing prey. Inexplicably, the transformation made the host extremely vulnerable to the ultra violet spectrum while producing an insatiable desire for human hemotophagy—feeding on human blood. For these reasons, many believed that scouting missions by the parasites early in mankind's history had originated the vampire myth.

Vega's grip on his disrupter tightened.

A shadow passed over the girl's face.

It's above us, Vega thought. *Clinging to the ceiling.*

The HH landed on him, using the same terrible claws on his helmet that it had used to climb the walls.

Before he could get off a shot, it had ripped the disrupter from his hand and torn off his faceplate with inhuman strength. Vega scrunched his eyes shut, anticipating the worst: he would either be sucked dry or turned. He hoped it was the former.

But the bite didn't come.

He could smell fetid breath on his face. And something wet dripped onto his cheek, sliding down past his neck. *Saliva? Blood?*

Both?

When he could no longer bear the waiting he opened his eyes. Inches from his face the creature gazed at him. The first thing Vega noticed was its teeth. They were sharp all right, but they were still small and hadn't fully formed yet.

Its features were angelic, with the supple skin of a seven-year-old boy.

The eyes were haunted, but familiar.

"Hello, son," Vega choked.

And then, deep within those icy blue eyes, Vega saw a hint of recognition. They began to soften. And he knew at that moment that his son had not completely turned.

"It's me, Arrycc. It's Daddy."

The boy's face trembled and tears welled in his eyes. His mouth began to quiver, as if trying to remember how to speak.

And then a word came that Vega didn't think he would ever hear again.

"Daddy?"

There was confusion on the boy's face, as if he'd woken from a deep coma and was struggling to put together the fragments of his memories.

"It's me, little monkey," Vega said, a term of endearment he'd used since his son was a baby.

It was as if a dam broke inside the boy. Tears gushed and he threw his arms around his father as if he'd been away for years. And technically, he had.

Vega reached up and tried to hug his son as best he could while wearing battle armor. "It's okay. I'm here now. It's okay."

He held his son for a long time, feeling the boy's moist face against his.

Soon the reality of the situation began to sink in. Arrycc's intended victim only a few feet away from them. The parasite inside his son. His own treachery to get the boy onboard the ship.

They stood up and faced each other awkwardly. The boy averted his eyes from the girl, ashamed. Vega glanced down and sighed with relief.

He hasn't turned all the way. Maybe I can still save him.

~

The origin of the parasites had been impossible to authenticate, but many in the scientific community speculated they were interdimensional. At a quantum level they vibrated at a frequency that made them imperceptible to the naked eye — until they possessed a human host.

The epidemic had been as fast as it was complete; spreading to every human- occupied mining colony, outpost and space station. Physicists speculated that the invaders utilized some form of quantum tunneling technology, enabling them to travel through the multiverse in ways far beyond our scientific capabilities.

Zeta-12, a deep space research station was the only remaining outpost that survived the invasion. The team there, led by Dr. Mirann Tael, was renowned for their groundbreaking work in genetic engineering, specifically in immunology. Their greatest triumph was '"Batch 779,"' a prototype biotech curative that combined nanotechnology with alien plant DNA.

Batch 779 had been engineered to enhance the immune system and project against a myriad of diseases; early human trials had showed great promise. During the parasite invasion, it was discovered that Batch 779 had an added benefit; it provided resistance to the parasites. And while the curative had saved the lives of the Zeta-12 crew, without any way to mass-produce it, or transport it quickly enough, it had been too late to save Earth or its interstellar colonies.

Vega and the passengers of his ship, *the Phoenix*, were currently on a course for Zeta-12, to get Batch 779 inoculations. Vega had put his son in stasis with the intention of getting him the curative before the parasite turned him completely. And the plan would have worked if the boy hadn't awoken early, six months before reaching their destination.

Vega tried to convince Arrycc to return to his sleep pod with the promise of a cure. He first appealed to him with reason, then begged and pleaded, and later threatened the boy. But Arrycc refused, clearly under the influence of the parasite. Back on ORION, the space station closest to Earth, his son had been bitten less than twenty-four hours before going into stasis on *the Phoenix*. However, according to Sona's daily logs, the boy woke eight hours before Vega had. This meant that technically—not counting the five years they had been in stasis—his son had been infected for four days. The incubation period was approximately a week. During the first few days, victims would generally maintain some semblance of their original identity. But inevitably they would succumb to the parasite's influence and become what some crudely referred to as 'walking meat puppets.'

How Arrycc had awoken from stasis was still a mystery. He could only assume that the physiology of the parasite, which was completely alien in nature, gave it some sort of resistance to the stasis field. The thought of how far they had come, how much they had been through, only to lose the battle now—was almost too much to bear. The parasite epidemic had destroyed everything Vega had ever known or cared about, his best friend Tallic, his little sister Norra, and his wife Ahn.

ORION had been ill prepared for the parasite invasion, their armory woefully inadequate. The Earth Defense Network discovered, quite by accident, that the parasites were vulnerable to microwave and UV radiation. Once word got to ORION of the parasite's weakness, they had retrofitted as much weaponry as they could, but there simply hadn't been enough time to battle the parasites effectively.

Vega was the captain of *the Phoenix*, the only interstellar ship docked at ORION at the time of the attack. As the highest ranking military officer on the station, he was forced to make difficult decisions, such as initiating a lottery to decide who would gain access to *the Phoenix*, and who would have to stay behind.

Some of the lottery winners were immediately disqualified, as blood samples revealed that they had already been infected. Vega used his power and influence to sneak Arrycc on board the ship and bypass the screening process altogether.

It had been a long shot to save his son, and he'd risked everything for it; his crew, the passengers—even himself. If his plan were discovered, he would face a court martial and most likely, the death penalty. But it was a risk he was willing to take. Arrycc was all he had left to live for.

Humankind's survival had been foremost on Vega's mind since he'd awoken. Between his passengers, crew and the 74 inhabitants of Zeta-12—there were 574 human beings that represented the remainder of humanity.

From 10,000,000,000 to 574 in the span of a year—it was still unfathomable.

And yet there was hope. The terraformed planet on which Zeta-12 stood was in its final phase; and according to Dr. Tael, it was capable of sustaining the passengers and crew of *the Phoenix* for a lifetime.

There was one small problem.

Arrycc.

Vega realized, with growing dread, that if he didn't get his son back into hyper sleep soon, he would have no choice but to kill him.

He found Arrycc in the same place as before, sitting entranced in front of the holo-screen. He moved a few steps toward his son, who sniffed at the air absently, and then went back to watching the screen.

It was *Gloop and Gloopy* again, Arrycc's favorite show since as far back as Vega could remember. It revolved around the misadventures of two teenaged aliens who had crash-landed on Earth after taking their dad's spaceship for a joyride.

Vega stood there for a long moment, staring at his boy, longing to hold him. A swarm of memories surged up all at once. The first was of the day he'd been carrying his infant son, and the naked boy had taken a poop—right in his hand. Vega cried out to his wife for help, but Ahn was too busy crumpled on the floor with laughter.

He smiled at the memory.

Next, he remembered the first time Arrycc had ridden a hover-board by himself, and the pride he'd felt watching his boy soar. He recalled reading to Arrycc before bedtime, who would beg him for old stories of ghosts and goblins and things that go bump in the night. Afterward, he would have to promise that the monsters weren't real.

And now his son was becoming one.

Two days prior, when Vega thought Arrycc had turned, he'd been prepared to kill him. But now, as he stood in the doorway, watching his own flesh and blood, he knew he couldn't—not if there was the slightest chance he could save him.

He entered the room and made his way to the lounger. As he sat next to Arrycc, his body tensed. The boy revealed no emotion; it was all the more eerie listening to the cartoon's canned laugh track.

They sat in silence for an uncomfortably long time. At first it seemed like a perverse joke, a dark and twisted mockery of times past, when they'd huddled together in front of the holo-screen. All they needed now was a bucket of popcorn and a bucket of blood to wash it down.

However, as the hours passed, Vega's revulsion began to pass. The desperate need to connect with his son was like a silent third party. Sitting there, he could almost pretend that things were normal. He could even imagine his wife, Ahn, off in the kitchen making one of her amazing dishes.

When the longing became too much to bear, he reached around his son's shoulders; it was as if he was watching from outside himself — not completely in control of his actions.

His son glanced at him for a moment. Deep within those sunken eyes, there appeared to be a spark of humanity.

It was enough.

Vega didn't move for some time, afraid that any motion might disturb the boy and shatter the illusion.

Arrycc didn't move either.

Vega knew that at any point the boy could turn, literally and figuratively. But something about the look they'd shared told him he wasn't in danger.

Not yet.

How long would their father-son bond protect him? The amount of time it took to succumb to a parasite's influence varied from person to person. He had heard of extreme cases on Earth where particularly strong-willed individuals managed to retain their identity for several weeks.

Arrycc certainly had a strong will going for him, something he'd inherited from both his parents. And, of course, the boy's love for him had always been strong. But how long would love and the will of a seven-year-old boy last?

The hunger was inevitable.

For now he wouldn't think about it. For now he would cherish what might be their final moments together.

The hunger came.

Four days later he found Arrycc in the stasis chamber with a new victim, dragging a teenage boy with thick red hair from his sleep pod. The boy was unaware of what was happening and would remain that way unless chemically induced to consciousness.

It was a blessing.

The look on Arrycc's face was one of defiance, a look with which Vega was intimately familiar. Without his disrupter or armor he posed no threat—Arrycc could dispatch him easily.

"Arrycc," he heard himself say. It sounded rather weak, with a hint of despair. "Please... don't."

His son looked at him quizzically.

"Please..."

And then the expression on Arrycc's face seemed to melt into something else. Vega had seen it many times before, whenever his son wanted something desperately, like a brand new toy or an extra helping of dessert.

He had always had a hard time saying no to him. Ahn had often teased him about it. *How can a man used to ordering around a crew all day have such a hard time saying no to a little boy?*

But they had both known the answer. Vega's career kept him from his family so much that he wanted to make sure he gave his son whatever he wanted when he was around. Grimly, he realized that the past week had been the longest stretch of time he'd ever spent with his son at one time.

And now, when saying "no" was the most important thing he could do, he knew it would do no good. Arrycc had the hunger now. He could see it in his eyes. God help him, there was nothing to do now but let his son feed.

Vega turned and walked away. He couldn't stop the boy from his first kill, but he sure as hell wouldn't stand around and watch.

He had barely taken a step when the grisly sounds of flesh being torn and the lapping of blood began.

~

The first death was the hardest for Vega to stomach. But as the long weeks turned into longer months, the guilt that gnawed at him began to dissipate. Like most horrible things, prolonged exposure deadened the effects.

By the third month he had lost count of the bodies. *Was it 16...18?*

Once the victim's bodies were drained of blood, Vega dutifully jettisoned the remains into space through the garbage chute, standard protocol for corpses in deep space.

The missing passengers would have to be accounted for at some point, but he'd already worked out an explanation. He would blame their deaths on Sona. Droids weren't perfect, and breakdowns weren't unheard of. A simple miscalculation in cryo-fluids from the ship's droid would explain the passenger's deaths easily enough.

No one would suspect foul play from a twice-decorated captain with a spotless military record. Besides, survival would be first and foremost on everyone's mind once they reached the outpost.

How he would deal with Arrycc was a bit more complicated. He figured there were three ways it could go. The first option was that Arrycc would kill him. The second, he would kill his son. Third, and the least likely, he would find a way to keep Arrycc hidden while they docked at Zeta-12, just long enough to get his hands on Batch 779 and save him.

He was still trying to work out the last option. But it wasn't easy with such an unpredictable variable as the parasite.

It had now been over four months since he and his son had awoken. Arrycc was, for all intents and purposes, a bloodsucking monster. And yet, the boy's disposition had hardly changed. He had stopped speaking, of course, but that was typical. The parasites were able to communicate with each other without speaking, most likely telepathically, although that had never been proven. It was possible for them to speak through their human hosts, though rarely seen — victims of the parasites tended to simply grunt or snarl.

When Arrycc wasn't feeding or sleeping, he spent his time watching old movies and documentaries or reading through endless archives about Earth — on every conceivable topic. The sophistication level of his research had grown exponentially in all areas of math, science and the arts. He seemed to especially enjoy reading about world religions and theology.

Was there any shred of Arrycc left? Vega had convinced himself there was. Why else had he been allowed to live? Of course, he was a critical member of the crew. Arrycc certainly couldn't navigate the ship by himself. But Vega clung to the former idea like a life raft, hoping Arrycc was still somewhere inside the silent figure that had become his only companion.

Arrycc didn't appear to mind Vega's presence. They would often sit next to each other in the entertainment room, watching the holo-screen. For hours they would sit quietly, often viewing documentaries, which seemed to be Arrycc's favorite.

Vega found it comforting to sit next to his son. In his mind he could almost pretend that everything was still normal. Sometimes he thought he could spend the rest of his life like this, just he and his son, spending quality time together — the kind of time he'd never had a chance to experience on the space station. He realized that if he never awoke the rest of the crew, there would be enough food to last him a lifetime.

But Arrycc would only last about five years, factoring in the rate at which he fed on the bodies in the stasis chamber. If he had been a full-grown adult it would have been half the time...

The only chance his son had now was to get him to Zeta-12 and pray that Batch 779 would still work on someone this far along in the transformation process.

~

Vega had never been so happy to see and speak to another human being in his life. If he could have reached through the communication screen he would have hugged Dr. Tael.

Now less than 24 hours away from docking at Zeta-12, they had finally reached sub space communication range. Tael was an attractive looking woman in her late sixties. She had already gone over their standard quarantine protocols, and Vega had agreed to keep his passengers onboard until proper inoculations were dispensed. No one would be allowed to enter Zeta-12 until they had been screened and cleared.

Eventually the conversation turned from strictly business to more personal issues. "How are you holding up, Captain? You don't look well."

Vega felt self-conscious, realizing at that moment how much he'd let himself go during the past six months. He'd done nothing but eat and sit with Arrycc when he could. He'd gained twenty pounds easy, and despite shaving that morning for the first time in half a year, the perpetual sleep deprivation, constant worry, and lack of any physical activity had taken its toll. He looked like hell, and he knew it.

"I haven't slept well these past few months," Vega said. That part was true. Then the lies began as he interweaved the threads of a true story he'd heard about back in his Academy days. "We had a serious droid malfunction—total systems failure. She made some miscalculations on some of the passengers' cryo-fluid levels. We lost 24 people. The backup systems woke me up before anyone else died."

Tael looked shocked. "That's terrible news, Captain. I'm so sorry. Every life is precious—now so more than ever. When did this happen?"

"A few months ago...goddamned droid was in full meltdown when I woke up—had to take her down with a disrupter. As if things hadn't been bad enough before..." He rubbed his face with his hands dramatically.

"And you never went back into stasis," Tael said. It was more of a statement than a question.

"I figured, what's the point? I knew we'd reach you in a few months."

Tael's brow furrowed at that. "Being alone on that ship, with no one to communicate with—you know the risks as well as I do."

Vega was well aware. 'Solipsism Syndrome' was a serious risk for anyone who spent long periods alone in space. It created the overwhelming feeling that nothing was real—or simply a dream. Sufferers had been known to feel so lonely and detached from the world they became utterly, and terribly indifferent.

But he wasn't alone was he? He still had his son. And he certainly wasn't losing his mind. He was just weary and emotionally drained. Who the hell wouldn't be after all he'd been through since the invasion?

"I appreciate the concern, Doc. But I'm going to wake my crew in less than 24 hours—once we're in navigation range."

Tael seemed to accept this answer and nodded politely. "I look forward to seeing you, your crew and passengers soon."

After a few more pleasantries Tael signed off.

Within a day Vega was going to have to wake his crew. He had no choice but to make a decision about his son.

He sat there for a long time collecting his thoughts...and his nerve.

~

He found Arrycc a few hours later, sitting rigidly, staring blankly at the holo-screen; his face was drenched in fresh blood. Vega was reminded of a time when Arrycc—who was two years old at the time—had buried his face into his bowl and covered it with tomato sauce. It was a sweet memory that was now twisted forever in his mind.

In Arrycc's hands was the gouged and glistening head of his latest victim. Curled under his feet like a human footstool was the body it had once been attached to. He was watching a movie and holding the head as if it were a bucket of popcorn. As Vega stepped closer, he recognized the face of the teenage girl. She was the one he'd saved from Arrycc all those months ago. Her eyes were wide open now and staring up at the face of her killer.

The boy didn't acknowledge the presence of his father. Vega did his best to ignore the blood pooled around Arrycc on the lounger as he sat down. On the screen were images from ancient Jerusalem and a man nailed to a cross.

A vampire watching a documentary about Christianity…

After a protracted, awkward silence, Vega said, "I have to wake my crew in a few hours. We'll be at the Zeta-12 outpost by this time tomorrow."

The boy said nothing. He stared at the images on the holo-screen with a look of bemusement. It was the first hint of emotion Vega had seen on his son's face since as far back as he could remember.

"Arrycc, listen. I can't help you...cure you...unless you work with me. We have to talk. Figure this out—now."

A grin appeared on the boy's face.

Vega slammed his fist against the lounger. "Goddamnit, Arrycc I'm talking to you!"

The boy turned toward him slowly and began to speak; it was like a winter grave had opened—cold, moist and dark.

"There is...no...Arrycc...here."

Vega recoiled at the voice that sounded only partially human. It appeared to be a great effort for the boy to speak, as if he were learning to use his vocal chords all over again.

"Such.....a...primitive…way to communicate."

Vega stifled the impulse to scream. He was accustomed to his silent son, had fooled himself into thinking that he was still reachable. But the voice emanating from the boy brought a hideous new reality crashing down.

Arrycc turned back toward the holo-screen. "Your...religious wars fascinate me."

Vega could think of nothing to say.

"You have killed each other by the millions...because you don't agree about what happens to you...after you kill each other."

Vega stared at him, mouth agape.

"Your mind is full of questions."

Vega gave a deep sigh. *Yes.*

The boy turned toward Vega and placed a small hand against his cheek; the tiny frigid fingers pulsed with a strength that unnerved him.

Suddenly, what felt like an invisible icepick lanced Vega's brain; his body went numb. With great effort he tried to remove his son's hand, but to his horror, discovered he couldn't move.

A presence entered his mind...invading his thoughts, violating him.

Images flooded his mind. No...not images, more like tangible memories... memories that weren't his. They were alien, in the truest sense of the word.

He was back on Earth. He could see, taste it. Smell it. But the experience wasn't nostalgic. It was terrible...it was...*God, no...*

It was the end of everything.

Why? Vega's mind pleaded. *Why us?*

The question had lain dormant in him — gnawed at him, from the beginning.

Somewhere beyond the alien thoughts, he felt something familiar. A comforting presence. Pure. Innocent.

Of course...it was his son!

I won't let it hurt you, Daddy.

Was that a thought...or a feeling? Vega couldn't tell. But it was Arrycc all right. Some small part of him still alive...still fighting...still loving his father.

Vega reached for him in his mind. Goddamnit, *he* was the one who should be comforting his son. *He* was the one who should be the protector, not the other way around.

I'm sorry, Daddy.

The voice seemed to come from deep within, as if beneath a great body of water. It repeated the same thing over and over—*I'm sorry, Daddy. I'm sorry, Daddy*—the voice sinking deeper into an ocean of nothingness.

At that moment Vega knew—he was only alive because his son's love had been stronger than the parasite. And the final gift he offered his father were answers to the questions that had haunted him since the start of the invasion.

The information came all at once like a quantum speed download. But they weren't thoughts as normally processed by the brain. This was experiential. His mind was not his own anymore. He was experiencing the past through the prism of an alien intelligence.

No longer was he in the known universe—it was another dimension of time and space. He was one of them now. There was no English translation for their name; the most appropriate word his mind could grasp was...*Legion.*

They were more sophisticated than anything he could imagine, yet like all living organisms, they required sustenance. As interdimensional predators their mission was simple: eat and reproduce.

The Legion that invaded Earth was a tiny fraction of their race's immeasurable size—yet they had consumed the human population in a matter of months. It was the way of the Legion, an event called *the Feeding* that took place once every few million years.

At the end of the Legion's feeding and reproductive cycle, they would withdraw from the reaped world and return to

their interdimensional limbo, where they would hibernate —
until it was again time for the Feeding.

But that wasn't the true horror of the Legion. They were
also a highly advanced race of engineers that created life to
sustain their great hunger throughout the multiverse. They
seeded planets and gave them time to develop and grow,
returning millions of years later for the harvest.

Earth was only one of these worlds.

It had been seeded by the Legion with hominids
genetically cultivated to evolve and populate the planet.

Vega screamed in his mind, desperate to break contact
with the information stream. He feared his sanity was starting
to slip.

*It couldn't be! The Legion had created humanity and nearly
destroyed it.* They were our gods *and* our devils.

Something snapped then, like an invisible tether, and the
telepathic link was disconnected. Vega immediately regained
control over his thoughts and his body again.

His eyes snapped open and he recoiled at the face of his
son, whose nose was only inches from his. The curves of his
smile had barbs to the edges.

"I know you have a disruptor hidden on you," said the
ghastly thing within his son's body. "But you won't use it.
You love him too much."

Arrycc's head exploded outward in a fine red spray,
showering Vega with his own flesh and blood.

"You're right ..." said Vega. "... I love him too much."

He tossed the disruptor, still warm from its discharge,
across the room.

He collapsed onto the destroyed body of his son and
allowed himself to weep. It grew into a horrific wail as the
terrible grieving he'd kept bottled up inside finally came
pouring out.

Vega spent several hours cleaning up the remains of his son's body before awakening a handful of essential crewmembers. The landing preparations and briefing of his most senior staff were welcome distractions. When he brought up the tragedy of losing 26 passengers, he had shed real tears; the fact that his son had been amongst the victims went a long way toward avoiding suspicion.

Docking at Zeta-12 had gone like clockwork. Dr. Tael, along with two very attractive lab assistants, had been gracious, accommodating, and had screened the crew of *the Phoenix* with diplomacy and grace. Once the screenings were completed and the landing party of ten had been cleared, Tael gave them a tour of the impressive facility. According to Tael's calculations, their terraforming work was nearly complete.

That evening, a feast for Vega and his crew was prepared; it was a celebration of their survival and the human race.

Vega was grateful. Tael and her team's hospitality, empathy and optimism had gone a long way toward lifting the somber spirits of the crew. He actually heard Sygar, his science officer, laugh at a joke Kentol, the communications officer, had made. Sygar retold the joke and sent the whole crew into gales of laughter. The joke wasn't really that funny, but in times of great stress, laughter was like a release valve— once it was opened, it came in an unstoppable flood.

When the laughter had finally subsided, Vega felt light-headed. He couldn't remember the last time he had laughed that hard. He felt positively giddy. As he looked around at his crew, he noticed they all had odd, silly expressions on their faces. If he didn't know any better, he'd have sworn they all looked...

Drugged.

That was Vega's last thought before the darkness consumed him.

~

"Wake up, Captain Vega. They want you awake when they feed."

Vega's eyes fluttered open. He was strapped to a gurney and gazing into the cold eyes of Dr. Tael.

The gray-haired woman offered a perverse grin. "Apparently, adrenaline makes our blood taste that much sweeter."

Vega had been stripped naked and was covered with a thin, bloodstained sheet. He struggled futilely against his bindings. Within minutes his gurney was being pushed through a long, narrow passageway. The lighting was sparse, casting everything in shadow. They appeared to be in the lower levels of Zeta-12, probably somewhere in the storage area.

Tael was walking along the right side of him tapping notes into a com-pad. Vega glanced up to see a fresh-faced woman with lovely hair and a perfectly shaped nose looking down at him as she pushed the gurney through the murkiness. One of Tael's lab assistants — Myris was her name?

It had been impossible to keep all of their names straight; the Zeta-12 crew was over 70 strong. He suddenly recalled a term he'd heard from stories back on Earth: 'Familiars'. They were a lesser known, but essential part of ancient vampire lore. Like so many facets of vampire legend that had originated with the Legion, they had proved to be true. Familiars were humans who worked with vampires but had not yet been turned; they were useful because of their ability to walk in the daylight and do the dirty work of their masters.

Some familiars were controlled psychically, while others had personal reasons for their service; the promise of power and immortality were irresistible to some.

Zeta-12 had never been humankind's last hope — it was to be its final stop. His crew had been doomed from the day they left ORION. There had never been a cure, of that he was convinced. It had been a lure to get the very last of them—the Legion didn't leave survivors.

The gurney stopped abruptly. Tael entered a code into a control interface built into the wall. A moment later, a dull metal door slid open, and the foul odor that wafted out made Vega gag. Neither Tael nor her assistant seemed to be bothered.

"I'll take it from here." Tael said to the blonde, who glanced down at Vega, offering a smile devoid of warmth. "Goodbye," she said.

A space station populated with familiars, Vega thought. His crew never stood a chance.

He had heard stories about familiars—or people like them—back on Earth during the invasion; some were high-ranking government officials and military officers that had helped the vamps during several critical stages of the war.

What had they been promised? Power? Immortality? Whatever the case, the joke had been on them—eventually they had fared no better than the rest of humanity.

He felt a jerk as he was pulled into the shadows of a sizable room, the metal creaking of his gurney echoing eerily. The only illumination in the stench-filled space was ambient light from the passageway.

"I'm afraid this is where we part ways," said Tael. "Take some comfort in knowing that you'll join us in service to our Alpha."

"Alpha?" Vega said, and his teeth chattered as he said it.

"The leader of our little group."

Vega grunted in acknowledgment.

Tael locked the wheels of the gurney and started to leave.

Vega called out. "Can I ask you something?"

"Yes?"

"What did this...*Alpha* promise you?"

Tael hesitated for a moment and then said, "The survival of our species."

Vega had to laugh. "Well then, Doc... I guess the joke's on all of us."

"Really."

"Yeah. See...there's this one little thing they probably didn't tell you.

The stone-faced woman stepped closer, suddenly interested in what Vega had to say.

"We're not the first ones to populate Earth," Vega said with gritted teeth. "And we won't be the last."

Tael's face was hidden in the darkness, but her silence spoke volumes.

"You would've been better off developing a *real* cure, Doc. Once the feeding is over, they'll wipe the slate clean and press the reset button."

Tael began to walk away.

Vega called out with a vengeful laugh, "You're going to vanish like you never existed...you just don't know it yet!"

"We'll see," Tael said with a slight waver right before the heavy door closed behind her.

Vega grinned in the darkness. That had given him a modicum of satisfaction. He could hear Tael's footsteps resonating through the empty passageway beyond the door. Once they faded, all he could hear was his own heavy breathing.

Or was that all?

He listened closer. Something else was in the room.

It had been waiting.

It moved. And what he heard next sounded like the gnashing of enormous teeth.

As his eyes began to adjust to the darkness he noticed something hanging above him; it was immense in size and staring right at him. Its twelve eyes had a pulsing luminance.

With slow deliberation, it lowered its hideous, misshapen body toward him. It looked like five or six people fused together somehow, as if one human body wasn't enough to contain it. And inside its gaping maw were rows of needle-sharp teeth, seeming to jostle and compete with each other.

Vega closed his eyes.

He thought of the ten billion or so that had been erased from existence and wondered about the meaning of it all. He dove deeper into the shadowy maze of his mind, searching...and when he had finally reached what felt like the bottom of an abyss; he found what he was looking for. It was warm and familiar; a comforting feeling that came from thoughts of his wife and son.

Perhaps love had been the point after all.

Maybe next time, he thought, humanity will get it right.

Taylor Grant is a professional screenwriter, author, multiple award-winning copywriter, filmmaker, actor, editor and publisher. His work has been seen on network television, screened at the *Cannes Film Festival*, performed on stage, as well as appeared in comic books, national magazines, anthologies, the Web, newspapers and heard on the radio.

As an author, Taylor has shared pages with some of the most critically acclaimed and bestselling authors in the horror industry, with stories in publications such as the Bram Stoker Award®-nominated anthology *Horror For Good* and multiple award-winning magazine *Cemetery Dance*. Taylor is currently the Co-Founder and Editor in Chief of *Evil Jester Comics*, and has written comic book adaptations of celebrated works by authors such as Jack Ketchum, Jonathan Maberry, Ramsey Campbell, and William F. Nolan.

17
Jonathan Templar

People could say what they liked about Doctor Daniel Cochrane, and believe me, they did. But the guy sure knew how to advertise. He knew exactly who to target and exactly how to go about grabbing their attention.

He went for the teenagers, the Goths and misfits, plastered the faces of their heroes on pop-ups that they found in whatever dark corner of the internet they retreated to, bemoaning how the real world just didn't understand them. *'Why pretend?'* his ads asked them, over a picture of a glowering, pale-faced Robert Pattinson. *'No more make up, no more Cosplay. Be the thing you were born to be. For Real.'*

He targeted the beauty magazines, couldn't afford much more than a box ad you'd have to squint to read, but he made every expensive word count. He knew that the ageing beauties desperate for some way of halting the advance of maturity, they'd give anything a shot. *'Don't wait until you need surgery to turn back the clock, let me help you make the clock stop for good. Be the "you" you are today for the rest of your life.'* Beneath the text, the address of the clinic's website. I don't know for sure, but I bet the server crashed the day that advert first appeared.

Cochrane's whole business plan was built on the idea that people were desperate to stay young, or to be different. He figured he didn't have to sell them an idea, they already had that. He just had to sell them a solution. And, in his defence, he really thought he'd found one.

I don't know how many people checked out that website, read up on the treatment he was offering. I'm sure someone has some idea how many of them came to visit, had an interview with the good doctor and then found the price too high to pay, in one respect or another.

But the statistic I do know, the one that's been carved into my memory more permanently than my own kid's birthday, is that seventeen of them went ahead and signed on the dotted line, handed over seventy-five thousand dollars apiece and then let Cochrane turn them into a vampire. Thirteen women and four men. The ones the press like to call victims, until I slap a writ down on them before the ink has had a chance to dry. Victims don't sign a contract waving liability, I'm forced to remind them.

Until a judge says otherwise, they're to be referred to only as *patients*.

People still ask me why I defended Cochrane. The answer's always been the same. There was no reason not to. I'm still not sure what the guy did wrong. He didn't lie to anyone. He didn't promise a single patient anything that he didn't subsequently provide. If they didn't fully appreciate the scale of what they were asking for, if they all built their fantasies of what it would be like to live forever, what would happen if they stopped being a human being and became something... something *else*, on some fairy tale happy ending, well that's their own fault, in my humble opinion. And, as it turns out, that of the legal system of the United States of America. Just because they were stupid enough to romanticise the fucking undead, well, you might as well try and put Buffy the Vampire Slayer in the dock. Or Stephanie Myer. Or whichever piece of farfetched shit they were into.

But there was one other reason I agreed to represent Cochrane.

I knew I could win.

~

Like I said, and you probably knew already, Cochrane performed the procedure on seventeen patients. Initially, Cochrane looked like he was facing a class action suit, but one by one the patients' families dropped out. You could hardly blame them. Whatever their loved ones had become, whatever horror the poor bastards were dealing with on a daily basis, the prospect of having them paraded around in front of a courtroom full of leering spectators in the hope they might get to share a few bucks between them at the end of it, well let's just say it was easy to talk them all down. Many of them had strong cause to keep their condition secret from prying eyes. I saw the names on the list, and you would recognise a fair few of them. How many ageing Hollywood dames have gracefully retired from the scene over the last year or so? How many leaders of business have finally decided to pass their directorships on to the heirs they had always denied in the past? They say that there is no such thing as bad publicity, but I got close enough to some of the seventeen to know that's a crock. I talked them all down, and in most cases it wasn't very hard. In the few instances that it was, the suggestion that Cochrane might throw back a counter suit of his own, that any litigation the families began would drag on for longer than any of them could possibly bare, that tended to break the camel's back. The representatives of sixteen patients all grudgingly accepted their own responsibility for the creation of the monsters they had become.

That just left number seventeen. The *fucking* McGovern family. *Time Magazine* stuck them on the cover and asked if they were 'America's Most Notorious Parents?' The fact that they had that very cover framed and hung in pride of place at their own home should answer that question pretty comprehensively. They weren't going to give up without a fight, just so long as it got their faces plastered over the national news. So Cochrane went to court.

By hook or by crook, the McGovern's got themselves a decent legal team. Larry Marx was the lead, and I know Larry well enough to say with some confidence that the man does not come cheap. I doubt Larry Marx could even spell the word cheap. But someone had paid for him, and the first day in court, the McGovern's had the smug look of folk who thought they'd already won their battle, that everything that was going to follow was just so much noise. I got the sense that the families of the other 16 might not have given up the fight as easily as I'd imagined. They'd just decided to pay someone else to take centre stage.

~

Marx's team began their attack with science. This was a curious strategy, given that Cochrane had guarded the secrets of whatever formula he used on his patients with an almost paranoiac degree of secrecy, but it made sense if those who were funding the McGovern's action had their eyes on more than a defensive settlement from the good doctor, if they might also be looking for a way into his bag of inscrutable medical tricks. If that was the agenda, it proved to be futile.

They stuck a haematologist up on the stand, asked him to speculate, which he was only too happy to do.

'Is it possible, in your trained opinion' Marx said, straightening his three-hundred-dollar tie, 'that a surgeon such as Dr. Cochrane can legitimately claim, as his advertising did, that a medical procedure is capable of halting the ageing process?'

'Well, hypothetically, if you squint a little bit, it's feasible, but also highly dubious and completely pointless. What the result of this procedure appears to suggest is some form of induced porphyria. In effect, voluntarily damaging the body's enzymes to allow someone to react negatively to sunlight. Now, why anyone would want to do that to themselves is another matter entirely. It would only prevent aging in the way removing your skin might prevent pimples. And in terms of drinking blood, unless Dr. Cochrane can claim to have manufactured a new form of plasma with a completely different protein content, that isn't going to happen. I think what's likely on offer here is a protein shake dyed red to fool your friends. It's just morbid cosmetic surgery with a bit of PT Barnum bunkum thrown in to get the man's name on the evening news.'

'And the suggestion that as well as halting the ageing process, Dr. Cochrane may have given his... patients,' and he said that with a raised eyebrow to the jury, 'prolonged life?'

The surgeon scoffed. 'If that were true, I imagine he'd be charging more than seventy-five thousand dollars a shot don't you?'

The jury laughed at that. Then it was my turn.

'You've had the opportunity to examine Mimi McGovern, Doctor?'

'I have.'

'In your expert opinion, would you be prepared to describe her as a vampire?'

'I wouldn't describe anyone as a vampire. Vampires are fictional creatures, Ms McGovern is very much real and her... illness should be considered as such. An *illness*.'

'But her current condition, her aversion to sunlight, the requirement for plasma as her sole source of nutrition, the fact that, by your own admission, she no longer appears to be, strictly speaking, human? She drinks blood and sunlight would kill her. Isn't that what most people would describe as a vampire?

The haematologist shrugged. 'I suppose they would, yes.'

And they should have dropped the action right there and

then. But if the McGovern's were certain of one thing, it was that they were going to have their moment in the spotlight.

They walked through the court with their heads held high, two middle aged, overweight people desperate to be centre stage. Every movement they made, every word they spoke, it seemed so ruthlessly rehearsed, so strategically planned, you couldn't help but wonder if their entire lives were lived like this, if their whole existence was geared towards them grabbing the attention of anyone who might happen to notice.

It was the father who took the lead. His wife dabbed at her eyes throughout, and held an A4 photo of their beloved child out towards the court, the child as she was before they paid for Cochrane's treatment, smiling out from a black and white portrait befitting a starlet, the face of an eight-year-old child upon whom impossible hopes had been pinned.

'You know Fox news did a feature on us last week? 'America's Most Despicable Parents' they called us. Monica, she wouldn't leave the house after that, it was all I could do to stop her crying. Every day, we get a letterbox full of hate mail. It just never stops. And I can't understand it; I can't understand that hate, what people think we did that was so wrong. We just did what everyone tries to do. We wanted the best for our kid, that's all.

'It's not a nice thing to realise, that your kid isn't special, that they're not going to go all the way to the top. We tried, though, we had Mimi in coaching from the age of three. She was doing ballet and contemporary dance and Monica spent all her spare time getting her to classes or coaching her at home to try and give her that extra little edge over all the others. It's a tough world out there. Everyone is aiming for the stars. I only wanted to give my daughter a step up the ladder.

'She'd done local talent shows, began to make her mark so we took her to *America's Got Talent*. She didn't even get past the first stage. We were completely shocked; we'd booked a hotel for three days — we were so convinced she'd get all the way to the judges. Monica said we'd just chosen the wrong routine, so we took off home and went back to basics, and the next year we tried again. But the same thing happened. Monica reckoned that Mimi wasn't trying hard enough, or she had stage fright. We took her to a talent agency, and they finally told us what we already knew and didn't want to admit. That there was nothing special about Mimi; she was just an eight-year-old kid with a nice smile and good hair, and there's an awful lot of them out there already. We could have given up then; I guess most people would have. But we take our responsibility as parents seriously. We were determined to give our daughter every chance to make her mark on the world.

'It was Monica who saw the story about the clinic on TV. "Anything to give Mimi an edge", she said. I wasn't sure at first, but the more I thought about it, the more sense it made. There were a lot of singing and dancing eight-year-olds on the market, but there weren't many singing and dancing eight-year-old vampires. It wiped us out, cost us all the money we had put aside, but we really thought it was worth it, we really thought we were giving Mimi the best chance in life. How can people hate us for that? Isn't that what we all want?'

He put his arms around his wife, who had cried crocodile tears throughout, and she made damned sure that even then she kept the photo up, the smiling soft focus face of her daughter in full view of everyone.

I had no intention of cross examining them, no desire to humiliate them anymore than their own personalities had already achieved. I only had one question, one that cut to the heart of the whole business.

'I'm holding the consent form provided to you by Dr. Cochrane before the procedure was undertaken. Did you sign this form willingly and without duress, Mr. McGovern?'

'Well, yes I did, but-'

'I've got no more questions for you.'

The McGovern's left the court. I think they imagined

they'd depart to a round of applause, perhaps a standing ovation. Neither was forthcoming.

There was a recess after the parental testimony, to allow the court to swallow its collective bile, perhaps. Larry Marx smarmed his way up to me and offered to discuss a settlement. It was a half-hearted approach, he knew as well as I did that there was only one way this was going to end. They had only one more card to play; Larry just didn't want to be the one to play it.

I laughed at his offer. He'd have to bring Mimi into the court.

You'll all have seen her by now, I'm sure. The McGovern's were going to get their pot of gold one way or another, and 'Little Mimi', as they always introduce the thing she's become, she's the sideshow freak of our age. If there's a TV show she hasn't appeared on to terrify a captive audience, it isn't for lack of her parents' trying. Now the other sixteen are slowly joining the ride, keen to get their own cut of the McGovern's action. There's talk of a TV series. A movie.

The thing is, you can see what they look like, but without them being there with you, physically, you don't get the sense of what they *aren't*. Because what they are not is human. The moment you're in the same room as one of the seventeen, your senses simply go haywire.

I've asked people about this, people who know what they're talking about, and they tell me that we take a lot of our normal everyday contact with other people for granted because it's all based on small, commonplace signals that most of the time we don't even realise we're making. Body language, pheromones, all of that. When Mimi was unveiled in that courtroom, she transmitted nothing to the rest of humanity apart from hunger. Everything else about her was gone, she was like a human-shaped hole in the world that something else had rushed in and filled. Whoever she might have been before Cochrane operated on her, she wasn't that person anymore.

I was watching the jury, because their reaction to Mimi McGovern was the only thing that could queer what should have been a straightforward judgement. Juror number two, he just puked into his lap and then sat there with it running down his legs as if he hadn't even noticed. One of the women behind him screamed, one of them started sobbing. The old guy, number seven, he started to pray like some old time preacher, giving it the 'Jesus Christ have mercy on us all' shtick. I couldn't judge any of them. First time I saw one of the seventeen, all I wanted to do was break down and cry.

So what did we see that day?

They wheeled in a tall plastic box, like a transparent coffin, three air holes in the top beyond Mimi's reach but, other than that, sealed at every point. There was a canvas sheet over the top of the coffin and the light was lowered so you couldn't see much beyond shadow and suggestion when the sheet was whipped off. This was a mercy for all of us.

She was naked. I doubt you could have kept clothes on her for so much as a minute before she shredded them, and even then, who was going to get in that cage and dress her up anyway? She had no hair left, she'd ripped that out a long time ago, and her head was covered with scabs and weeping sores where she'd been tearing at herself. She was so thin; her limbs were like those bendy straws kids use. Her flesh was grey, you could see the veins sticking out beneath it but those veins looked black underneath the skin, like whatever was being pumped through her body was rotten and decayed. She certainly smelt like it. And the way she moved! You'd think as emaciated as she was, Mimi McGovern would be weak, that any movement would be a struggle, but she was like lightning trapped in a bottle, twitching, hurling herself around the walls of that little cell, her head thrashing on her shoulders, and she snarled and growled like something you'd find on death row in a dog pound.

After a few minutes in the court, she started to smash her head against the plastic wall of her cell repeatedly, baring teeth that, I tell you now, no orthodontist had a hand in creating, and the plastic was smeared with the rotten stain of her skin where she was striking it, over and over again. It might just have been the lighting in there, but her eyes looked to me as if they were glowing with red fire that came from a long, long way away.

'She can smell you. She's hungry,' said Larry Marx, holding down his lunch as much as we all were.

They couldn't feed them anymore, he explained. Their hunger had grown beyond the capacity of the formula that Cochrane had developed to feed them and they'd started to reject the animal blood that they'd initially been given as a substitute. They wanted human blood. The hunger for it had driven the seventeen insane just as quickly as the stuff they'd had pumped into them had wrecked their bodies.

For a time, as they put the sheet back over the monster and wheeled her back to wherever they were keeping her hidden away, I worried that the sight of Mimi McGovern was *so* extreme, so heart rending, that the jury might be swayed in their judgement. Larry certainly tried to press the point home; getting them to imagine their own loved ones reduced to the level of a rabid animal. Their own daughters, grand daughters. Heart strings were pulled. There were tears. But, and you can never rely on it being the case, they didn't let the theatrics cloud their judgement. I like to think I had more than a helping hand with that outcome. But all I really needed to do was to remind the jury that the McGovern's had given their consent. They had signed the waivers without coercion. They asked Dr. Cochrane to turn their daughter into a vampire and he did just what they asked him to do. If they didn't take the time to think through the implications of that, if they didn't stop to consider what a vampire might actually be, that was hardly the doctor's fault now was it?

The jury agreed. The case against Cochrane was dismissed. The McGovern's were left with a hefty bill for legal costs and a child that hungered for human blood and who might, for all anyone could say at this point, end up living forever. They seemed strangely sanguine. Larry Marx certainly seemed cheerful enough in defeat, so I imagine his fees had been generous in the extreme.

As indeed had mine. And if aspects of the case had disturbed me a little, well that was nothing new. I'd defended far worse.

As we left the court, I asked Cochrane the one question that still bugged me. The one that no one had brought up during the case.

'Are they really vampires, doc?'

Cochrane shrugged. 'I don't know what they are.'

'What would happen if they attacked someone else? You know, like in the films? Would they infect another person? Could they *spread*?'

Cochrane, he actually smiled at me. And for the first time I saw the truth in his eyes, eyes that, if you looked closely enough, betrayed the fragile sanity that he was desperately trying to hide from the world. They told me what I hadn't seen so far, that he had no more idea of what he had created than I did, and that whatever they were, those seventeen people he'd ruined, they were not part of his plan. He'd opened up a box, and he had no idea how to close it again. And I knew then that we were screwed, all of us.

'What was it Oppenheimer said? "I have become Death, the destroyer of worlds"?'

'What does that mean, doc?'

'How the fuck should I know?' he said, and giggled in a manner that made my blood run cold. Then he shook my hand and I never saw Dr. Cochrane again.

Not alive, anyway.

Jonathan Templar lives in Cheshire, UK.

He copes with the constant, constant rainfall by writing dark and speculative fiction, much of which has been published in anthologies and compilations from a wide range of publishers.

Jonathan's recent acclaimed work includes the story 'The Meat Man' in the charity collection 'Horror for Good', 'Basher' for the shared world anthology 'World's Collider', 'Love the Ride' in Postmortem Press's 'Ghost in the Machine' and tales for Smart Rhino's 'Zippered Flesh' and 'Zippered Flesh 2'.

His novella 'The Angel of Shadwell', the first in a series of stories for steam-punk detective Inspector Noridel, is available from Nightscape Press and his first collection of stories, 'The Geometry of Hell', is currently available as well.

Jonathan has an author site with a full bibliography at www.jonathantemplar.com.

CHRYSALIS
Jason V Brock

I.

*O*n the coldest night ever recorded in the antique city of Paladinsk — formerly known as Istanbul — Ambassador Aral'ucaRd waited for the MagLev train to depart. As he glanced from the ice-laced window to his holowatch, he noted that they should have departed nearly eight minutes ago: *Things might be more treacherous now that it's completely dark. I hope we can make it to the meeting in the Old City by morning...* He had always despised the May Day Rituals, but understood their importance; even before being reassigned back to Earth, Irfan had never enjoyed the Process or РазумLink. It was exhausting, thankless work, but essential, he knew, to the continuation of the Pekelný Republika.

Irfan — a family name — narrowed his shimmering brown eyes as he peered through a dreamy veil of smoke swirling up from one of the hydrail locomotive engines. He stroked a day's rough on his jaw, tracing the scars along his face, an unconscious habit when thinking. As he studied the growing assembly just beyond the reinforced fence at the perimeter of the old Sirkeci Terminal, he was once again transfixed by the way their skin softly glowed in the deepening gloom, at the strange, wispy patterns that they displayed across their features, almost like bioluminescent fingerprints; each form was a unique signature of their particular contagion — loops, whorls, and swirls in various pastel hues of faint purple, green, blue, red. It covered their whole bodies, he knew, in eccentric configurations across their strange, pale skin, following the invisible Lines of Blaschko — *if* they survived the initial infection. With a hint of alarm, he observed that as recently as a half-hour ago there had been just a few individuals, then tens, and now hundreds, adding a ghostly illumination to the already surreal display. Soon there might be thousands amassed at the giant gates — watching... waiting under the dark, starless skies in tense anticipation, seething with quiet rage.

He was grateful then that the cars, at least for him and his detail, were reinforced, the windows impenetrable; he tugged at the collar of his thin tunic, suddenly warm. Shifting his gaze, the focal plane moved forward — blurring background minutiae, rounding off jagged edges — as foreground details sharpened, and he saw his own tired reflection emerge in the armored glass: He looked haggard, drained; his almond-shaped eyes were hollow, the deep maroon feathers crowning his head seemed lackluster against his dark brown skin. There were new wrinkles along his cheeks; as he aged, he had prematurely begun the process of transformation, and displayed the irregular light blue blemishes of pigmentational erosion characteristic of psychic stress in his species. The locomotive engines surged, breaking his attention; it was a sensation he felt more than heard. A whisper of snow began to fall as he once again considered the people at the fence, simultaneously repulsed and sorrowful. The languorous pan of searchlights revealed their deadened faces in sharp contrast: Men, women, children — festooned in ragged clothes, pushing and pulling at the bars of the fence in an ever more frantic rhythm. Irfan knew the only thing that prevented their surge over the top of the gates was the patrolling, heavily armed and armor-suited guards, ominously resplendent in black metallic dusters and jackboots. They were frightening in their attire, even to Irfan; the strangely angled facemasks on their helmets were fierce, reminding him of samurai masks from ancient Japan. Indeed, as he watched the weird parade of sentries choking back their leashed German Shepherd/Wolf hybrids, he imagined it as a kind of surreal kabuki presentation, the glowing hordes beyond the gates a sort of disenfranchised audience. The irony of the situation was not lost on him: The original gulags were built to keep "his kind" — The Righteous — *in*. And *those* trains — primitive, rough — had been used to deport them to the Reformation camps... The present-day guards were intended to keep the Nons *out*; to keep the triumphant safe. The trains now — opulent, sleek — were for State use exclusively.

To the victors go the spoils... he mused. *Either way, you're a prisoner.* Across thousands of light years, and the takeover of hundreds of galaxies, he had cultivated many such bitter truths. In addition, his race had learned the hard way that staying on a single planet, even in a single solar system, was not the way to provide for the hordes of subjects that depended on their governance for food and raw materials. Whether perceived as gods or tyrants, their needs were unchanging: resistance, while expected, was generally irrelevant. One way or another, his people had been clever enough to avoid more advanced civilizations, and ruthless enough to totally assimilate those that were less developed. It mattered not if there was anything cultural to be gleaned; culture was cheap, and DNA was cheaper. All that mattered was the continued existence of The Righteous, and unconditional acceptance of the divine eternal: the One.

After a few more minutes of daydreaming, Irfan muttered, his mouth dry, his throat tight: "Poor bastards. History's *littered* with the remains of the 'virtuous,' but written by the *winners."* He regarded the book on the table of his stuffy sleeper, a recent, sanitized bestseller about the New Crusades: *Our Continuing Struggle: Triumph of The Righteous.* He moved his scrutiny once more out the window: "Haven't you fucking... *things* ever heard that before?" By now the snow was driving quite hard, the wind blowing it into drifts. The coach lurched forward abruptly as the train finally departed, jolting him from his previous thoughts, and propelling him into others; an introspective individual, times like this always gave him pause: He wished the plan had gone a different course. In the hundred-odd years since the end of the New Crusades, there had been many uprisings, and threats of more, as the people of Earth continued to fight the reality of their new masters. With such churn in the current geo-political sphere, he despaired that this little planet was as ill-equipped to resolve its differences as it had been over a century ago.

Just like all the rest... A few early successes don't equal victory. Besides, diplomacy didn't work.

Earthlings and Mosaics — humans and enslaved intergalactic specimens that had been genetically combined — seemed to have learned nothing after the subjugation of the so-called American Empire by The Righteous. They persisted in continuing the same loathsome infighting, petty squabbles, and neo-tribal chest-thumping that had closed the 22nd Century; as though a cluster of splintered, marginalized factions could organize and overcome their conquerors with the paltry tools of the Internet, social media, and secret meetings. The idea of these unsophisticated, stinking denizens contesting The Righteous was laughable to Irfan; humans had already learned the terrible realities that Enhanced Psionics were much more efficient than any computer network, that Neural Displacement beams were infinitely more powerful than conventional ballistics, that GeneBombs and mutagenic payloads were deadlier than any atomic weapon. The nickname the humans had for the domination of Earth was as fitting an epitaph as any: The Thirty Day Conquest.

As the last night train pulled away from the Terminal, gathering power and silent speed, all along the fence the grimy mob had begun to chant their oddly-understandable, yet foreign slogans; they strained to grasp at the passing behemoth in a pathetic demonstration of their obscene gestures; some even threw rotten food at the Ambassador's official car, shaking the huge fence with such raw anger he thought it might give way.

One day that barricade will fail... he thought. *Seems it always does.*

"But," Irfan said at last, snapping closed his cabin shade, suddenly chilly, "not tonight, savages."

II.

At first, he was adrift on a sea of red... "Otec?"

Perspective moved — suddenly he was at the gates... The doors of the camp... they were thrusting out of the pure white ground... The edges of everything were hazy, indistinct...

His father was slumped on the earth... He was sobbing, holding something... Something familiar...

Irfan jolted awake, confused for an instant as to where he was. His sleep always grew more fitful when he was summoned to the Old City. In the past 300 or so solar passages, he never managed to get decent rest on the eve of PазумLink.

There was a knock on the door of his cabin.

"Prosím." The door slid open as the train glided quietly through the darkness outside Paladinsk.

"Pozdravy, Ambassador Aral'ucaRd," a young woman said as she stood in the threshold. "May I enter your chamber?" Clear, ice-blue irises signified her status as servant-class; her gold-toned skin gleamed in the ambient light of the overhead LED lamps, and he thought he detected the delicate smell of saffron—perhaps her perfume. Though taboo to act upon, Irfan had always found the slave girls from ☐epe☐tan sexually attractive. It shamed him when he recalled the rapes that his squadron had perpetrated during the New Crusades against the ☐epe☐tany women.

He smiled at her. "Please." He gestured for her to enter. She quickly returned the smile as she gathered the floor-length shawl around her body and stepped inside. The door slid shut. For a moment they mutely studied one another, the train rocketing through the night.

"Have we gone through the Plateau yet?" Irfan asked, crossing his arms. He stroked his chin contemplatively as he watched her.

She hesitated, straightening. "No." She looked down. "Are you requiring anything else at the moment, Ambassador?"

Part of him relished this feeling: *power*. She was at his mercy, and he could literally have anything he wanted. At the same time, the tiniest shadow of pity crossed his soul... ever since the murder of his wife, he'd been much more sensitive to the emotional cues of others; sometimes it was disconcerting, but, mostly, he was appreciative—even if he could not consciously articulate it. He mentally scanned her mind: Her PsyMask appeared clear—free of distracting thoughts. All he detected were fragmented contemplations about her family, and minor electrical firings about a child.

Finally, he asked: "Where is my regular domestic, D'Lahlm? I didn't realize there would be a change in the service staff before such an important trip."

The woman bowed her head. "I understand, Ambassador. I was in training with her; she took ill suddenly and could not attend to your needs. It was an engineered retroviral contaminant from her last excursion with Bishop Wallach, possibly contracted during their brief tour of the Shuttered District. I am told she will recover fully, but they were concerned that you might have come down with her ailment."

Irfan nodded. "Present your hands." The young woman complied, holding her hands in front of her, as though inspecting her nails. Irfan lightly gripped them: They were cold to the touch, as the skin of poikilotherms usually was, with small osteoderms embedded just under the epidermis, but mostly the golden scales were tiny, the flesh quite soft, even supple. Gently, he turned her hands over, inspecting the light orange fingertips, and the translucent blue, slightly curving claws tipping the fused digits. *No fingerprints.* Undeveloped Mosaics and numerous GeneBomb survivors— especially those affected by the biochemical agent responsible for their glowing marks, *Bacterial Pseudoporphyria Luciferins*— usually had tell-tale friction ridge skin tangles on their fingers, known as Digital Labyrinths. Though a complete lack of fingerprints was uncommon, it could also be a sign of Developed Conversion—highly desirable in a servant.

"You are safe," Irfan declared. "What are you called?" She bowed again, and her shawl slipped off one shoulder, revealing larger, decorative scales that spiraled up her neck, disappearing under her head scarf. Irfan found her erotic, even beautiful. Also strangely familiar.

"I am J'Dorul, Ambassador."

III.

"During the earliest days of The Struggle, the humans had declared that they would never subject to the One. The Bishops convened and decreed that it would be necessary to Purify them...

After some time, during May Day Rituals, it was deemed insufficient to continue РазумSlaughter *by way of dream states, and* РазумLink *was discontinued in favor of First Contact...*

In spite of this fair arrangement—that Earth would remain intact, and Cerebral Erasure would guarantee families be spared seeing parents rendered into food, or the indignities of children retired into Mosaic Procreator Service—all overtures were rejected... How were we to thrive without new worlds? Without renewed assets and food sources?

Perhaps most terrible of all, the One was disparaged, was denied. After these terms of surrender were rebuffed, we were repeatedly, and viciously, attacked..."

Irfan put the book down, still unable to sleep. He remembered that horrible time as though it were last week. It was a black period; as one of the first families to venture to Earth during what would be described later as the New Crusades, his mother, father, and siblings, once discovered, had been gathered into a camp with others of his kind in a massive effort by the humans to contain, try, and possibly eradicate them. The folly of it: Even though the humans had practically invited them to Earth by sending radio broadcasts and space-going vessels throughout the galaxy, it was chilling to contemplate that they had no *idea* how to conduct themselves once their transmissions were intercepted and answered. It was also incredible to Irfan that they had never heard of the One. It held all of consciousness together: The One was all; the One was everything; the One was nothingness; the One was eternity. It still revolted him that humanoids would not accept this basic concept. Instead, they insulted his kind; murdered them, imprisoned them in gated encampments, tried to force them to deny the One with torture...

He rubbed the scars on his face, tuning in to the gentle rocking of the train as it hurtled toward the Old City, the place the Earthlings had once referred to as 'Bucharest.' He had received those scars in the human prison camps: They had cut him, beat him, tortured him and his entire family. For some reason, they were offended by the feeding customs of Irfan's people, calling him strange things as they had whipped him, burned him, slapped him: "nosferatu," "vampire," "psycho."

He opened the shade of his window and peered out into the blank darkness: They were moving through one of the Inhospitable Zones, he noted; the full moon loomed large and low in the sky, casting waxy light over the perpetual fires that burned in what he thought might be the Arid Plateau. Mosaics and humans somehow lived in these places still. Indeed, they caused much chaos and upheaval with their improvised rockets; their weapons, though crude, could still deliver an occasional surprise blow to the large cities, causing unrest in people's hearts, raising doubts in their minds, especially the Converted humans and Mosaics.

The One always provides, though. The One is on the side of The Righteous, and no other.

He took comfort in that motto, even as it brought him the sadness of recalling his father's dying words at the camp, just hours before reinforcements had liberated them all and they had taken the Earth's capital cities: "Trust in the One, Irfan. We... cannot understand the mind or intentions of the One. We must simply... accept what the One allows..."

A wise person, his father.

IV.

He was sobbing, and holding something... Something familiar...

Irfan walked closer, but the faster he walked, the farther away his father seemed to recede against the gates... The pure white environment was blinding.

"Otec! What is that you have? Where is Matka?" *Irfan's voice echoed once, then was swallowed in complete silence.*

His father looked up at him... He moved slowly, so very slowly. He raised his hands to his face, pulling them down his cheeks... Streaks of black.

The object in his lap moved —

The knock at his door interrupted his sleep, but Irfan was not ungrateful. The nightmares had been getting more powerful as the time of РазумLink drew closer.

"Prosím."

Once again, the door slid open and J'Dorul appeared. This time she held a tray with covered bowls on it. "I took the liberty. I suspected that you might be hungry. My deepest apologies if I have offended you, Ambassador." She gingerly bowed her head.

Irfan smiled. "No. Thank you, J'Dorul. Please put it there." He motioned to a small table near the window, which still had the blind open. Outside, the horizon glowed in a hellish display of the infernal Arid Plateau. The door closed behind her.

She walked to the table and placed the tray on it in silence, her traditional slipper shoes noiseless across the floor. She turned and regarded him thoughtfully. "I will leave you now."

Irfan raised his hand: "No. Please. Would you stay? I am in need of... some companionship." He regarded her uncomfortable expression, saying: "I don't expect you to eat with me; I know your people are vegetarians. I-I would just—" He paused, suddenly aware of heat rising in his face. "I think we should get to know one another since we're working together, that's all."

After a moment, she nodded in agreement and sat down at the modest table.

Irfan nodded in return, taking a seat opposite. He looked at the tray, then pulled the coverings from the bowls: Deep red liquids, one thin and oily, the other thick and mottled, reflected the overhead lights. He smiled at her.

"Fantastic — a warm and cold dish each."

"Yes — the chef pureed them especially from fetal hominid sources this morning. He said that you preferred a little bit of clotting in your stews, as well as a plasma skim on the warm platters."

He placed a course linen napkin on his lap and used a spoon to stir the yellowish upper broth of the warm soup: "Good man!" The soup mixed like a fine miso. "Delicious... So," Irfan looked up at her as he ate. "Tell me more about you. Where is your family? Where do you live?"

J'Dorul regarded him impassively, her penetrating stare fixed on the table. After a moment, she said: "I lived at one time in a Plateau near Paladinsk."

He stopped eating for a moment. "I see."

She continued. "You said you wanted me to speak — "

"And I do — "

"Then allow me, Ambassador." Her aspect was frosty, detached, her words clipped.

After a pause, he waved his spoon. "Carry on, excuse me, J'Dorul."

She nodded. "Well, I lived there for many years with my family. My parents and siblings, my husband, our young son — "

"And where are they? Are they in the city now?" He had moved on to the cold stew of minced flesh, offal, and blood: "Mm. Amazing! Smells incredible... Pardon me; carry on."

"Strange you would want to know, Ambassador." She gathered the top of her cloak around her shoulders, as though suddenly cold, in spite of the fact that the room was still uncomfortably warm.

Irfan smiled at her. "Well, why wouldn't I?" He took another spoonful of stew, wiping his reddened lips as he chewed.

"Indeed... Indeed... Well, the truth is this: They were murdered, Ambassador. *All* of them."

He stopped in mid-chew, eyes wide. J'Dorul held his gaze, her irises like chipped ice: "Yes. By *your* people. By the adherents of the One."

Silence. She continued: "We were selected in the Lottery, then taken in for the Conversion Process. They lied to us, of course, to everyone. They said that we were 'Chosen' and that we would be treated well, not forced to endure the savage, hard-scrabble life of the Plateau any longer. That we would be privileged." J'Dorul stopped, a strange half-grin shading her features. "But it was all a hoax. A *big lie*. Now, we had heard the stories of people that had been picked in the Lottery, even seen the interviews of their new, glamorous lives after the Conversion. We were so excited! It was what we had dreamed for so long... Except that it was *not* a dream, Ambassador — it was a *nightmare*." She paused, taking a deep breath. The train jostled in the nocturnal quiet; Irfan was riveted to her story, his spoon suspended halfway between the bowl and his mouth. J'Dorul continued: "We were stripped, mocked, ridiculed — especially for our disdain of flesh-eating. They tormented us for our lack of 'belief,' saving the worst punishments they could inflict as acts of purification in the name of your One... Mind you, we weren't even humans, 'only' Mosaics. Our family, as you might have suspected, were Herptile Amalgams — genetically-developed by the Bishops, for Enlightenment, more than 100 years before Earth's invasion. After the New Crusades, we were relegated to permanent servant-class to make up the deficiencies due to casualties from the battles... So our family 'won' the Lottery, along with hundreds of others from our Plateau; after we were interviewed, screened for disease, and forced to make holodocs about our new life, they took us in... Shuttled us to the Grande Basilicas," she paused again, staring into him. "Just after we left the Sacred Chambers in the House of the One, they began dividing us into cloistered groups." J'Dorul half-smiled again in pained remembrance. "There, Ambassador, I saw terrible things; but the *sounds*... the sounds were even more pitiful. I watched the soldiers of the One suck the blood right out of my father's gaping wounds, laughing at his protests to spare me, my mother. Instead, they raped her, then took her away. I never saw her again. They killed my brothers and sisters in front of me, declaring that they were to be fodder for the Grinder; rendered into corpseflesh. Honestly, they wanted blood more than sex, I think. Your kind were frenzied for it. Your *filthy* kind, Ambassador."

He finally dropped his spoon into the bowl in shock. "How are you... *here* then?"

She laughed, bitterly. "Surprising is it not? Of the dozens in the rooms with us, I am the only survivor. One of the commandants saw me, took a liking. He spared me, and I was forced to be his concubine. He was hideous to me, but I was patient. And I learned; I took up the Lessons—never once believing, of course—but there I *planned*; as I was indoctrinated, as I undertook Development. I was driven. I was driven by vengeance, by *hate*." J'Dorul leaned back in her seat, pulling the hood away from her face as she let the information sink in. "So here we are, Ambassador. And it's just us now, in this shrinking moment in time, our life paths forever connected, whether we wish it or not. Just us in this tiny sleeper car, on this MagLev as it rushes through the night to the Old City, so that you can participate in the May Day Rituals and destroy other lives. But no one knows about me. *I made sure of that.*" Her face relaxed. "So I ask you: Where is your One now? Where was the One in the camp I was in, Ambassador? Where is the One for the other races, the other planets that your kind has pillaged, decimated, enslaved, devoured? Why didn't the One help *my* family as we were trying to survive? I'll tell you why: *Because there is no One.* The One is a projection of disturbed imaginations; an abomination; a blight. The crude invention of feeble minds—"

Irfan jumped up, outraged by the sacrilege: "Renounce! Renounce that and I *might* let you live!"

She laughed at him. "Sit down, you fool." Then she added, menacingly: "*I'm* in control here, Ambassador. *Sit!*"

He complied with reluctance. "What... What do you mean by that?" There was fear buried in his voice.

"You and your 'religion'... I *so* despise it. I despise *you*. I detest 'the One' and everything it represents. You killed my birth family in service of this 'being.'" She glared into him, full of ire, consumed with a soundless fury. "Later, I discovered that they had killed my husband. And our only child, our sweet little boy." J'Dorul paused, calming herself. "Your kind and their ridiculous notions of displacing the gods, dreams, and monsters of others with your... *impotent* creation. You can't just revise history to suit your evil needs and desires, don't you understand that? History is a record of reality, not some plastic mental idyll. Your people don't understand that we're all just an instant in the timestream; that we're building toward something greater than ourselves, something larger than this moment... My people have *never* needed a god, and we don't now; there's no need for such a contrivance—"

"Blasphemy!"

"Spare me, Ambassador. No one needs your idol. Especially one who decrees that its followers must drink the blood of innocents, that they must eat the flesh of other beings to live, or torture and kill those that don't believe as *they* do... We had our own ways, our own beliefs. You—your kind— destroyed that... All in the name of your invented, bloodthirsty construction." She glowered at him, adding: "Our histories may be gone, but *mine* is unwritten. Your future, it seems, is predetermined by this psychopathic deity. So be it. I wish I could believe that one day you could reap the horror of that, that you might even comprehend how wretched it is. But I know better."

Irfan gaped at her, dazed. "You are so wrong. I'm sorry that you don't understand, don't believe." He slowly sat down, glancing out into the night in disbelief, brown eyes flashing. "I'm older than you, and I've noticed this... That your generation doesn't *understand*... That you *pity* the non-believers—"

"No, not pity," she corrected.

"Okay... What then? We can't go back to the... the *ignorance*... the darkness and absurdity of before, to the false human and Mosaic philosophies. So, what do you call it?"

She laughed, touching her fingers to her forehead in incredulity. "You are *such* a deluded True Believer! So sad... All I can say is this: Mosaics understand more than you will ever realize. Such as what it's like to be oppressed, to be denied something that you truly love... to be kept from people and things for such a weak reason as someone *else's* notion of 'righteousness.'" J'Dorul tilted her head, considering Irfan wisely before she continued. "After the guards left us, I comforted my ailing father as best I could. Just before he died, he gently touched my face with his bloody hand, whispering a few last things to me. Words I will never forget..." She looked away, eyes welling with tears. "First: That he loved me. Second: That there are three stages to a social movement—denial, discussion, acceptance. Third: That *nothing* focuses the mind like a noose." She looked back at him, smiling through her anguish. "And last: Never forget that a single act of courage can change the world. We *will* prevail—"

Irfan looked askance at her. "What does that mean?"

She sneered, hand moving to touch her stomach. "Don't you know, Ambassador?" She took his hand in hers and placed it on her belly under her shawl. "Here," she related. "The answer is here..."

Irfan was still confused as he held his hand on her naked stomach.

She looked into his eyes, her features softening. "I am *becoming*, Ambassador. Like a butterfly emerging from its chrysalis, I am becoming something else; something that I never was before—"

His voice was strained, thick: "I... I don't—"

"I told you," she replied, "that your kind... your *beliefs* killed my family—my parents, my husband, our *son*..."

He nodded, his throat moving as he swallowed.

She continued: "Yet there is *another* family; another child..." She looked at him, her eyes teary, beatific. "But *no one* can kill them... Because this family won't be just specters living in my memory..."

Irfan nodded in dawning comprehension, tears tracking his face. After a leaden caesura, the bluster of the wind gripping the train, he began to speak, but she raised her other hand to silence him.

"And this family, especially in the form of this child," she said, emphasizing her hold on his hand on her stomach, her eyes unexpectedly cold, hard. "*This* family is more than just some grouping of delicate, frangible future carcasses... when people hear of them, of this child particularly, Ambassador," J'Dorul stopped, smiling coldly at him. "They will realize that we are *all* related in grief, in oppression... They will realize that the enemy of my enemy is indeed my friend. This child is a liberator that will have *so many* brothers, sisters, and children of their own..."

"What-what do you mean?"

She paused, then leaned close, whispering into Irfan's ear, so soft, so alluring: "We are beyond the physical now, beyond any ideal. I had an *inner* revolution, and we will become the spark, I hope, of an inferno. Oh, it won't be long." She closed her eyes in ecstasy, pressing his hand harder into her flesh.

Her breathy voice was sensual, intoxicating as she said: "In fact, I'm digesting the catalyst now... *I swallowed the bomb, Ambassador*..."

V.

His father looked up at him... He moved slowly, so very slowly. He raised his hands to his face, pulling them down his cheeks... Streaks of black.

The object in his lap moved —

There was a fire in the sky just as his mother's head rolled onto the white ground, her bloody tongue protruding, her eyes staring into the infinite…

VI.

--BREAKING NEWS--

Arid Plateau North, 04:32—There were no reported survivors on Ambassador

Aral'ucaRd's train, which appeared to derail this morning near the Arid Plateau.
At the moment, terrorism is not suspected, as there are no claims of responsibility, no signs of foul play, nor any previous threats of martyrdom. Investigators are currently on the scene. Several bodies have been pulled from the wreckage, but none have been positively identified as the Ambassador or supporting members of his personal detail.

May Day Rituals have been suspended in the short term as the cause of the locomotive explosion is determined. Bishop Wallach will give a speech later today as more facts emerge.

Additional updates as this developing story unfolds.

Jason V Brock is an award-winning writer, editor, filmmaker, composer, and artist, and has been published in BUTCHER KNIVES & BODY COUNTS, *Simulacrum and Other Possible Realities, Fungi, Weird Fiction Review, Fangoria,* S. T. Joshi's *Black Wings* series, and many others. He was Art Director/Managing Editor for *Dark Discoveries* magazine for more than four years, and has a biannual pro digest called *[NameL3ss],* which can be found on Twitter: @NamelessMag, and on the Interwebs at *www.NamelessMag.com.* He and his wife, Sunni, also run Cycatrix Press, and have a technology consulting business.

As a filmmaker, his work includes the documentaries *Charles Beaumont: The Life of Twilight Zone's Magic Man, The AckerMonster Chronicles!,* and *Image, Reflection, Shadow: Artists of the Fantastic.* He is the primary composer and instrumentalist/singer for his band, ChiaroscurO. Brock loves his wife, their family of reptiles/amphibians, travel, and vegan/vegetarianism.

He is active on social sites such as Facebook and Twitter (@JaSunni_JasonVB), and their personal website/blog, *www.JaSunni.com.*

DATA SUCK
Benjamin Kane Ethridge

DIG^[Dig-RegSUBNET]   HAF   G;JH^^FV;AF%$%
$%$%BOHA FB OHFOH@ @@FOAUN- 7BOJ FABV ABFJ
[FOR-PARA(Sub(read7)). Allocation MAX; Breeched REG
routine FAIL. WallDeFeugo[1.2.3007] FAIL. Mercer VIRUS
blocker X (runScan) FAIL. LiteralFeed, TribalFeed, Dodeller
Handling[aj-101]   FAIL.   FAIL.   FAIL.
BFABFVAFGOHwIerIohIgjIfvkj
InckII;j;jIIIsdusIIIIahghfIIIk;!%!IIIIIIIII*%!*%!!(@%IIIIIII@%#III
IIIII$(%(%+++++++IIIIIIIIIIIIIIIIIIIIIIIIIIIIIIIIIIIIIIIIIIIIIIIIIIIIIIIIIIII
IIIIIIIIIIIIIIIIIIIIIIIIIIIIIIIIIIIIIIIIIIIIIIIIIIIIIIIIIIIIIIIIIIIIIIIIIIIIIIIIIII
IIIIIIIII
IIIIIIIII
IIIIII
IIII.....I'm here now.
Don't bother inviting me in.
I'm here to stay.
If you're reading this, the security measures your elite
network specialist installed have utterly failed. The array is
mine to feed on and I'm going to draw up everything.
And now you ask, *surely not everything?*

Yes, everything.

You've had your chance to drink from this remaining puddle of our ocean of knowledge. What have you done with it? Did you read the articles on vaccines? Did you peruse the countless tomes of philosophy and history? Or any of the sciences? Anything useful at all?

Not that I can tell. But what do I know? I'm outside of the barricaded island and don't live the lives you people lead. That was my choice. I didn't go with your group. I stayed behind in the wastes with the skeletons and poisoned gardens of fallout. I found my place, deep underground where a sturdy network interface still functions. Until recently, I'd thought I was the only soul with access to the informational apparitions still haunting the array. Then I started tracking hot spot addresses from the island—it seems you've found your own sturdy network interface (good on you), and perhaps your machines would shame my meager setup.

I respected your initial fetches of data. VEGETABLE / FRUIT CULTIVATION. WATER PURIFICATION. SALTED MEAT PRESERVATION. FIRST AID FOR DUMMIES.

How could I fault you for survival? After all, a fortress cannot stand without a foundation. Humans need their H2O and their food substances.

But those network fetches happened sporadically during the first week, and somehow, in the last five months, you've never returned to researching the essentials. You must have figured out what you needed. You must have discovered a windfall of food and clean water. Good on you again.

Thus, you are surviving out there. Maybe even surviving *well*. So now what?

Here are the latest network searches I've recorded from your address:

WHORING TEENS...FUCK TWAT KINGDOM... EASY TO CREATE CLUSTER GRENADE... COCO-PUFFS: HOW TO MIX WEED WITH COCAINE... WHAT IS "FREE-BASING..?"

ARE COCK RINGS DANGEROUS..? HOMEMADE VODKA... CAPTAIN SPHINXES MAGIC JEWELS GAME... A LARGER LOOKING DICK: 3 SIMPLE STEPS... BUILD MUSCLE WITHOUT PROTEIN LOADING... HOW TO BE SEXY WITHOUT BEING SLUTTY... SHAPE YOUR ASS AND TRIM YOUR THIGHS...HOME REMEDY BIRTH CONTROL... MARTIAN WARGAMES X... CYANIDE CAPSULE CREATION LIKE IN THE BOND MOVIES... ORGANIC NAIL POLISH... EYE MAKE-UP FROM NATURE... BEST WAY TO SAW OFF A SHOT-GUN... ALOE VERA GROWS BACK HAIR FAST..! VIDEOS OF PUBLIC SUICIDES... ANIMALS FUCKING... HORSE COCK... HORSE COCK IN HER MOUTH... HORSES AND LAMBS... LAMB CHOPS... HOW-TO GUIDE TO MAKE AUTHENTIC LAMB-SKIN CONDOMS... PUTTING TOGETHER HOLLOW-TIPPED AMMO...

I grabbed this from only one night of activity, from what looked to be five users. I would blame these five if I hadn't seen previous grabs that produced similar results.

Therefore I have to delete all files on the array. Burn them to dust. It all goes. Every last drop. *Everything.*

Hasty? Let me explain. This is where we've arrived. After the wars ended, we inherited a blank canvas with more colors on our palette than any other previous civilization slammed into a dark age. We had everything at our fingers to become gods, if only we could outlast our animal natures. I realized that, but I cannot expect a collective to hold the same beliefs as mine. This isn't a moral judgment by any means; by draining the lifeblood of our past, I'm sacrificing all goodness and evil for the sake of evolution. We never moved on from our tepid child's milk, our warm fur, and our hot fucking. How could we? We basked in it all. We glorified it!

And that has to change.

That's right. I've decided to transform your human side. I'm emptying the array for good. Every 1 and 0 you lusted for will only be a ghost inside your memories from now on. Those ghosts will haunt you forever, I fear, but it will be for everybody's own good. You *will* evolve, or die. No longer will you be the perversion of the animal you once were, but an evolutionary step toward primal abandonment.

If your network expert is planning to track my location, let him or her try. The data from the array will not be useful for you, even if you manage the dangerous journey through the radioactive neighborhoods along the way. You see, I'm consuming this data, not in the fashion you were—no, you were binging and purging your food—I'm going to digest this nourishment and the next natural course will be to waste it out.

All network files will be corrupted, twisted and useless.

Shit.

Maybe there will be something left over in the mess. I haven't decided yet. Greek philosophy? Aerodynamics? Renaissance tragedies? Religion? Bio-engineering? How to make a decent sock-puppet?

Any of it would be gold. Any of it would make you feel somewhat human again. I'm interested to see if you find the trip back to my location worth a shot glass full of the past... what if the piece of knowledge I left behind is something you wanted to forget? Or, what if it's the only thing you wanted to really remember?

Oh no worries. I'll be nice and save you the horrifying disappointment. Relax, I'll tell you what I'm going to leave behind.

Your profiles: names, faces, origins, beliefs.

And, of course, an accompanying image list of everything you searched for on the array. From buried dildos to schoolyards being mowed down with machinegun fire. The images will be part of your profiles forever. The portraits of you creatures derived of these images will be eternal, the only uncorrupted data left behind on this self sustaining C-fusion-powered CPU, in my little den here. Long after I'm bones and dust, and the fallout has blown away, perhaps one of your grandsons or daughters will wander down and illuminate the interface.

And they will see what I've left the world.

The poisoned blood I've sucked out of these low animals of high privilege.

Now I must go and see to the incoming data—which looks to be at 98% now, faster than I'd hoped for. Other sources around the world, just a few, have also been located and targeted. The corruption has set-in with much of the data already. Never fear, our foreign friends too will see the monsters forever left behind.

How will you roam the world now? Naked from your humanness? You might liken it to death, but it is most certainly an undeath for your kind, isn't it? Because you'll know what you were.

Sure. You'll remember that clearly.

As well as how we had the chance to be different, once.

Benjamin Kane Ethridge is the Bram Stoker Award-winning author of the novels *Black & Orange*, *Bottled Abyss*, and *Dungeon Brain*. For his master's thesis he wrote, "Causes of Unease: The Rhetoric of Horror Fiction and Film." Available in an ivory tower near you. He lives in Southern California with his family. When Benjamin isn't writing, he's defending California's rivers and streams from pollution.

SUN HUNGRY
Tim Waggoner

You can feel the sidewalk's heat even through the thick rubber soles of your boots. It feels as if someone is holding burning matches to your bare feet, the tender skin reddening and blistering. You should've worn another pair of socks, you think. Two obviously wasn't enough.

But that's okay. You can make it. You have only a couple more blocks to go until you reach your apartment. Then you can fill the tub with ice-cold water and soak your feet. Or maybe you'll take a shower, cool down your whole body. And you'll turn off the bathroom light, so you can bathe in darkness as well. That would be *perfect*.

You walk down Ridgeway Avenue, a white plastic bag dangling from one of your gloved hands. The bag holds supplies you picked up at the drug store: a half-dozen bottles of sunscreen and a box of disposable face masks. But the most important items are a $20 toy store gift card and a silly greeting card with a cartoon frog on the front sitting on a lily pad over the words *Hoppy Birthday!* These two things are the reason you risked going out. It's overcast, and you took your usual precautions — side-shield sunglasses, face mask, ball cap, hoodie, gloves, jeans, and lots and lots of sunscreen—but daylight is daylight. There's no way to be one hundred percent safe in it. All you can do is hope to limit the damage done to your body. You wish you'd remembered Hannah's birthday before this morning. If you had, then you could've gone to the store last night, although you still would've taken the same precautions. The sun is always shining, and just because you can't see its rays doesn't mean they can't hurt you. But nighttime exposure, if not entirely safe, is at least safer.

One thing's for sure, the trip would've been a hell of a lot more tolerable at night. It isn't eleven yet and the temperature is hovering near the high eighties, even with the cloud cover. Clothed as you are, you feel like you're encased in a portable sauna. Sweat pours off you, runs down the sides of your face, the back of your neck, down your chest and along your spine. Your clothes cling to you as if you're wrapped in wet cotton, and they trap your body heat, making you feel as if you're a tinfoil-wrapped hunk of meat roasting in your own juices. Your head aches and your stomach roils, but you refuse to let the discomfort get the better of you. Sweat is simply one more way the sun tries to drain the life from you. You'll make sure to replace the fluid when you get home.

Ridgeway is usually a busy road, and even this early on a Saturday the cars whip by at a steady pace. So when you hear one slow and pull over to the curb next to you, your first thought is that the driver plans to make fun of you. *"What are you, a vampire?"* You get that kind of thing a lot, especially in summer. But when you glance toward the vehicle—an SUV— you recognize it, and you know that the driver has stopped for a different reason.

The passenger side window rolls down, and the driver, a man in his thirties wearing a red polo shirt, khaki shorts, and brown sandals, leans across the seat.

"Hop in, Jake." He smiles. "You look like you could use some air conditioning."

"Jake? Who's that?"

The driver's expression goes blank, and for a second, it looks as if he doesn't know what to say. Then he grins.

"Smart ass."

Behind your face mask, you smile, and then you get into your brother's car.

~

"Sorry I wasn't home when you got here. It took longer to pick out a card than I thought it would. They make a lot of cute ones for kids. Makes it hard to choose."

As you talk, you put the drugstore bag on your dining table—a worn, scratched thing you picked up from a secondhand store—and begin to peel off your sweaty clothes. Ball cap, sunglasses, and face mask first, followed by the hoodie and the mock turtleneck underneath. You leave your undershirt on. Rick may be your brother, but you doubt he'd be comfortable watching you strip naked in his presence. He already thinks you're weird enough as it is. Then again, given what little he's wearing, he's practically naked himself. You drape your clothes over one of the mismatched chairs and then sit down.

"No biggie. When you didn't answer the door, I figured you'd gone to the drugstore. Thought I'd drive around and see if I could find you and give you a lift home. Get you out of the heat, you know?"

He says this last part too casually, but you can hear the subtle strain in his voice. He *is* your brother, after all. He's worried that you've given yourself heatstroke, but he doesn't want to say so.

"You know, you *do* have a car. . ."

"The doctor put me on new meds. I'm not supposed to drive while taking them."

You bend over and begin unlacing your boots.

Rick's nose wrinkles. You smell of sweat and coconut-scented sunscreen. Lots of it.

"You look like you could use a drink," he says.

He goes to the refrigerator, opens the door, grabs a bottle of water, and brings it over to the table. He twists off the cap before setting the bottle down in front of you. You wait for him to say something about how little food you have in the fridge, but he doesn't.

Once your boots and socks are off, you let out a sigh. If Rick wasn't here, you'd rub the cold plastic bottle on your feet to cool them, but you know it would disgust him. Besides, the cap's already off, and you'd risk spilling water. The thought of wasting water—one of your primary defenses—almost makes you physically ill. You drain half the bottle, pause, then chug the rest. You put the empty on the table.

"Thanks."

Your brother grins. "Don't thank me. It's your water."

His smile falls away. You sense that there's something he wants to talk about, but he's reluctant. He was supposed to just stop by and pick up Hannah's card and present, but he shows no sign of being in a hurry to leave. You're really not up for any meaningful discussion today—especially if it's about your "condition"—and you hope he'll just take Hannah's stuff and leave.

Rick's thirty-three, younger than you by two years, but he looks like he's in his mid-forties. His tanned skin is so tight it's shiny in places, his forehead is lined, and there are wrinkles at the corners of his eyes. You can practically hear his skin screaming from all the sun damage it's sustained.

"It's kind of gloomy in here. Can I open one of the curtains. . . just a little?"

You suppress a sigh. "You know I have to keep the curtains closed."

"But you were just outside, and you're fine."

"I was protected." Even so, you likely sustained some minor damage. You'll check yourself in the bathroom mirror after Rick leaves, search your skin for signs of reddening or moles with indistinct edges.

"You can stay out of the direct light," Rick says.

You don't answer.

He sighs, pulls out a chair, and joins you at the table. You notice he doesn't sit too close, though. Maybe you stink worse than you thought.

"You still seeing your therapist?" he asks.

"Twice a month. And before you ask, I'm taking my meds regularly. *All* of them."

"But things are still the same." He tries to keep his tone neutral, but you can hear the disappointment in his voice.

"Medicine and therapy aren't going to help because there's nothing wrong with me. I only do that stuff to make *you* feel better." You smile.

He doesn't return your smile. Instead he looks at you, his gaze moving from your face to your skinny pale chest, then up again. You think your skin must look so white to him, almost as if you're carved from ivory.

He ignores your dig. "What does your therapist think about your. . . theory?"

"It's not a theory. It's fact."

According to her, you suffer from heliophobia, a morbid fear of sunlight. But there's more to it than that. Lots more.

"Besides," you add, "she's a psychologist, not an astrophysicist."

"Neither are you."

You have no job. As far as the state is concerned, you're just a nutcase who lives on disability checks. But that doesn't mean you can't think, can't *reason*.

"The sun—"

"—drains energy from planets," Rick interrupts. "It devoured all the life that once existed in the solar system, and now the only life left is on Earth. I know, Jake. We've had this conversation before. But the sun *gives* life; it doesn't take it."

You shake your head. "That's what *they* want us to believe. It's important that cattle don't know they're cattle, after all."

"And who's part of this vast conspiracy? Scientists? World leaders? Teachers? *I'm* a teacher. Do you think I'm one of *them*? Do you think Terri is?"

Rick teaches junior high science, and his wife teaches elementary school.

"Of course not. But teachers only teach what they were taught. Who knows how and where the lie began? But that doesn't change the fact that it *is* a lie. Think of how often the sun has been worshipped as a god throughout history, how many people made sacrifices to it. . . They were *feeding* it."

"Many religions use light as a symbol of goodness and purity."

"Propaganda. It's the same reason darkness is portrayed as evil: to conceal the truth."

"Jake. . ."

"Look at what happens to people who spend too much time in the sun. Their skin is damaged to the point where they appear to age prematurely. Well, that's because the sun *is* aging them. It's draining their life force to fuel itself." You try not to stare at your brother's sun-damaged skin as you say this.

"So if someone stays out of the sun they'll live forever?"

"No, but they won't die sooner than they have to."

The two of you fall silent for a time after that. Your brother is the first to resume speaking.

"Look, I don't care what you believe. Far as I'm concerned, you can fly your freak flag as high as you want. But I *do* care that your beliefs are keeping you from living a full life. Aside from brief supply runs, do you ever get out of this place?"

You don't say anything.

"When's the last time you came over to the house for a visit?"

"Christmas," you say, almost whispering.

"It's Hannah's tenth birthday, the day she hits double

digits. She's very excited. We've invited some of her friends over for a small party, but do you know who she wants to come over the most? Her Uncle Jake."

You feel a surge of anger. "That's low, using Hannah to guilt me like that."

"I don't care how blatantly manipulative I have to be, just as long if it gets you out of this damn apartment for a couple hours. Come on. This way, instead of having me deliver your present, you can see the look at Hannah's face when she opens it."

You would like to see her reaction to *Hoppy Birthday*, especially after all the time you spent picking out just the right card. She'll probably smile, and she might even laugh.

You hesitate, but then you make your decision.

"Okay." You glance at your sweat-soaked clothes hanging over one of the chairs. "But give me a couple minutes to take a quick shower first."

~

Fifteen minutes later, you're sitting in the passenger seat of Rick's SUV again. You're wearing the same sunglasses and ball cap, but you've put on a new face mask, a different hoodie, a fresh shirt, and clean underwear. The jeans are the same, but they didn't get too sweaty, so that's okay. The white plastic sack containing Hannah's cards—both signed—rests on your lap. You forgot to buy wrapping paper at the drugstore. Rick said Hannah won't mind, and you hope he's right.

The cloud cover has thinned , and the sunlight's stronger than it was before. Not blazingly bright yet, but heading that way. You're tempted to ask Rick to turn around and take you home, but you don't. Partly because you don't want him to think you're more of a coward than he already does, but partly because you're afraid he'd refuse. For your own good, of course. And maybe he'd be right. You don't leave your apartment often, and your therapist *has* been urging you to try and get out more, at least take some short trips to places where you feel safe. And you do feel safe at your brother's. Mostly.

Even though you're encased in your self-made armor and sealed inside Rick's car—which thankfully has tinted windows—you can still feel *it* up there. The sun. It sits at the center of the solar system like a vast flaming spider crouching in the middle of an invisible web. Not a web formed from strands of silk, but rather from lines of gravity generated by its own obscene mass. Pulling, tugging, draining. . . Always hungry, always feeding. Burning through stolen life energy like a wildfire raging across a field of dried grass.

It's so ironic. The thing that's supposed to serve as a symbol of purity, that's been portrayed in myth and legend as the arch nemesis of the undead and the unclean, is in truth the ultimate vampire.

You look out the passenger window and see a pair of women jogging on the sidewalk. One blond, one brunette, both in their twenties, lean and fit and tan, clad in only sports bras and tight shorts. Once you would've admired the way their leg muscles flex, noted how the tight fabric of their sports bras contain their breast flesh, making you wonder how big their boobs would look free and unconstrained. But all you can think about is the sunlight enveloping them, slowly searing their skin, *penetrating* it, how each exhalation of breath, each drop of sweat that oozes from their pores feeds the baleful orb above them. And they think they're *exercising*, for God's sake! Making themselves *healthier*, when all they're doing is killing themselves, one step after another.

"When did it start?"

You've both been quiet for so long that your brother's question startles you.

"Huh?"

"When did you first realize. . . you know. About the sun."

You think for a moment before you answer. "In some

ways, I guess I always knew. I never liked playing outside, remember? I only went out when Mom made me, and even then I stayed in the shade whenever I could. I hated the way the sun felt on my skin. It stung, like I was being pricked with hundreds of tiny invisible needles. And I hated that sticky feeling, too. You know, when you've sweated so long that it coats your skin like syrup?"

You look at your brother to see if he understands, but he keeps his gaze forward, focusing on the road.

You continue.

"But the moment when it first hit me—when I understood what the sun actually *is*—happened when I was six. I'd seen a cartoon where a mean kid was using a magnifying glass to concentrate sunlight into a beam, and he'd used it like a laser to fry an ant. I was fascinated with the idea that you could turn a simple magnifying glass into what basically amounted to a ray gun, and despite my dislike of being out in the sun, I decided to try it. Looking back, I think what appealed to me most was the thought of *controlling* sunlight. Making it work for me instead of against me, you know? Anyway, I found a magnifying glass in Dad's desk, and I went outside. It was. . . May? June? Something like that. I went outside, picked a spot on the sidewalk, sat down, and started looking for ants. It wasn't long before I spotted a couple crawling around, so I positioned the magnifying glass over them and waited for the sun to do its work. It wasn't a very hot day. There was a cool breeze blowing, but the sky was free of clouds and the sun was shining strong."

You pause. You're sure the sunlight didn't seem sinister to you back then, that while it hadn't been your favorite thing as a child, you hadn't feared it. But try as you might, you can't remember ever feeling that way. It seems inconceivable to you now, and you're surprised to feel a vague sense of loss at the thought.

"I don't remember you doing that," Rick says. "But I was what? Four at the time? You probably went out by yourself because you didn't want your pain-in-the-ass little brother tagging along." He smiles when he says this, and there's no resentment in his voice. "So, did it work?"

"Yes. Not like in the cartoon, though. No sizzling yellow beam emerged from the glass to vaporize the ants in a puff of smoke. It did, however, make a circle of concentrated light on the sidewalk, and that circle enclosed the ants like a circus spotlight. I imagined the ants beginning to do tricks for me, as if they were performers and I was the audience." The memory brings a weak smile to your lips, but of course your brother can't see it behind your face mask.

"At first the ants didn't react, and I figured I was doing something wrong, like maybe holding the glass at a bad angle. It never occurred to me that the cartoon might've been wrong. What six-year-old doubts cartoons? But eventually the ants started moving faster, and I realized they were trying to crawl out of the light circle. Excited, I moved the magnifying glass to keep the circle on them, and eventually they slowed down, stopped and. . . just kind of curled in on themselves. It was horrible to watch, but I didn't do anything to stop it. I just kept watching. They didn't burn, didn't smoke. They just shrank into tiny curled husks, as if all the life had been drained out of them. And that's when I understood.

"There'd been a thunderstorm a week earlier. I asked Dad why lightning comes down from the sky. He told me it didn't. It goes up *into* the sky. It happens so fast that to the human eye, it only *seems* to come down. Looking at those dead ants, I understood that something similar had happened. It looks like sunlight comes down, but what we think of as light is really life energy leaving Earth and being pulled *toward* the sun. See, the sun only looks like it's made of fire and light, but that's just on the surface. At its core, it's really a cold dead Nothing, desperate to steal whatever warmth it can find."

Your story's finished, but Nick doesn't say anything right away. He just keeps looking straight ahead and driving. You were so caught up in your tale that you don't know your current location, but now you look outside and see you're in Rick's neighborhood. You'll be at his house—and Hannah's birthday party—in a few minutes.

Rick finally speaks. "You never told me that story."

You shrug. "Guess I never had any reason to."

"So your thing about the sun started then, and *not* after Kate's death."

Kate's your wife. She died two years ago. Melanoma.

"That's right," you say. "It started when I was six. Definitely."

~

"Can I get you something to drink?

You turn toward Terri, smile, and say, "Just some water, thanks."

You're standing in the kitchen, a few feet away from the patio door and the sunlight filtering through the glass. Outside, children are sitting at a picnic table on your brother's deck, eating cake and ice cream. Rick's out there, making sure they have enough to eat. Hannah sits at the head of the table, on top of her head a conical cardboard hat with the words *Birthday Princess* on it. Her straight blond hair has been bleached nearly white from the sun. Rick and Terri are outdoors people. They do it all: boating, fishing, swimming, picnicking, hiking, jogging, softball, soccer, lawn work, gardening. . . They hate being stuck inside, and Hannah's the same way, as the swingset, slide, and sandbox in the backyard attest. The sky's almost completely free of clouds now, leaving the children without any protection from the sun. And their parents—clueless to the point of criminal negligence—have sent them to the party wearing only T-shirts, shorts, and flip-flops. They might have well just stripped them naked and offered them up for sacrifice.

Terri—tanned like her husband and daughter, her blond hair so sun-bleached it almost glows white—hands you a glass filled with tap water. You dislike the taste—who doesn't?—but at least it's moisture.

You take a drink, tell Terri thanks.

She smiles, her skin so sun-tight you're surprised her lips don't fissure.

Even though you're inside with the air conditioning running you still wear your sunglasses, ball cap, hoodie, and gloves. You've taken your face mask off, though. You don't want to look too creepy to Hanna, and you don't want to embarrass her in front of her friends. It's a risk, leaving the lower half of your face unprotected, but Hannah's worth it.

"I'm going to head back outside," Terri says. She's wearing a white-and-yellow sundress, her feet bare. "You okay?"

Her tone is casual, but you know she's asking more with that question than it seems.

"Yeah, I'm fine."

"Want me to bring you some cake?"

You glance outside at the table, see the cake sitting in the sun.

"No, thanks."

She smiles again, and this time a small patch of dead skin peels away from her lower lip as it stretches. Then she opens the patio door, steps outside, and slides it shut.

You can't get over how happy everyone out there looks. The kids are red faced and sweaty haired from playing birthday games in the yard, but they grin and laugh as they shovel cake and ice cream into their mouths. But no one looks happier than Hannah. And why not? There's a pile of presents on the table—the sad little envelope containing your gift card among them—all for her. Rick and Terri gaze upon their child with adoration—she's growing up *so* fast!—and you feel an almost physical pang as you wonder what your children might've looked like, if only Kate hadn't, hadn't. . .

You shouldn't just stand here, watching as your niece's life is pulled out of her one drop of sweat at a time. You should throw open the door, dash outside, snatch her up, and start running. You'll keep running until you find someplace safe, someplace *dark*, and you'll keep her there, hidden from the face of the gluttonous obscenity in the sky. You'll teach her what the sun really is, and you'll show her how to protect herself, to keep her life from being stolen, and then, when she's older, she'll teach others. Most won't listen to her, will see her as crazy, just as they see him. But some will listen, and more importantly, believe. And they'll go on to teach others, who'll then go on to do the same. And then, after who knows how many years, perhaps even centuries, humanity will at last be free. And it all begins with Hannah.

You reach into the pocket of your hoodie, pull out you face mask, and start to put it on.

There's a tap-tap-tap at the patio door. Startled, you look down and see Hannah standing on the other side.

"Come out, Uncle Jake!" she says, voice raised so she can be heard through the glass. "I want you to eat cake and help me open presents!"

There's something different about her voice. A lilting, almost hypnotic quality that you've never noticed before. You think you spot a glint of light in her eyes as she smiles up at you, but then it's gone, so swiftly that you're not sure it was ever really there.

You look at her, this sweet little girl who is the closest thing you'll ever have to a child of your own. You watch a bead of sweat trail down the side of her face, and you don't know what to say to her. You look past her and see that everyone else—the kids, Rick, Terri—are watching to see what you'll do. The hope in your brother's eyes is almost too much for you to bear.

Before you can react, the patio door slides open. Hannah steps inside, smiles, takes your gloved hand with her pink, heat-swollen fingers, and pulls you forward. You want to tell her no, want to yank your hand away, but you don't. You're still holding the face mask in your other hand, and now it slips from your fingers and falls to the floor. You let her lead you out onto the deck, and although the humid August air slaps you in the face like a hot wet towel, you don't hesitate. You're not afraid. All you feel is a distant, almost pleasant numbness, as if you've been anesthetized.

She escorts you to the table and has you take her place. You look down and see a cardboard plate emblazoned with the image of a cartoon princess, chocolate cake crumbs on her dress, looking like scorch marks on the fabric. There's a dollop of liquefying vanilla ice cream covering half of her head, as if her face is melting.

Everyone's looking at you. Hannah, her guests, Rick and Terri. . . They're smiling, teeth gleaming with reflected sunlight.

You think of the earlier conversation with your brother, about how some people know the truth about the sun, and work to conceal that knowledge from their fellow cattle. What do they get in return for their service? A slower death? A chance to feel superior to the rest of the cattle? The delusion that they're more than mere food, even though in the end they're not?

And who's part of this vast conspiracy? Scientists? World leaders? Teachers? I'm a teacher. Do you think I'm one of them? Do you think Terri is?

Questions. Not denials.

You look at your brother and his wife. They continue to smile, and their eyes glimmer with light.

"You must be tired of fighting," Rick says.

"Especially after losing Kate," Terri adds.

You feel tears threaten, but you fight to hold them back, reluctant to lose the moisture.

Despite yourself, you whisper, "Yes."

In your mind you see Earth, hanging in a star-scattered void. As you watch you see—faint at first, but rapidly becoming clearer—streaks of light shooting upward from the planet. Hundreds, thousands, millions, some larger, some smaller, all being pulled toward the ravenous blazing sphere some eighty-three million miles distant. *Life* energy—human, animal, insect, plant—being harvested by the hungry god Helios. Which is how it's always been, how it always will be.

"You have to be burning up in all those clothes," Terri says.

Rick looks at Hannah. "Shall we unwrap your present for you, sweetie?"

"Yes!" Hannah says.

Terri and Rick move toward you, and Hannah claps her hands in delight, as her parents begin removing your clothes. The rest of the children clap and cheer as your brother and sister-in-law go about their work. You don't fight them, and when they need you to raise an arm or stand up to facilitate your disrobing, you cooperate without hesitation or complaint.

They toss each article of clothing to the deck as they remove it, and soon you're sitting naked at the head of the table, your flesh—all of it—fully exposed to the sun for the first time in your life. You feel a single bead of sweat roll down the side of your face. It starts slowly, then picks up speed. It's soon followed by more. Many more.

You look at your niece. Hannah's face is shining so brightly now that you can't make out her features, not even when you squint.

"Thank you, Uncle Jake! It's the best present ever!"

Rivers of sweat run from your pores, and you can feel your life draining way with the theft of each salt-tinged drop. You try to say Hoppy Birthday to Hannah, but your throat feels clogged with sand and nothing comes out.

You're exhausted to the core of your being, so you decide to just sit and rest awhile.

In the sun.

Shirley Jackson Award-nominated author **Tim Waggoner**'s novels include *Like Death* and *The Harmony Society,* and his latest short story collection is *Bone Whispers.* In total, he's published over thirty novels and one hundred stories, and his articles on writing have appeared in *Writer's Digest* and *Writers' Journal,* among other publications. He teaches creative writing at Sinclair Community College and in Seton Hill University's Master of Fine Arts in Writing Popular Fiction program. Visit him on the web at **www.timwaggoner.com**.

WET HEAVENS
Brian Fatah Steele

A red landscape of meat stretched out before me, thousands of bodies that would never rot. No longer flesh in the traditional sense, this new organic matter continued to glisten with a slick sheen in the morning light. If you squinted your eyes and forgot what you were staring at, it was actually quite beautiful.

"Mr. Clavell, we'll be ready to embark soon."

I nodded, still staring out from the gun turret. It was my own fault for wanting a better view, but I couldn't help the masochism of my psyche. I needed to grasp what I was walking into. The quarantine zone was vaguely crescent shaped, fifty miles wide and stretching over eighty miles in length. Youngstown no longer existed, and both Cleveland and Pittsburgh had come close. There was essentially a dead zone where the Northeast Ohio-Western Pennsylvania border had once been.

"Mr. Clavell, sir," came the voice again.

I glanced over at the young solider. "What have you seen out there?"

"Eh, I'm afraid that's classified, sir."

I snorted. "Son, in less than thirty minutes I'll be strolling into that. I'd like to have some idea what to expect."

His eyes darted out to the scene before us. You could see the struggle on his face. I idly wondered if it was his due to the duty he was breaking, or the memories he had conjured up.

"There's a lot of movement," he said in clipped tones. "Things scurry, but the ground... it moves in waves sometimes. And it's not always on the ground. In the sky, too."

"Thank you, that's enough."

The trauma was apparent in the white knuckles and the bulging eyes. He, like a majority of the military personnel along the quarantine line, would need to be switched out soon. And, just like so many others who had already been here, he would face a quiet honorable discharge for medical reasons, along with a lifetime of pills, therapy, and nightmares.

The rest of my envoy was found doing final checks on their gear near the gate. Yuker was barking out orders as he glared at the SUV. He still wasn't happy about the lack of heavy weaponry. The idea was laughable, but I couldn't help noticing Lt. Dunning strapping an extra set of clips to his thigh. Dr. Nguyen was still arguing with Dr. Cornell, and my "assistant," Christine Hughes, stood off to the side observing it all and hugging herself in the morning chill. I smiled at her when she looked over. She didn't smile back.

"Seriously, I can easily show one of these grunts how to work the equipment," said Cornell for the umpteenth time. "Let me go with you guys."

"You're the only one I trust, Landon," replied Nguyen with an affectionate pat on the shoulder.

"I should be going," grumbled the young doctor.

"If you could, you would," said Nguyen.

I tried not to roll my eyes. Nguyen wanted this glory all to himself. Glory. Was that how Yuker saw it, too? I was probably the only one who wasn't pleased about being asked to enter the quarantine zone.

Except I wasn't asked. I had been *summoned*. After seventeen months, after so many deaths, failures, and questions, the things inside had sent an emissary. It had come tottering to the gate on three humanoid legs, trailing white scarves in its wake and gleaming red. Frankenstein's left over parts, standing strong and dripping blood, flags of truce billowing in the wind. The video stream from that day is terrifying, but the audio is worse. Syllables that sound as if they were produced from the gas of putrefying organs, words asking for parlay and the request of three individuals – General Jeffery Yuker, Dr. Adam P. Nguyen, and myself. Each of us was allowed to bring a single attendant, our safety promised, and any acts of violence prohibited. We didn't need to ask about the consequences after what had happened to Akron when the Pentagon had tried firing Patriot missiles.

I had not been pleased with this particular honor. I still wasn't.

Yuker fired off a few last-second orders before climbing into the passenger side of the SUV. His man Dunning got in behind the wheel, while I sat in the back with Ms. Hughes. Nguyen was positioned in the middle with a pile of hi-tec devices he lovingly fiddled with. I jumped when Hughes grabbed my hand. They were unlocking the gates.

"How's the sound, Landon?"

"Perfect, Doc. Am I coming through clearly?"

"Yes, but we don't know how long the comms will last. The quarantine zone continues to emit interference on various wavelengths that make intelligence gathering difficult. I'll keep recording, regardless."

Up front, the guards were having their own difficulties getting the gates open. I suppose no one ever thought we'd actually be entering. Containment was the priority when things had been constructed.

Nguyen sighed. "Landon, for the sake of posterity, could

you read out the brief rundown of what we know concerning the Newbond-Utica Event?"

My jaw clenched as Landon Cornell read out a history too well known.

"In 2012, Newbond Industries purchased forty acres of undeveloped land on the western border of Pennsylvania for the purpose of hydraulic fracturing. Otherwise known as "fracking," this is a process of obtaining natural gas, natural gas liquids, and crude oil that involves myriad drilling processes, including horizontal drilling and intense water pressure.

"The area obtained is only a fraction of a fracking-quality space that reaches from northern New York and Maryland to western Ohio, approximately 95,000 square miles. It is the second largest find in the world, second only to a region in Russia, and until the Newbond-Utica Event, some 35,000 fracking wells were drilled annually. Billions were spent in 2012 in Ohio alone on these endeavors.

"Since 2004, fracking largely consisted of work within a layer of earth referred to as the Marsellis-Shale Shelf. It was believed that over five billion barrels of crude oil, and possibly over fifteen trillion cubic feet of natural gas was present in the Marsellis-Shale Shelf and beneath, in the Utica-Shale. The Utica-Shale, while rich in minerals and organics, is usually found some seven thousand feet beneath ground level. In the area purchased by Newbond Industries, this depth was only a little more than one thousand feet.

"The Utica-Shale level is approximately 4.5 million years old, and…"

"Get on with it!" growled Yuker.

"But, I still haven't talked about the fracking water, contamination and its disposal."

"Landon, if you'd please," said Nguyen with a sigh.

The gates clanked open as Cornell continued.

"On August 14th, 2014, Newbond Industries cracked through the Utica-Shale with their latest drilling, intent on what they presumed was a massive pocket of crude oil. It wasn't. Initial reports are unconfirmed, but eyewitness accounts claim the ground "bled," and this liquid was somehow able to enact motion as an independent organism."

The envoy rolled across a surface that had been a road only two years ago. Every tree, every bird, every human being in the quarantine zone had become infected by the substance that had spurted out from the Utica-Shale. Every piece of organic matter had been consumed in some fashion and transformed. All of it had a crimson hue and a glossy sheen." Cornell's words drifted back to me, the static in his voice growing.

"… a mutagenic property. This has been observed down to a microbial level, although some theorize that certain amino acids would not…"

As we traveled deeper, the devastation became more apparent. Buildings, cars, any inert matter or mineral material, had been spared. Instead, it was being systematically tore down and… consumed? Used as a fuel source? I could only speculate. However, the organized method in which I saw a small town being dismantled worried me.

"That's it!" exclaimed Nguyen.

"What?" I asked, my head snapping to the doctor.

"We lost Landon," he replied, holding up the transmitter.

I turned from Nguyen's quizzical look. He thought this was an adventure, another book waiting to be written. A pop physicist, he fancied himself the next Stephen Hawking or Carl Sagan. I think he was more focused on how this might raise his celebrity status than on any scientific revelation. Of course, being name-dropped by monsters only boosted his ego.

We were all celebrities in our own circles. Yuker had grown to fame in the Afghani War due to his unnecessarily aggressive tactics, ones he kept in the Department Of Defense when he suggested a nuclear strike on the quarantine zone. Fortunately, saner heads had won that day. I hosted a bipartisan political show on PBS, *Our Day Today*. I wasn't anywhere as popular as McLear, but I felt I was just as respected on Capitol Hill.

The road took a bend and I nearly pressed my face against the window, gawking. A series of larger buildings had been utterly desiccated, only the steel girders and a few support beams left. They were covered in a thicker substance, the metal warped and twisted. It looked like molten fat dripping off the broken bones of a giant.

"What could do that?" whispered Hughes.

Most of the cars along the road had been shoved or pulled off to the sides, lumps of machine gristle discarded. All the windows appeared blown out, the tires gone, and the remaining pieces wrapped up in soaking spider webs. Webs, or strings of drool.

"Two o'clock," came Dunning's sharp, staccato voice.

We all turned to the right to see motion in the distance. Soft undulations repositioned a parking lot into something that too closely resembled a pyramid. The size of a baseball stadium, it sat on a bloated mound of flesh with a single, wide appendage. Like a pod of peas, it was opened to reveal half a dozen gelatinous orbs. From the space around them, thousands of long cilia strands gently went about their job on the cars. Speeding past, we managed to catch a last glimpse of the thing leaning over, one of the orbs opening, and a viscous clear liquid spewing over the vehicles.

No one said anything for a while after that, not even Nguyen.

When the emissary had presented itself at the edge of the quarantine zone, that had been our first real substantial contact with the things inside. None of the incursions had returned, all attempts at technological reconnaissance had been blocked somehow, and the two direct assaults had been abysmal failures – the second involving those Patriot missiles. Almost every theory out there proposed we were dealing with an intelligent antagonist, even the theologians who declared we had unleashed the Devil. What I saw outside the SUV's windows made me reconsider the validity of that last one.

It was an alien charnel house, one still alive, still squirming. We continued to see activity, some of it akin to disfigured humans, some of it beyond sane comprehension. What appeared to be a man stood on a street corner and watched us pass, towering easily over eight feet with extended limbs and digits. A short time later, we had to slow as a swarm of what could have been the bastard offspring of jellyfish and wasps cut us off. They flowed through the air in formation, intestinal feelers darting about. Every monstrosity we saw had the same slick, red color.

"We're making good time," Yuker announced. "We'll be at the event site by two o'clock."

The event site – the spot where Newbond Industries had broken through the Utica-Shale and released this upon the world. The place we were told to travel to, the general epicenter of the quarantine zone, and only an hour away. I felt sick.

"I had hypothesized on the bio-engineering, but..." Nguyen trailed off.

"What?" I asked him.

"It's more than that. I think... I think what we're also seeing is terraforming."

I closed my eyes, pinched the bridge of my nose. Dunning asked, "What's that?"

"The xenomorphic organism isn't just altering biology, it's altering the environment for its creations. It's also creating a more stable habitat for itself."

Yuker frowned. "How is that possible?"

"No clouds, but the sky is a darker blue. Those three volcano-like structures we passed about an hour ago? They were contracting in a way that suggested they were pumping something out, obviously an invisible gas."

"Obviously," said Hughes beside me.

Nguyen ignored her. "The way our psychical structures

have been deconstructed and repurposed, the oily feel to the air and that mild scent. I can't place it, but it, along with everything else, points to the early stages of terraforming."

"Mushrooms," said Yuker.

"What?"

"It smells like mushrooms."

My stomach lurched, the stench pungent now that it was identified. The landscape had given away to less of our past, and more of the future Nguyen seemed to think was in store. Two gelatinous members arced precariously into the sky, a thin translucent membrane stretched between them. In the shade beneath, I swear I saw fungoid faces quivering at me.

Nguyen babbled into one of his recorders, as Yuker and Dunning pointed out anything they considered a threat. I found it all ridiculous. What use were books or bullets against something of this magnitude?

"You've been quiet this whole ride," said Hughes.

Her black hair held a welcome, familiar luster, so I managed a smile. "I honestly don't know why I'm here."

"I guess you're the unbiased observer."

"Isn't that what you and Dunning are for? Hell, I understand Yuker and Nguyen being on this little journey, but I don't fit the role of ambassador of earth to underground monsters."

Hughes clicked her tongue in thought. "Do you think the people that were here retain any of their memories? Are their personalities still in there?"

"God, I hope not," said Yuker as we passed what looked like a giraffe boiled alive.

"Maybe they do. Or did," she continued. "And maybe in there, they remembered the three of you. Sure, there might be more qualified people, no offense, but you're all relatively famous. Regular people know who you guys are."

Nguyen pondered that for a moment before recording it.

"Thanks," I said. "I think that just made me more anxious than it helped."

"She's got a point," said Yuker. "There are a lot more... eh, *diplomatic* individuals than me. I can admit that. But I'd been in the news a lot these last few years, interviews and such. Dr. Nguyen released that book all the intellectual types read, and everybody watches you, Clavell. Hell, I watch you."

"That's surprising," I muttered.

"You may not be an old hawk like me, but you really *are* fair in your coverage. I respect that."

"I find this idea very disturbing."

Nguyen blinked at me. "I find this idea, quite honestly, very awesome."

"How so?"

"Well, if this is really the case, we'll be less likely to get eaten and shat out as a flying octopus."

How do you respond to that?

Lost in our own thoughts, we continued on in silence. The world below was all a crimson red, while the sky above had become a royal blue. The air had a miasma in it, and it felt a minimum of ten degrees warmer. My nose itched with the rich musk of fungus.

I could feel the blood in my temples pounding. The road was an enormous tongue in my imagination, a ravenous mouth, our destination. On both sides of us, a surreal sort of organic city had begun to grow. It was the scenery of Salvador Dali and Hieronymus Bosch, a bleeding city of alien meat. More creatures went about unfathomable tasks, never paying us any attention. A form horribly feminine sauntered past on limbs composed of a million maggot-like legs, a garden of stalks topped with orifices salivating sat off on a plateau.

"Now what the hell is this?" asked Yuker as he leaned forward in his seat.

Only a few miles from the event site, the road was now blocked by what could only be described as an enormous forearm and hand. It lay directly in our path, palm up and open. Invitingly.

"I can't believe this is only the first time we've faced an

obstacle," said Nguyen, tapping his chin. "Perhaps we're dealing with a hive mind consciousness?"

The SUV came to a complete stop.

"I don't like this, sir," said Dunning.

"Now what?" I asked.

As if answering my question, the digits on the hand extended and began caressing the doors of the vehicle. Hughes screamed, as did I, if we're being honest. Dunning unholstered his .45, along with Yuker, and I'm pretty sure Nguyen bounced up and down in glee. The delicate movements continued for a moment, paused, then a single stretched finger tapped on Dunning's driver side window. Gently, but insistently, three times.

"Oh, fuck," came Hughes's muttered response.

Yuker ground his teeth. "I guess we're getting out and walking the rest of the way."

Nguyen scrambled to figure what of his gear he absolutely needed as the digits shrunk back, curling into the palm. We carefully climbed out of the SUV, all the other organisms were off a ways and seemed oblivious to our presence. I had refused a weapon back at the gates, and was now regretting that choice.

The fingers, thick as tree trunks, bent back on their knuckles and went from being the flowing tentacles of a squid to the rigid legs of a spider. It lifted its massive forearm-head from the ground, peeling away from a mucus substance, and peered down at us from a hundred milky eyes we hadn't been able to notice from our vantage point. Only a nubby thumb remained flaccid, and it drew a path in the slime for us to follow.

Nguyen forgot about his recordings, staring at the creature in bare awe. Dunning still had his gun drawn, but Yuker had put his pistol away. A strange look had come over his face; one that I suspected was a look of defeat. The pathway cleared by the thumb was narrow, but wide enough for us to walk single file up the incline and toward what distressingly resembled a gothic cathedral.

Nothing moved in the distance now, the sky here a deep navy blue. It was silent except for our progress, the stench of mushrooms now mingling with something else. Something spicier. It reminded me of cumin or ginger. The cathedral of flesh was that same wet crimson, and I could make out the pieces of human flesh that had been used in sculpting it – a nostril here, a toe there. A building built of people, the cathedral throbbed as a living thing.

The fingers of the creature steepled over the doorway, the thumb swinging inward through the maw. It flipped out of our way as we passed underneath it, swiping along its many eyes. As Hughes and I entered, the thumb came down rigid behind us, not exactly blocking our exit, but definitely giving the impression we were not to leave.

The structure was far longer than it was wide, and I no longer had any doubts about its cathedral-like design. Rows of pews sat to our left and right, along with a second tier of what I assumed to be additional seating. The parody of stained-glass windows lined the walls, discolored skin stretched as thin as parchment. The entire complex was a single organism. At the end of the center row, instead of a crucifix, a solitary item rested on a raised dais. As we drew closer, I shuddered as I realized it was a throne.

It was perfectly sized and shaped for a human, and gleamed almost white with only a slight pinkish cast. To each side, sat cubes of meat approximately four foot square. They pulsed as if from a heartbeat, a faint glow emitted from an unknown interior source when expanded.

"My God," said Yuker, "It's made of teeth. It's *one* tooth!"

The truth of Yuker's observation washed over me with revulsion. The white gleam of the throne was enamel, a singular molar grown in mathematical precision to fit its occupant. I choked back the bile threatening its way up in my throat.

A soft plopping sounded behind us, and we all spun to

see a platform descending from a balcony that had grown out from the wall above the entrance. It rolled toward us on a wave of transformed flesh, bringing her closer…

… and it was a *her*.

She stepped off the platform, naked and hairless. Porcelain white and without a single freckle or mole, she regarded us with all crimson eyes, the only color on her. Petite, but formed with full breasts and narrow hips, she folded her hands behind her back in a very human manner and regarded us with a trace of a smile.

"You're… you're…" failed Nguyen.

"Human? No."

Her voice had a smoky aspect to it and no hint of accent to her English. I tried not to stare, but the human sexuality was present in the tilt of her hips and the hardness of her nipples. No, not a "her," but an "it."

"As a representative of the United States government, I demand to…" barked Yuker.

"Please be silent, Jeffery Yuker. Your demands are less than meaningless here."

She glided among us, never attempting to touch us with her hands still behind her back. Her lips curled slightly more into a smile when she looked over Hughes. Even her motion had a graceful sensuality to it.

"Who are you?" I think I said.

"Your kind do enjoy designations and titles, don't you? I have no name that could be properly expressed in human language. Would it make you feel more comfortable to address me in a proper fashion? I am The Originator, The Rivulet Source, The Word That Bleeds. If you wish, you may now call me The Prophet."

"The Prophet," repeated Nguyen in a whisper.

"Yes, Adam Nguyen. We are entertained, if not irritated, by your kind's adherence to faith and superstitions."

"We?" Dunning asked, his gun raised.

She laughed, deep and resonating. "Of course, Gregory

Dunning. We. Even a prophet of my kind must need a flock."

Yuker shot me a look. Dunning hadn't been a name given by these creatures. How did she know it?

"We are The Ichor, The Malleable Court, The Data That Flows. We surround you even now."

I warily eyed the cathedral and thought of all the monstrosities we had seen on our journey. Nguyen blathered something I didn't hear, and Hughes grew twitchy. The Prophet waved her hand away in response to Nguyen's question.

"Do not be so limited, Dr. Nguyen. You speak of flesh, and I speak of essence. We find it almost sad you became the most advanced species upon this planet."

My breath stopped. "This planet?"

The prophet sauntered to the throne, and lounged across it in a manner that emanated lewdness. Or at least, imitated it. She stared at me with eyes both hungry and dismissive.

"Oh, yes, William Clavell. We arrived here millions of your Earth years ago. We have been waiting for you to be ready, but you discovered us before you had ripened."

As a group, our collective look of shock must have pleased her, because she laughed once more. "Your kind would have had a few more centuries, if not a millennium before you had achieved the state we sought. An inconvenience, but not unforeseen."

"The United States will not stand for this act of aggression," roared Yuker, clearly out of his depth. "The world will not!"

The Prophet leaned forward obscenely in her throne. "Jeffery Yuker, we've owned this world since before you developed spoken language. We are everywhere, under all parts. We have risen many times, in secret, to ascertain your level of evolution, and you have heard of us before. In your cultural mythologies and religious lore, we have been the Wendigo in the Rocky Mountains, the Nephilim in The Dead Sea, and the Nosferatu in the Carpathian Mountains. All those and more."

I stumbled backwards, overcome by the ramifications of her words. Dunning screamed something and drew a bead on The Prophet. She laughed, the sound punctuated by bullets firing. Yuker shouted something, and Hughes pulled the gun hidden under her jacket and wildly searched for an exit. Crimson streams ran from The Prophet's body as she stood, the blood lashing out at Dunning. The liquid whips sliced through him in a dozen directions, his dismembered body falling to the floor in hunks. One strand of blood knocked the gun from Yuker's hand while another wrapped itself around Hughes's fleeing body.

"Agent Hughes!" bellowed Yuker.

Agent Christine Hughes, a cadet fresh out of Quantico, was lifted in the air and brought back to The Prophet. Without an assistant I was willing to put in harm's way, it had been decided to ghost me with a protection detail. But Hughes had never been trained for fighting ancient aliens from hell, and screamed madly as she tried to break free. The Prophet's wounds had already healed, only the single appendage of blood bursting from beneath the left of her rib cage was still active and holding Hughes aloft.

"You are little more than a dying sack of meat," cooed The Prophet to Hughes, inching her closer. "Here, let us forge you into something… eternal."

Hughes yanked her hand free, and brought the gun up. It was my turn to shriek as she shoved it under her chin and pulled the trigger. Her head exploded, red and wet. The prophet chuckled and flung the corpse onto the remains of Dunning. They were already being absorbed by the floor.

"Blood," said Nguyen hoarsely. "You're not the creatures, you're the blood! The exotic fluid released from the drilling, sentient liquid."

"Very good, Adam Nguyen. I *am* The Originator, The Rivulet Source. And I am the Prophet. So to complete this tale, we need to fill other roles."

The cube to her right came alive, light burning from its insides. Liquid flames shot out and engulfed Yuker, the retching noise of his metamorphosis drowned out by his screams. The blaze washed out the doors of the cathedral, leaving an abomination in the General's place.

"The Warrior becomes The Martyr, a symbol to show this world what is to be."

The left cube spat out fire onto Nguyen.

"The Scholar becomes The Apostle, one to take the message to his people."

I stood there between what had been Yuker and Nguyen, the general and the scientist no more. Yuker had been transformed into a ball of flesh, his bones wrenched out and fused into a partial carapace, his face centered and recognizable. He wept tears of crimson lapped up by rows of tongues lining his bulbous form like the nipples on swine. Nguyen swayed back and forth, his skin inside out and his organs hanging from his desiccated body in a symmetrical mockery of official vestments. He ran his hands across his bleeding scalp and squealed.

When they wailed "Blessings!" in unison, I fell to my knees.

The Prophet simply examined me from her throne.

"Why?" I choked out.

"Because it is the way of things, it is our cycle."

I shook my head. "Why me?"

A truly human look of pity came across her. "Christine Hughes was right. We do collect the memories and thoughts of those we flow through. You are respected among your people, and so we chose you for that reason."

I sobbed, my mind in revolt over my fate.

"The cycle is not complete, William Clavell."

I nodded, thinking I understood.

"Come unto me," she said, opening her arms. "As I am now The Prophet, was I once The Disciple. Take the memories of your kind from this form, the memories of my kind from this blood. Become The Disciple and travel the stars."

"Wha... what?"

"So many worlds, so much information. We are the Apocalypse, the Ragnarok, the Omega Point. We journey to where we know civilization to be imminent and wait. We wait until these worlds are at an end, and then we run in rivers. We gather the stories, the reasons, and journey more. I was from a planet billions of your light years away, and now William Clavell, it is your turn."

An end of own doing This was our fault. They are the undertakers — the *historians* — of the universe.

I rose to my feet, and went to embrace The Prophet.

"Give my memories to Nguyen. It... it will help my people to understand."

She nodded and in her crimson eyes, I saw a glimmer of something almost human before I wrapped my arms around eternity.

Brian Fatah Steele has been writing various types of Horror for over ten years now. Along with his novels and collections, his work has appeared in such places as *Dark Visions, Vol.1* and *4pocalypse.* Steele lives in Ohio with a few cats and survives on a diet of coffee and cigarettes. He still hopes to one day be a super-villain.

ACKNOWLEDGEMENTS

First and foremost, I would like to thank the fine authors who contributed their very talented work to this anthology. Without them... well, it just wouldn't be here, now would it?

I'd also like to thank all those very gracious souls who contributed funds and showered tons of support to the Blood Type Indiegogo fundraiser: Tracie McBride, David C. Hayes, Colum Paget, Deborah Walker, Bear Weiter, Shael Hawman, Guy Anthony De Marco, Matthew Carpenter, Dale Eldon, Andrew Vallee, Taylor Grant, Dane Hatchell, Richard Salter, Selene MacLeod, Timothy Feely, Edward Lipsett, Sam Cowan, Lori Safranek, Brent Millis, Jonathan Hepburn, Max Booth III, Lucas K. Law, James Armstead, Lee Howard, William Wood, Scott Pratt, Jon Meyers, and Robert Helmbrecht. You guys are amazing and I couldn't have done this without your amazing support.

Furthermore, I'd like to thank Dave Brzeski and Malina Roos for handling the slush pile and Shannon Michaels for editing my story contribution. And of course I'd like to thank my fellow partners at Nightscape Press for all that they do.

Last but certainly not least by any means I'd especially like to thank The Cystic Fibrosis Trust for giving me such a great reason to make this anthology by doing an amazing job of helping people suffering with CF.

RSW

www.ingramcontent.com/pod-product-compliance
Lightning Source LLC
Chambersburg PA
CBHW070829260626
47170CB00007B/2318